Nemesis Circle

Nemesis Circle

A CONNOR BROCK THRILLER

Emerson Cole

severn
House

This first world edition published in Great Britain 2007 by
SEVERN HOUSE PUBLISHERS LTD of
9–15 High Street, Sutton, Surrey SM1 1DF.
This first world edition published in the USA 2008 by
SEVERN HOUSE PUBLISHERS INC of
595 Madison Avenue, New York, N.Y. 10022.
This first trade paperback edition published 2008 by
SEVERN HOUSE PUBLISHERS, London and New York.

British Library Cataloguing in Publication Data

Cole, Emerson
  Nemesis circle
  1. Brock, Connor (Fictitious character) - Fiction 2. Human
  trafficking - Europe, Eastern - Fiction 3. Pharmaceutical
  biotechnology - Fiction 4. Suspense fiction
  I. Title
  823.9'2[F]

  ISBN-13: 978-0-7278-6537-3   (cased)
  ISBN-13: 978-1-84751-034-1   (trade paper)

All Severn House titles are printed on acid-free paper.

Typeset by Palimpsest Book Production Ltd.,
Grangemouth, Stirlingshire, Scotland.
Printed and bound in Great Britain by
MPG Books Ltd., Bodmin, Cornwall.

Reader, take note:

Yesterday:

'The great Konstantinoupolis began to take fire, and well do I, Geoffrey de Villehardouin, Marshal of Champagne, bear witness in the year of our Lord 1204, that never, since the world was created, had so much treasure been won.'

Geoffrey de Villehardouin (1160–1213), *Memoirs of the Fourth Crusade*

'With the richest city of the world at their mercy, these Western barbarians massacred the population; destroyed a thousand years of palaces; stole priceless sculptures – smashing those they could not steal – crushed by a crusade of envy.'

Nicetas Choniates (1155–1217), *Memoirs of Escapee and Refugee*

Today:

'Contract killings and human trafficking, particularly the increasing problem of trafficking newborn babies, are major hurdles to overcome.'

European Commission Report on entry by Balkan States

'Thousands of Eastern European children are disappearing, harvested for their organs and body parts.'

La Terre des Hommes

Tomorrow:

'The value of human trafficking is over $12 billion a year, yet no substantial study on the trafficking of Eastern European Children has emerged.'

UNICEF

'Our accomplishments in genetic engineering, stem-cell research, medical advancement, disease eradication, life extension and cloning are progressing us towards a tomorrow, which, history will record, justifies our research today and all our yesterdays.'

A shareholder report

'. . . winged balancer of Life . . . daughter of Justice . . . unnoticed you walk in our tracks . . .'

Taken from 'Hymn to Nemesis Mesomedes', Hadrian's poet

Prologue

'Your uncle will have you excommunicated!'
'Then it will be the only thing the blind old fool will have ever done for me!' spat Count Marcus Dandolo in retort. 'These past two years I, nay, we have risked all and for what? His ambitions, his coffers, his titles, which all, by my father's rights, are mine!'

Giuseppe Montefiori, recognizing the rising anger of his battle-weary liege, sighed inwardly and mollified his tone.

'My lord, your uncle Enrico is our Doge of Venice. We return, as I would counsel you, and he hears directly from your lips what you have accomplished this night on his behalf, then I believe he will announce publicly his praise. If, however, he learns from another . . .'

'And how could my intentions be revealed?' interrupted Dandolo. 'Look around you, my men are loyal and they can now be richly rewarded.'

'There is your inheritance to consider; the Doge is old, you have proved yourself worthy and—'

The headstrong young count again cut across Montefiori. 'My father was worthy yet his inheritance was stolen!'

'I can only urge you to reconsider, my lord,' said his counsellor.

Dandolo turned slowly to survey the men he had chosen. These were, supposedly, his most loyal, certainly the finest. He listened to the muted coughs coupled with the occasional gasp of pain punctuating the moist pre-dawn air as comrades-in-arms tended to their wounded. He closed his eyes.

The arguments with his uncle had escalated since they had departed the shores of Venice. There had been too much talk, too much political rumination on strategy. The old Doge's earlier scheming had already put the Flemish into his debt. Whatever excuse would later be cooked up it was clearly the intent of the Franks to take as much as their barbarous hands could gather. When Constantinople inevitably fell – and fall it would as the ports Zara and Dyrachion had already done – then the only Venetian benefiting would once again be the direct heirs of his uncle.

Weeks of boredom, coupled with wanting to keep out of his uncle's presence, had motivated him to take his troops on scouting exercises. His timing this evening, now positioned close to the northern passes of the Bosporus straits, was perfect. By chance they had waylaid a local seaman who, being part of a crew tasked with bringing boats away from the port bustling with loutish crusaders, had taken the opportunity to steal away from the others and visit a woman he knew in the area. The man revealed, under duress, the totally unexpected: that the pretender, Angelo Alexius, had fled the city upon the arrival of the first boat. The Emperor had been secretly waiting, in disguise with one of his daughters.

'So despite negotiations in his favour, the damned usurper has abandoned the people he so fervently claimed wanted him; and we let him slip through!' Dandolo had cursed with frustration. Furious at the missed opportunity of personally capturing the errant ruler, Alexius III, and certain that his uncle would place the blame on him, he had ordered that the bearer of such tidings be put to death. Desperately the seaman pleaded for his life, claiming that the other boats they had ferried to this point were intended to convey the Emperor's personal treasure to his retreat in Thrace, under the protection of Alexius III's personal guard. Why otherwise would a covert convoy of boats be required, the man argued, with Emperor Alexius already escaped?

Here was the opportunity Dandolo sought.

It had been a couple of hours after midnight when the soft trundling of a covert convoy was heard. From their vantage point Dandolo and his men silently observed a number of heavily laden carriages each pulled by four horses, their hooves wrapped in sacking, moving slowly toward the moored boats. They counted six carriages in all. For over an hour they had watched as sea chests and man-size wooden frames were loaded aboard the three single-masted, flat-bottomed merchant cogs and two fishing dhows.

With the advantage of surprise, a ferocious, co-ordinated assault allowed his troop to ambush the convoy on all sides before an alarm could be raised. In the ensuing close-quarter fighting even the most hardened remnants of the procession were put to the sword. With adrenaline-fuelled fury, he had scythed his way to the centre, his sharpened blade slicing through leather, flesh, sinew and bone with every lethal swing.

Instinctively parrying a heavy blow aimed at his left side his swinging momentum gave him an advantage over a much lighter defender who crumpled to the ground, as their exposed side caught the retaliatory blow. Frantically the fallen bodyguard tried to scrabble up again, holding up hands in a plea for surrender.

Too late.

In the frozen second that his heavy blade, swung with the force of both arms, delivered a mortal blow to the other's vulnerable neck, Count Marcus recognized his adversary. Unable to halt his strike to the exposed throat, the plainly dressed young woman was killed instantly. Glancing to see who had noticed, he'd caught the eye of his loyal companion defending his left side. Giuseppe looked at the bloodied head stuck at an awkward angle to its prostrate body, he too recognizing the shocked youthful visage that stared back. He simply nodded in emotionless acknowledgement.

The Emperor's personal treasure, covertly taken from the city he was abandoning, was beyond anything Count Dandolo could ever have imagined. Inspecting each of the boats in turn had strengthened his resolve. He was determined that such a prized booty would never fall into the coffers of his uncle, who would surely take credit for capturing it, leaving his nephew with the crime of killing the Emperor's daughter.

'Giuseppe, my friend,' Count Dandolo said. 'The Doge will not learn the truth of this night. My mind is set.'

Montefiori sighed inwardly again, this time holding his words, knowing any argument would be poorly served at this moment. 'Set, my lord?'

'Yes, as I swear are the minds of the old Boniface himself; and Baldwin, Villehardouin, Blois and La Roche – indeed all the Franks!' retorted the count, his voice rising in cold anger.

'You know, Giuseppe, as well as I that in setting their replacement puppet emperor upon a powerless throne they have intent to bleed him dry. And what will they do then? I will tell you! They, in their Frankish fashion, will be first to sack Constantinople, treating Venetian requests with derision. They will choose and distribute titles amongst themselves. And why? Because they know well that Pope Innocent threatens excommunication to any Venetians who violate the city, its emperor or any members of his family. If what had happened here is discovered I will be both penniless and excommunicated.'

Montefiori respectfully held the other's levelled gaze. 'It could fall in your favour. Alexius was a usurper. I understand—'

'Politics, Giuseppe! You don't understand politics!' interrupted the count. 'You think old Baldwin, with his eyes set on the rich prize he surveys glinting in the sun each morning, will honour Rome's edicts in the name of reinstating the rightful emperor? Ha! Think again! The Franks are on their own crusade of enrichment. Listen, my friend, we must look to our own and not return to Venice. Stay and we are excommunicated and penniless, for we are but pawns in a game. Vanish and the future is ours to carve.' The count placed his hand on the other's shoulder. 'Tonight was destined, Giuseppe. I believe it with all my heart. Are you with me?'

'When have I not been?' answered Montefiori, more in statement than question.

'Then bring the men to order, for we must be long gone before sunrise. We follow our new destiny.' The count looked into the distance and back to the young woman he had just slain. 'Giuseppe,' he added quietly.

'Yes, my lord?'

'I once spoke with this fair lady while my uncle and her father feasted, before negotiations were soured. She was quick-witted, and strong-willed; I liked her.'

'As I well observed, my lord,' said Giuseppe.

'We mused that our lives followed a similar path,' continued Dandolo not hearing the comment. 'Yet in opposing directions; for it was indeed her father who stole from his saintly brother. But such misguided loyalty is common to us both; a loyalty that took her life as easily as it could have taken mine.' The count removed his blood-spattered cloak and placed it over the

4

slaughtered girl. 'Bring her, Giuseppe; we must dispose of the cowardly pretender's brave daughter properly.'

Without speaking Montefiori wrapped the cloak tighter ensuring the head was covered, and easily lifted the body on to his shoulder.

With the first sprinkling of warm light stimulating swirls of mist to form along the Bosporus, the boats carrying the self-exiled Count Dandolo and their priceless cargo became disappearing specks on the horizon.

'It is two weeks since the flight of that pretender,' boomed the elderly Doge, Enrico Dandolo, 'We are agreed that our protégé be crowned emperor tomorrow, being the first day of August and the feast of St Peter?'

'Agreed,' responded Baldwin of Flanders. 'And then, as Alexius IV, he must fulfil a covenant to pay dues.'

'Indeed!' replied the Doge. 'With half the sum immediately repaid to Venice as payment for your own debts. Are we agreed on that too?'

Baldwin looked at the wizened old blind man across the table from him and across to his fellow Franks who nodded and smiled in turn. They were fully aware that after he'd appealed to the Venetians for transportation and food, the Doge had later used the crusader's indebtedness for his own political ends. But why should they care? With the three-score armed warships he had also contributed they had seen their wealth and titles increasing with every port taken. And now the greatest prize in all of Christendom beckoned.

'Agreed,' he said with satisfaction. 'By all.'

With only a portion of the huge demand raised, through land confiscation, emptying the public treasury and imposing taxes, Enrico of Venice, openly grieving his lost nephew, insisted on half before forcing the new Emperor to depart the capital, under escort, to seek the money in the empire. When he returned empty-handed the Franks stripped the Emperor of all power and threw him in jail. Having persuaded the crusaders two years earlier to come to his aid, Alexius IV was discovered strangled in his jail. His disabled father, the former Emperor Isaac, blinded by his disloyal usurping brother, met a similar fate within days.

The great city was ransacked, Baldwin was crowned emperor; Boniface became King of Thessalonica; and the vast riches and lands stolen by the old Doge established the Venetian Empire.

Count Marcus Dandolo was never seen again.

Donaueschingen, Germany, 17th July 2003

'Esteemed colleagues, my warmest welcome and thanks for gathering here this evening on what must surely be one of the warmest days in Europe's history. And for us the timing could not be more perfect nor the place more appropriate.'

Professor William Steinwright gazed with exhilaration at his audience, comprising some of the world's most distinguished scientists in their field, including no less than two Nobel Prize winners, and Europe's most powerful patrons from industrialist families and bankers.

'So why are we here?' Steinwright paused expectantly before answering himself. 'Not in the evolutionary sense, of course, as each of us acknowledges that we humans are not the goal of evolution for there can be no such thing. We are just one stepping stone in the river of life.

'However –' he paused again, pointing his index finger at nothing in particular – 'from this point on we can decide on the direction in which as a species we grow and evolve. We can choose new health, longevity and new states that benefit us, our children and future generations, rather than benefiting our genes.

'That is why we are here!' he continued enthusiastically. 'To research, stimulate and grow the catalytic seed from which wondrous new generations will evolve without fear of degenerative diseases including Alzheimer's, Parkinson's, the myriad of senile ailments and, above all, stave off cancer and heart disease, which afflicts young or old. Altering the genes that fight the effects of our bodies' free radicals will eliminate genetic dysfunction, improve well-being, support organ, spinal and bone regeneration and, of course, slow ageing.'

Steinwright paused again, pushed his dextrous fingers through his grey thinning hair, sighed and adopted a graver tone. 'We are all aware, of course, of the affect that brain implants have on restoring motion to the paralysed and sight to the blind, and agree that such techniques must be allowed to develop. However,

6

not everyone understands and welcomes such progress. Even as we scientists continue to break new ground there are cries of acting against nature. Such medieval suspicious thinking has always existed and will no doubt continue to restrict progress, as it seems that nature has allowed the naysayer's vocal chords to be the loudest. And, of course, the political and moral debate will, we can be sure, continue until acceptance of the human benefits forms a new status quo.

'Our strategic goal, therefore, must be to raise awareness of the radical accomplishments being made in genetic engineering, stem-cell research, life extension and cloning and in doing so separate myth from fact, encouraging those who do not understand to both embrace and celebrate genetic evolution.

'And now, at last, through the mutual merging of our industry's leading laboratories, the vehicle for achieving this goal and for the realization of our overriding vision of life enhancement through biological genetics has been accomplished.' Steinwright gestured his arms towards his audience expansively. 'Sincere thanks must, of course, also go to our patrons. Their generous investment, matched by the valued support of our loyal bankers – all of whom I am delighted to see are present to witness this historic moment – is of vital importance.

'So, my dear and esteemed colleagues, right now, right here, at the very source of the Danube, that historic river which has stimulated profitable trade between western and eastern Europe for thousands of years, will witness the dawn of a new era, for it gives me immense pleasure to introduce you to BioGenomics Research.'

The professor left the podium to enthusiastic applause as the lights dimmed and a giant screen electronically sprang alive to display a lavishly prepared corporate video entitled 'The Future is Now'.

PART ONE

Seedlings of Another Day

One

Witnessing the rape of her elder sister was not the worst nightmare. Being sold by her mother a few minutes later to the same violators had taken that prize. At nine years old she had been unable to read her mother's face as it had seemed devoid of expression. She liked to imagine it as one of remorseful resignation. Pausing in recollection by the full-length mirror, she studied her own image.

It amused her that male admirers took every opportunity to lavish praise on the adopted daughter of Conrad Lefrington. They almost paid homage to what they referred to as her stunning Slavic figure, clothed in ethereal skin. With a distinct facial beauty framed by shoulder-length blonde hair that accentuated high cheekbones, and a finely chiselled nose above a uniform and sensual mouth, she allowed her expression to bestow a warm visage on the beholder. Only in moments alone did she allow her pale-blue eyes to reveal the anger, pain and humiliation she inwardly felt.

For a moment she enjoyed the amalgamation of such emotions as they recharged her resolve, which had been channelled into her work, before a light tap on the door announced the arrival of her father. As she turned, her sparkling eyes complemented the light sapphires interlaced into the designer gown.

'You look stunning, Sophia.'

'Thanks, Papa. This is it then.'

'Yes, except how can I possibly just give you up?'

Sophia looked into the eyes of her tall, aristocratic father. 'Whoa – hold back! This is an engagement party. You promised me a year working for you in Europe before marriage.'

11

'Well, I can't disagree with that. However, you must admit Stephan is a great guy – a rare find, even though I say so myself.'

'And well you should, considering you introduced him to me.'

'Ah, but what does it matter what I think? Could I have persuaded you to do anything other than what you choose? I don't think so.'

'Ah, but . . .' mimicked his adopted daughter. 'Where do I get that from, eh?'

The first-generation Swiss-American, with a magnetic personality and a network that had assisted in building his fortune, laughed. 'Come on, or you'll be later than what is fashionably accepted.'

Stephan de Brouwer stretched from head to toe, enjoying the luxurious feeling of the sun warming his well-toned, tanned body. His brown eyes surveyed the glistening form of his fiancée as she returned from her brief dip in the Pacific.

'So, Sophia,' he welcomed her. 'How does it feel to be engaged?'

Sophia smiled as she reached for the towel. 'Just right, as though we were planned for each other; how about you?'

'Perfect! Though do we really have to fly off to Europe tonight? Why don't we cancel it for a few days and then take our time crossing by sea?'

'That is not the Atlantic, Stephan,' she retorted, pointing at the ocean. 'If we take that long then I miss the start of my project, and anyway I will at last meet your parents, the famous de Brouwer family.'

De Brouwer felt a moment of concern. Though he greatly appreciated capturing the heart of such an incredible woman there were times when he wondered if he had only succeeded in attracting a workaholic. Naturally he had been delighted when she'd agreed to marry him, yet he wondered how much their respective parents had planned it behind the scenes.

'How am I going to give you up?'

The woman cast a cursory glance at her watch and, with a wry smile, leaned down and kissed him. 'You're not. Now come on or we'll miss lunch.'

'You sound like your father,' said de Brouwer, making a face.

Sophia smiled. 'Me? Listen to yourself; you're starting to sound like him too.'

MUNICH, GERMANY

Herr Duisen blew a deep breath through his pursed lips and looked at the time that appeared in the bottom right corner of his laptop. He stretched out his arms, hands clasped backwards, until one of the knuckles cracked in relief. It was just past midnight. Though heavy-hearted about the message he had to deliver he was satisfied with the speech he had just finalized. It was alarming to both investors and media but the truth must out, he repeated in his head. In preparation for its delivery in about ten hours' time he pressed 'save' and 'print' in quick order and stood up, walked to the French windows to the side of his study and noted how the Munich lights twinkled in the rain-soaked city.

Tomorrow, in his position as chairman, he had the mandate to implement the changes he so strongly believed were necessary for both the protection and the future growth of the Duisen Foundation. Then he would take the train to his weekend home close to Obersdorf and decide how to address the much larger issue that beset him.

Thirty minutes later he had reread his speech and got ready for bed. As he cleaned his teeth with his electric toothbrush he felt a slight tear of his gum. He chided himself in the mirror remembering how his wife had always warned him about brushing too vigorously. He thoroughly rinsed his mouth before getting into bed. A shortness of breath caused him to promise himself, once again, to make a commitment to lose weight. Lying back he stared at the ceiling for a few minutes thinking that there would have to be many changes from tomorrow; then he switched off the light and closed his eyes.

The following morning a small, expectant audience of broadcasters, trustees, benefactors, investors and lawyers were informed that Herr Duisen had died unexpectedly a few hours earlier of natural causes. The broadcasters lamented the loss of the distinguished man who had worked tirelessly for European interests; the establishment organized a memorial service in honour of their esteemed colleague; the investors suddenly had alternative interests to honour; and the lawyers sought fees to honour the beneficiary's interests.

The de Brouwer family exemplified European colonial wealth that had successfully multiplied with the new technologically driven age. Simon de Brouwer was a rotund, jovial man who, though proud of what he liked to call his 'Old Europe' heritage, had an innovative business acumen that was razor sharp; his darting eyes rarely missing an opportunity. His distant cousin, Simone de Brouwer, had not even required a change of name when they'd married. Nor was a change in initials for their only son, Stephan, necessary in relation to the countless heirlooms engraved with their family crest.

The family heritage and wealth was founded in rubber plantations in Dutch Indonesia and cane plantations in the Belgian Congo. During the twentieth century the de Brouwers moved into banking and real estate, leasing huge areas of land to form new technological parks. There was hardly a significant investment that Simon and Simone de Brouwer were not directly, or indirectly, involved in. Their influence, or lack of it, could cause shares and reputations to rise, or fall, respectively.

Their Monaco registered yacht, Simone, had departed the Port of Fontvieille for a two-day return trip to Portofino. Apart from the reduced crew they were the only party on board. The de Brouwers had wanted a quiet time together, initiated by Simone, to address a major disagreement between them. The crew, holding to the rumour that it related to the couple's son, kept a discreet distance.

Within a few hours of the discovery of Herr Duisen's demise Simon and Simone de Brouwer failed to return to the Port of Fontvieille for a scheduled luncheon meeting. When contact with their vessel proved unsuccessful the alarm was raised and within the hour their smouldering burnt-out yacht was located close to its last reported position.

Investigators confirmed that four crewmen had died of smoke suffocation. The scorched bodies of Simon de Brouwer and his friend the captain were in the galley, where it seemed that faulty gas bottles had exploded. Simone de Brouwer's

14

bloodied nightgown was found floating in the water, caught on the partly submerged bow of the lifeboat, which was tilted on end due to one of the release catches failing to function. What was left of the nightgown had been torn to shreds as if her body had been subjected to a frenzied shark attack. A verdict of misadventure through crew ineptitude was recorded.

Two

'Another day!' shouted the nine-year-old girl to herself as the sun made its early-morning appearance, rising atop the ragged Carpathian escarpment that haphazardly bordered Romania from Ukraine, north of Transylvania. She ran towards the fenced, bleak-grey building that she and the other children called home.

'Another day!' cried out the young girl again.

'Good!' came the usual reply the girl habitually waited for upon their return trip from town for bread. 'And what of it?'

'This could be the day father comes?'

Mother Govrovych reached out gently with her free hand for the blonde bright-eyed skinny girl who bounced around her, just touching the jaded but clean dress she wore. Govrovych recalled how it had been a favourite with its previous owner, who had since outgrown it. 'It could be, little Anna, but for now, be my little helper, help me with our breakfast. Everyone will be waiting.'

'You know that my father said he would come another day! And that I should look out for him each morning?' argued the girl, persistently, her short haircut and pre-pubescent body giving her the appearance of a young boy, were it not for the pretty floral pattern of her dress.

Govrovych put the three plastic bags full of bread she was carrying into her other hand and gave the little girl a broad smile, displaying a row of uneven teeth as she grinned. Hearing the enthusiastic morning ritual, so full of hope, was actually infectiously uplifting. 'Well, perhaps he will, another day, Anna.'

The girl turned to make her usual plea in response. 'It might be today . . . wait, what is that sound?'

16

'It sounds like someone is having a party,' answered Mother Govrovych, trying to hide her surprise as she walked quickly towards the building, wondering as to the reason for such a commotion.

Having worked for most of her adult life in a Romanian state orphanage, Valentyna Govrovych had enthusiastically embraced the offer to be matron – or mother, as the role was known – soon after the orphanage had become part privately funded six months earlier. She had expected huge improvements to follow the promises and was saddened that nothing had changed. Moreover, it was no longer possible to maintain contact with children after they had left. Indeed, she had taken the opportunity to voice her concerns during the brief visit of the director of the region's state orphanages the previous week. Marku Dudnic had waved her concerns away as he would shoo an annoying moth attracted to his light.

'Matron Govrovych! Look, how many orphans enter foster-homes now? Families which have been found by our new patrons. What do you call that if not improvement? Is this not a good thing? Surely you must agree this is positive improvement?'

She had smoothed down her grey coat trying to contain her nervous frustration. 'Of course, Director Dudnic, though do you not agree we should know where and receive news?'

'Yes, yes, we should,' the balding director had quickly replied, peering at her through his thick black-rimmed spectacles, 'but what of the children? Should we not be fair to them? Should we not give them a chance to acclimatize to their new home without our being overly protective, however well-meaning?'

'Of course, of course!' she had said, feeling more hurt than surprised this time by his response. God knows how many children she had learned to love and then never seen again.

She entered the door that Anna pushed open, placed down her bags and looked around her.

'Ah, here is our good Mother! You have arrived just in time to hear our wonderful news.'

Valentyna looked up to see the administrative representative of the region's five state orphanages, Boris Bulkorsky. Even at the three paces that separated them she could smell his usual odour of tobacco interlaced with alcohol. But, she admitted to herself, the man did seem to be interested in the children's welfare, so who was she to judge. Perhaps she was becoming overly protective. 'What news?' she enquired expectantly.

'The resources we are so desperate for. We have them! Not just for you, Mother, but every one of our little people in the region.'

'That is . . . wonderful news! Our patrons have delivered what they promised?' Valentyna Govrovych blinked as she felt an involuntary tear prick her eye with delight. 'When do we receive the funds?' she added, inwardly chiding herself for her earlier cynicism towards the director.

'That's the best part!' shouted Bulkorsky. 'Our current resources will be sufficient because six out of every ten of our family will be leaving. Right after breakfast, a great celebratory breakfast I brought for the occasion. That is why everyone is singing.'

'What do you mean?' said Govrovych trying to make herself heard over the children's crescendo of excitement. 'I know we should have waited for you but how could we with such news? Look, the transport arrives as we speak!'

The matron's head swivelled round to watch a convoy of minibuses pulling alongside the rusting perimeter fence; and back to the happy faces crowded into the eating hall. She had never seen everyone so happy. In contrast she started to feel rising panic as she blurted a series of questions. 'Boris! How can this be happening so quickly? I have received no information at all. What about release forms? Which children are going? Boris! Where are they going? Answer me!'

'I am not the one to ask,' replied Bulkorsky quickly. 'I know little more than you do now. Director Dudnic informed me personally just yesterday that all arrangements were made and paperwork attended to. I could not tell you earlier as I had to attend to my other regional responsibilities first. Indeed, two of our orphanages will now close and be amalgamated into our remaining three but we retain our current resources. Don't you see how the news is good for everyone?'

Learning that two orphanages had already closed put Valentyna Govrovych momentarily into a state of shock. 'So many children, where are they going?' she repeated after Bulkorsky had walked off to meet with a man and woman who had exited the first coach. Valentyna watched as the man, dressed in a long black leather coat despite the morning warmth, walked directly towards her.

'Ah, Matron Govrovych!' said the man in an overly welcoming voice. 'I have heard much about you from Director Dudnic. So, I understand from our good friend Boris that you have many questions. Of course you do! Now where is your office? I will explain everything.'

Valentyna involuntarily shuddered as she looked at the tall thin man with jet-black shoulder-length hair. She noticed how his easy smile did not reach his dark, almost hypnotic, eyes. She felt another shudder as he placed his arm around her shoulder and guided her away from the others.

The glint of field glasses remained unseen on the shaded Carpathian escarpment two hundred metres away. The light blue eyes of Sonja Brezvanje did not leave the binoculars as she spoke. She watched the convoy of minibuses arrive, two people disembark and walk towards the orphanage. 'It seems your persistence has paid off, Natalya, good work!'

Former orphan and escaped street girl, sold into prostitution before being recruited by Brezvanje's anti-trafficking group, Natalya Toruk beamed a brief smile in response to the praise, before resuming her frown. 'Let me see,' she asked.

Natalya watched as the two people stood talking with a third. At one point the man seemed to gaze directly towards her as if sensing he was being observed. Natalya hastily passed the field glasses back.

Jakiv Teslenko, younger cousin to Brezvanje, placed his hand on the girl's shoulder. 'You recognize him, don't you?'

Natalya involuntarily shivered as her fingers, nails bitten down to the quick, touched the deep scar on her face. 'It is him, Jakiv. He is Pied Piper.'

Three

Tears of frustration stung the woman's dark eyes as she surveyed the high wire fencing that prevented any further access to the cliff face or the medieval fortress.

Cassie Kaligirou's expedition had started out with promise. Flying from Athens she enjoyed the scenic flight: soaring over the Macedonian Relief before hugging the Black Sea coast and landing north of the Dobrudzansko Plateau at Constanta's airport in Romania. The two-hour bus ride skirting the Danube Delta to Tulcea in the Dobrogea region had been interesting as locals had been eager to share histories of their region. As an archaeologist she had welcomed it. The ferry trip had been pleasant too with more locals taking her under their frantic talkative wings. The only other foreigner was a balding, tight-lipped man who, seeming uncomfortable in the heat in his tailored suit, totally ignored her when she caught his eye.

'Still, you should have rested after checking in, and not been in such a rush as usual.' Cassie chided herself out loud, as she often did in an effort to re-channel her increasing annoyance. 'But oh no, you had to press on and take the ferry to the Ukrainian side, where you were delayed. Yes, but how was I to know the person in front would take so long? Not having a passport.'

She breathed deeply, knowing that the truth was that she had been unable to contain her excitement, feeling so close to fulfilling her father's and grandfather's life work. Stretching her arms behind her head to repair her long curly black hair into a new ponytail, she once again walked the perimeter of the fence, trying to recognize the exact location.

'That is the third time she has walked the same route and

20

now she is talking to someone, though I cannot see who or what. She holds no phone.'

'Perhaps the woman is mad,' mocked Hristo Amaut to his security operator who had called him. 'Keep monitoring.'

Director General Amaut pondered to himself as he returned to his office. Since opening the clinic three years ago he had at first questioned the need for such high security. People did not travel to this Ukrainian naval base, which is exactly why they had seized the opportunity to acquire the lease to this section of the fortress. Impenetrable since its construction in the thirteenth century, they had ensured that all their conversion and research work was kept that way too. And their work, he admitted to himself, did require high security. He was sure the strange woman offered no threat, yet in view of where she was, he considered it prudent to utilize the sensitive authority of the Ukrainian Sea Guard as usual. Amaut smiled to himself. Operating under their nose was so convenient.

Cassie was so involved in studying the cliff wall that she did not hear the approach of two guards who roughly grabbed her arms and frogmarched her away from the cliff, towards the jetty. Ten minutes later, without anyone taking the slightest heed of her protestations, she was impolitely pushed into a small room, empty save for a chair, table and phone. The two guards forced her to sit.

'Why have you brought me here?' she demanded indignantly, her Greek heart beating furiously after such treatment, yet also from a little fear.

The grey-uniformed officer, with matching grey hair and a deeply lined face, studied her. 'You were entering a restricted area. Why?' he asked in English.

Cassie swallowed. Her permit for archaeological research had not yet been sanctioned, though she was sure it would only be a matter of days. She chose to stick to the absolute truth. 'My name is Kaligirou. I am an archaeologist with a pending permit from your government. So, I am on an advance trip for a couple of days to survey the area prior to our dig. I was not aware of entering a restricted area, I saw no signs.'

The officer nodded, looked at the passport that had been taken from her, lifted the receiver of the phone, spoke in measured tones and replaced the receiver. 'Ms Kaligirou, I am Commander Christoui. This is a naval base and like most military bases carries restrictions. It was noticed that your behaviour was unusual and you were not on a tourist route and I suggest—'

'But I saw no signs.'

'What you mean is that you noticed no signs, I assure you that they are attached to the perimeter fence you were so close to, a fence I might add that is a restrictive sign in itself. However, I have to instruct you to leave Ukraine immediately and return only when you have your permit of authorization.'

Cassie was about to protest when the phone rang. The officer answered, listened silently for a few moments before replacing the receiver. He stared again at her for a full ten seconds, as if contemplating, before speaking to the two guards in his own language.

'Let go! I can leave unaided,' cried Cassie, struggling as her arms were once more pinned behind her.

'You are to be detained, Ms Kaligirou, or whoever you are. Goodbye.'

'What do you mean?' demanded the archaeologist, outraged, as Christoui left the room. 'You cannot detain me!' Cassie got up to leave too but the two guards instantly stopped her, forcing her back to her seat. Five minutes later the door reopened and a woman in a white coat entered. Cassie immediately stood, whereupon the two guards once more restrained her. This time as she struggled in a futile attempt to free herself, the white-coated woman strode purposefully towards her. Cassie's eyes glanced questioningly at the woman as she experienced a sharp jab in her arm. She felt herself shouting but could not actually hear the words; distorted colours filled her dizzying vision, culminating in utter blackness.

ZURICH, SWITZERLAND

The slight whitening of Dr Paul van Lederman's knuckles was the only visible evidence that the ICE director's legendary emotional discipline was being severely tested. Though he had been one of the first to learn the news, every fibre of his being was still gripped with shock and anger as he watched again the repeated news announcement on his desk's built-in console.

Carl Honstrom breathed out slowly through pursed lips. 'Both too perfectly accidental and coincidental,' he said in measured tones.

'And we don't believe in such things, do we?' said van Lederman emphatically as he switched off the console and turned to look at his chief of field operations.

Honstrom made no comment, waiting with patient expectancy for van Lederman to continue.

'Carl, I have been a friend of Hans Duisen for over twenty years. And I am also one of the executors to his estate. The last time we met was at the banking seminar last week; he was one of the guest speakers. His speech was interesting, but he did not seem, to me anyway, to be his usual self; and I commented that he seemed preoccupied with something. It prompted him to share that he was increasingly uncomfortable about an issue which directly involved his foundation.'

Honstrom shifted in his seat. 'What was it?'

'He didn't say. Naturally I pressed him, but he felt it would not be prudent to discuss anything at that time, as he had no tangible evidence to share. But he was working on it and promised to tell me at the right time. But you know, Carl; I remember thinking that he seemed uneasy about even being with me.'

'Well, with all due respect, Paul, when you have a major issue in business, the last thing you want is someone like you asking questions – depending upon what the issue is, of course.'

'I appreciate that, yet even so I insisted, as his friend, that he let me know if there was anything at all we at ICE could do to assist. He said he would and then joked about such problems at our age. We both laughed as we confirmed to each other that we were fitter than most men half our age, and no more was spoken about it. But my feeling is that, knowing Hans, he was about to be a reluctant whistle-blower. Damn it, Hans Duisen has been professionally disposed of. As for the de Brouwers we can only imagine they met a similar fate, which is a bit too close to home, Carl. Simon de Brouwer was one of ICE's founding members!'

A Swedish Navy flying instructor and later NATO field operations director before being head-hunted by van Lederman, Honstrom combed his fingers through his short, almost crew-cut, greying blond hair. ICE, or Investigation of Corporate

23

Espionage, was the brainchild of van Lederman, created with his legendary network, which included Simon de Brouwer. Originally founded for the purpose of investigating potentially damaging corporate governance issues and fraudulent acquisitions, its reputation for integrity and effectiveness quickly grew, allowing it to provide early warning of either terrorist or passive espionage against industry, which jeopardized trade and investment or risked economic security.

The advisory board of ICE, of which Simon de Brouwer had, until now, been an active member, comprised business leaders of proven integrity. Honstrom knew that any intimation that such a member had been professionally disposed of would be jumped on by certain bureaucratic departments of the European Union, still smarting under van Lederman's scrutiny. He picked his words sparingly.

'Are we able to request a post-mortem?'

Van Lederman leaned back in his chair smoothing down his signature well-groomed moustache. 'One for Hans has already been requested, Simon is a charred shell, though his estate will probably insist upon it anyway. Simone of course . . . well the coastguard will look out for remains but . . . shark attacks, in the Med?!'

'There are more than are generally known about, suppressed for reasons of tourism,' said Honstrom. 'They travel from the Red Sea via the Suez as well as the Gibraltar Straits – and if the lady had been injured, well the chances of any remains turning up are slim. And with the frequency of North African refugees' bodies periodically being washed up onshore it is not unusual for it to only make local news, but for good measure I will alert the coastal patrols to be vigilant and report anything they hear.'

Van Lederman, his elbows leaning on the table, hands clasped with thumbs supporting his chin, looked thoughtfully at his colleague. 'Thanks, Carl,' he responded. 'And I want to know within the hour every commercial interest that Hans Duisen and the de Brouwers shared, whether patron, investor, director or shareholder. And whatever interests they shared I want to know everything about it. In particular, get our tech wizard Peter Kenachi to turn up everything he can on BioGenetics Research.'

'Will do; any particular reason? It is one of Europe's shining

24

lights and becoming a global heavyweight – we'll have to tread carefully.'

'Because it is one interest in which I know for a fact Hans, Simon and Simone were all board directors and significant founding investors a few years ago. To lose one director is unfortunate, two is irresponsible, but three director investors – in twenty-four hours? To me that's just damn suspicious.'

Honstrom rose from the table to leave the room. 'Good enough, I'll get right on it – anything else?'

'Yes. I must remind you of something.' Van Lederman's steel-blue eyes shone in the overhead light as he looked up at his chief operations officer. 'I am chairman of the advisory board for BioGenetics Research.'

Four

Januz Kastrati glanced at the minibus dashboard clock as he drove swiftly through the usually congested arterial Knez Mihailova Street. He nodded in self-approval. The timing to enter the city known as the Balkans Gate and the Door to Central Europe had been well planned. Following behind within a space of ninety minutes were similar vehicles that had either started the journey with him in convoy or had joined from different destinations.

His group had travelled the furthest on this trip, following the Carpathian range as it curved towards southern Slovakia, before leaving Romania via the impoverished Severin region, where the local border guards were once again pleased to benefit from his visit. Next month he would change the route, he promised himself.

A few minutes later he entered the long steel-girdered Brankov Bridge spanning the great river, which teemed with an array of battered barges and a few heavily painted tourist vessels, and conveyed them from the city centre to the swarming suburb of Novi Beograd, a concrete ants' nest, densely populated with humans scurrying along the banks of the Sava and Danube. The minibus drove towards a towering mound and entered into its depths via a steep access ramp.

Kastrati turned to his companion after parking. 'I want to make the selections quickly, Leka. We total a large number this time and the sooner we get it split and underway, the better it will be for everyone.'

Leka Varoshi looked into the dark eyes of Januz Kastrati. There was nothing she would not do for this strong man she utterly adored. 'All will be ready on time,' she replied before standing and turning round. 'Right, everybody,' she addressed the passengers in a sing-song voice. 'I want you all to follow me, quickly and quietly. For those who are good, you will be going on a boat trip.'

Kastrati took the elevator and opened the door to one of the ten apartments occupying the eighth floor that he indirectly owned. The one he entered had interconnecting doors to flats either side. Another six did not. They were his holding pens, each with mattress floors and recently barred windows. Though several jumpers had not attracted any unwanted attention from their suicides, it was a costly and unacceptable inconvenience to him. He'd named the last apartment the entertainment room, which was arranged as a filming studio.

Kastrati threw off his long black jacket, pulled off his T-shirt, revealing a wiry torso that bore numerous scars, and threw it next to his jacket before dialling from his cellphone. From his own unbarred window Kastrati immediately recognized his two small river ferries, marked 'Prince of the Danube Scenic Tours', both licensed to dock at a third of the sixty European cities through which the Danube flowed. Later today, on one of their frequent departures from Belgrade, one would go upstream and the other downstream – when fully loaded.

'*Të marrtë dreqi Petri*,' cursed Kastrati harshly when he heard the call answered.

'*Ta qifsha tokën tënde, Januz*,' came back the immediate reply, before both men laughed. Their habit of swearing at each other in the Albanian Tosk dialect had strengthened the bizarre bond they had built since they had been thrown together in their country's capital, Tirana.

'Good to see you have arrived, Petri; any problems?'

'None, apart from the *qifsha* heat in the shitty sardine can that you put me in!'

'Petri Paloka, how else could you have earned the reputation as the ferryman?' laughed Kastrati before turning serious. 'This is our heaviest cargo to date. I want you underway immediately after we have loaded. You are to go west again, I will take the eastern.'

'Always a pleasure for me, you know that.'

'Yes, but Petri, remember not to spoil the Berlin consignment. You are ready to prepare documents?'

27

'The genius of Santos is flawless – he simple awaits the photos.'

'Good, see you later.'

Kastrati took a long shower, changed into a fresh shirt and matching black jeans, poured a large drink of vodka, and continued to make calls. Ninety minutes later Leka Varoshi entered the apartment, quickly removed her clothing and stepped into the shower. After five minutes she walked, dripping over the floor to the fridge which had been pre-stocked with ready meals. After placing two in the microwave she moved towards her Kastrati, standing in front of him, her hands on her naked hips. 'All that selecting has made me hungry; do we have time?'

Kastrati looked at the slim woman who once more made herself available to him without asking and he wondered when she might realize that he didn't take things that were offered to him on a plate. He liked to take what was not available, by force if required. 'For food, yes,' he answered inwardly smiling at the woman's self-humiliation. 'You are pleased with your selections?' he added.

'I have followed your instructions to the letter. I believe you will be pleased, Januz. They await your final approval,' the woman replied cautiously.

Kastrati walked over to the young woman and placed his hand around her neck, gently stroking her vulnerable throat with his thumb. 'I have confidence in what you approve, Leka. If you are content with your choice, then I am content to accept it. Are you content?'

Leka felt her heart beat faster. 'I am content, Januz,' she replied quietly.

Within two hours of the cargo arriving, either abducted, lured, bought or taken from neglected, former war-torn ghettos, poverty-stricken villages, impoverished market-towns, grimy urban streets and desperate orphanages, it had been selected into two groups and boarded on to the boats.

In the group on the smaller craft, due to head downstream, Anna was crying. She had missed saying goodbye to Mother Govrovych and was hungry, having also missed breakfast. All the others, including those she knew well, did not speak to her, instead meekly staring out of the window. Only one, a girl older than herself, had caught Anna's eye and taken the opportunity to walk towards her soon after they had boarded.

Immediately, one of the chaperones of her group, a short stocky man with a week-old beard, shouted at the older girl. Turning her head Anna witnessed the man smashing the frightened girl's head and face against one of the iron cabin doors. After a horrific shriek the girl fell silent and her body was dragged away.

Nobody would answer any of Anna's questions and everyone's former excitement had turned into fear. None were allowed on deck and instead had been placed in small iron-walled, windowless cabins that smelt of urine. Shortly after that Anna heard the noise of engines and felt the boat lurch into motion. She curled tightly into a ball, scared, hungry, and miserable. 'If my father comes tomorrow,' she whispered to anyone who was listening, 'how will he find me?'

Five

The thickset Irishman sitting in multi-pocketed safari trousers and a green button-down shirt, long sleeves untidily rolled to the elbows, shot a bewildered look at his colleague. 'Connor, you never cease to amaze me. We both get pulled without notice to meet here. We travel all day in blistering heat without air-con or a decent drink to get to a hotel that resembles a nineteenth century boarding house and you say: "Aren't we lucky to be in such an unspoilt haven."'

Matt Ferguson slapped his wide hand against his red neck at the high-pitched whining noise he suddenly heard. 'It's a haven for bloody mosquitoes, that's what it is!'

'Well, there are over two million unspoilt acres with hundreds of bird species, including massive colonies of pelicans; countless lakes, channels and islands blanketed in wild flowers right on our doorstep.' Brock stretched his long jean-clad legs in front of him, looked at his watch for the second time in ten minutes and leaned back in his chair. He pulled at his stone-coloured short-sleeved shirt in an attempt to circulate some cooler air before clasping his hands behind his head to survey the bustling market square in front of their hotel. 'And this town, which has been inhabited for two and half thousand years would you believe?'

'Yes, by bloody mosquitoes, I bet!' Ferguson quipped, slapping his forearm. 'Why do they always seek me out and leave you alone? That's what I want to know, Mr Walking Tourist Guide.'

'Not me; according to the brochure I picked up from the hotel' – Brock leaned forward again to pick up his drink – 'apparently we are at the gateway to the two-thousand-two-hundred-square-mile Danube Delta wetlands.'

No sooner had he leaned back again than a heavy object crashed right on to the table, collapsing it into pieces. Brock and Ferguson were momentarily stunned as they surveyed an overweight naked body lying on its back, arms bound, mouth tightly gagged over a face distorted in agony, and a bloody mess where a male's genitalia had once hung.

Brock's jaw tightened further upon recognizing the face of the contact they had agreed to meet there.

Ferguson's habitual sardonic sense of humour, developed in conjunction with seasoned training and experience, in order to lighten the stress of such events, kicked in.

'Well, that puts a new angle on the old Irish sentiment of "just drop in as you are".'

Brock jumped, cat-like, from the raised terrace down into the square. His eyes narrowed as they swept the hotel, gauging which window would reveal evidence. 'Fourth floor!' he shouted to Ferguson, as he began racing towards the hotel entrance. 'Check back-door exits!' A moment later he reached the solitary and centrally located elevator, which opened on first press. Brock grabbed the information leaflet stand, from which he had selected the enlightening 'Danube Delta' brochure ten minutes earlier, and threw the stand on to its side and into the opening door, preventing further calling. Hitting the stairwell door he then pounded up the stairs two at a time.

On his third flight of steps Brock literally ran into a couple walking casually down the stairs, hand in hand. All three went down into a sprawling heap, the man cursing in pain. Brock extricated himself, shouted an apology and had started on the fourth flight before suddenly stopping. He had noticed spots of blood on the woman's sleeve. He turned back. The woman was standing with a glazed look, as if waiting for the man to take her hand before continuing. The man caught the assessing look emanating from Brock's azure eyes, realizing from the level gaze boring into him that he had been found out. In the seconds that followed the woman continued to stand stock-still while the man pulled a knife from his waist and swung viciously at Brock.

With the advantage of a higher step position, Brock retaliated with a well-aimed kick, catching his assailant on his swinging arm. The knife stayed in the tight grip that held it but the man's own momentum, assisted by Brock's kick, caused him to topple over the low railings. Brock heard two distinct cracks followed by a sickening thud.

With outstretched arms frantically flailing, the survival instinct stimulated the falling man to reach out to the lower stairwell railings on his descent. Both his arms had snapped as they ricocheted off the first balustrade, which bounced him to fall on his back on the second, breaking his spine and neck in numerous places. Death was instantaneous.

Brock turned to the girl, who had not moved, still with a vacant expression. No cry of concern or shock had emitted from her lips.

'What is your name?' Brock asked in English to no effect. He repeated the question in Russian, still with no response. He took hold of her arm and she obediently followed him back down the stairs.

The crowd that had curiously gathered around the body backed off as police arrived. Handing over the mute girl, Brock explained that she was not compos mentis, perhaps drugged, and that her accomplice, in his eagerness to get away, had tripped over the stairs to his death. The police shrugged as if this were a common occurrence, clearly more interested in removing the bodies as quickly as possible.

One man did rush over. 'Mr Brock, I am hotel manager, you recognize, yes? This is the height of tourist season, which we depend on,' he explained. 'Police believe this is matrimonial dispute, horrific, motivated by jealousy. But we cannot allow it to spoil harmony of our haven.'

Feeling slightly more bewildered than Matt had earlier, Brock went looking for him, reaching for his cellphone to call him. Despite the signal being intermittent he tried calling a couple of times without success. After ten minutes of circling the hotel from the square to the river there was still not the slightest trace of Ferguson.

Ferguson arrived too late to block an earlier exit at the rear of the building, but had glimpsed a short stocky man jumping the last few steps of the external metal fire exit and racing away. Ferguson gave chase, following the fugitive down a number of narrow streets to the port before cornering him on a jetty.

A number of small motorized fishing boats were moored,

with one, occupied by an elderly man, just returning. Spotting a convenient escape route the man ran and jumped on the boat without stopping, knocking the surprised occupant overboard with his clenched fist. The displaced boat's tenant fell backwards, hitting his head on the side of one of the adjoining boats. The fugitive then opened the throttle and the boat swung away from the jetty.

Without hesitation, Ferguson jumped into the neighbouring boat; he threw the top part of his body over the side and yanked at the bobbing scruff of the sinking man's neck. His thick arms swung his sodden catch on to the boat, where it lay unconscious. Within a minute Ferguson had started the requisitioned boat, and was once more chasing after his quarry, some eighty metres ahead. Ten minutes later the distance had widened and the boats had entered a confusing network of channels and islands. Ferguson's wet passenger, now conscious, was sitting, looking around in pained confusion. After a further five minutes the target they were chasing had disappeared; all around was an area that reminded him of the Florida Everglades. He heard Brock's words in his head – 'two-thousand-two-hundred-square-mile Danube Delta wetlands'.

'Well, ain't that just dandy, Ferguson! You've bloody done it again. Gone and got yourself stuck in a mosquito-infested haven.'

His alarmed, reluctant passenger let out an incoherent babble, started a violent coughing fit, then whispering after it had passed: 'English?'

'Irish, which is even better. Matt's the name; how are you feeling?'

Before the recovering man could reply they both heard a shout emanating from ahead of them. As their channel passed a reed-covered island Ferguson saw their quarry standing in his stationary boat, pointing a gun at them. Ferguson guessed what had happened.

'Out of fuel, eh?' he shouted, while slamming his own engine into reverse and hit the deck, as the expected bullet whistled through the air above him. 'Well that's no way to thumb a lift, is it?' he said to his alarmed passenger, dragging him on to the deck beside him.

Adrenaline at last kicked into the veins of the twice-assaulted victim, 'I not lost, know way back. We go now.'

'Ah, that's music to the ears,' replied the Irishman, as he guided the boat once more behind the rushes. 'I just have a little something to do first,' he added, cutting the engine as the boat touched the channel bank. 'Stay here and I will be back in a few minutes. You don't want that nasty man who tried to drown you to get away, do you?' The dubious look the man returned prompted Ferguson to increase motivation. 'And you don't want to be losing your fine boat, when we can just as easily tow it back; will you wait for me?'

The man nodded, reached to his belt and handed over a small fish knife. 'Name is Anton, take this,' he answered in reply. Ferguson removed his shoes and began to slip over the side. Anton put his hand on his rescuer's arm, pointing with his other. 'That way best, you will see.'

The crystal clarity and warmth of the water surprised Ferguson, who had expected it to be cold and unpleasant. Within a minute he was positioned slightly behind his target, who was presently shouting towards where he thought his hunter was. 'I not shoot, I give up! We go back now please. Hey, this truth! Talk me. You see is truth!'

Taking a deep breath, Ferguson swam the short remaining distance to beneath the boat, surfacing astern by the outboard. A moment later, he yanked with all his strength down on the side, immediately pulling it up as the water reactively pushed back. The unexpected unbalancing had the desired effect of causing the gunman to topple into the water. Despite gasping for air as his head broke the surface he swam decisively to the bank, still holding the gun in his right hand. His face turned once more to shock as he felt himself being pulled under. Kicking wildly, he felt his legs trapped and turned the gun towards them, firing off a shot. He screamed. The panic shot had missed the Irishman's arms, holding on in a bear-like grip, and ripped into the shooter's own thigh.

Ferguson surfaced through water clouding with blood, his vice-like forearm swiftly moving to curl around his opponent's neck. Grabbing the wrist of the weapon hand with his other arm he swung it hard against the boat. The gun sank as smashed knuckles forced its release. Pushing to the bank while maintaining his grip, Ferguson gained his footing and dragged the struggling assassin to the ground, before slipping on the wet reeds. Immediately taking advantage, the man moved his head and sunk his teeth into his attacker's forearm. Reacting with hard-won experience Ferguson used his fingers to gouge the man's eyes. The vicious biting stopped as the man screamed in agony and fear; Ferguson slammed a fist into the side of his head for good measure. All was silent.

Six

Returning to his room, Brock did not feel undue concern for Matt. The possibility of there being a further assailant was not remote. He was confident of Matt following up the lead and chose to continue directly with his own. Checking the voicemail of his cellphone from the hotel room revealed a lengthy, disturbing and horrific message.

Twelve hours earlier van Lederman had called Brock directly requesting that he and Ferguson travel immediately to Izmail on the Ukrainian border and investigate a research clinic that was affiliated as a supplier for BioGenetics Research. The clinic's shareholders included the de Brouwer family and the Duisen Foundation.

Van Lederman had already contacted BioGenetics Research and had been directed to talk to one of the scientists he knew, Ron Patrowsky, currently visiting Izmail. Patrowsky had been shocked by van Lederman's news about Herr Duisen. Van Lederman learned that Patrowsky was there at the behest of Duisen. Brock had called him direct upon arrival. Patrowsky said that he had been expecting his call but first wanted to follow up on an idea that had come to him following his conversation with van Lederman. They agreed to meet in two hours at Brock's hotel.

Brock's blood ran cold as he listened to a stilted conversation, culminating in muffled cries of tortuous pain recorded from Professor Ron Patrowsky. Clearly the unfortunate victim had made a call which had been interrupted: 'Mr Brock, it's Patrowsky. I'm already here at the hotel. I took an earlier ferry. Upon reflection it's better to meet you in my room . . . it's um . . . it's not . . . well I'll explain when you arrive. Come straight up when you arrive . . . room four-o-five . . .'

The message had then recorded the sound of knocking, a door opening and then a crash as if someone was pushed across the room, followed by a clunk as if the receiver had been thrown. Then a heated conversation: 'What are you doing here!' shouted a frightened Patrowsky.

'Strip him and search him,' said a gravel voice. 'He has it somewhere.'

'Leave me alone, stop it! What are you doing?' A series of crashes and shrieking protestations followed.

'I have it!' answered another higher voice.

'Listen to me, toad man,' continued the gravel voice. 'You are from Poland; I am from the western Ukraine. The dilution of my language with Polish means you understand me; either in Polish or English. No?'

'I am an American citizen! I don't speak Polish! Leave me alone . . .' Another shriek.

'Or else what, toad man? Your government will strongly object? Ha! They don't even know where Ukraine or Poland is. How will they find you? Or me? And why would they care to? We have nothing they want. Now, tell why you have taken this little stick. No doubt packed with the stolen information, no?'

'It's not stolen,' cried Patrowsky desperately. 'It is my research . . . my analysis. Let me show you.'

'It is of no interest to me. I just came to return it. And collect this lovely young patient too, who you took away from her bed. She is one of your special patients, no? Perhaps I can ask her to assist me, eh?'

'What do you mean?'

The gravel voice switched back to Ukrainian. 'Gag him, keep the fat toad quiet.' A series of muffled shrieks followed. 'I think we should try an experiment of our own, no? What they call in America a win-win one, eh? I get information and we make good test of your patient. Now, Tila, listen carefully. I want you to hold this sharp knife. Good. Now, I am going to ask your doctor a question. If he does not answer, then I command you to castrate him. Do you understand?'

Silence.

'Good. So, Professor Patrowsky, tell me, what is plan?'

Inaudible shrieking followed by a short laugh.

'What, no answer? The cat has got your tongue? OK, no matter we have what we came for. Tila, castrate him.' The sound of struggling followed by a muffled agonized screaming. 'You are genius, doctor, experiment works. With such reputation you will soon be flying. Have a good trip.' The gravel voice became quieter as if the speaker's head had turned. 'I go now, throw him out window and leave.'

Brock heard a door opening and closing, followed shortly afterwards by the scraping of a window being opened and a huge distant crash – the inhuman muffled cries stopped.

Brock went to the police station to see if the drugged girl, the catatonic Tila, had spoken, only to discover that she had been moved to another location. 'By men in white coats, no doubt,' he commented lightly.

'Yes,' the officer at the desk replied flatly, before turning to answer another enquiry. Brock walked back to the square and followed the road to the port to check the ferry times to Izmail. Across the river on the town outskirts he recognized the medieval citadel from the brochure he had perused earlier. Fixed to the quay was a telescope, a recently installed tourist accoutrement requiring one Romanian lei, about thirty cents. Inserting a coin, Brock brought the lens to focus on the citadel, stoutly positioned on its rising cliff. He was disappointed to see the incongruous appendages that had been constructed into the integrity of the former fortress, distorting its original shape into a prefabricated factory.

So, twenty-first century meets thirteenth century, he mused to himself as he shifted the lens on to what resembled a school outing moving in a crocodile fashion towards what he knew to be the clinic. A wide window overlooked the series of private, public and military jetties that were intermittently constructed along the riverside.

As the shutter clicked and he walked past the series of similar jetties on his own side of the river, he decided to go to the clinic himself. Hearing his name hailed he turned to see Ferguson mooring two boats. Within two minutes of joining him they were heading back up the river to one of the many hidden islets out of view from the town.

Brock looked at the bound, wounded man sprawled out on the deck, the tourniquet secured tightly around his leg having stemmed the bleeding. Dried blood was still evident around his puffy swollen eyes.

'I know that you have it,' said Brock to him without emotion. 'Does anyone have anything sharp?'

Ferguson looked at his colleague in bewilderment as he handed over the short knife loaned to him by the fisherman, who threw a dubious, then resigned look towards his unusual passengers. The gagged man began to struggle frantically as Brock sliced the blood-soaked trousers off and pointed the blade at his now vulnerable manhood.

'Here's a man who believes in action before words, Matt. So I thought we should play it his way. He has what was intended for us, and we will take it, but first we will leave our mark. Is that OK with you, Mr –? Oh sorry, you're unable to talk. Did you want the opportunity to speak? Now why should I allow you that? Did you give that luxury to Dr Patrowsky?' Frantic nodding ensued. 'You didn't, and I know you didn't . . . however . . . search him thoroughly, Matt, then perhaps we can let the man speak.'

Matt found a small memory stick. 'It's damp, but it should be OK with a hairdryer,' Matt said flatly as he pocketed it and then removed the gag. Immediately the man cursed. 'You have no idea who you are dealing with. You're dead. All your family are dead for what you have done!'

'So he's attended that course on how to win friends and influence people, I see,' Ferguson quipped. 'And does the fella have a name so that we can quake in our shoes when we hear it?'

'Well,' added Brock as he pushed the blade against the man, 'what is your name?'

The man's eyes widened as he saw the blade so close to his exposed privates, but he tried to maintain bravado as he answered. 'Doroshenko, cousin to the Mortician,' he shouted with pride and glee, his expression changing to surprise when not the slightest recognition was forthcoming from his audience.

'Look Dory, your accomplice is dead – he fell downstairs – is that who you mean?' offered Brock.

'That fool, Lenser . . . of course not! You will learn soon enough.'

'I'll look forward to it.' Brock pressed his blade against Doroshenko's groin. 'For now I would like to know why you killed Patrowsky.'

Doroshenko gave a half-smile. 'I not kill the toad. Girl slices him, not me! That fool Lenser kill him, I am innocent.'

'Why was he killed?' repeated Brock, pressing his knife so that the delicate skin was broken and blood appeared on the knife point.

'Because it was ordered, dead man! Go ahead and slice, you dead man. You run. There is no place to hide!'

'Who ordered it?' asked Brock quietly as he pushed the knife, ignoring the man's bravado. Blood appeared and then seeped over the blade as the knife opened the soft skin.

'Goryachev, the Mortician, of course!' screamed the hit-man. 'I get call to locate, retrieve and dispose.'

'Your cousin,' prompted Brock, releasing his pressure on the knife. 'And where do we find him?'

Doroshenko laughed. 'He will find you!'

'Well, let's hope he does, because dealing with lowlife sadists like you and your boss are my speciality.'

The man began to curse once more. 'You'd better gag him, Matt,' concluded Brock.

Seven

Following the convoy had proved a challenge after it had split up in Belgrade. Yet deciding to pursue the largest of the three buses and keeping it in sight, due to its size and inability to move quickly across Belgrade, had proved a good choice. Sonja Brezvanje observed it parking next to a tower block and unloading its passengers; she was certain she had at last located the Pied Piper's holding station.

Her strategy of waiting had also proved to be correct, yet she was shocked to see so many children and teenagers walk quietly in order down to the waiting boats. There had to be at least two hundred. She had split the team: her cousin, Jakiv Teslenko, would go upstream with the most recent member of her team, Natalya, and Georghe Enescu, who had been with her and Jakiv from the beginning; Sonja herself would go downstream with her partner Radu Raducioiu.

'Remember, Georghe, you are only to follow and observe. No heroics.'

'But there are so many. We should do something,' Enescu argued.

'In understanding their planning and routing, we are. I urge you to be patient. We must gather evidence.'

The latest call with Jakiv had reported yet another stop. The first had been Budapest in Hungary. Georghe had followed the small group of six teenage girls and one adult woman that had disembarked. The second had been Bratislava, in Slovakia, which Natalya had followed. This time it was Vienna and three separate groups had disembarked. Her team was frustratingly small and she had agonized over whether to have Jakiv follow a group or stick with the boat.

41

'Stay with the boat,' she instructed, 'and stay in touch.'

Radu Raducioiu turned towards her, a strong wiry young man of few words, his weariness evident; the small cabined motor-boat had required constant supervision. During the past twenty-four hours the tour boat had docked at six cities and small towns. First at Dobreta in Romania, where three children had boarded; then Nikopol and Rousse in Bulgaria, where one child and three older teenagers had joined respectively; then for one girl at Oltenita in Romania and finally the city of Braila, where two more teenagers had been taken aboard. What had surprised both her and Radu was all the teenagers had swollen bellies, as if in the medium stages of pregnancy.

'They are docking again, Sonja. The map indicates Izmail,' said Raducioiu.

Sonja glanced at her watch. Almost midday; the high sun reflected off the silver-grey naval and coastguard vessels anchored beyond the port. The port itself was an array of barges and tour boats of all sizes. High above the bleak town stood the ancient Izmail Fortress she had heard of, but until now, never seen. Born in an overcrowded communist tenement in Kiev, the very centre of Slavic civilization, she had never travelled to her country's southernmost port. Her mother had worked in a downtown bar on the Dneiper River. Her mother had long disappeared; she had never known her father. There had been two older brothers, now she was the only remaining sibling.

Sonja looked into the dark, haunted eyes of the Romanian man she had known for eight months now. He had been searching for his young sister when they had met. He had immediately joined her group and had become the most dependable friend she had known. She placed her hand on his. The look that passed between them required no words. They had become lovers only a few weeks ago, yet their passion was their joint mission. Each knew how the other felt with their mutual sense of injustice at the suffering of so many innocents from their countries.

Sonja reached for the field glasses. 'There is a bus waiting for them.' She counted forty children, obediently walking along a quay towards it. 'They are so docile' she said to Radu.

*   *   *

Januz Kastrati mentally praised his foresight as he swaggered arrogantly next to the Izmail clinic receptionist who accompanied him to the director general's office. Upon entering he plumped himself down on the chair in front of Hristo Amaut's desk before being invited to.

'You will enjoy your lunch today, my friend,' said Kastrati.

Amaut spent a few more moments studying the laptop computer in front of him, annoyed at the intrusive way Kastrati made his entrance. 'And why should today be any different?' he enquired, looking up.

'Because I bring a selection of all blood groups, including a rare rhesus negative and six ripening pregnancies all under your preferred twenty weeks – a bundle of life-enhancing assets all in good working order. And, I might add, eager to be of use to you.'

Amaut raised his black bushy eyebrows, his hooded eyes perusing his visitor without emotion. 'Are you presuming to know my requirements?'

'I took the precaution of setting up my own little laboratory on board.' Kastrati grinned broadly, the smile not reaching the black eyes that he levelled at the director general. 'To save time in our negotiations, you understand.'

Amaut paused before answering. 'Amateurish tampering does not save time. Perhaps the order is no longer acceptable.'

'You want I should take them away? OK, no problem.' Kastrati kept his emotions hidden as he got up to go. No one would play him along.

'There is no need to react so hastily my friend,' said Amaut calmly, getting up from his desk and moving towards a coffee machine in the corner. 'I expect you have been revising your remuneration requirements also. Coffee?'

Kastrati slowly returned to his seat. During the past three years building his trafficking network he had learned never to compromise and also to hold the best cards. Information had been the key. Approached in January to provide specific orders for this clinic he took it upon himself to find out why. His brand of trafficking was for the sex industry, plain and simple. Supplying the network of brothels across Europe was highly lucrative. Every asset carried a fairly standard purchase and sales price and generated a set income, which, as it depreciated, would have to be replaced. But Amaut's Izmail clinic, if what he learned was true, was maximizing each asset in ways he had never imagined.

Last year he had taken a percentage of the Internet company which used the assets he filmed for the porn industry. They had been forced to agree in order to receive a regular source of videos that would meet the increasingly bizarre demands of their logged-on members. He would simply apply the same strategy with Amaut.

'Yes, I will take a coffee; and you're right: I have a desire to simplify our current agreement.'

Amaut gave his visitor a measured look. He did not like him, but had to tolerate him. 'And how would that be?'

'In plain and simple terms? Well, in addition to our usual finder's fee, I now want a percentage of your end value; say twenty per cent? There, plain and simple, don't you agree?'

Amaut shook his head in disbelief. 'Well that's twenty per cent of nothing. We are a research centre. You are a supplier of a raw material. Which I might add, is our biggest outlay.'

'Do you take me for a fool, Hristo? One asset alone with "matching criteria" can be worth two hundred and fifty American dollars.'

'Criteria?' asked Amaut blankly.

Kastrati's face clouded over. 'What do you take me for? Organs of course! In the form of kidneys, heart, liver, lungs! Then there's marrow, essential for leukaemia, I understand, and blood. Then there is your requirement for pregnant girls, whether to carry to full term or not, for your precious research. Oh, don't look so shocked, I know what you are doing. Forty specific candidates every month! Have you any idea of the risks my organization has to take to deliver such an order?'

'I do have an idea where you are getting such ideas from – science fiction. And a little knowledge is, as they say, a dangerous thing.' Amaut stood up and walked across to the window; he could see Kastrati's moored vessel. 'Listen, Januz, we pay you top dollar and the young people we acquire from you are not ending their lives on the streets or in some drug den.'

Kastrati's face broke into a broad satisfying grin that turned to a cold sneer. 'Not on the streets, maybe; but they're still ending their lives, Mister Director General.'

Amaut paused to consider the supplier in front of him. He

could tell that his words were to no avail. The man's hypnotic eyes seemed verging on the fanatic; certainly there was an under-current of sheer ruthlessness present. He would play this game as he had before. He carried the two coffees he had prepared over to his desk, and sat down behind it. 'Listen, Januz, even if it is possible for us to form some new agreement, I am sure that you also know, as you seem to be so well informed, that any such agreement is hardly reliant on my sole decision.'

Amaut momentarily paused to take a sip from his coffee. 'Unlike you, I have to answer to shareholders and discuss with a board of directors. This takes time. So you can choose to be patient or you, as you say, can choose to leave with your consign-ment. What will it be?'

Ignoring his own coffee, Kastrati placed his hands behind his head, leaned back and disrespectfully placed his feet on the director general's desk. 'Listen, Hristo, I will take my delivery fee on account now. If you cannot get agreement by the end of this month, then any future consignments will be diverted, as you said, to the street.'

Amaut nodded. 'Agreed; anything else?'

'Yes, there is. I have a question relating to the drug you have supplied me with. The one I have called the Pied Piper.'

'What is it?' enquired Amaut.

'It appears to have less effect on our older candidates. Can I administer a stronger dose?'

Amaut sat down. 'You must be careful. The high metabol-isms of young candidates are affected quicker. Someone in their thirties for example will not feel anything untoward. Too high a dose, however, can be dangerous. The intention is for plia-bility, not to have living mannequins.'

Kastrati laughed. 'That's exactly what we want, isn't it? The drug is great. It has allowed me to increase supply while main-taining minimal supervision.'

'Which also increases your income? It would appear that you view all elements of your trade as a one-way street in your favour,' offered Amaut disdainfully.

'Correct. What other way is there?' answered Kastrati flatly.

Amaut stood up again. 'I insist that you use the drug we give you as directed. It is to facilitate our requirements not termi-nate them.'

45

'Is that not what you do, in the end?' Kastrati sneered.

'You know the difference between you and me, Januz? You do what you do for money, plain and simple, to use your words. I do what I do for the greater good of mankind.'

'Ha!' Kastrati scoffed rudely. Pushing his chair back he stood up and moved slowly into the other's space until his face was a few inches from Amaut's. 'No, my friend,' he said coldly, 'the difference between you and me is that I do not deceive myself. I am a live meat-trader fulfilling an insatiable demand. And so are you, plain and simple.'

Eight

T he group of six girls and their new chaperone, who had met them at their disembarkation, exited the minibus taxi that had driven them the nine kilometres from the Danube, entered the rectangular glass structure topped with the sign Bratislava Airport, and passed smoothly through security at Slovakia's international terminal. Once again the timing had been perfect, checking in forty minutes before their 14.15 departure for Luton Airport, just forty minutes north of London. The chaperone passed their passports, all expertly produced on board the *Prince of the Danube* during the past twenty-four hours, to the clerk at the check-in booth to locate the booking. The chaperone received all boarding passes into her hand where she retained them with the passports.

For the next inspection at passport control, the chaperone called each girl in turn while she passed over the corresponding passport and boarding pass. All duly received a peremptory glance. Their small matching backpacks displaying Summer Camp Holiday stickers passed the X-ray without event. Each contained the right size of short dress, a change of underwear and a wash bag – all given along with the jeans and coloured blouses worn for travel. Only one girl had her bag randomly searched while her companions dutifully waited for her. The chaperone then purchased and handed out a bottle of water to each girl as they waited in a group for boarding.

Natalya Toruk clenched her fists as she continued to fight against what she really wanted to do. Sonja had insisted that she must observe only. 'I know it hurts, Natalya,' Sonja had said when they spoke on the phone while the girls were checking in. 'You know I understand. But you must concentrate on

47

observing all details so that we can advise our network to continue tracking in the UK.'

'But the girls themselves, Sonja, they seem almost robotic. Whatever is asked of them they just nod their heads. I don't understand. I fought and always tried to escape. What have they done to them – stolen their minds?'

Sonja received a similar story from Georghe Enescu in Budapest. The group he had followed had also been met by a chaperone at disembarkation, who had then adhered to a similar procedure. They boarded a discount airline, again departing with perfect timing, for Berlin Schoenefeld airport at 12.50. 'They are too good to be true,' related Enescu. Their chaperone says stop, all stop; go, all go; sit, all sit; laugh, all laugh. They don't seem human, more like willing robots. I think it is best that I follow.'

Sonja had been afraid of hearing such a reaction. Enescu disliked the feeling of helplessness when he could not follow things through because their numbers would not permit it. 'No, Georghe, you know we can't. That is not our role,' she said firmly.

'Just what is our role, Sonja?' Enescu argued. 'In London we can rely upon the team we have an alliance with; but we have no one to pick up the trail in Berlin. Once these girls get on that plane that is the last we will see of them.'

'I know, Georghe, but listen to me. I need you to return to Bucharest. Please understand I will need you there.'

'Sorry, Sonja. It is too late. I have a ticket. Boarding is now. I will call you from Berlin.'

'Georghe, no!' implored Sonja, but Enescu had already terminated the call.

After the Danube tour boat had dispensed several groups in Vienna, a European hub for transcontinental flight, Jakiv had stayed with the vessel as instructed, advising Sonja each time more groups were despatched from Linz, Passau and Regensberg.

'All locations conveniently running discount airlines,' Sonja had commented.

'Or on arterial routes,' added Jakiv. 'From Linz to Prague; or Passau to Munich; and Regensburg to Frankfurt. There are too many for us to follow, Sonja. All tiny organized pockets easily concealed in Europe's big overcoat.'

Jakiv's gift for simile was jolting. How could she and her small band stop such a flow of illegal traffic? Yet once more the thought served to strengthen her resolve. She would block the very source. Everything led back to the Pied Piper.

'After Ulm, we are almost at the source,' continued Teslenko, interrupting her thoughts.

'Sorry, Jakiv, can you repeat that?'

'I said it's turning around now. I would imagine it is too big for further passage. After the city of Ulm only riverboats the size of mine can make further passage.'

Sonja wanted to confirm all the docking stations. 'Stay with the boat.'

'OK. Oh, hang on, Sonja. A smaller boat, looks like a fast speedboat. I think it has just come alongside it.'

'What's happening?'

'I can't see, it's on the other side. Just a minute.'

Sonja waited.

'No, it's gone off again, heading upstream, though there's no way this hire boat is going to be able to follow it.'

Sonja bit her lip again in frustration. 'OK, Jakiv, stay with the main boat; and keep a safe distance. You don't want them to know that you are following them.'

A late summer afternoon sun was casting long shadows over a turreted former residence of the Princes of Furstenberg in Donaueschingen. Nestled on the Baar plateau in the Black Forest where the confluence of two rivers, Brigach and Breg, formed the source of the Danube, the tiny city of 22,000 inhabitants continued its usual orderly calm. Inside the former French military barracks, utilized during the 1990s by the US as a hospital and facility for Eastern Bloc refugees, there was an air of anticipation amongst a gathering of world press mingling with elite scientists. The great hall had been restored to its former eighteenth-century splendour by the palace's new owners, BioGenetics Research.

William Steinwright paused as he reached the podium, as always, to raise gravitas and expectation. Though there was little need as both were at an all-time high. 'Thank you for your warm welcome, yet it is I that must sincerely thank you for your valuable time in coming here this evening. Though our intended announcement has been planned for a month now, it is with great sadness that it must also act as an occasion for another.

'As most of you will have heard, three of our close colleagues, all BioGenetics founding patrons and board members, cannot attend. Such great people as Hans Duisen, Simon de Brouwer and Simone de Brouwer have been untimely lost to a world that will greatly miss them. I fondly recall the first time all of them stood in unison in this very room four years ago, all sharing a vision of a healthy world eradicated of degenerative and cancerous disease.'

Steinwright paused again as a lump involuntarily formed in his throat. 'We will all miss their wisdom, inspiration and courage. We will miss their friendship. I will miss my friends.' Another pause, as Steinwright removed his glasses and wiped them.

'What is comforting, however, is that before their passing they knew that the daunting wall, which for years has held back progress in our world and cast a shadow over its people's quality of life, has started to weaken. Through its widening cracks we are at last able to envisage the future they dreamed of and we all hoped for.

'My friends, esteemed colleagues, ladies and gentlemen of the press, I am pleased to announce that we have made such a breakthrough. BioGenetics Research has discovered – which we hold to be both revolutionary and evolutionary – a longevity drug with recuperative powers for Alzheimer's sufferers. And tests on other degenerative diseases, including Parkinson's, are already proving positive.'

Steinwright beamed as his audience applauded. A moment later a myriad of questions were fired at him.

'Kate Drew, CNN. When will this drug be available?'

'Most of your questions will be answered in the press pack you will receive as you go. However, we anticipate launch in both the US and Western Europe in January, following the licence approval and registration in those sectors. From next year all countries will follow, as soon as licence approval and registration is granted.'

'Bill Tollins, *New Scientist*. Could you explain the extensiveness of your testing, and do you have a name?'

'Neurofribiline, and yes, all research data are attached to your press pack, which adhere to all the strictest requirements.'

'Dr Matthew Penfold, *The Lancet.* How does your drug differ from current cholinesterase inhibitors that prevent the breakdown of acetylcholine?'

'The short answer is by preventing the development of amyloid plaques and neurofibrillary tangles that characterize such degenerative disease. But, please, Doctor, all technical answers are available in the usual manner. Let us not blind our non-technical guests at today's general announcement. So I will take one more question before passing over to my colleague to continue our presentation.'

'Dagmar Stahl, Börse Online. Professor, I have a non-technical question for you. Three of your leading shareholders and directors all died within a twelve-hour period. How does this affect ownership of BioGenetics?'

'You must have expected such a question William,' said van Lederman, who had driven from Zurich in time for the announcement. 'The point is, who is in line for the thirty per cent? Will you be looking for the institutional market to take it up or partnering with one of the pharmaceuticals? With the share value certain to rise, it would be the right move.'

Steinwright placed his glass of champagne on a passing tray, untouched. 'Correct, Paul, but in fact de Brouwer's nineteen per cent holding will stay where it is, with the family. As for the eleven per cent Hans Duisen controlled, well you probably know more than me, being an executor to the estate.'

'For Hans, I am, yes; though not for the Duisen Foundation. But only this morning the estate lawyers informed me that there was an ongoing discussion with a private investor introduced by Simone de Brouwer. Apparently Hans had been considering whether to cast his vote to liquidate their investment in BGR.'

Steinwright sighed. 'It comes as no surprise. The last meeting we had was in fact a little heated. For some reason Hans felt there was something going on he didn't know about.'

'Is there, William?' van Lederman invited.

Steinwright jerked his head up like an annoyed bulldog, 'Of course not! You know yourself Hans was a numbers man, insisting that they told a story. He argued our research investment was not adding up. But come on, Paul. You, of all people, know that research in our field is almost entirely made up of intangibles. We invest fifty million dollars in a hundred thousand permutations and can be no closer to what we think we are looking for.'

Something caught Steinwright's eye and he smiled. 'Anyway, at the risk of changing the subject, there's someone I want you to meet.' Steinwright guided van Lederman by the arm towards a couple who had just entered the room. 'Stephan, it's so good to see you, and you too, Sophia. Paul, allow me to introduce you to Stephan de Brouwer and his beautiful fiancée, Sophia Lefrington from the US, with an offer to assist with our research here. Stephan, Sophia, this is Paul van Lederman.'

'It's a pleasure to meet you, Stephan. And please permit me to extend my sincere condolences at your recent loss. Your father was a dear friend of mine. He always spoke very highly of you. I believe that both your mother and father would be immensely proud of you, representing them here today.'

'Thank you, Paul. It has been a huge shock; tonight was going to be very special for us as a family.' Stephan paused for a moment before adding, 'My father spoke very highly of you too and valued your advice. Perhaps I too could call upon it when needed?'

'It would be both an honour and a pleasure,' smiled van Lederman. 'And what a pleasure it is to meet your fiancée Sophia. Though I have not met him, I have heard of your father's reputation.'

'Thank you and we must put that to rights, for he is here.'

'I would welcome that and you must share with me the research you are interested in. Who knows, perhaps while you are visiting Europe, you will allow an old-fashioned gentleman to assist you.'

Van Lederman allowed Sophia to confidently take his arm, leaving her fiancé with Steinwright. 'Well, thank you, kind sir, come on.'

Van Lederman listened as the girl chatted to him, with half his mind on his own research compiled earlier that morning on the private investor who would soon own over a tenth of BioGenetics Research: Conrad Lefrington.

Nine

A maut looked down towards the river from his elevated position. He clenched his jaw as he recognized the man's arrogant gait walking along their private jetty below. Kastrati was yet another dangerous loose cannon who would have to be dealt with. Perhaps one too many, he thought. Perhaps he should get out and, if what he had learned from that archaeologist was true, there might just be the opportunity.

Then he shook his head. 'Ah, but pipe dreams,' he said to himself aloud. He knew the unpredictability of truth serums. Designed to reveal the dominant thoughts that preoccupied a person's mind, they often only revealed delusional fabrications – those things that people so wanted to believe, they did in fact believe to be factual. The information extracted from the girl was disjointed. Still, it was interesting, perhaps tomorrow he—
The shrill ring of his desk phone interrupted his thinking as he quickly moved to his desk, knowing it was the call he was expecting.

The refined voice that opened the conversation was not concerned with preliminaries. 'You wanted me. What do you have to report?'

Amaut kept to the point. 'Our Pied Piper wants us to pay him more: twenty per cent of what he considers our end value to be.'

'I take it he has delivered a consignment?'

'Itemized, in fact, thanks to a new onboard laboratory he has installed, hence his demand.'

There was a pause; Amaut waited. 'Has he? Very well, thank you for bringing it to my attention; I will think about how I want to deal with this. But the consignment itself – it is good?'

'He has actually exceeded our expectations this time. There are even some rare types.'

'Good, keep me informed on which types. Now tell me, what of our visitor?'

'Patrowsky?' the director general asked.

'Are there others I should know about, Hristo?'

'I thought you meant Neumann,' recovered Amaut before adding, 'who arrived for his monthly visit also.'

'Yes, Patrowsky,' said the voice coldly.

'I contacted Goryachev, as required, to deal with the matter. Unfortunately I understand from our friendly officer that it was in Tulcea's market square.'

'Such details are his to choose. Have you retrieved what was stolen?'

'The girl he took with him has been collected, but we are still awaiting recovery of the memory stick, which Goryachev's team must have.'

'It's a pity your surveillance did not catch him earlier storing files. This was the infernal man's second visit in a month; it was no doubt he who caused us unnecessary problems earlier.'

'But his neurological work was in our interest,' countered Amaut, attempting to alleviate the blame put upon him. 'How could I know that he was?'

'Because it is your responsibility!' interrupted the voice. 'It is your responsibility to monitor every visitor who is not directly employed by you. Now, tell me about Neumann,' asked the voice flatly as it moved to another subject.

'He arrived Tuesday, placed his biggest order to date and returned immediately.'

'You are able to fulfil it?'

'With the assets just received, yes.'

Amaut felt the tension in the pause that followed. 'And my personal order?' enquired the voice quietly.

The director general saw an opportunity to ingratiate himself. 'It will be fulfilled, and we are hopeful about the other development we are researching.'

'Good, Hristo, I shall look forward to that.'

The phone clicked off.

* * *

54

The elderly man ran to inform the police of the man lying in his boat, who had inadvertently shot himself while trying to hijack it. Sharing how the thug had attempted to coerce him to help make his escape and how he, a man in his late sixties, had valiantly smashed the fugitive's face with a boat hook, knocking him out, made the fisherman a local celebrity. 'Bravery of local man foils foreign criminal' would read the morning newspaper, delighting both the police and the mayor of Tulcea.

Brock and Matt had returned to their hotel. With most of the files password-protected, Brock had forwarded all the data from the memory stick directly to resident technical wizard Pete Kenachi at ICE. Formerly on the FBI's wanted hackers list before Carl Honstrom had recruited him, every file would soon open to his dextrous mind and fingers. The files Brock had opened successfully appeared to substantiate the information that van Lederman had already relayed.

Brock's view, influenced by the past twenty-four hours, was that the exclusive clinic was a façade for something untoward. The death of Patrowsky, linked with the appearance and disappearance of a catatonic young woman – in turn both linked to the clinic – added up to more than what these files contained. One thing both he and van Lederman were in agreement on was that all such events were always worth addressing head-on. By late afternoon Brock was shown into Director General Amaut's office.

Amaut had been assessing his unexpected visitor via reception room monitors. There was a quiet confidence about him – perhaps former military. When he moved it was with a relaxed intensity, as a panther would noiselessly track its prey. And amusement too, coupled with determination, in the eyes that turned and stared, as if instinctively, at the hidden monitor. With his personal assistant away from her desk he had gone to meet Brock personally, using his key card to open and close the series of security doors that led up to his office.

'Good of you to see me, sir, at such short notice,' said Brock after they had made their introductions.

'Please, Connor, call me Hristo.' He directed Brock to be seated while he moved towards an area in the corner of his office. 'You are more than welcome. Naturally, as soon as I learned you were representing the estate of one of our patrons

I instantly cleared my agenda. It was good of you to call. The news was a great shock. Now allow me to insist on you trying a special coffee? I can promise you every cup is freshly made with this little luxury I have indulged myself with here, particularly when one's secretary is away on maternity leave.'

'Thank you, sounds like a very practical indulgence,' replied Brock pleasantly. 'Yes, it is shocking news for us all,' he continued. 'I sincerely hope that their deaths will not adversely affect your clinic. Will they?'

Amaut paused while he prepared two cups of coffee and placed them on the table between them. 'A good question and indeed one we are still waiting to find out about, though, as you will be aware, the Duisen Foundation recently decided to transfer their shareholder status. We can only hope that the de Brouwer's estate, which is substantial, will retain their holding. The family is renowned for keeping its investments for generations, so we remain optimistic. In our field, and as a privately funded clinic, stability is important.'

'Smells interesting,' commented Brock as he brought the cup of coffee under his nose. 'What field are you in exactly?' asked Brock.

'It's Arabic blended with a little Turkish.' Amaut imitated his guest's action. 'Primarily, we research cancerous and degenerative syndromes. We have patients, though we are not available for general admission. Predominantly our patients are terminal cases, who come to us on a voluntary basis seeking relief from their conditions. In receiving it they allow us to – how do you say? – guinea-pig them in return.'

'Sounds like a good working relationship, though I was surprised how young your voluntary admissions are. I noticed a group arriving earlier today. They could only have been teenagers.'

A look of surprise momentarily flashed across Amaut's face. 'Very observant of you, Connor, though they are not for admission.' He chuckled. 'The nature of our work requires very limited visiting to our patients. Therefore we can only permit the closest of kin, a patient's children for example. Once a month we collect them and bring them here for the weekend. We even arrange that the children's visit includes an excursion down the Danube. It can be very hard for a child to know they are losing or have lost a parent, so naturally we try to alleviate their stress.'

Brock's mind instantly flew to another time and place. Losing his wife in a hit-and-run. At the time their baby daughter had lost a parent, but being raised by Heather's sister, the child, now aged ten years, had not been told. 'Very thoughtful,' he commented.

'Of course for that very same reason, I am sure you will understand that I cannot offer you a tour of our premises,' continued Amaut.

'I understand, but may I just impose a little more on your time with a couple of other questions?'

Amaut glanced at his watch. 'Yes, continue,' he said as he reached again for the coffee cup in front of him.

'I represent the executor of Hans Duisen's estate, and as I explained, I am tasked with verifying what interests are attached to it. My original intention was to actually make an introduction through an associate of Herr Duisen, a Professor Ron Patrowsky. Perhaps you have heard of the neurologist?'

'Of course! He was a guest of ours yesterday, in fact, though he never mentioned anything. If I had known I would have had him join us.'

Brock leaned forward. 'Then you would be truly providing miracles at your establishment, Hristo, because his naked corpse crashed on to my breakfast table only this morning.'

Coffee spilled all over Amaut's shirt as he jolted upright. 'What! That's . . . that's . . . oh that's shocking news! Terrible, terrible!'

'We know there were three involved in his murder; one is dead, another accidentally shot himself and is in custody,' continued Brock.

Amaut stood and began to pace around, finding it impossible to hide his agitation. The spilled hot coffee on his chest was ignored. 'This is outrageous. Why would anyone do such a thing? Do they know why? Was it a mugging or something? Crime is rife in the towns around here. Abject poverty meets tourist wealth.'

'Well, bizarrely, he had been castrated just prior to being launched out of a fourth floor window,' said Brock, flatly. 'An unusual practice for muggers; wouldn't you agree?'

Amaut stopped and grabbed Brock by the shoulder. 'But what of the third person – did they get away?'

'Well, that's the odd thing,' answered Brock. 'A young female, suspected of actually performing the castration while in some bizarre controlled, almost catatonic state, was released by the police into the custody of – well, your clinic, would you believe.'

Brock let the information, which he had embellished upon, sink in, observing the increased pallor of his host before adding: 'Apparently she was one of Patrowsky's own patients, or should I say neurological experiments?'

'I'm sorry, Mr Brock, I must ask you to leave. Your news has shocking implications.'

'I'm sorry too, Hristo, but I must insist that I stay. How can I report back to shareholders if I have not had the opportunity to inspect your operation here?'

The director general looked aghast. 'Impossible! We don't disturb our patients under any circumstances!' he shouted.

Brock pointed at the director general's desk console. 'Then perhaps you would allow me to see your array of monitors, so as not to disturb your patients?'

Amaut went an apoplectic shade of purple. 'How dare you! You do not even represent our shareholders. I have already told you that Duisen had agreed to sell out his interest. As for the de Brouwers, I know for a fact that you do not act for them. You come here uninvited and cast aspersions on my clinic! You will either leave my office now, or I will have you thrown out!'

Brock got up to leave. 'Well if you put it that way, Hristo, I suppose, as I am already here, I will have to opt for a third option.'

Amaut's confused look turned to one of acute pain after he went to shake the hand Brock proffered. The man spun in a circle as his arm went behind his back and Brock's well-aimed hand chopped down hard against his carotid artery. A few moments later the unconscious Amaut was slumped in his chair, hands deftly tied behind his back, mouth gagged with his own socks tied together, the knotted area inside his mouth.

Ten

Sonja Brezvanje had witnessed the procession as it disembarked and walked along the jetty. Once again the orderly crocodile fashion of the group intrigued her. All the most recent passengers and the children from the orphanages were just too quiet. Observing some of the older girls among the group, through her field glasses, confirmed that they were indeed pregnant, some almost at full term. Later in the day they had seen the Pied Piper returning to his pseudo scenic tours boat. The woman's frustration and anger intensified as she recognized his arrogant swagger.

Attempting yet again to call Georghe Enescu on his cellphone, but unable to receive a signal, she looked up at the military fortress, of which the clinic was part, cursing. She noticed a tall rugged man dressed in light blue jeans and stone-coloured shirt gain admittance to the clinic, then realized how hungry she was. 'Radu, I must go ashore to find a call box. I am convinced that the signal here is being influenced by military suppressors or call monitoring from that naval station.'

'Perhaps that café on the quay will have one,' suggested Raducioiu. 'I could do with something more to eat.'

'Then I will bring you something, but one of us must stay here, Radu, sorry.'

The man looked into the stunning blue eyes that he always drowned in whenever she gazed at him. 'I know, but please bring two of something for me; in fact make it four of something, Sonja.'

Sonja smiled and threw a wave acknowledging that she understood and left the jetty, unaware that it was her turn to be observed.

'So the little bird that follows me has finally left her nest,' said Kastrati as he focused on the woman through the field glasses. 'Good.'

As he regained consciousness the director general's expression slowly changed from one of confusion to anger when he saw Brock was activating the private monitors. The real-time images displayed on the six computer monitors showed various wards full of patients, some of whom appeared to be motionless as if sleeping or in a comatose state; others were youthful patients either sitting in quiet groups on their beds or on the floor. There were two dimly lit but empty operating theatres and an unlit room where it was impossible to make out anything.

His arms securely tied to the chair with his own telephone cord, Amaut settled for the only resistance open to him: he kicked at his desk with his bare feet. The high-back swivel chair reacted, moving quickly across the floor on its five-wheeled base to whack against the door. While Amaut's eyes widened in a desperate hope that his ploy would have the desired affect of attracting attention, Brock took four long strides, toppled the chair over backwards, opened the door and smiled at the woman looking expectantly from behind her desk.

'Sorry about that,' said Brock, coyly smiling with embarrassment. 'I tripped against the door.' The temporary part-time assistant smiled back.

Brock closed the door and returned to operate the remaining monitors, which relayed a different story. Two wards displayed beds occupied by females, sitting up. From their swollen bellies Brock surmised that their pregnancies were nearing full term. A third ward contained a series of cots and incubators. Brock could see tiny babies covered in tubes and sleeping babies in laboratory cots. Further rooms were laboratories, full of high-tech equipment, and others empty. Two rooms were each occupied by solitary individuals; one young woman was sitting on the floor, her arms wrapped around her folded legs, her forehead resting on her knees; another female, whom he recognized as the woman he had seen on the hotel stairwell, presumably called Tila, was lying motionless.

Brock whistled soundlessly as he turned to look at Amaut lying like a turtle that had been turned upside down on its shell. 'Well, every picture here tells a story – though it would seem a different one to yours director. It appears your inmates are more prisoners than patients.'

The director general tried to get up, only succeeding in falling over on his side. With his florid cheek pressed against the floor he helplessly watched Brock do something to his monitors before putting on his own white coat. The tall man calmly knelt down beside him. 'Well no doubt we'll meet again soon. Thanks for the coffee and' – he saw Brock hold up the key card he must have removed from around his neck – 'for this too.' Brock pressed the electronic door indicator to read 'engaged', left the office and locked the door using the key card.

The temporary assistant once more rose from her desk expectantly. Brock replied with another warm smile. 'Please don't disturb Mr Amaut before I return,' he offered, placing his finger on his lips. 'He is just working on something very important for me.'

Brock reached the wards, picking up the chart from the base of the nearest bed. The few nurses present paid no real attention other than a cursory nod or polite smile. The only sound was light classical music that was piped throughout the building. Brock's first-hand inspection intrigued him more and more. None of the inmates involved themselves with the usual activities associated with clinics: reading, talking or watching television. They just lay there staring at the ceiling. One nurse spoke to a girl of about sixteen, who slowly got out of bed and followed her.

Brock witnessed the same scenario in the adjoining wards. With no one in attendance in the one occupied by pregnant girls he took the opportunity to speak to one. 'How are you?' To which he received no response. *'Kak posj ba-ait?'* he asked again in Russian and the girl's eyes turned expectantly toward him. 'Get out of bed,' he continued in Russian. The girl obediently got up. 'Return to bed,' commanded Brock and the girl returned to her former position.

Brock went from room to room with the director general's key card. For over five minutes Brock calmly walked all of the floors until he reached the lower level. He entered one of the solitary confinement rooms. The girl Tila lay motionless on the bed. 'Get out of bed,' he commanded in Russian, to which he received no response. He waved his hand in front of her open eyes. No response. He placed his cheek next to her slightly opened mouth

61

and, feeling her breath, confirmed for himself that the girl was still alive, albeit in a comatose state.

Exiting the room Brock closed the door, walked down the hall, and used the key card to open another door. Recognizing it as the unlit room he had observed on the monitor his immediate thought was that he had entered a games room, with its low-slung lighting fixtures and billiard-size table. Brock turned to exit then he noticed how cold it was.

The security guard stood up to take a short break of nature when a habitual cursory glance at his screens caused him to stop. He recognized the man he had first monitored when the director general met him at reception. He thought it unusual that a guest would be on the lower levels, but then it was also unusual that the DG would go to meet his guest directly; usually they were sent up. Perhaps this was one of the new doctors they were expecting, and by the look of things, he was getting to know his way around.

He observed Brock using his key card to open one of the solitary confinement rooms, which confirmed his suspicion. There were only two keys that opened those rooms, the one kept in this security office, as the responsibility of all shifts, his included, was to open the secured doors whenever required, and the DG's, who would never loan it to a guest or a new employee. The guard punched the button for the DG's private office line. No reply. He punched the button for the DG's office line, usually diverted to his secretary. Getting voicemail he left a message: 'This is security. We need to speak to you or the DG urgently. Please call us.'

His eyes on the screen, as he replaced the receiver he began to convince himself that the stranger was more intruder than guest. In the three years he had worked here he had questioned the need for a security presence. Nothing ever happened, and if it did they simply called their military neighbour to resolve it. A couple of days ago he'd noticed that woman pacing around talking to herself, whom the DG had had detained by the naval guard. He knew she was currently under observation in one of the confinement rooms. And now this man was entering rooms in that secure area. He watched as the man exited the room holding the other girl currently under observation. He reappeared on the hall monitor and continued down the corridor and entered another. The security guard pulled off the safety strap of his holster and left to confront the guest directly. Better to be safe than out of a job, he reasoned.

Brock located the switches he felt for by the door and flicked them down. The bright lights that bathed the room transformed the perceived recreation area into a pathologist's laboratory. The table top was covered in a form of white sheer plastic. Lifting one of the table sheets revealed a clinical stainless steel surface. Against the wall were three closets.

Brock opened one, confirming to himself that they were in fact walk-in cold rooms. They reminded him of the Moscow abattoir he had been thrown into two years earlier. Removing Amaut's white coat he wrapped it around the door edge, preventing it from being slammed shut. Set into the wall were large sliding drawers.

Brock slid one open.

Eleven

Brock was not a stranger to morgues or cadavers. Personally, he'd been called to identify his own wife, when she had been the victim of a hit-and-run. Professionally, he had been called upon for identification following post-mortems. In those cases the body had been put back together, irrespective of what had happened to it, in preparation for burial. What he saw here was not like that and caused bile to rise to the back of his throat.

The corpse of the body in the drawer was unrecognizable. From the size of it and remaining locks of hair Brock estimated that it had been the body of a teenage girl. Everything conceivable had been removed, and recently. The still-open body had been emptied of its organs like a gutted young dolphin.

Brock quickly checked the other drawers, three of which contained body parts, two untouched corpses. In another cold room, the similar drawers revealed packages of stored blood and organs.

Cassie felt dazed. It was only in the past hour that she had regained her balance and was able to stand up. She rubbed her arm and noticed the small red mark. She looked at the date on her watch – two days she had lost! She vaguely remembered someone in white talking to her. Where the hell was she? The door opened without warning and a tall man in jeans stood in the entrance. She involuntarily stepped back into the corner. 'Why am I here?' she shouted instinctively in her own language.

'Do you speak English?' enquired the man.

'Why am I here?' said Cassie once more, this time in English.

'I was hoping you could tell me,' replied Brock instantly stiffening as he heard the sound behind him.

'Who are you?' shouted the security guard.

Brock turned slowly around and looked directly at the gun that was pointed at him. He made an expression of shock followed by indignant surprise. 'What do you think you are doing?' he questioned loudly.

The guard lowered his gun slightly, looking uncertain; the man's authoritative response was not what he had expected. 'Security, sir; doing my job. This is a restricted area. I need to see your identitification.'

Brock continued to look indignant before turning back to the woman. 'Would you excuse me?' he said as he shut the door.

'Wait!' shouted Cassie, wondering what the hell was going on.

Casting a look at the security guard that conveyed he was annoyed at the interruption, he held the key card in his fingers, pulling it away from his chest as he confidently closed the gap between himself and the man confronting him. The guard, now wrong-footed by the stranger's confident manner, as it did not match the behaviour of an intruder or someone doing something wrong, focused on the approaching key card, as Brock intended.

'You will see that this is the director general's own pass, which he has loaned to me while I make my inspection at his bidding,' said Brock in measured tones. 'I am sure that he will be delighted to learn that you are holding a gun on his new colleague.'

'I have called the director general.'

'Good, so you already know who I am,' offered Brock, maintaining his bluff command of the situation.

'I cannot get hold of him. I'm sorry, but I have not been informed of who you are.'

Brock rolled his eyes in exasperation. 'I expect because his secretary is away. Here,' said Brock as he offered his hand with an understanding smile. 'We will have to make our own introductions. My name is Dr Brock.'

Brock noticed the man's guard visibly relax for a moment before a fleeting doubt passed across his face. He did not shake the proffered hand. 'I had better receive confirmation, Doctor.'

'OK,' Brock sighed, 'let's get it. Where is your office?' Brock's acquiescence at last gave the sense of security the guard sought, albeit a false one. As both men fell into step, Brock's hands shot around the guard's wrist and elbow in a vice-like grip, followed with a jerking twist. There was an audible crack as the ulna and radius tore apart fracturing the arm in two places. The gun dropped and the man screamed in pain. A split second later Brock's knee ploughed into the nerve area between the rectus femoris and vastus lateralis muscle groups on the thigh, dead-legging the guard, who dropped like a stone.

When Brock reopened the door, dragging the immobilized guard behind him, Cassie looked to the agonizing grimace on the face of the guard, before looking questioningly at the man who had spoken to her a minute earlier. 'If you want to get out of here we had better leave now,' he said.

As Cassie ran to keep up with Brock down the corridor she breathlessly fired questions at him: 'Are you rescuing me? How did you find me? Where are we going? Who are you?' They reached an emergency exit, Brock slammed his foot against the metal bar and the door opened with the accompanying wail of an alarm.

Sitting at one of the small tables that were haphazardly arranged outside the plain concrete café gave Ferguson a clear view of the clinic, one hundred and fifty metres distant. Nevertheless he allowed his gaze to be diverted by the distinctively attractive woman who had recently arrived. After ordering a pile of breaded products she sat down at the available table adjoining his, stared up at the clinic before tapping out a number on her mobile phone with a preoccupied agitation.

'The fortress is imposing – thirteenth century apparently, though the modern addition is ugly.'

The woman ignored the approach as she put the phone to her ear. A moment later she looked directly at Ferguson with her pale-blue eyes: 'You are English?'

'Irish.' Ferguson cocked his head to one side and winked. 'Can you not tell the difference?'

'Do you know where I can find a payphone? I don't get a signal,' she asked holding up her cellphone.

'Same story with me – and no, I'm sorry, I haven't seen one. But you seem like a nice lady, so I may be able to help.'

The woman's eyes narrowed. 'How?'

'Well I do have a satellite phone, not reliant on unreliable local networks.'

The woman looked into the tanned broad face. The green eyes gazing back seemed friendly and sincere. 'That is a help. Do you often put yourself out for strangers?'

'It's this big soft Irish heart,' replied Ferguson, tapping his chest. 'It's never more content than when it's being of service to a lady. Matt is the name, Matt Ferguson.'

'Sonja Brevanje. Matt, please I need to borrow the phone now? I promise to be quick, but it is very important.'

Ferguson melted at her accent and eyes. 'You will have to be very quick.' Ferguson watched as the woman quickly dialled and waited. She left a message: 'Georghe, where are you? You must call me!'

'Romanian?' enquired Ferguson, when the woman had terminated the call.

'No answer; I may call voicemail?'

Ferguson gestured his consent and returned his gaze to the clinic entrance. 'Nothing,' said Sonja a few moments later, her eyes glistening. 'Thank you,' she said passing the sat phone back, before levelling her gaze once more at the clinic.

'You seem as interested in that building as I am.'

Sonja levelled her gaze on the Irishman expectantly. Before Ferguson could continue an alarm started, filling the air with its undulating wail. 'It seems another will be requiring my assistance right now; excuse me Sonja, I must fly.'

As Ferguson took to his heels, Sonja watched as a man and woman exited from a side entrance a level below where the orphans had earlier entered. The man tried to close the door behind him then walked calmly but briskly with the woman down the steps towards the jetty. No one seemed to be following them, and then when they were over half the way down, a figure in a white coat appeared at the door, hesitantly ran a few steps before returning and once more shutting the door. The alarm stopped as suddenly as it had started.

'Calm before the storm, Matt,' Brock said as he met Ferguson. 'We need to get lost.'

'Over here!' shouted a voice.

Brock gave Ferguson a quizzical look as a woman beckoned frantically at them. 'I won't ask,' he said as they ran toward the jetty.

Ferguson looked at the dark curly-haired woman standing at

67

Brock's side. 'Oh, I will,' he said as he returned the quizzical look.

Sonja reached the small cabined boat, her home for the past twenty-four hours, first. Ferguson boarded a moment later turning to assist the two women Brock was guiding towards him.

'Radu!' shouted Sonja, quickly stepping into the cabin. 'Where are you?'

Brock directed Cassie into the cabin, before turning to Sonja. 'I suggest we leave this jetty now; introductions can wait.'

'But where is Radu? He would not leave the boat.' Sonja pushed past Brock, returning to the jetty, her eyes shielded with her hand, scanning the café she had left a few minutes earlier.

Ferguson went to start the engine while Brock went forward to release the mooring. 'Hang on, Matt,' shouted Brock as the engine coughed before rising to a consistent tone. 'The anchor is down.'

'We can't leave without Radu!' shouted Sonja, stepping back onboard. 'This is our boat and we go when I say!'

Brock wondered as to the reason for dropping anchor while moored at the jetty while he struggled to pull in the chain. He bent his legs and pulled hard before peering over the side at the boat to gauge his progress. The anchor had broken the surface; its chain appeared to be wrapped around a log until it became recognizable as a human neck and head skewed at a grotesque angle; eyes stared unseeing at a darkening sky. A moment later Brock let the chain pass through his fingers before returning aft. 'I found Radu,' said Brock grimly as he put his hand on Sonja's shoulder.

Twelve

Kastrati steadied himself as he felt the familiar lurch of his vessel leaving the jetty, his binoculars trained on the small craft he had visited a few minutes earlier. His plan to confront the remaining occupant to find out who they were had not gone as intended. As the young man on board had exited the cabin in response to Kastrati's introductory hail, his display of shock recognition, blending horror with hatred, was clear evidence that the young man knew he had been confronted by an enemy. Kastrati had reacted with a habit born from using ruthless attack as the only form of defence. Within a minute he had concealed the body, searched the cabin, removed the camera he had found, and then waited to intercept the woman.

A shout had drawn his attention, first to the woman and then to the group of two men and woman she was beckoning. As the group bounded toward the jetty he had nonchalantly returned to his imminently departing vessel. He focused on the woman when she returned to the quay in search of her companion. He then directed his field glasses towards the tall seasoned individual pulling the anchor. He committed both their faces to memory.

Sonja sat in stunned disbelief while Ferguson directed the boat through the delta wetlands. The body of her friend, colleague and recent lover dragged alongside just below the surface, as pulling it aboard ran the risk of attracting further unwanted attention. Radu Raducioiu, his mission to find his younger sister unfulfilled, was laid to rest with short ceremony in a channel abutting an island blanketed by summer wildflowers. 'It was the Pied Piper,' began Sonja in a voice bereft of emotion, as she recounted recent events.

'Six months seeking information that would lead us to him!

In the last seventy-two hours I finally obtain photographic evidence of him involved in trafficking and he wins again. Radu, everything lost, and what of Georghe, Jakiv; and where is Natalya? What have I involved them in?'

'A cause which your friend Radu believed in enough to give his life for,' said Brock as he sat down in the stern next to her, studying her for the first time. Her red-rimmed eyes, tear-stained cheeks and river-swept blonde hair could not hide her natural beauty; the regal Slavic cheekbones curving elegantly down to her evenly formed mouth with slightly pronounced lips. Brock gently took her two hands in his. 'What are you involved in?'

'My name is Sonja Brezvanje,' she replied, raising her head to look into his eyes. 'For three years I was attached to La Strada-Ukraine, founded to prevent trafficking in women in central and eastern Europe, but a personal involvement led me to set up my own group protecting children: La Strada des Enfants. With support from UNICEF and La Terre des Hommes we are trying to stop the trafficking of young girls endemic in the poorer areas of the Black Sea states. Unfortunately with little success; people do not talk.'

Brock stayed silent as Sonja paused. 'And why?' she added. 'Because in my Ukraine, Romania and Bulgaria there are eighty million people with the lowest earnings in Europe, huge unemployment, with little concern when another mouth to feed disappears from illiterate villages. Relatives, fearing that their child, promised a good life, will suffer, or worried that they will have to return money, won't talk.

'Others, especially our self-serving officials, don't talk! Thousands of children are abandoned every year. Without birth certificates or consent from the abandoning parent they cannot be fostered or adopted. Orphans are state supported until the children are fifteen. After that they fend for themselves, homeless. Countless girls disappear every year, never reported as missing. How can they be when they do not belong to anyone? Orphans are recruited, despite our efforts, before they leave; offered attractive positions of work, money, even fame in the West. They are never heard of again. Then three months ago we heard rumours of state orphanages in Romania and Ukraine receiving private funding. Good news, we thought, only to learn

70

that soon after, half the orphans, those aged between ten and fifteen years, were mysteriously disappearing.'

Brock looked past Ferguson at the helm into the small two-berth cabin. Asleep on the bunk lay the other woman still suffering from the after-effects of being drugged, kept against her will and rescued unexpectedly. He wondered about the young girls who had filled the wards. 'And this Pied Piper, who is he?'

'It is the alias that a member of my team, Natalya, said he was known as. We know that he is a major trafficker. We went to the minister, who demanded evidence, arguing that it was not unusual for philanthropists to insist on secrecy. We argued back that this was against the Hague Declaration and even went to the press, who printed a brief story which was ridiculed by the local councils as untrue, before an injunction prevented it from being aired by national television. Apparently, without evidence, it was contrary to Romania's interests.'

'So you went out to get it,' prompted Brock.

'By luck and chance more than design,' said Sonja. 'Our budget does not run to regular national bulletins, but we do post as many notices as we can. Last month we were contacted by Natalya. Her orphanage, at Brasov, was visited six months earlier by a man and woman recruiting for a German modelling agency. She was told that her distinctive beauty would reward her with a highly paid modelling job in Munich, or Paris.'

'Perfectly designed to appeal to a young girl's dreams,' interrupted Brock with a sigh.

'Yes, and despite our efforts to warn in advance, it is a ploy that works without fail. And the perception of risk is lessened whenever there is a woman involved in the ploy, as regretfully there always is in my experience. Natalya accepted the invitation to go with them to Brasov for auditions, and then awoke two days later in a crowded apartment with eight other girls of similar ages. None of them could remember a solitary second of the past forty-eight hours.'

'As if under some hypnotic influence, hence the Pied Piper,' said Brock. 'Entices them with exciting prospects, lulls them into a false sense of security, then commands them to do his bidding as if under their own volition.'

'Exactly that! It is what we have all witnessed independently during the past few days. Girls provided with identity are crossing borders as easily as crossing a road.'

'And we can assume the Pied Piper has numerous identities. How about Natalya – what happened?'

'When they moved again, she recognized the man everyone referred to as the Pied Piper as the one who had promised her the modelling career. Natalya pleaded with him, reminding him of his promise. And you know how he replied? He looked at her, smiled, took out a short-bladed knife and slashed her across the side of her face, telling her she was not there to be a model. It was incredibly courageous of her but she kicked out at him in pain and anger. He then raped her.'

No response was required. Brock looked into the woman's light blue eyes, waiting for her to continue. Sonja pulled her hand away and wiped her eyes. 'Later Natalya learned she was actually in Istanbul; she had no idea how she had entered Turkey. For two days she was abused, raped and beaten into submission by her captors, then forced to service clients day and night. After five weeks she managed to escape, went straight to the police where she was promptly placed in prison for thirty days before being deported. With no family or friends she went to Bucharest and contacted my colleague Georghe Enescu via one of the posters. She joined our team and directed us to the address she'd gone to audition at in Brasov. Four days ago Natalya bravely volunteered to watch the place. It was highly unlikely that the Pied Piper would return, but Natalya insisted on doing something.'

'And you were in luck,' offered Brock.

'Yes, we thought so. Now I question it. Anyway, yes, someone arrives. The woman Natalya met before. We follow her and she leads us to Pied Piper.' Sonja put her head down. 'Now Radu is dead. I must contact Georghe.'

Thirteen

'There is no negotiation. You knew that the price was to be whatever it had to be. Yours is a rare match for which I have two other clients in the queue. Take it or leave it.'

Friedrich Neumann had been continuously on the phone upon returning to his office two hours earlier. He reached for the cigar smouldering close to his first, now embedded in its black crystal tray. He studied the distinctive Cohiba label, indicating its Cuban authenticity, while he waited for the expected reply.

'I will transfer the money today,' his client breathed with resignation. 'But I want fresh delivery in twenty-four hours. I can confirm with my surgeons?'

The lawyer's thin lips stretched into a smile. 'You are in Geneva now?'

'Of course, as per your instructions,' came back the reply.

'Then, as soon as I have received confirmation your transfer is complete, I will arrange for the consignment to be delivered. The price reflects the rarity of your case. Transplant will be affected simultaneously. So, at the time I receive your transfer I will assume that you have your team fully prepared.'

'Your assumption is correct. What the hell else do you expect?'

Neumann did not reply.

'I'm sorry, I don't mean to take my frustration out on you. It just is so scary waiting, just waiting. I'm not used to not being in control of my life.'

'I can imagine. Still, all will be well; you are very fortunate,' Neumann said without expression.

'Thank you. Tell me, who is the donor?'

The lawyer rolled his eyes at the expected question. 'Now, you know I do not divulge that information. However, the young person with the unfortunate terminal illness is content that their strong healthy heart will be providing for their family. I repeat, you're a very fortunate man, Mr Saeed; goodbye.'

Neumann replaced the receiver and moved towards the ebony drinks cabinet, poured himself a glass of the fifty-year-old malt whisky, sent by a satisfied client, and stretched himself out on his black leather chesterfield.

'A good morning's work deserves a little indulgence,' he said to himself as he swirled the amber nectar around the heavy crystal glass before sipping it. His brief visit to Ukraine had exceeded his expectations. Though there was no need to visit, he had made it a policy to personally verify product availability. How else could he personally vouch for the items his clients demanded? And now, culminating in his final and most lucrative call of the day, he had confirmed orders amounting to almost three-quarters of a million euros.

These rare-blood requests were the best, plus his choosing to deal with only the best clients; but € 250,000 for a heart! *Mein Gott, das ist gut!* He toasted his negotiating skills: four kidneys at € 50,000 a piece, each with a wholesale price of € 20,000; a liver at a profit of € 65,000; and four corneas at € 30,000 each. Perhaps he would no longer have to involve himself with time-consuming peripherals associated with blood, skin, lungs and less valuable body parts.

Neumann placed his drink on the polished ebony low table and leaned back, clasped his hands behind his neck and recrossed his outstretched legs. His gaze rested on his patent shoes as he considered an idea. Perhaps he should be more involved in the actual identity documentation relating to the assets. Every time there was a customs refusal, it cost him both money and credibility, proving very expensive if it affected clients like Saeed. If the live donor was refused entry, the alternative was a non-simultaneous transplant which allowed only a four-hour window to ensure delivery was received as fresh.

The lawyer picked up his glass, did his habitual swirl and took a large slug, enjoying how his throat glowed as the fiery liquid coursed smoothly down. He stared at the glass as he rationalized the idea. On the other hand, he argued with himself, if he did take over the documentation and it was ever scrutinized and proved to be forged, he ran the risk that it would lead directly to him.

He placed his glass down heavily on the ebony table, having come to a decision. No, it is best to be a middleman. In that way I am always acting in good faith. How can a lawyer be blamed for the untoward motives of his clients? He was simply fulfilling their instructions. He pushed his drink further away, removed his spectacles, placing them on the table in front of his empty glass, smoothed his balding head with his hands and closed his eyes.

Georghe Enescu had closely followed the six girls and their attendant chaperone since they landed at Schoenefeld airport, ending at a private house off the Bachenhofstrasse in the south-west quadrant of the city. The recently renovated property was enclosed by an original stone wall and wrought-iron gates. From the size of the house, Enescu thought it might once have been an official government building, as it reminded him of similar ones in his home town of Bucharest that were now embassies. It was warm and he was not hungry, having purchased soup and a sandwich on the flight, but with the approaching evening coupled with a slight smattering of rain he was prompted to go in search of accommodation.

An hour later Enescu cursed. He had walked a round trip of three kilometres, softened by the fact that he was wearing comfortable trainers, jeans and a light khaki anorak. He looked like a tourist but it had not helped. The big hotels had been way beyond his meagre budget, and the cheaper ones, even the abundant guest houses, had no vacancies, all enjoying the benefits of the trade fair that had taken over the city. Finding himself back where he had started he decided to stay and observe for a few hours before taking a bus back to the airport, where he could sleep before boarding the early-morning return flight. He continued to watch the house, thinking of the new occupants, frustrated at not being able to do more.

Enescu was about to leave when a convoy of gleaming black Volkswagen people carriers approached the entrance. A moment later the gates opened to allow entry. Enescu, his heart beating furiously, watched them pass through and waited. Unable to stop himself he impetuously left the sanctuary of his chosen observation post, hurriedly crossed the road and slipped through the closing gates.

Remik Kostina never smiled. Though his skin was pockmarked and his broad, heavy-browed head with its thick grey crew-cut hair may have borne some resemblance, that was not the reason he had held the nickname 'the Crocodile' with his Bulgarian brethren. He had earned the title for the tears he bizarrely shed whenever he disposed of his victims, and the cold ruthlessness of his reputation for striking ferociously without warning went before him.

The atmosphere in the exclusive establishment Kostina termed his 'Berlin Flagship' was as tight as a drum skin stretched to breaking point. A number of provocatively dressed female occupants forced inviting smiles, desperate to appear appealing, though they could not prevent their eyes relaying the submissive apprehension that had been beaten into them. The new arrivals stood in the centre of the entrance hall. The drugs they had unwittingly imbibed at breakfast three days earlier had worn off leaving behind a stupor of confused fear.

'Strip them,' hissed Kostina to the elegantly dressed woman who stood beside them, keeping his black, slightly protruding eyes on the females, measuring their value as though they were livestock at a market. 'I have paid for six virgins and will accept nothing less.'

Though attractive, the expression of Mira Luga, the madam of the exclusive brothel, was hard as stone. She commanded them to remove their clothes immediately so that she could make an inspection. The girls looked at each other in horror, their frightened faces uncertain what to do. One girl began to scream. Luga smashed the girl hard in the face with the back of her hand and tore the girl's new blouse off with the other.

'Take your clothes off now!' she shouted. 'All of them.'

Another girl tried to run away and was immediately punched in the stomach by one of the Crocodile's six attendant bodyguards. She doubled up in pain as the bodyguard tore her clothes off. Within minutes the other girls, assisted by the bodyguards, were sitting on the floor, quivering in shame and abject terror, vainly trying to cover themselves.

Kostina nodded to Luga to continue with the inspection.

Luga's eyes bore into each girl as she approached them. She

firmly pushed each one in turn on to her back for inspection, taking her time over the youngest girl, still winded from the stomach blow. 'There are five. This one is not, but I think from another cause. It happens.'

'I own you now,' hissed Kostina, addressing the girls. 'You belong to me. You are not even allowed to think; if you do then you are no good to me and I have no further need of you.' He slowly crossed over to the girl who had failed the inspection. 'Let me explain so that you fully understand what I mean,' he added. Kostina gently lifted the girl up and looked into her eyes. Slowly he moved his hands down to her throat and began to squeeze. The girl used every muscle in her delicate body to fight until her frantic eyes glazed over, her young life extinguished. Kostina wiped his eyes and looked towards his remaining assets. 'You understand now, yes?'

Georghe stood transfixed at the window. Every instinct shouted at him to get out of there immediately. Just then his mobile phone rang. Desperately he sought to silence it.

Fourteen

With her father and fiancé having flown ahead to Brussels to finalize funeral arrangements for the de Brouwers, Sophia focused on setting up the project she had been planning, intending to join them in a couple of days. A small part of the converted former military hospital had been converted to high-tech offices, the greater portion devoted entirely to state-of-the-art laboratories. A recent postgraduate in biogenetics, Sophia was in her own private paradise, eagerly commencing her work before the arrival of any of the resident scientists or technicians.

She had learned of BioGenetics Research's pioneering reputation in the two years she had studied at Stanford. Already they were leaders in addressing the very source for disease prevention through gene modification to gain immunization from cancer even before birth. The enormous investment in research and development always meant that such preventative cures were available only to the very wealthy.

Her personal mission was to develop a cloning procedure that would allow vaccines to be duplicated at negligible cost. Now that her father was soon to be a major shareholder, it would ensure the support for her research. Soon after her adoption he had shared with her that her two elder brothers had died from a disease that had been easily preventable, but her mother, a single parent, was both poor and illiterate. That had been the reason her mother had resorted to selling her – so she could have a better life. She had enquired why her mother had allowed her sister to be raped. He had gently suggested that being so distressed at the time caused her to imagine such a scenario. Sophia pretended to agree but she knew that such a vivid memory was never imagined.

Arriving at the station she had been assigned the previous day, she was about to sit down when she heard an annoyed exclamation in a language she did not recognize. She leaned to peer over her cubicle. 'Hello, you are certainly out to catch the worm.'

The man jumped in surprise, looking at the cause as if it was a strange life form. His wide dark eyes, enlarged from the refraction of thick bottle lenses in black frames, slowly focused. 'What do you want?'

Sophia smiled. 'Just saying hello. I am Sophia, arrived yesterday.'

'Oh.'

'And you are?' prompted the girl.

The man stood up, though he did not gain much height in doing so. 'Jon Su-Yeong,' he said, offering a small bow.

'Dr Su-Yeong.' Sophia flushed, already aware of the renowned Korean specialist in stem-cell research. 'It is an honour to meet you, sir. Your biogenetic work is ahead of its field.'

Su-Yeong was already sitting back staring at the three screens in front of him. 'This is not right.'

'What did you say?'

'This is not right. These results have changed. These damn machines.'

Sophia went around to the increasingly agitated specialist. 'Which results? Perhaps I can help.'

'No, no, no! I have already backtracked and checked. Yesterday they were all the same, now they are all different, which they should be, but not as they were.'

Looking at the screens Sophia recognized the highly magnified embryonic stem-cell structures appearing like fishing nets haphazardly rolled into ragged piles 'But aren't they meant to be the same structure but individually unique?'

Su-Yeong looked at the strange alien that now stood next to him. 'The specimens must have been tampered with. I do not make mistakes.'

Quickly surmising the uselessness of the current one-sided dialogue, Sophia adopted the open-ended-question psychology that her science teacher utilized to make her explain her postulations. 'And how do you think that happened?'

The scientist's brow furrowed as he channelled his concentration on the question. 'These are recent batches which I had collected myself from storage. Usually my colleague Dr Seokhung arranges it but I did not want to wait. They immediately caught my attention of course. Now there is no sign of it. But I did notice it so they must have been like it at the beginning.'

'What exactly caught your attention?'

'Their slightly lighter green colouration indicating contamination, possibly non-virulent and it would seem temporary, but there was identical contamination in three separate sealed batches. Now, this morning, I find no evidence of any contamination whatsoever – as if they are completely different specimens.'

'Then they must have been like that at the beginning,' prompted Sophia repeating Su-Yeong's own words.

'Exactly what I think! Tampering with evidence!'

'What about the regenerative ability of cord blood stem cells?' Sophia asked. 'Could the contamination introduced to all batches, before sealing, have corrected itself thus removing evidence of such contamination?'

'Regeneration does not happen that quickly!' The scientist suddenly looked right into Sophia's pale-blue eyes as if seeing her for the first time. 'Unless . . . oh my . . . no, it's not possible . . . how . . . why did I not think?'

'Unless what, Doctor?'

'Stem cells generate fastest in an early incubatory state. For such speed these cannot be cord blood specimens. These must be derived from an early ante-natal environment.'

'You mean unborn foetuses?' whispered Sophia as she clarified the scientist's thoughts to herself.

Su-Yeong's olive skin had turned a whiter pallor. 'I mean live specimens, which have sought to survive from an introduced contamination.' He grabbed Sophia by the arm tightly as he jumped out of his chair. 'I have heard rumours at conferences, but always ignored it as the ill-humour of scientists frustrated at slow progress through moral restriction.'

Sophia did not attempt to remove the arm. 'What rumours?'

Su-Yeong looked around him before whispering his reply, as if not even wanting to hear the words himself: 'Foetus farming.'

'You must be mistaken, Doctor. You've talked about contamination and tampering, perhaps another option is that you are mistaken?'

Su-Yeong gripped her arm even tighter. 'I don't make mistakes,

I make tests, hundreds of them, if necessary thousands, and then I cross-check. I know when I see contamination; I know when there has been tampering; and I am experienced enough to know what my results reveal.'

PART TWO

The Harrowing Harvest

Fifteen

Hristo Amaut's back shivered again as if someone had slowly dragged ice-cold fingernails along his spine. 'I fear we have been irretrievably compromised,' he added in conclusion to his flustered discussions detailed during the call.

'Then you must all ensure immediate containment,' returned the voice in a higher tone than its usual controlled one. 'What I have told you has to be executed right now.'

'It is an excellent foresight of yours to plan for such a contingency,' offered Amaut submissively, in an effort to soften the news he had just relayed. 'We deeply value your support.'

There was a pause on the line. 'It is more a case of having to address your incompetence than foresight. The premises you will relocate to were not intended to provide an alternative to Izmail; they were in addition! Still, what has happened means we must look to protect our work at all costs.'

'I understand,' Amaut said, feeling both angry and embarrassed at his open humiliation in front of his colleagues.

'Good, then call me when it is done,' came back the final reply before the line clicked off.

Amaut glanced at his watch and then looked at the faces of the three people sitting around his table in turn before addressing them. 'We have four hours. Each of you knows what to do; any questions?'

Tereza Ditschec, her greying hair harshly pinned back in a bun, leaned on her elbows, her bespectacled eyes returning the director general's gaze. 'I need to select only a third of my candidates for transportation. But I was due to take leave tomorrow. Can Ivan cover for me until I join you next week?' she said, turning to the slightly built colleague sitting on her right.

'Absolutely not,' answered Amaut, looking incensed at his gynaecologist. 'Each of us must attend to our responsibilities.'

Ivan Karnovitch, former army surgeon, shrugged his slim shoulders. 'We have been cooped up here like prisoners for some months now. I for one am looking forward to a change. But are we to change one prison for another? Is it that these increasing responsibilities of ours will not allow us any freedom?'

'Each of you earns more in a week, than your peer group earn in a month. How do you like the idea of giving that up and going to a real prison?' offered Amaut coldly.

'What do you mean?' Karnovitch began to argue. 'It is you who has brought this on us. Why should—'

'Where are we going, Hristo?' interrupted Ditschec. 'We must be allowed to know.'

'You will know when you get there. I have already said that it is vital we maintain secrecy in this immediate relocation.'

'We will have the same facilities?'

'Everything will be in place for you, Tereza; in fact I understand the internal apartments are larger.'

'You know where we are going?'

'I know of the place where we are going.' Amaut rubbed his chest, slightly flinching as his hand touched the sensitive area where spilled hot coffee had burned the skin. 'As you have just learned, though, it was not specifically prepared in case of the eventuality that currently challenges us; the overriding factor is that any long-term interruption of our operation, beyond a few days, is not an option.'

Karnovitch looked dubious. 'But you did imply that not relocating, immediately, may lead to us going to a real prison. I thought we were guaranteed protection from—'

'This is for your protection, Karnovitch,' interrupted the fourth member without expression. 'And going to prison, alive, is also not an option.' The others turned towards the heavy-set man who had spoken, the overhead spotlight behind his shaved, scarred head casting a dark shadow into the centre of the group. 'Each of us heard the instructions from our employer who is now having to spend a fortune in sorting our problem. I insist we stop wasting time.'

Goryachev stood up and leaned against the table with his knuckles; the others were wary of the dark eyes void of emotion, staring at each of them in turn. 'Enough questions,' he added. 'If you do not have yourself duly organized in time, I will consider you part of my disposal duties.'

'Thank you, Gregor,' acknowledged Amaut as the others scurried out of his office.

Brock gently shook awake the woman he had rescued from the clinic as they docked at Tulcea. During their brief conversation he had learned that she was an archaeologist and was staying at the same hotel as he and Ferguson. 'Let's get you straight to the hotel, perhaps get a doctor and we can talk later,' he said helping the woman to her feet.

'The last person I want to see is another doctor,' she replied. 'I want a shower and something to eat!' Seeing she was still unsteady on her feet Brock supported her out of the cabin on his arm.

Ferguson was already standing on the quay, having securely moored the boat. 'I think someone wants to carry on upstream,' he said lightly, tossing his head in the direction of the other woman still on board.

'I must follow Radu's murderer,' answered Sonja determinedly as Brock's eyes swept towards her. 'He must not be allowed to get away again!'

'OK, Matt, you go ahead and take care of this lady,' said Brock, passing the seemingly drunken woman over to Ferguson's outstretched hand. 'We'll meet at the hotel.'

Brock turned back to Sonja. 'You found him before and we will find him again, almost certainly at what you discovered to be his holding station in Belgrade. He knows this boat and will be watching out for you, so it would be—'

'I don't care what he knows,' argued Sonja passionately, 'he must be stopped!'

'But it is because you care that you must curb your anger. If not, you will make mistakes and end up like Radu. How is that going to help your cause, eh?'

Sonja's pale-blue eyes appeared cold as ice. 'All my life I have had to fight to survive each day. But I do so on my terms. They threatened to kill my little sister unless I worked the streets. They did anyway. It is because of men like this Pied Piper who remove all choice from their victims that I must destroy him.

While governments pour millions into anti-prostitution, misguidedly believing that in doing so they are addressing the source of trafficking, I believe that we must remove the key perpetrators. History has proved countless times that it is the only way in the end, preferably with capital punishment. So I must destroy him, even if it means I destroy myself. That is my cause!'

Brock placed his hands gently on her shoulders. 'I respect your courage and your conviction. But from what I discovered in that clinic this man is involved in bigger crimes than you could imagine.'

'What could be a worse crime than trafficking a fellow human being, removing all vestiges of dignity and honour?'

'All in due course; first I need to make some calls to get some back-up.'

The woman looked at Brock, who returned her gaze. 'Backup? Where from, the authorities? Waste of time! In Belgrade, if he is going there, the Serbian bureaucrats will not lift a finger to help until it has been well greased.

'Over there' – Sonja jerked a finger in the direction of Izmail – 'the Ukrainian military are all neighbourly and uninvolved, guarding their own rackets. Romania, prostitution is strictly illegal; therefore how can any trafficking exist! Bulgaria, it is also strictly illegal, yet the economy almost relies on crime. In this business, there is a simple rule: profit from looking the other way!'

'Which directly involves my work,' said Brock.

'Which is . . .?'

'Investigating corporate espionage.'

'A spy?'

Brock gave a broad grin. 'No, not at all. It involves ensuring economic security for industry.'

Sonja stopped to look at the tall man in front of her. She had been around many men; most of them, due to the nature of her experiences, were insensitive or oafish. Loutish and employing bullying tactics to hide their insecurities always stemmed from ignorance or a lack of confidence. This man was different. He displayed confidence; not the arrogance that she encountered in the bureaucratic halls of pseudo power, but a quiet, strong self-confidence. Though his eyes were a little wild, she registered the integrity that shone from them.

'How?' she asked.

'Well, to put it simply,' replied Brock, 'I investigate potential economic terrorism.'

Sonja furrowed her brow in puzzlement. 'Terrorism? Then why is your interest here? Trafficking is not politically or ideologically opposed to government. Other than the point that governments in this part of the world may use it as a political lever to win or deny membership to the European Union, they mostly ignore its existence. I fail to see why trafficking should attract the interest of people involved with corporate espionage.'

'Listen, Sonja, terrorism may be predominantely politically motivated, though UN members have never been able to agree on a definition for it. However, economic terrorism,' repeated Brock, 'is defined by my organization, ICE, as a pre-meditated, economically motivated violence against individuals, business and industry. For me personally, Sonja, and in relation to what you have shared with me, any profit-motivated action that contravenes basic human rights is economic terrorism. In which case ICE will be your back-up.'

Sixteen

A maut pressed the 'send' button and watched as his selected database emailed to a specific address. Holding the two-gigabyte memory stick stirred his memory of a similar stick. If he had been more vigilant with Patrowsky he would have saved himself from being on the receiving end of such an enormous setback and personal humiliation.

There was nothing else for him to remove and he was ready to leave in the clothes he was standing up in. He looked around his office and the view it offered over the twinkling lights of the distant port. He had enjoyed its lofty position and cursed his egoistic stupidity for allowing Brock into his clinic. He had underestimated him and paid the price.

But it had not been entirely his fault; what about Goryachev? His brutish methods had caused the problem. To have dealt with Patrowsky in such an open fashion was beyond stupidity. The man never considered consequences, as if he was untouchable. Yet their mutual employer would not have a word said against him. Amaut pushed at his chair, remembering how Brock had tied him to it. He would not complain of Goryachev's brutish methods when it came to dealing with that man.

Karnovitch had finalized his current series of small cylindrical metal containers, they had been sealed, collected and taken to the small airfield north of Izmail with the prepared consent documentation. There two aircraft were waiting to courier them to their specific destinations. The surgeon now looked around his operating theatre, concerned that the state-of-the-art equipment he had compiled over the past year would be damaged or simply destroyed. He recalled the time he had spent cutting his teeth repairing mangled bodies during a two-year period in Chechnya. Goryachev reminded him of the implacable CO of the unit he'd had the misfortune to be attached to. The man was a ruthless, ignorant bully, deriving pleasure from destroying things or people, irrespective of whether they were for or against him.

The money they offered to head up a team specializing in removing, maintaining and transplanting organs and body parts had exceeded his expectations; and taking from terminal candidates to preserve life was good. At times he knew that the reality had not been quite that, yet each time guilt had raised its accusing head, he had smothered it, disliking even more intensely the thought of losing the income he was earning. The director general was right, it was a fortune.

He pushed the idea of losing the income out of his head as he departed his operating theatre and made his way down the corridor. It was too late now for him to not do what he did, and at the very least his work was making a difference to the lives of some, but certainly his own. He was lucky to have survived Chechnya so he would do whatever he had to do and that was that.

'I have finished, Tereza, are you ready?' he said as he entered his colleague's theatre.

Ditschec look worried. 'Relocating at such short notice is really inconvenient, Ivan,' she whispered in a low voice.

Karnovitch shook his head. 'Forget it,' he chided. 'We have always been well catered for. OK, we have to move. So what? An operation that can move smoothly from one base to another at short notice is worth a great deal. After all, money seems no object.'

Ditschec closed the metal case containing her professional equipment and picked up the small bag she had taken from her quarters. 'You're right, of course, but I fear our freedom is being lost because of it. Do we no longer care about that?'

'This is more than serious, Paul,' said Brock nearing the end of his conference call to van Lederman. 'The clinic is nothing more than a bloody human farm. Wards are full of drugged young women. They are being harvested for their organs and body parts. If I had not seen it with my own eyes I would not have believed it.'

Van Lederman's lengthy pause added to the gravitas of Brock's words. 'I'm afraid it could be the tip of the iceberg, Connor. Though they are water-damaged, we have managed to recover some of the files from Patrowsky's memory stick. Among other things, they outline a network of adoption agencies, hospitals and private clinics specializing in organ transplant spanning the globe. Hans Duisen must have learned what he was unwittingly involved in and was about to blow the whistle, while trying to mitigate any fall-out that would incriminate him or the Duisen Foundation. In view of your eyewitness report we must assume that the whole supply operation is illegal.'

'That's putting it mildly, Paul. It's inhuman, but bizarrely the man running it seems to genuinely believe his work is providing huge benefit! He heads a team of pathological liars hooked on the business of wealth equals health. If you can afford it they can provide it.'

'Which is why it is an increasing global industry,' replied van Lederman. 'The US, Europe and China are the biggest markets. Right now there are over a hundred thousand patients registered in the US waiting for a genetically suitable organ donor to die. The unregistered number is probably greater. In Western Europe there are fifty thousand registered patients of which thirty per cent die annually. Desperate patients will pay up to two hundred thousand euros for an illegal kidney transplant irrespective of the risks. Macabre websites Pete Kenachi has been tracking offer organs harvested from China's executed prisoners. The Chinese government claims that prior consent is obtained but refuses to provide evidence. We contacted Kidney Research and they confirmed that many of their supplies come from donors originating from Eastern Europe, particularly Romania, Bulgaria and Turkey. All arrive with consent documentation all in order.'

'Which is forged, no doubt?'

'Impossible to tell and when time is of the life-saving essence no one is going to study it too closely. The harsh fact of life and death is that black-market organs save lives.'

'A case of the poor giving to the rich, eh?' said Brock sarcastically. 'Another fact, Paul,' he added coldly, 'is that we need to close this operation down, and right now.'

'Agreed, Connor, yet there is no way we will get civil jurisdiction over military-owned premises. The Ukrainian navy are the landlord. We will need a couple of days.'

'Paul, first a group of trafficked girls just entered the clinic; second we just met a representative of UNICEF who confirmed some had been abducted from orphanages, which she witnessed, while others, most of them pregnant, were collected en route through the Danube; and third, their organs are about to be ripped out of them! We have to do something, damn it! And as for why so many pregnant girls are there, I don't dare to think!'

'I will try and persuade the Ukrainian navy to enter, in their capacity as landlord, and get back to you within the hour. Is there anything else?'

'OK. Yes there is, Paul. Sonja Brezvanje is an anti-trafficker; she is, indirectly, the UNICEF representative we met. We owe her a big favour too, and right now she requires our support.'

'How can we assist?'

'Help her collate evidence of the trafficking racket that abducted and sold the children and teenagers to the clinic, though in my opinion we should help her to smash it. It would seem, Paul, that the Izmail clinic is just one of many clients supplied by this operation. Sonja believes this operation is responsible for thousands of missing girls being trafficked.'

'Smash it?' asked van Lederman. 'That is more than going beyond our brief, Connor. Our role is to bring it to the notice of the authorities, not deal with it ourselves.'

'Paul, you know as well as anyone that authorities prefer to deny than get directly involved. They want the credit after the situation has been resolved.'

'It is politically useful to take such a view. In the same vein, should I know what is in your mind?'

'It would seem that some self-styled Pied Piper character operates a network across the Balkan States using the Danube as a route for collection and delivery for clients across Western Europe, including the UK and possibly the US. Perhaps catching this Pied Piper rat would be an effective resolution that will benefit all. After all, we need to ask him questions relating to his interest in the clinic, which may directly be linked to the deaths of Duisen and the de Brouwers, don't we?'

'It will be useful, admittedly. I will contact you immediately I have spoken with the Ukrainian navy.'

'I want to accompany the visit,' added Brock.

'We can only request for observation purposes, but you know the answer will be no.'

'Tell them I brought the complaint. That might swing it. In the meantime Matt will be accompanying Sonja to Belgrade.'

'To locate this Pied Piper?'

'Correct. He is directly linked to the murder earlier today of Sonja's partner. They are leaving for Constanta airport right away to reach what Sonja has told us is one of his bases. She believes it is some type of holding station. With luck they will be there ahead of him and I will join them as soon as I can leave here. If we get to the source of the supply chain we stand a good chance of learning what links who together.'

Van Lederman paused again. 'OK, Connor, agreed. I'll call you within the hour.'

Seventeen

Though Kostas Vladimic had retired from the Ukrainian navy two years earlier, his influence was such that he persuaded the commanding officer at Izmail that it was in his interest to verify all was in order with their clinic tenant without delay. With the services of Vladimic, van Lederman successfully leveraged his legendary network. Brock was granted observation status and a surprise entry was agreed at dawn in the morning. No warrant would be required as the military would be applying their usual method: a critical situation requiring immediate entry – a bomb threat being the most common interpretation by non-military personnel.

Having briefed Ferguson, who had just departed with Sonja, Brock glanced once more at his watch before looking at the other person who now joined him at the dining table.

'Feeling better?'

'Yes, though whatever they gave me is certainly disorienting – and look,' said the woman holding out the inside of her arm. 'That local doctor you brought to the hotel thought I was a junkie!'

Brock looked at the blue and red blotches starting to yellow into bruising. 'Certainly indicative of a lot of recent shots; I think we're lucky to get you out of there alive. What did he say?'

The woman pushed her black curly hair behind her as she sat down. 'He refused to give me anything, said I had had enough, should rest and stay off the drugs. But why me? One minute I'm minding my own business, the next I'm locked up, drugged to the point I can't even think straight. Now I'm accused of being a drug addict! How dare this happen to me! I'm an archaeologist!'

Brock poured a glass of water from the almost empty carafe

remaining on the table, caught the attention of the barman and signalled for him to come over. 'Well, it did for some reason and, as the best way to calm down is to eat and debrief, I suggest you order something and tell me, from the beginning, what happened; starting with who you are and why you are here.'

'That's what people keep asking me! Why should I go through it all with you again?'

'You don't have to. It's your choice. However, remember I chose to rescue you, which I didn't have to. There were others incarcerated who have not been so fortunate. So why not give me the benefit of the doubt? First, I am interested. Secondly, I may be able to help you further; or you may be able to help me, as two heads are usually better than one. But I do not have a whole lot of time, so what's it to be?'

Cassie looked at the rugged handsome features and broad shoulders of the man in front of her, his bronzed forearms leaning on the table, palms held outward waiting for her answer. The wide smile he gave her which deepened the etched lines around his penetrating blue eyes stimulated her decision. 'You're right and I've not even thought to thank you for getting me out of that place. How did you know I was there anyway?'

'Start at the beginning,' repeated Brock. 'Like what is your name?'

'Sorry; my mother always said I would infuriatingly answer every question with one of my own. Right, my name is Cassandra Adrasteia Kaligirou. My friends call me Cassie for short.'

'OK, Cassie, now what would you like to eat?' offered Brock as the waiter came to their table with more bread and another pitcher of water. 'The special is a local goulash-type fish stew. I ate it earlier. It seems OK.'

Cassie looked briefly at the menu, suddenly realizing how hungry she was. 'I'll take it, with the tomato salad.'

'That's all, thanks,' said Brock nodding to the waiter before looking again at Cassie. 'I would of course like to offer you something else to drink but it may be advisable to leave that for another time,' he added as the waiter left the table. 'Sounds an interesting name and you are an archaeologist, right?'

'Yes, like my father and grandfather before me. Both of them were quite famous in archaeological circles and of course were passionate about Greek mythology. They chose my names, though both of them died before I was born. But my mother honoured their wish, albeit calling me Cassie, which sounds less ancient.'

'I am sure they would have been very proud that you followed them into their field, in keeping with family tradition. It's a pity you were never able to meet them.'

'In a way I have,' replied Cassie. 'I studied all their recorded journals and my mother shared many stories about them.'

'Is she still alive?'

'No, she died earlier this year, which is what led me to come here in fact.'

Brock raised his eyebrows, 'How come?'

'Well, to start at the beginning, as you say' – leaning forward in a playful conspiratorial fashion – 'means going back to 1976. That was the year I was born and my father and grandfather, Adonis and Andreus Kaligirou either went missing or were killed. Either way they were never found.'

'Killed?' said Brock, pouring fresh water into their glasses. 'An accident?'

'Well, my grandfather's colleagues at Athens University were convinced it was something like that. They pushed for a full enquiry into their disappearance but at the time both the Ukrainian and Romanian communist authorities never bothered to reply for a whole year. Finally a local enquiry, right here in Tulcea in fact, concluded that they must have lost their lives in the delta wetlands. The Greek media wanted to believe it was something more sinister, suggesting that they could have been robbed and killed as the area was so poverty-stricken and under a communist regime at the time. Even today this area, as you see, is incredibly poor, though I have only experienced friendliness. How about you?'

Brock looked non-committal. 'Some friendliness, some not so friendly, like anywhere in the world, I suppose; but tell me, what brought them here?'

'Lysippos,' replied Cassie briskly before drinking half her glass of water in one go.

'Who?'

The woman looked surprised. 'Lysippos of Sikyon of course. You must have heard of him, no?'

Brock shook his head, 'Sorry, should I have?'

Cassie leaned back as the waiter arrived with a large steaming bowl of fish goulash, yet more bread and her salad.

'I suppose because I have lived with the name and am Greek I assume everyone must know him as well as I do,' she said, immediately tearing off a piece of bread and dunking it into her stew. 'But I am sure you must know of his work, have surely seen copies of it, even if you do not recall the name. He is the greatest sculptor that ever lived. He set the standard that all others have attempted to emulate.'

'Michelangelo was pretty great, wasn't he?' Brock put in, in an attempt not to look entirely ignorant of the subject.

'Lysippos was that Italian's role model,' scoffed Cassie with a mouth full of stew before swallowing quickly in order to continue. 'His pupils include Chares of Lindos, who constructed the Colossus of Rhodes, one of the seven wonders of the ancient world. So perfect were his creations that Alexander the Great made him his personal sculptor; Tiberius caused a revolt in Rome when he removed one from the city to his own chamber and Nero coveted them, covering them in gold.'

'Sounds like something Nero would do,' said Brock, refilling her glass with more water.

'Thanks. The point is they were all in bronze,' continued Cassie, 'and Lysippos was prolific. It is said he created one thousand five hundred works of art, all of them so uniquely skilful that each of them alone made him famous. But not one survives. Today each one would be priceless. Finding one would be like, well, as if you had Mona Lisa and it was the only surviving work of da Vinci.'

'Hmm . . . that is priceless,' agreed Brock. 'None have survived? There must be some in museums?'

'The academics argue over what is attributed to him or not. A bronze, found by a fisherman in 1964, and revealed to the public only last year, renamed the Getty Bronze, is believed to be one. The famous Venetian four bronze horses have been attributed to him, but were more likely to be from his school. Nero took them to Rome from Greece; Constantine the Great moved them to stand at the great hippodrome of Constantinople. Stolen by the crusaders, they were taken to Venice, where for centuries they ornamented the façade of the Basilica de San Marco, facing out to San Marco Square. Napoleon transported them to Paris until they returned to Venice, after his fall. You must go and see them. The museum keeps them indoors on the second floor to avoid further corrosion; copies of them now stand on the façade.'

'I will make a point of it next time I am in Venice,' said Brock.

Cassie swallowed another mouthful. 'Hmm, this is good. Yes, you must! Marble copies of his work, of course, are everywhere. The British Museum attributes its Eros stringing the bow to Lysippos. A copy of one of his many sculptures of Alexander the Great still exists at the Louvre; the lifelike bust of Socrates is at Naples. The resting Hercules which inspired Michelangelo is also there. Lysippos of course did statues of all of Hercules' twelve labours of which there are fourth- to first-century BC copies from the Lysippos school. You must see them too! What makes Lysippos unique is how he described his own work. He said that where other artists made men as they are, he made them as they appear. He was able to project their character. You must have seen pictures of the bronze copy of his original work of Alexander on horseback in Florence?'

It was clear that the food and the talk about a subject that she was passionate about were restoring the woman's energy. 'I have been fortunate to see a few original works relating to Alexander. However, you said that Lysippos was the reason your father and grandfather came here. Tell me about that,' prompted Brock.

'Yes. Well, I believe so because of a journal my grandfather sent my mother and something I found among her personal items.' She put down her fork and bread and stretched down to the bag she had retrieved from her room. 'Look, let me show you.'

After ensuring that all the patients had been transported to the boat and safely secured in the containers, Goryachev continued supervising his disposal team. Everything that could provide any evidence relating to the clinic's use had to be destroyed before dawn. The furnace that had been purposefully installed years earlier during the conversion cremated all the hard drives, file copies, monitoring videos. Any evidence of human remains followed, including the unfortunate comatose candidates who

99

had not passed selection. Goryachev personally lowered the last item into the intense heat. Whether the girl Tila, carried like a lifeless rag doll from her enclosed room, felt the flames as they began to incinerate her body, no one would ever know. The man never gave it a thought. His mind was already turning to the remaining element that required urgent elimination: Connor Brock.

Two kilometres downstream an ex-naval captain reassuringly patted his breast pocket and thanked the stars for luck as his vessel left the Danube on its scheduled return voyage via the Black Sea. By 08.00 they would be docked in Odessa. To think that just six months earlier he had been forced out of the service, saving the navy the embarrassment of a court martial for his ferrying of non-military cargo. Yet, true to his word, the man who had in fact first caused his dismissal had supported him, securing him a great position with Izmail's food-processing plant. The thrice weekly trip even allowed him to spend time in Odessa, in the bars away from his nagging wife and her mother. No one would even know that two of the empty containers were returning full. And they would be empty again long before the dawn reloading. Patting his bulging pocket once more he blessed his friendship with Gregor; a whole year's pay in one night! And even a little something for a bonus if he wanted. And no one would know. He chuckled to himself as he thought of what the containers carried.

Uncertain whether she was awake or asleep, Anna tried to open her eyes, but there was nothing but blackness all around. The air was hot and stuffy and the world seemed to be in motion again. Convinced she was trapped in the recurring dream that so frightened her, she tried to move. Her legs and arms would not respond and her chest felt heavy. Someone called her name. Anna desperately tried to shout a reply.

No one cared to listen.

Eighteen

T he gates reopened at the front of the house at the same time as the phone rang. The mobile had been stopped, though not before its shrill tone had sounded off for what had seemed an endless five seconds. Horror for what he had witnessed blending with the fright of being discovered stimulated a surge of adrenaline to course through Georghe Enescu's veins, prompting him to action.

He knew he had to get out and quickly. Yet everything seemed to move in slow motion as he turned away from the window. Inexorably his eyes seemed compelled to look once more; inevitably locking with those of the man whose attention had been attracted. Though it could only have been a millisecond, the look seemed to last an eternity. The sounds of warning cries inside the building filled his ears, coupled with the noise of wide tyres crunching gravel, as two incoming heavy cars swept along the drive.

Clutching his cellphone tightly in his hand Enescu ran for the gates, which were already beginning to close. His heart pounding in his chest he could see the gap to his freedom narrowing, but he was certain he could make it. In the final two paces remaining he heard someone or something right behind him. As he threw himself through the tightly narrowing space he screamed in pain. The jaws that clamped around his forearm were like no other pain he had experienced before, crushing bone and sinew as if they were papier mâché. Enescu desperately tried to free his arm, pulling the Doberman through the gate with him. The tightly muscled beast, its target won, instantly halted its previous momentum and began to pull back.

A second later the Doberman yelped in distress as the gates

closed on either side of its taut neck. Like all high-security gates the automatic safety sensors installed to prevent accidental crushing had been disabled for added security. Instinctively the animal sought its own escape, instantly releasing its trapped prey. Enescu ran across the street, intent on crossing the park opposite; then towards the town and trams.

Kostina kicked the limp dog aside as the gates reopened. The dog, its head falling loosely to the side, made no sound. He strode over to the cars that were parking, having dropped off their passengers. A minute later as their headlights swept past him something reflective on the ground caught his eye. He stooped down to pick up the silver object that was lying on the gravel.

'Technology is wonderful,' he said to one of the remaining men who habitually stuck to him like ramora, the quasi-parasitic fish that spend their lives swimming close to sharks. 'As long as man is the master of it and does not become its slave.' He tossed the mobile phone to the ramora. 'Here, I want to know who he is. Now, we do not want our visitors becoming impatient.'

The VIPs were shown into the overly sumptuous lounge, festooned with heavy black and deep-red drapes, a room which Madame Luga affectionately referred to as her parlour, an elegant yet seamy reflection of her own couture that was overly scented with sweet, yet spicy perfumes. They were then served a glass of Cristal champagne by scantily dressed females. When Kostina entered, Mira Luga smiled at him, conveying in her look that none of the four guests had any idea of the earlier commotion. He imperceptibly nodded back, continuing his stride towards the three visitors, who stood apart from each other. The anticipation that emanated from two of them was clear to register.

'So good to see you all here!' said Kostina in a relaxed friendly manner. 'My dear friends. It is so good of you to accept our humble invitation for dinner.'

Not mentioning names was a rule of the house, though Kostina knew all of them. The man nearest shook Kostina's proffered hands, blissfully unaware of the callous deed they had recently completed. 'It is we who are delighted to be here. No doubt you have some perfect entertainment planned, as promised.'

Kostina smiled at the government minister before him.

102

Tonight would be a culmination of the special relationship he had been developing over a six-month period. 'Of course!' he replied before leaning into the minister to whisper: 'Perfect untouched delicacies, of which you have first choice, as promised.' Kostina saw with satisfaction the glint of avaricious lust in the man's eyes as he turned to the others. 'But first you must enjoy the delightful delicacies which we have specifically prepared for your gourmand taste.'

'You are both a gentleman and a scholar,' flattered the largest of the three visitors, an obese man hungrily pawing the scantily clad rear of the girl attempting to pour a fourth glass of champagne for him. 'And the perfect host, as ever!'

Kostina placed his hands on the man's shoulders, preferring their flaccid softness to the clamminess of the usual limp handshake, wondering yet again how such a slovenly individual was able to earn the millions he had. He smiled, thinking how the man had already paid the sum of one hundred thousand euros for what he was so salivating for: a virgin who would only ever know him; one who would then be disposed of when he had grown tired of her.

'Good to see you, Remik,' said the third visitor, who, after taking Kostina's hand, firmly gripped it while pulling him to one side. 'Everything is all right, I take it?'

One look into the tall distinguished man's eyes confirmed to Kostina that the situation with the intruder had been observed. Kostina squeezed back, knowing that, although there was little reaction, his grip was having an effect, and not caring that it did. 'Good to see you too, my old friend,' he replied, at first ignoring the question and turning back to the room. 'Come let us eat,' he added to his guests.

Feeling less inhibited after the champagne and heavy scent the other visitors followed Madame Luga out of the parlour, each accompanied by a girl on their arm. Kostina turned back to his third visitor in a softer manner.

'Come, my friend, there will be plenty of time to talk later. Do not concern yourself with my minutiae. I assure you all is as it should be. Why should it not be?'

'It is the little things that have always bothered me, Remik. Each one of them tells a story like a bad stitch in a wound that can scar us.'

'Always a way with words,' laughed Kostina. 'Remember, you and I have always been our own cutting edge. Now come on, perhaps you need a little honing this evening.'

The tall visitor looked at the pockmarked face of the man in front, knowing that it had been splashes of acid, poured from the man's own hand, which had caused the marks. He smiled, revealing a set of perfect teeth. 'Perhaps you are right.'

Kostina recognized the familiar glint in the other's eye. 'And I have the perfect solution.'

Enescu winced from the pain in his savaged forearm. As soon as he'd reached the other side of the road he'd entered the park gate and run fast, frantically looking over his shoulder. His peripheral vision caught sight of someone appearing directly to the side of him, and he tripped as he tried to take evasive action, falling heavily to the ground. He held up his good arm, in anticipation of a forthcoming blow, but none came.

Momentarily stunned he tentatively looked up at the person gazing down on him. He scrambled to his feet, the realization that he was in a graveyard flooding him with relief; he had tried to avoid the statue of an angel. His relief instantly vanished a second later when he heard shouts from the enclosed courtyard he had just managed to vacate. Crouching down behind the angel he watched as two vehicles shot out of the entrance in opposite directions.

Enescu prayed that was all they would do; perhaps they would assume the intruder they were seeking had come by car. Hearing the clang of the gate quashed his hope and he knelt closer to the ground. Each following second passed as though it were a minute, certain he was about to be discovered. Then he heard another clang. What if they bring the dog?

His imagination shouted at him as rising panic began to take him over. Struggling to control himself he risked peering from his hiding place, straining his ears for the faintest of noises.

Nothing.

Perhaps they had given up, he reassured himself. No, they have gone to get the dog, he argued. He began to move, running low and carefully until he reached a wall, noticing another gate further along it opening on to a street. He ran down the street, dodging into entrances or hiding behind gate pillars whenever he heard a car approaching. Fifteen minutes later, his coat, jeans and trainers covered in grey-black dust, he saw a bus slowing to a stop. Despite hurrying towards the bus as it dropped off a passenger, the doors were closing when he pushed his injured arm through them, causing a renewed bolt of pain to shoot through it.

The driver threw a disdainful look as the doors reopened before driving off. Enescu used his good hand to locate a coin among the loose change in his jacket pocket, inserted it into the dispenser, retrieved a ticket and sat down. Neither knowing nor caring about the bus's destination he sank low into the seat as though asleep. He would stay like that until it returned to the depot and there he would hide until the morning before going to the airport.

Enescu knew he had to call Sonja and felt for his phone. With an increasing sense of renewed panic he went through his pockets again, suddenly remembering where he'd last had it. It had been in his hand when the dog had grabbed him. He felt a wave of despair. He could not call Sonja. He could vaguely recall some of the digits but her numbers were stored in the phone memory, along with everyone else's.

Enescu took a deep calming breath. He looked at his arm. It felt worse than it looked; his now torn jacket had protected it from being punctured. But it would have to wait before it received attention. His priority was to get to Bucharest; Sonja would already be there, waiting for him. He was sure of it; tomorrow.

Nineteen

B rock looked at the faded photograph Cassie presented to
him. 'Look, that is my father, Adonis; and that is my grandfather, Andreus. And look what is between them.'

'The person or the object?'

'The object of course!' Cassie said, impatiently. 'That is an
original Lysippos.'

Brock studied as requested. 'It looks like he's been in a fight.'

'Of course it does! It is identical to what is argued to be an
authentic surviving Lysippos bronze: the Boxer of Thermon.'

'This one?' asked Brock, waving the photo.

'I believe so.'

Brock raised his eyebrows. 'Why? You said yourself only copies
survive.'

'Because I went to see it, of course!'

'Of course,' said Brock, mimicking the girl patiently. 'Might
one enquire where?'

'Rome! Immediately after finding the photo, I needed to
confirm for myself. I had only seen photos before, but after
comparing this one to the museum piece, I am sure it is the
same one.'

Brock studied the photo. The piece of art was indeed impressive. It was as though the creator had captured the moment when
the athlete, sitting exhausted with elbows resting on knees, was
about to hear if he had won or lost. The boxer's facial wounds
were lifelike; his head was turned as if, unable to hear due to his
injuries, he was looking at the judges and crowd to verify the
result.

Both her father and grandfather bore a family resemblance
to the increasingly impassioned woman before him. Behind the

boxer a third, younger man stood. And behind him Brock recognized the backdrop. 'And that is Izmail fortress, I take it, which is why you came here.'

'My father must have enclosed the photo with a letter to my mother. Unfortunately the letter was missing; perhaps it was only things my mother wanted to read, I don't know. But there were some numbers on the back.'

Turning the photo over, Brock saw the faded numbers that had been written in pencil: 45 21N/28 50E. 'A couple of map references . . .'

'But enough for me to go back through my grandfather's books and read again the notes he had written in the margins. I had noticed and read them before, but they only described what to me had previously been meaningless. With the photo and the reference my father sent I put two and two more easily together.'

'And still probably came up with five, by the look of these co-ordinates.'

A flush of anger passed over Cassie. 'I do know that exact references are in degrees, minutes and seconds. I'm not stupid. But as the seconds were not included I relied on what my grandfather had written, which talked about a location in a fordable part of the Danube in the lee of a fortress and gave step measurements as to the possible location. I immediately came here to see for myself, of course!'

'Of course,' mimicked Brock again, 'but you have to admit trusting to a little research, a big assumption and a lot of luck, though.'

'What do you think is the basis of archaeology? Most finds are the result of luck, assumption and research, in that order,' replied Cassie cuttingly.

Brock held up his hands. 'OK, but on such a basis you come alone to the lee of a naval base and, correct me if I'm wrong, start walking around a restricted area. Why did you not just hold up a sign saying, "Please arrest me"? It would have been better—'

'A permit was being processed,' interrupted the woman indignantly. 'I was just—'

'Impatient to get started,' interrupted Brock in turn. 'Hey, I understand, and I am on your side, remember? I am sure I would be impatient to get to the place where at least this photo was taken. So what happened?'

'Well I was taken for questioning by the navy guard. All seemed OK and I was about to leave when without warning I am restrained, injected with something, and the next thing I remember is waking up in that room you found me in.'

'Who's the third person in the picture?' asked Brock, studying the tall young man with collar-length hair, its blondness in contrast with the dark curly hair of Cassie's father, who had rested his arm on the other's shoulder.

'I don't know – one of grandfather's team perhaps. He looks like a student.'

Brock leaned back in his chair and stretched. 'Well, Cassie, I strongly recommend that you get straight back to Athens, wait for your permit and come back with some of your students to help you out.'

'I know, but it seems so unfair. I want to know what happened.'

'Well, it would be interesting to know how this boxer came to end up in Rome, if it is the same one.'

'I am sure of it. My grandfather devoted his working life to following up clues relating to the crusade's sacking of Greek heritage from Constantinople. The journal he sent to my mother with its added margin notes is a complete catalogue of what he believed was stolen or destroyed. His own crusade related to Lysippos and he was convinced that such priceless works of art were too beautiful to be just destroyed. They would have been hidden, never intended to be found by such barbarians.'

'Well clearly he found something,' offered Brock, pointing at the photograph. 'Look, my organization employs some of the finest technology available. What if I arrange for you to take all your research material and take advantage of it? Perhaps, with luck, some further assumptions may materialize while you are waiting for your permit. Maybe even some hunches – who knows?'

The woman looked puzzled. 'Why are you helping me?'

'Well you could call it old-fashioned chivalry,' smiled Brock. 'Seriously though, I'm interested because it concerns the clinic, and I'm interested in your story. You were apprehended and drugged in the same place where your grandfather and father disappeared thirty years ago. You and I both know that history

108

is continuously repeating itself, but this seems an unlikely coincidence to me. And investigating unlikely coincidences is the basis of my work – along with research, hunches and luck, of course, in that order.'

Too early for the first ferry, Brock crossed the Danube in the small boat Sonja Brezvanje had hired from Belgrade. At 07.30 he was at the clinic, the entrance already barred by two stone-faced young navy guards. He calmly waited until the door was reopened by an officer in a grey uniform, with matching hair. His deep-lined face was tense. 'Mr Brock?'

'Yes, Commander,' replied Brock observing the decals on the other's arm denoting his rank.

The man raised his eyebrows. 'Military,' he said, relaxing his expression slightly. 'Navy?'

'Former Royal Air Force, squadron leader, retired from active duty.'

'And an observer today.' The officer put out his hand. 'My name is Christoui. You're early.'

'The early bird catches the worm, though it seems you have already started,' replied Brock.

'It was decided to give notice of our unscheduled morning visit last night. We sought to confirm at 07.00 but received no reply whatsoever. So we entered, and, well, to use your metaphor, the bird had flown. Come in and observe. It is absolutely bizarre. The place is empty.'

Brock spent the next sixty minutes revisiting the rooms he had entered the day before, confirming Christoui's statement that the place was empty. There was neither a paperclip in Amaut's office nor a clipboard in any of the wards. The macabre mortuary closets were spotless. Perhaps forensics would reveal evidence of what he had earlier witnessed, but he was there as an observer.

Brock shrugged, thanked Christoui and returned to the boat. He was midway across the river deep in thought when the approaching roar of a powerful engine broke his reverie. Turning to his left he saw that a heavy motor launch was on a direct collision course with him.

Braced against the bow railing for support, Goryachev signalled to his helmsman. Immediately the powerful twin motors responded to the turn, slamming into the port side of the smaller craft. It was impossible to take evasive action in time; Brock looked at the large man standing on the bow only two metres from him. The man was raising something the size of an anvil above his head.

Goryachev threw the heavy anchor directly at Brock, who instantly dived away from his console. Missing him by inches the anchor smashed on to the decking. Immediately the launch pulled away, the chain tightened, forcing the anchor into the port side, where it held like a medieval grappling iron. Wood began to splinter and break like balsa as the hook bit into the boat's side like a vicious jaw determined to crush its prey. Brock was thrown back towards the wheel console while the boat tilted to its side at a dangerously steep angle. Dragged into the wake of its powerful captor by the deadly improvised hook, the smaller vessel was quickly swamped with hungry waves intent on swallowing it whole.

With the throttle of Brock's inboard motors still open, the water between the two craft appeared to be boiling as the two pairs of engines screamed, fighting against each other. Quickly calculating that any resistance would only speed up the capsizing process, Brock pulled himself back up to the console, grabbed the wheel and swung it hard to port – towards his aggressor. He then slammed the engines into full throttle and lessened the treacherous angle as he came alongside again. The other boat's helmsman turned his wheel further to port, reasoning out what his victim was trying to do. Once again the tilt increased. Brock saw the other salute him with his middle finger, recognizing him as Doroshenko. He saw the big man clinging hard to the railing, moving back from the bow.

His legs already knee-deep in water, Brock once again swung the wheel hard to port to compensate. This time as the degree lessened he quickly swung the wheel back out to starboard while slamming the engines into reverse. Doroshenko, as Brock had hoped, swung his own helm to port to keep the angle sharp and on course for the smaller boat to capsize. He had not anticipated Brock's action. The chain slackened then immediately tightened with double intensity, causing the heavy launch to unexpectedly lurch. Goryachev almost lost his balance but managed to maintain his hold with one hand. Yet the action of increased momentum activated Newton's third law of motion, causing the anchor to reactively tear the side of Brock's boat away. The sudden release of tension sent a shock back to the launch and Goryachev was catapulted into the water.

Brock paid little heed to his aggressor's predicament; water continued to swamp his own boat. Keeping the engines at full throttle he headed for shore. With less than four hundred metres to go Brock knew he was not going to make it. He donned his life vest, shut down the engines and jumped overboard. The boat sank quickly as Brock kicked away and began swimming. He had covered a quarter of the distance when he once more heard the increasing throaty roar of powerful engines behind him.

Brock spun round as the launch pulled back on its throttle and halted a few metres from his position.

'You're lucky, Squadron Leader, that we were observing you this time.'

Brock looked resignedly at Commander Christoui as sea guards threw a grappling net over the side for Brock to pull himself aboard. 'Much appreciated, Commander,' said Brock as he took the towel offered. 'I thought I was about to be fish bait.'

'Well, perhaps you would like to still go fishing,' offered Christoui pointing in the direction of the other launch, which was fast becoming a speck on the horizon. A moment later the launch's four powerful engines surged up to full throttle, its bow rising out of the water in full chase. Ten minutes later, the distance shortened to one hundred metres, the pursued boat entered the wide delta racing toward the Black Sea.

'If she turns starboard towards the Romanian wetlands we will be out of our jurisdiction,' shouted Christoui. Two minutes later, with the distance between craft reduced to twenty metres, the fleeing fugitive suddenly turned to starboard into a wide channel. The navy vessel swung to starboard to head it off.

'It's difficult to know exactly where Romanian boundaries start,' Christoui shouted to Brock as they closed in on their target. Brock saw the wiry Doroshenko as they raced alongside. Or how far they stretch, thought Brock, recalling how the man was meant to be in Romanian police custody for murder.

Directly ahead lay one of the numerous reed-covered islands, haven for the thousands of pelicans indigenous to the wetlands.

111

With the channel inexorably narrowing ahead, Goryachev, at the helm, swung his boat hard to starboard, literally bouncing it out of the water into the approaching navy vessel. A heavy dull clang of metal shook both craft, the shock of impact travelling through the hulls to jar the bones of the occupants.

Brock recognized Doroshenko's scream as he was thrown against the side, clutching the wounded leg he had accidentally inflicted on himself the day before.

Christoui, his face set in controlled rage, immediately took over the helm, swung out in as wide an arc as possible before returning to a sharp collision course. The heavier four-engined vessel struck the other launch like a battering ram, bouncing it on to a trajectory directly towards the island. Goryachev took evasive action but with little effect as both the rudder and engines were momentarily out of the water. The reed-layered sloping bank accommodated the projectile like a ramp launching a boat, only in reverse. For a split second the sound of screaming propellers punctuated the air, followed by the discordant crescendo of a thousand Dalmatian pelicans forced ungracefully airborne in fright. The boat slid to a stop and keeled over. Immediately Christoui reversed engines and began to turn. Brock looked at him enquiringly.

'Fishing in Romanian waters may be overlooked,' Christoui explained. 'Hunting on Romanian shores is strictly forbidden. We haven't been here. I will put you ashore at Tulcea.'

Brock looked back at the crumpled wreck and nodded. 'OK, Commander, works for me. Oh, and I owe you one.'

Twenty

William Steinwright looked ashen as he listened to Sophia Lefrington and his scientist Jon Su-Yeong. 'All recent samples are contaminated?' he said quietly.

'All,' repeated the doctor. 'We have spent the last twenty-four hours retesting. All current and recent – up to six months – supplies of embryonic stem cells and cord blood stem cells contain varying levels of the same contamination.'

'Jon, what do you exactly mean by contamination?'

'A foreign body introduced directly by the host, in other words from the mother's blood contaminated by drugs.'

Steinwright balled his hands tightly into fists as he spoke. 'Any such evidence of drugs will strike us with a two-edged sword,' he said slowly. 'First, from the moral view, current law only allows voluntary donation of aborted foetuses and umbilical cords. The fact that they are contaminated is evidence that the donors have been coerced to donate under the influence of drugs.'

'And second, from a scientific point of view, it will influence all our results,' added Su-Yeong. 'Including our critical period of testing for Neurofribiline.'

'Which we have just announced,' said Sophia, immediately biting her lip for stating the bitterest pill for Steinwright to swallow.

The professor audibly swallowed. 'Quite. Have you identified the contamination?'

'Not completely, but on preliminary investigation it appears to be a blending of Flunitrazepam and Sodium Thiopental. The former impedes victims physically and erases all memory of an event; it is more commonly referred to in layman terms as—'

'The date-rape drug, Rohypnol,' interrupted Sophia coldly. 'Used for drug-facilitated assault, where victims are unable to refuse sex and can't remember if they did or didn't.'

The doctor nodded in agreement before continuing. 'And the latter, more commonly known as Sodium Pentothal, interferes with judgement and higher cognitive function, allowing automotive control over the person.'

'The effect being that a candidate is compelled to perform what is commanded of them without recollection,' simplified Steinwright.

'It would appear to be the case. And I believe that further investigation will reveal Ketamine, which induces hallucinations, a dreamlike feeling, and a complete loss of time and identity. A person under such influence would feel they were willingly experiencing what was performed on them or enacted by them. The side effect of Ketamine is aggressive or violent behaviour.'

'Is it legally or readily available?' asked Steinwright.

'Legal yes, in the US, for use as an animal anaesthetic, though not readily available for general use. Indeed, veterinary clinics in the US are frequently robbed for their Ketamine supply. Also, it is a long-lasting drug which can remain present in the blood system for weeks. Those, together with other as yet undefined elements, are the sources of the contamination.'

Steinwright's pallor became florid as his anger rose. 'If what we have here is a drug that has been specifically developed from these three, and other elements, then it immediately begs the question of not only why, but who?'

'With heightened security awareness since 9/11 there have been major advances in such drugs for use by the intelligence services, or so I understand,' said Sophia. 'At Stanford we heard rumours of new truth drugs being tested by unknown persons on unknown persons. The Cold War continues even though it is behind closed doors. Perhaps this drug has found its way into other hands.'

'I hate to think why,' said Steinwright.

'I think we both know why, Professor. To ensure that our not-insignificant demand for embryonic stem cells and cord blood is fulfilled,' said Dr Su-Yeong, who then paused and looked at Sophia. 'Which leads us, I'm afraid, to another concern.'

Steinwright remained silent, slightly nodding his head for the scientist to continue.

'As you know, Professor, a maturing cell structure begins to develop an immune system. The more mature the cells the more they are able to dissipate any foreign influence, though not in all cases of contamination, depending on the addictive influence introduced. For example, a pregnant woman's continued use of heroin will inevitably influence the same addiction in her unborn baby. We have identified varying degrees of regeneration from our test samples, different absorption abilities relating to the contamination. Which means that the material we are working with is not only embryonic; it is evolved to mature foetus.'

'I don't understand! How can that be possible?' blurted Steinwright.

'It has either been requested or accidentally supplied. Professor, though I am inclined towards the moral standards of acceptable and indeed voluntary donorship, as a scientist I hold little concern for any religious outcry. My concern is that I have conducted my research with contaminated material. Effectively all my clinical trials and cloning experiments during the past six months must be considered void.'

Steinwright's florid complexion returned to ashen white. BioGenomics Research had already recognized that the Vatican's threat, to which he knew Su-Yeong was alluding, to excommunicate scientists who carried out embryonic stem-cell research using eliminated embryos made them good fodder for sensationalist media. The slightest evidence of drug-induced donors forced to provide supplies, and more mature ones at that, was more than newsworthy. Their recently announced Alzheimer's cure would be ridiculed and shares would drop like a stone. Steinwright shut his eyes. Reports of such an ongoing investigation would threaten to wipe out their current $100 billion capitalization.

Steinwright pinched the bridge of his nose with his forefinger and thumb before using them to smooth down his bushy eyebrows. He looked at Sophia and Su-Yeong and breathed out slowly. 'We are all fully aware of the utmost seriousness of what you have brought to my attention. And I give you my word that I will now focus all such attention on the matter without delay.

115

But I want your word right here and now that you will not reveal even the slightest of your concerns to anyone. This has to be handled with extreme delicacy. This could ruin more than six months' clinical trials. It could ruin our work for good. Do you understand and do I have your word?'

'Of course, Professor Steinwright,' said Sophia.

'And that must include your father, and husband. Both are now major shareholders. There will be a time and place and it will be of my choosing.'

'You have my word,' replied Sophia without emotion.

'Mine too,' said the scientist, again without emotion. 'I want to continue with my research. But William, I suggest you focus your attention close to home because whether I was to have the sample I first received, I don't know. But someone later tampered with those samples, and irrespective of legal, moral or religious relevance, someone is conducting their research utilizing the rich regeneration cells indigenous in almost fully formed foetuses; so someone had to place and receive the order first. Someone in our organization.'

Steinwright watched as the two left his office, shutting the door behind them before pulling his platinum mobile from his pocket and pressing a preset number. He could feel the sweat forming on his brow as he listened to his phone ring once, then twice.

'William?' said the voice which answered. Steinwright could not hide the stress in his voice. 'You were right. I will need your help,' he said.

BELGRADE

Kastrati smiled with satisfaction as he read the current balance on his Internet banking account. Coupled with the usual amount of cash received during the last month, it meant he was now in a position to complete his final payment for the yacht he had ordered. He leaned back in his chair, placed his feet on the desk and stretched. The yacht where he would run his expanding operation, moving between the Black and Mediterranean Seas.

He would delegate his current day-to-day running around to Leka Varoshi and Petri Paloka; and promote some others from the ranks. That would leave him free to focus on the bigger

116

deals. Too many operators were getting involved in the prostitution rackets, resulting in far too many percentages being diluted. In France alone he had provided several thousand girls for European streets, including those of Nice, Paris and Marseilles, yet after sweetening the Russians his cut was hardly worth the effort. But taking a percentage of the clinics would be an entirely different story.

He smiled broadly as he thought of the millions it would net him. When he'd started providing selected candidates to order and couriering between Donaueschingen and Izmail six months ago he'd had no idea that the demand for body parts and organs was so immense; nor had he realized that the demand for newborn babies was so big. Why else would Amaut want so many pregnant girls supplied? And with his street girls falling pregnant with such regularity it was so easy to supply. A win-win opportunity. Men wanted girls without protection; and he of course was being well paid for them to fulfil their fantasy and sow the essential seeds. Then rich Western women, desperate to adopt, paid again to reap the babies, with no questions asked.

The girls could then return to the streets to start another crop, until their usefulness was over; then they returned to be harvested for what was left of them. No, he would no longer just be a meat-trader as he had told Amaut; he would become a modern farmer, supplying seed, crop and benefiting from the rich harvest delivered to an insatiable market.

Twenty per cent on the price of organs from one delivery would bring him more than six months' income derived from supplying the sex industry, without the work or risk.

Let the Russians, Bulgarians and even his fellow Albanians control the rackets if they wanted, paying his delegated personnel for their continued supply. The future was farming. Kastrati laughed out loud, a deep belly laugh.

'Now that Romania and Bulgaria are part of the European Union, I should ask for a farming subsidy,' he said to himself. 'Why not? Did not their very ratification prove to be a grant in itself, with the market gates being thrown wide open. And with Ukraine and Turkey, in a few years, think how much produce I can bring to market!' But first, he reflected, he must insist on getting more supply of the Pied Piper drug. Perhaps he should work on getting a direct supply – cut out Amaut.

Ten years of ruthless drug crime evolving to the more lucrative business of trafficking had hardened Januz Kastrati to what a civilized world defined as human misery. The only rights he recognized were his own and how the world revolved around him. Ten years had also honed a predatory sixth sense, the uncanny cat-like ability to know when another predator is in the vicinity. As he surveyed the view from his office he had the feeling he was being observed, and swept his narrowing black eyes over the surrounding vista before shrugging and returning to his desk.

Though confident that it was impossible for him to be seen, Ferguson saw the man's eyes appear to look directly at him. The Irishman's powerful field glasses had already observed Kastrati departing the berth of the pseudo scenic tours boat and walk the short distance to the bleak tower block; and now they stared right into the only uncovered apartment window on the eighth floor. He passed the field glasses to his companion. 'And now we wait.'

Twenty-One

The Tarom-owned ATR72, its twin-turbo engines at full throttle, left Constanta runway, and climbed steeply before veering west on its twice-daily shuttle. Flying to the north of the Bulgarian capital, Sofia, and following the lee of the Carpathian Danube relief, the pilot maintained Romanian air space until the plane began its descent fifty-five minutes after departure; right on schedule. Brock recognized the distinct confluence of the Sava joining the Danube adjacent to the manmade arterial web that haphazardly spun across the city of Belgrade.

It was almost eight years to the day since his first visit to, at that time, the capital of Yugoslavia, seconded from the RAF by NATO, no doubt partly due to his father's influence, Cameron Brock. And it would have been his last had it not been for the intervention of another member of the Special Forces division, Matt Ferguson, during a covert operation. Brock considered that perhaps if providence had destined otherwise he would never have met and subsequently married Heather McCoy shortly afterwards. In that scenario he would have avoided the ongoing pain of having lost her in a hit-and-run accident, soon after the birth of their daughter – a daughter who knew him only as Uncle Connor.

Brock pushed the invasive thoughts out of his head as the plane touched down. Like Belgrade, no longer capital of the former Yugoslavia but of the Republic of Serbia, and recently awarded the accolade 'City of the Future' for south-east central Europe, he too must look forward, not back. Dwelling on the past, or what could have been, was nothing more than delusional.

After a speedy entry through customs and ignoring the entreaties offered by a variety of unregistered taxis, Brock strode directly to the number seventy-two bus that he knew would take him close to the address Ferguson had texted him. He paid his eighty dinars, the equivalent of one euro, and took a window seat. Scottish thriftiness was not the reason; arriving at his destination by taxi was simply too conspicuous. Brock felt pleased with himself, however, as he took his seat, in the knowledge that the inflated taxi tariff of fifty euros for western Europeans meant an ample saving.

The bus driver took a more circuitous route than scheduled in an attempt to randomly serve as many passengers as possible prepared to pay an extra thirty dinars for the convenience. Brock saw again how the Stari Grad, or old city, architecture of a grander Austrian epoch, unalterably began to change into the more recent structures of Novi Beograd with its assortment of bleak-looking edifices, constructed during a supposedly practical, though austere, communist era.

Yes, one must look to the future, but not disregard the lessons of the past, reflected Brock. Yet experience had developed an inevitable cynicism in him, which earlier thoughts coupled with recent events now stimulated. Ruefully he acknowledged that regimes inevitably grew to disregard whatever their predecessors had painfully learned, and to permit continued exploitation in the name of a brighter future. And always it was the innocent who suffered.

Three passengers, including Brock, exited the bus soon after it had entered the concrete city and stopped at its dilapidated heart. Adjacent to a treeless square, with uniform squat tower blocks on all sides, were a number of wooden kiosks, each offering limited stocks of whatever produce they had on offer. Behind them was a supermarket in the process of trying to be refurbished. Its wide window had been boarded up as if recently vandalized. Garish graffiti now crudely decorated it.

Brock felt his mobile vibrate in his pocket, alerting him to an incoming text. Thirty minutes later he'd listened to Ferguson and Sonja Brezvanje's report and briefed them in turn on the telephone conversation he had had with van Lederman before his departure from Constanta.

'So he expects us there tomorrow, does he?' said the Irishman. 'If we're supposed to be field operators, why can't we hold a conference call?'

Brock raised his eyebrows at Ferguson, intimating he knew

better than to ask why. 'Now, I propose we make the most of our time here by—'

'Applying the usual policy of grabbing the bull by the horns,' interrupted Ferguson to Sonja.

'Well, we do need to get the information from the horse's mouth,' said Brock.

The woman looked from one to the other in puzzlement. 'Bull, horse, animals? What are you two talking about? You promise help. Now you talk about leaving. This is bullshit.'

'No, it is not, Sonja. As time is short we need to get what we came for in the most effective way available to us, which means confrontation.'

'But it is too dangerous. Remember Radu.'

'I remember you wanted to destroy his murderer's operation, even if it destroyed you,' said Brock. 'You say that all the windows on his level are covered and secured with bars, except in what you believe to be his office. You have already told us that it is a holding station. How many young girls are up there now? We need to take action, now.'

'Two of you! He is not alone.'

'Yes, I am acutely aware that he will be accompanied by more bullies, but in our experience a bully fears being bullied more than anything. Matt and I hope to persuade them to take us for a scenic cruise.'

'Give bullies shit, eh, Connor?' quipped Ferguson.

'Yes, something along those lines, thank you, Matt,' said Brock.

As Ferguson raised his hand to his head pretending to touch his forelock, Brock recognized the familiar habit that his friend employed to diffuse forthcoming tension or stress. 'Ah well. I suppose you'll be after scuttling it then,' said Ferguson, reverting to his Irish vernacular.

'We need to do something to frustrate his operation. If as you say, Sonja, this Pied Piper is trafficking through discount airlines within hours of abduction, then he must have facilities en route. We already know that drugs are used and we can assume that there will be passport forgery when required. Now, we know the authorities will not move without evidence. So it seems to me that if we incapacitate his method of transportation and gather evidence of his trafficking, then you will be able to, hopefully, get the authorities to listen to you.'

121

Sonja listened gravely. 'OK, sounds good; what is your plan?'
'I'm working on it,' said Brock.

Four hundred kilometres due east another plane landed, on
schedule, at a place that had also aspired to the acclaim 'City
of the Future'. Recovering from a crippling sixty-year heritage
that included an earthquake during World War II, followed by
extensive bomb damage, another earthquake in the 1970s,
coupled with a communist rebuilding programme, had, however,
extracted too heavy a toll on the city, formerly renown as 'Little
Paris'.

To a certain returning passenger, being local made no difference to the almost lethal experience of trying to get through
the city. Teeth-jarring potholes, which the erratic driver repeatedly hit, aggravated his pain. The route was so tenuous through
the historic neglected ruins of Str Franceza, and his spirit so
low that the man mentally agreed with the opinion of the older
generation: Bucharest mirrors our whole country – beautiful but
ready to collapse.

Just a few yards from where it felt like he had been flung on
to the street, the man entered a jaded French-bourgeois corner
building, supported either side by smaller neo-Romanian structures. Slowly, yet without stopping, he plodded up the rounded
steps, his gaze fixing on each of the worn and chipped edges
in turn, until he reached the third floor. Pausing for a moment,
he then pushed open the tarnished door.

Sitting behind one of the metal desks in the high-ceilinged
room, festooned with posters and newspaper cuttings, was
Natalya, her head leaning to one side as she spoke into the
phone she had just answered. Instantly noticing her colleague's
dishevelled state, despite his earlier attempt to improve it before
his flight, Natalya immediately stood up, her free hand instinctively flying to her mouth. The exhausted man noticed how her
pretty eyes, hair and expression of sudden, yet worried, surprise,
mirrored those of the beautiful girl he had witnessed strangled.
A loud, involuntary sob erupted from the very depths of
Georghe Enescu's heart as he collapsed to the floor.

The linguist who had been delegated the task of dialling each
one of the numbers located in the phone memory listened

intently. With the Romanian international code prefixing almost all of the numbers the choice of the linguist had proved worthwhile. Twice she had asked to whom she was speaking, in order to verify the caller's initial answer of La Strada des Enfants. The response and the address subsequently given, following her request, were duly recorded electronically when she heard the phone drop.

The background conversation between a man and woman, though hard to decipher, was also recorded before someone retrieved the phone, and replaced it on its cradle, terminating the call. Curious, the linguist considered calling again, but as the brief was to obtain names and addresses for the various numbers she had been given, she continued to the next one. Upon hearing the engaged tone, she dialled the next on the list.

Sonja had answered the call from her Bucharest office as she watched Brock and Ferguson walk purposefully towards the Danube scenic tour boat. Living with the human misery which trafficking causes on a daily basis, had anaesthetized Sonja from the initial emotions of horror, dismay and revulsion that a person feels. Listening first to Natalya, and then to Enescu, renewed her frustration at her syndicate's weakness and vulnerability, as she had felt after Radu – before once again reinforcing the growing anger that fuelled her resolve.

'I could do nothing,' said Enescu again, allowing the guilt to take him over.

'We are not responsible for the actions of others, Georghe,' placated Sonja. 'We do what we can. You have already achieved more than is expected of us. And you have made a difference. We have their location. We can pass the details on to both the Berlin police and UNICEF. What is a priority now is that you get treatment for your arm and—'

'What is the point? It will be too late. They will all be dead.'

'Georghe,' said Sonja firmly. 'Listen to me. I mean what I say when I tell you that what we do does make a difference. You must understand that, however insignificant what we achieve might sometimes seem, there is always a point to what we do. Even if it is just one young person we rescue. Yet I strongly believe we are going to make a really big difference, and soon. I promise you we will. Now let me speak to Natalya.'

'Natalya, is Tomasina in yet?'

'No, she called in sick, says she will be back in tomorrow.'

'OK, did you hear back from London yet?'

'No. Do you want me to contact them again?'

'Later. First get Georghe to hospital; make certain he gets treatment for his arm. And watch him, Natalya; he's blaming himself.'

'I know,' said the woman, understanding.

'I am back in Belgrade, with Jakiv.'

'In Belgrade? Why? The Pied Piper?'

'To retrieve our transport,' replied Sonja without clarification. 'Then we will be returning. In the meantime, as Tomasina is not there, close up the office, get Georghe to hospital. I'll call you when we're almost back and we can meet back at my place. We all need to talk.'

'Radu too?' asked Natalya intuitively.

'He will not be joining us ... and Natalya,' continued her employer quickly to truncate further enquiry, 'before you ask, I prefer to explain everything later. I must go, now.'

Burying her grief deep in the catacombs of her heart along with the emotional tombs of her younger sister and the others she had known and lost, Sonja Brezvanje pushed the phone into her pocket and lifted the field glasses to her eyes. The plan, for all it was worth, was already in motion.

Twenty-Two

Petri Paloka lit a fresh cigarette with the burning embers of one to be discarded, pulled another beer bottle out of the cooler, leaned back in his seat and surveyed the concrete Novi Beograd ant nests for a few moments before closing his eyes, enjoying the noonday sun. Empty of cargo, except for the recently collected drugged girl locked in his cabin, and with two-thirds of his nine man crew ashore, he had just finished the large plate of pasta the ship's cook had prepared for him, and now looked forward to more beer and a sleep in the sun before returning to his cabin.

He stretched out his thin, wiry limbs, resting his feet against the rounded steel ridge of the boat side. This, he concluded, had been one of the best trips ever. Kastrati had been true to his word, as he had since first the streets and then the prisons of Tirana. He had always looked up to the man, holding his almost cat-like senses in awe. Having the Tosk dialect in common with his fellow Albanian, as well as speaking Romanian and a couple of other Slavic dialects, had ensured trusted positions for him over the years.

When Kastrati chose the Danube in his search for a trafficking route which was consistently overlooked and poorly monitored, and had acquired a couple of boats, Paloka was told he would be one of the ferrymen responsible for moving cargo.

A shout from the shore prompted Paloka to stand up and peer over the side; leaning his elbows on the white side he peered at the two strangers hailing him. His initial suspicion at their presence turned to bored amusement when they opened their mouths.

'Excuse me. Sorry to trouble you; do you speak English?' asked the taller of the two loudly.

Sent by Kastrati to London for two years, to support an

earlier fledgling prostitution racket, the wiry ferryman also understood and spoke the language well. It amused him how uniquely the people from that country politely requested service in an apologetic way. He'd witnessed it on a daily basis. With his own language, only another of his own countryman would understand his dialect, and then only swearing, never an apology. 'Enough. What do you want?'

'Well we would like very much to hire your boat for a short cruise.'

Paloka drew deeply on his cigarette before flicking it expertly into the narrow space between the ships buffering buoys and the quay. It amused him how frequently he was asked for hire. Grinning he delivered, in a pleasant-sounding voice, a tirade of coarse Tosk profanity.

'Excellent,' said the taller of the two again. 'How much?'

Paloka surveyed the two men standing near to the gangway looking up. Both were carrying bags, a fleeting thought crossing his mind that they were seeking to leave Novi Beograd for some reason. Relaxed from his heavy lunch and under the influence of his third beer Paloka decided to have some fun and changed his tack. 'One million dinars!' he replied, his smile broadening upon hearing the reply.

'Would that be for one or two hours?'

Paloka shook his head in amazement. 'One hour,' he said, wondering how far he could string these idiots along.

'OK, upstream,' Brock said.

The ferryman's eyes narrowed. He was now certain that they must want to leave unseen for some reason, not that he was surprised as the Danube was a conduit for such exits. 'OK, upstream; but it has to be cash up front,' he added mockingly.

'Great, we only want to touch Hungary; anywhere will do,' said Brock, walking up the gangway followed closely by Ferguson.

Paloka cursed again as he held up the palm of his hand to stop them coming aboard. 'Hold it! If you're serious then show me money first.'

Brock pulled a thick roll of money out of his pocket and held it between his finger and thumb for the other to see. 'Euros OK for you?'

Paloka recognized the € 500 note and shook his head in disbelief. Such luck, to be offered so much, yet knowing he couldn't

126

have it. No matter what trust existed between him and his boss, if Kastrati discovered he had allowed any unauthorized person to board his boat he would severely punish him.

He was about to swear in a seriously unambiguous way for them to go elsewhere when an idea came to him, wondering if they were stupid enough to go for it. The taller of the two men took a step closer. 'Wait,' Paloka said raising his palm up again. 'It is not possible to depart immediately. My crew is ashore and without a full complement of crew I cannot allow you to board. I am sure that you understand that.'

The two men standing on the gangway looked disappointed but nodded to each other, shrugged and began to turn. Both of them were already aware that the crew were ashore, having watched them leave.

'But you had better pay me now to secure our agreement,' added Paloka quickly, his thin body, jutting head and pointed innocent smile reminding Ferguson of how a weasel might regard a plump pair of rabbits. 'And then if you return in about an hour we can depart; but only for an hour, no more. Is that understood?' Paloka held out his hand in a friendly way, in the knowledge that there was no way they would get on board when they returned; he would simply get the heavy crew to deal with them.

Brock looked at Ferguson. 'Seems fair,' he said. 'It's only another hour to wait. Here, give it to the man.'

Ferguson stepped on board, his left hand passing over the thick bill roll, while stretching his right hand out to shake on the deal. The ferryman's satisfied expression changed instantly into a grimace of pain as his hand was crushed in the Irishman's vice-like grip. His eyes, focused on the roll, saw it also crushed into a closing fist before smashing into his sternum like a battering ram.

Unable to breathe, let alone utter a cry for help, Paloka collapsed on the deck. Lying on his side gasping for breath, he saw Ferguson peel off the solitary €500 note and throw the rolled up pieces of newspaper on to the deck.

'Ah, wanting something for nothing is a curse, to be sure,' Ferguson quipped.

'Greed is the best of door openers,' replied Brock. 'OK, Matt, let's move it.'

Ferguson dragged the choking man out of sight through the nearest doorway, along the corridor and into the first cabin he came to. He removed Paloka's belt, quickly tied the man's hands and closed the door before rejoining Brock. They went from cabin to cabin, which on the deck level were all arranged as offices. Four laptops, bundles of stolen and counterfeit passports, batches of printed photos and marked flight timetables went into their bags. Brock momentarily studied the marked maps and the printed series of addresses arranged on the wall, no doubt placed for convenience, before ripping them down and folding them into the bag.

On the lower level, the cabins, each containing three sets of metal bunk beds, were airless and emitted a rank odour of urine and sweat. Scratches were evident over the portholes, which had been sealed shut and painted over. The air was almost claustrophobic and the two exchanged grim glances at the mutual thought of such dire conditions to keep people under in the summer heat and winter cold. Sounds were coming from one of the cabins. Approaching it they heard a TV and then voices, shouting. Brock crept forward and stole a glance around the door.

The cook and another crewman were engrossed in watching a football match. In front of them were the remains of what had clearly been large plates of pasta. There were empty and full bottles of beer remaining on the table. Brock and Ferguson stepped quietly past.

Another cabin was occupied. A semi-naked girl lay on the bed. She appeared to be sleeping yet with her eyes open. Brock recognized the vacant look he had encountered before. Ferguson watched in amazement as Brock commanded the girl to get up and dress.

'Right, Matt, we have enough. We'd better head back up. Take her and the bags ashore; she will follow you. After you have given them to Sonja, go ahead as planned.'

The prime intent had been to board, collect evidence, as damning as possible, and get off. Brock's secondary objective was to apply the same procedure to the Pied Piper's stained ivory tower; gain access and collect evidence. Matt calmly left the boat, and walked like any departing passenger with their bags and companion along the quay, even waving and greeting

Sonja when he recognized her waiting by the agreed vantage point.

Brock returned below, entered the engine room and found what he was looking for. Taking a crowbar, hammer and gloves, he lowered himself into the bilge. A minute later he located the first of the tightly sealed seacocks. Wrapping the hammer in the glove, he began to strike at the crowbar he had pushed through the grooved valve. After four hits it began to give. Within one minute water began to flood the area he was crouched in. He smashed at the chain that held the seacock top so that it broke free from its base. On its own it might not scuttle the ship but without the lid it would be impossible to immediately repair.

His clothes soaking, Brock climbed back into the engine room. At the end of the room he located the large gas cylinders that directly connected to the galley for cooking purposes. Each one acted as a reserve for the other; when one was empty, the other could be switched over. Brock opened the valves on the two current reserves and the air began to thicken with gas. Closing the door he went up to the galley, which was directly above, and turned on the eight cooker burners. Quickly he fired up just one and calmly shut the door. Two minutes later he was ashore releasing the vessel's mooring ropes.

Kastrati's preference for dealing in cash had shifted with the increasing realization of the conveniences the Internet had proven to provide for his network of operations. He knew it had been instrumental in contributing to his business partner's wealth. Remik Kostina had first introduced it to him, through his insistence first on paying via Internet transfer, after delivery of consignments; and second through the proposals he had made which would ensure greater return for Kastrati's part of the operation.

He logged out of the final account he had just visited based in Andorra, and clicked on to one of the restricted sites they operated. Clicking on a live webcast he recognized the apartment that came into view and the recently selected, highly distressed, young star of the ongoing action.

He knew that the live and recorded pornographic webcasts, continuously downloaded by fee-paying members, delivered a monthly return more than equal to what even the apartment had originally cost. He had little interest in what was being cast, so long as it was vividly abusive enough to meet his members' demands, keeping them logged on.

His interest lay in how to negotiate a larger percentage of the action. All the candidates, crew and film were his, yet Kostina insisted upon control over all credit card transactions; ensuring Kostina's operation received an equal share just for administration. Yet how much laundering was required when all payments were seemingly Internet business? And since when had they ever encountered any challenge with any laundering? – it was what Balkan States founded their real estate growth on. He was learning fast. It was all about delegation and percentage. They were his two keys to do less, yet at the same time have more.

The soft thump against his window prompted Kastrati to pause and turn his head to listen. Curious, he stood up and moved towards the window. Intuitively his eyes were drawn to the riverbank. Smoke was billowing out from the side of his boat. He grabbed at the cellphone on his desk and pressed one of the speed dial keys, continuing to gaze back to the boat. The ringtone sounded seven times before it was picked up by voicemail. '*Petri! Marrtë qifsha!*' cursed Kastrati harshly into the phone before slamming it down and crashing through the door into the outer office, calling for anyone in earshot. 'Vladic, Leka, where the *qifsha* are you?'

No reply.

Kastrati cursed again. 'Delegate! How can I *qifsha* delegate?!'

Leka, feeling humiliated for being ignored after being refused again by her returning lover, had gone into town. Vladic was a simple-minded parasitic ramora who only hung around when he wasn't hungry, and with no food he had disappeared for lunch. Kastrati ran back to the window and dialled a second time. During the fifteen seconds he listened to the tone, before it once more diverted to voicemail, he was certain that his vessel began to very slowly shift from its mooring.

Twenty-Three

A s soon as Sonja saw the Pied Piper race out of the building, she pressed the call button of her phone. Jakiv felt his phone vibrate and looked at Ferguson. Both men, waiting on the seventh floor, had already heard the elevator pass and upon receiving signal of Sonja's visual confirmation immediately walked up to the next floor.

Brock reached the building's elevator in a few minutes. The door was closing when Sonja's arm stopped it. She stepped in as it reopened.

'It's better that you stay with the evidence; you don't want to lose it again,' he said.

'I need to do this,' said the woman.

Brock gently but firmly pushed her back from the door. 'I know, but I repeat, it is better you stay with the evidence this time, including the girl. Without it what can you do? And I need you to call me immediately you see our Pied Piper returning.'

Sonja, her lips tight with emotion, nodded once before turning on her heel and retracing her steps.

When the elevator reached the eighth floor, Ferguson and Jakiv were in the apartment directly opposite the elevator door. 'Our friend was good enough to leave the door open,' offered Ferguson as Brock entered.

Brock walked past him to the window and surveyed the vista it afforded. A moment later he saw a man race along the quay pushing through the small gathering crowd. He assumed from the description Sonja had given him that it was the Pied Piper. It had taken the man about four minutes to reach the stricken boat, now heavily billowing with smoke. 'Ten minutes and we're out of here,' he said, striding to the desk himself, and picking up the bundle of keys he noticed lying there. 'Just in case our friend decides to do a quick U-turn.'

131

'Hmm,' said Ferguson, reflecting on his earlier comment as he registered the laptop screen. 'I doubt if there is a good cell in his body.' Brock joined him. The image revealed in graphic detail the clear abuse that was being meted out by an overweight naked man upon a defenceless victim.

'No, no good at all, Matt,' said Brock curtly as he snapped the computer shut and pulled out the attached leads. 'So we'd better take good care of this evidence!'

His jaw set Brock tried to open each of the other apartments in turn before matching keys with corresponding door numbers. The smell that emanated from the first was the same that arose from the others: a sickly sweet odour of dried sweat and ammonia from urine, coupled with the more metallic hint of blood. Apart from stained thin mattresses strewn across the floor, the first five apartments entered were empty. Each was identical, with a living room, two small bedrooms, a kitchen and a bathroom.

The cheaply painted walls were marked with pitiful messages scratched in forlorn hope by earlier occupants. Brock looked at the heavy bars that had been crudely but effectively bolted to the inside of the windows, noticing the blood surrounding them where inmates had tried to unscrew them with their fingers.

Unlocked, the sixth apartment opened to Brock's testing. Though heavy blackout blinds completely covered the windows two powerful freestanding halogens bathed the room in artificial light. A man, dressed in baggy jeans and an off-white T-shirt, lay sprawled across the arm of a sofa closest to the door. He briefly turned towards the new arrival, before momentarily returning his focus to the centre of the room. His head instantly jerked back again when, upon his double take, he realized that he did not know the person entering. He started to get up, a questioning, puzzled look on his face.

What he instantly recognized in the centre of the room had been enough for Brock too. It was the original of what he had just seen transmitted on the laptop. The effect of seeing the young female victim, not much older than his own daughter, altered the direction of his controlled discipline. The tortuous image in front of him ignited the cold precision that had first been internalized during Special Forces training and then later reinforced during action. Confronted with the depraved suffering before him reignited in Brock what the Special Services had originally intended, an impassioned machine, which fought fire with fire, terrorism with terrorism, and inhumanity with equal emotionless detachment.

The man's expression passed from puzzlement to shock as Brock's fist smashed into his vulnerable Adam's apple. Any cry forthcoming was extinguished before it could rise as the heel of the other hand, driven with the full force of Brock's weight, connected with a protruding jaw, causing the head to whiplash with a dull snap.

The man operating the camera looked sharply around from his digital screen in annoyance as his colleague fell across the sofa behind him. His eyes widened as those of Brock, cold as blue ice, bored into them. A split second later, blinded, the cameraman crashed to the ground, his left leg in searing pain, broken, his cries also extinguished by a stunning blow to the temple.

The remaining man, overweight, naked and sweating after his exertions, half rose from his position, trying to escape. Brock caught his leg and dragged him backwards. His cry of discomfort as he was pulled across the floor rose to a shriek of agony as a targeted stamping blow to the mid-section of his vertebrae forced him flat to the floor, immobilized. Another crushing blow hit the exposed neck and head that stuck out like a giant turtle's from under its overweight shell.

'Connor!' shouted Ferguson, pushing aside a transfixed Jakiv, who had entered just before him. 'Time's up!'

Brock stepped towards the gagged girl, who recoiled as he tried to release her roughly tied bonds, which had already burned deep weals into her bound limbs. Jakiv ran to assist, softly pushing Brock away without speaking.

Brock strode over to the window and tore at the screens, the heaviness of the room lifting as outside light flooded in. He momentarily scanned the area, confirming to himself that it was not possible to see the quay from this apartment. He turned back to Jakiv, who was talking gently to the freed girl, cowering in a sheet that he had wrapped her in.

'She won't speak,' said Jakiv. 'I believe she is Romanian; I can't be sure but I think I recognize her as one of the orphans abducted a few days ago.'

Brock noticed how the sheet shook as the girl, her head

hanging low over her tightly hunched body, quietly sobbed in heart-rending anguish. He thought she looked about fourteen. 'Jakiv, there's no word from Sonja yet, so we can take it that the Pied Piper is otherwise occupied. We need to check the remaining apartments in case there are others and get them out of here.'

Stepping between two of the former camera crew, Ferguson roughly kicked the camera hard against the wall, smashing it, before carefully placing another laptop computer into his bag. The sharp noise caused the girl to quickly raise her head in renewed fear. 'Sorry,' he said as he noticed her react. 'But looking at the chaos we're leaving behind us, I suggest we make that very quick, Connor.'

Brock tried the apartment adjacent to the filming studio. The flat carried a similar stench to the others, only stronger, the reason being that it had current occupants. Five girls had quickly huddled together in the corner upon hearing the door open. Despite the pressure of time Jakiv spoke slowly and reassuringly to the group. A minute later Jakiv and Matt crammed into the elevator with them and descended.

Directly adjacent to the office, opposite the elevator and linked by an interconnecting door was a richly furnished, though garishly decorated, apartment, which Brock decided was the Pied Piper's personal rooms. Apart from the wardrobe of expensive leather jackets, jeans, shirts, T-shirts and shoes in differing shades of black and blue, there were few personal items. Brock felt in the pockets of the jacket thrown against a chair. There was a wallet containing numerous credit cards in several different names. The name that appeared most frequently matched the name on the Serbian driving licence also in the wallet: Januz Kastrati.

Brock pocketed the wallet and moved over to the window to once again survey the quay, before investigating the room further. Picking up the binoculars lying conveniently close, he scanned the area in more detail. The crowd that had gathered on the graffiti-covered concrete quay had grown, numbering over a hundred people.

With its belly full of water, the vessel, draped in a cloud of dense black smoke that allowed intermittent tongues of flame to poke through, was listing to starboard. A group of men were desperately trying to moor the stern, while its unsecured bow continued to be pulled inexorably round by the current. For a full minute Brock studied the scene. Januz Kastrati, alias Sonja's reviled Pied Piper, was nowhere to be seen.

Twenty–Four

T he woman could no longer contain the pent-up emotion that had been building over months culminating in the transatlantic crossing with her husband. She clasped Max Adler's hands in her own. 'I cannot thank you enough, Herr Adler,' she said, ignoring the tears that streamed down her cheeks. 'We have waited so long.'

The lawyer hated it when he had to shake hands, let alone when someone insisted on holding them. He didn't know why his palms were always wet with sweat; it wasn't as if he suffered panic attacks as his doctor suggested, though the fact was they were frequently clammy at moments like this. But at least the other fact was that, whatever he felt or thought, no one could ever read it in his face. He smiled.

'Mrs Williamson, it has been more than a pleasure,' he said, retrieving his hands and gesturing for her to sit down. 'And Mr Williamson, please sir, be my guest.'

A moment later they were standing again as the door opened and a portly woman dressed in white entered. She was carrying a baby which she placed into Mrs Williamson's arms then discreetly left the room without having spoken a word.

Adler allowed several minutes of adulation for the new arrival. As planned, the baby had recently been fed, changed and entered a calm period ready for sleep. Tiny eyelids heavy with oncoming sleep blinked once or twice, bright blue eyes too young to focus on anything in particular.

'Your son, Mr Williamson; I believe he has your colour eyes,' Adler said to the man, who was caressing his wife while she held the baby.

Williamson looked at Adler, a huge grin on his face. 'Susan's right: we owe you a lot.'

Adler placed his hand on the man's shoulder, gently guiding him back to his seat. 'Speaking of which, why don't we conclude the formalities? I believe your flight is this afternoon; you must be anxious to get straight back to Washington. I understand that this is the best time of the year to be there; perfect for a new family.'

Fifteen minutes later Adler left his office, walked ten minutes to Philharmonikerstrasse, entered the café of the Sacher Hotel and ordered his usual indulgence of a double espresso macchiato and large slice of the hotel's famous torte with apple strudel and melange. He smoothed the sides of his brown, slightly greying and richly oiled hair back, settled in the corner of the room and began checking his latest batch of emails on his Blackberry.

His nondescript suit and reserved manner allowed him to blend with other locals amidst the numerous tourists that filed in either to eat or look around. The returning waitress, recognizing him as a regular, momentarily dropped her aloofness to deliver a curt respectful nod of acknowledgement as she carefully arranged his gateau and coffee as she would a priceless *objet d'art*.

With no wife or children of his own to cosset, Adler enjoyed pampering himself. He considered his niche as an adoption co-ordinator specializing in newborn babies provided all the family he needed: gratitude without commitment.

Contentedly he placed a generous forkful of rich chocolate and apricot into his mouth, leaned back to read the email he had just opened and instantly began to choke on both. The refined elderly couple sitting adjacent to him formed the opinion that the puce-coloured man disturbing the civilized hubbub with an uncontrolled coughing fit was simply receiving just punishment for gulping back a sacred Sacher torte too quickly. The reality was that the lawyer's next five consignments, already ordered and confirmed with deposits paid, had just been irrevocably cancelled.

Twenty minutes later, a profusely sweating Adler was wiping his hands on his jacket as he listened to the ringing tone. He had already emailed a reply requesting immediate and further information, but to no avail. As the phone was finally answered he thanked his foresight in insisting on being given a variety of numbers in case of emergency.

'What can I say, Herr Adler?' said a voice the lawyer immediately recognized.

'Herr Amaut! At last! What is the meaning of your email? You can't just cancel. I . . . we . . . there are commitments!'

'It is not my choice,' said Amaut resignedly. 'We have had to relocate. The circumstances are unimportant but it means we have had to radically alter our own plans. As soon as we are reorganized I will contact you.'

'But that is unacceptable. What about my orders?'

'We no longer have them. We discovered that some terminations were necessary during our relocation.'

'Terminations? What do you mean terminations?'

'You know what I mean. I don't need to spell it out for you. I will contact you as soon as possible. Do not call again.' Adler looked at his Blackberry in horror as if it had just burned the wet hand it then slipped from.

He picked it up again, located another saved number, pressed 'dial' and waited. 'I'll call you back,' said a voice before the line clicked off. Adler paced around his office while he waited. Almost thirty minutes later he heard the special tone he had previously allotted to this specific caller. 'My order has just been cancelled!' He immediately bit his lip for being so precipitous.

'I am already aware of that,' replied the voice. 'So how can that be a problem for you?'

'These are different. They are for highly influential people.'

There was a lengthy pause. 'Who have naturally already paid you inflated deposits on agreed inflated sums, no doubt,' said the voice coldly.

'I was going to tell you, of course.'

'Of course you were. Well, Max, you can either refund their deposits, out of your own pocket of course, should you so choose. Or you can just inform them they will have to wait. Simply tell them there have been unforeseen complications. The deposit does not guarantee delivery – it is a finder's fee.'

'But you don't understand; I have commitments. I need these orders to go through,' said Adler urgently, again biting his lip.

'Commitments?' repeated the voice coldly. 'It sounds as

though there are several factors you are keeping from me. Indeed, I understand that there are two transfers overdue from you which amount to a great deal of commitment.' Another pause. 'This is what you are going to do, Max. You have already been told that you will be contacted when consignments can recommence. So you will be patient. In the meantime you will transfer those overdue sums to my account without delay. Do I make myself clear?'

Adler felt as though he was about to melt. 'Yes,' he whispered.

'Good, then don't call again. If I want to speak to you I will call you.'

As the phone clicked off, it immediately rang again. 'Herr Adler?' said an anxious voice. 'It's Mr Williamson. We're at the airport. It's our baby. He won't wake up!'

Six hundred and twenty-five kilometres south-west of Vienna, Umberto Giramonte was enjoying his own indulgence in Milan. The mushroom season ensured that his risotto was just to his taste. He sipped a final mouthful of the light-red Valpolicella he had chosen to complement the meal, wiped at the corners of his mouth and his pencil-thin moustache with his white linen serviette and gestured expansively to his guest.

'Your look tells me you are tiring of what you call our old Europe preliminaries and long lunches. So, let us get down to business, as you Americans are so fond of saying. How may we assist you this time?'

Mike Neubauer's smile did not reach his dark brown eyes, which he kept levelled on his host. 'You forget, Umberto, I am first generation and both my parents are Italian-Swiss. However, time, as ever, seems to be at a premium these days.'

The recently appointed head of one of Italy's leading family-owned conglomerates, Giramonte Pharma, looked sideways at his luncheon companion. Both in their late thirties they had met several years earlier at a meeting chaired by his uncle, the then head of Giramonte Pharma, after they had been approached by the American company. At that time it had been his uncle who had undertaken the special order, requesting that his protégé, Umberto, be present. 'Well, it is good to see you again, Mike. Now what do you want?'

'Our special product we paid you to develop and manufacture for us. You will recall, of course, that this product was exclusively ours.'

Giramonte inclined his head to one side, slightly shrugged his shoulders and nodded in agreement.

'You will also recall that we requested it be destroyed – insisted upon it in fact,' added Neubauer precisely.

'You mean, after certain unfortunate side effects were discovered at one of your "holiday camps", to put it politely,' put in the Italian.

'Correct,' came back the quick reply. 'However, information has reached us that raises concern.'

Giramonte leaned forward, his usually languid eyes widening in feigned astonishment. 'Concern?' he asked.

Trained to notice and assess even the most indiscernible signs that might reveal untruths or discomfort, irrespective of the often utilized expansive gestures to hide them, Mike Neubauer kept his own manner calm. 'My employers have reason to believe it has either been acquired or copied. So you can imagine the level of concern. Our product being used in the wrong hands for the wrong purpose is a big concern. Being traced back to us is another. And, of course, cognizance of the drug's undesired after-effect is in itself an additional concern.'

Giramonte cast glances to either side before leaning forward again. 'Listen, Mike; you cannot believe for one moment that Giramonte Pharma would break its contract with you. Not for one moment! Is there a chance that a copy could have been coincidentally developed?'

'Always a possibility, but as you know, my employer does not recognize coincidental outcomes.'

'Then it has somehow been stolen,' said the Italian animatedly.

'That outcome is accepted as a much more likely probability. However, at the risk of sounding indelicate, my company is currently leaning towards the more likely assessment that it has been sold.'

'The formula; but that is still theft,' offered Giramonte matter-of-factly.

'Hmm, a possibility perhaps. However, I have to inform you that my employer is inclined to believe that our product was

simply shelved, not destroyed, and subsequently has been manu-
factured and provided as a special order. I really don't think that
such a view is likely to alter, unless of course I am able to
persuade them otherwise.'

Giramonte went a sickly hue as though the risotto had turned
sour in his stomach. He leaned forward again. 'What do I need
to do?'

'Names within eight hours; do we have a deal?' The question
was made more in statement than polite request as Neubauer
pushed his chair back and held out his hand.

The Italian stood up, his habitual gesturing temporarily absent.
'We do,' he agreed, ignoring the other's proffered hand.

PART THREE

The Corrupted Crop

Twenty-Five

After deciding to park in the long-term car park at Nikola Tesla Belgrade airport for short-term safety, her minivan bulging with four bags containing electronic and paper evidence together with six first-hand witnesses, Sonja watched Brock turn to give a quick wave as he boarded the airport shuttle bus with Ferguson, bound for Zurich. Waving back she felt a strange emotion of sudden loss. She thought how the man had delivered everything he'd promised – which was a new experience for her.

All her life she had mostly encountered false promises or cowardice from men. And it seemed that no sooner had she felt able to give her trust and respect, perhaps even love, than it fell from her grasp. Radu gone; and now ...

Sonja shook the thought from her head. 'Well, Jakiv, we have our evidence; and now ... well, now the real work begins.' She looked at the young teenagers sitting with knees drawn up tight to their chests, each docile but with eyes so frightened Sonja felt her heart lurch, and again she remembered the desperate eyes of her little sister. 'First we must contact the Belgrade branch of UNICEF. These girls are Romanian and I would prefer to get them to UNICEF Bucharest, but I know them here at Markovica, and—'

'We can take them home, Sonja,' interrupted Jakiv holding up a pile of passports in his hand, 'with these.'

Sonja pressed her lips together for a moment before answering. 'We can't, Jakiv. I was going to say we have to deliver them to the country branch we find them in. It is not up to us to repatriate.'

'So they will stay here, in a detention centre, though they are only children, for a year until they are—'

'Jakiv, we must focus on our main objective. You know how

I feel – each and every rescue counts – but look around. What we have here is dynamite to blow the Pied Piper out of the water. If we travel as a group like this, and are stopped, then we are back where we started.'

Jakiv looked at his cousin. She had already shared with him what had happened to Radu and though he had been deeply shocked, his recent experience at the tower block had altered his view on taking action. He ignored an intuition not to press it further. 'Brock would take them back; as would Radu too, if he were here.'

Sonja gazed back into Jakiv's determined face and swallowed back the immediate reaction which rose in her throat. She noticed how the younger man had matured. Here was a man who had also never let her down; she had just not fully recognized it, had even taken him for granted.

'You are right, of course, Jakiv,' she said softly. 'Connor Brock does do what he is best at; and Radu did too. And because of that, we must do what we are best at. I promise you that if within three weeks these girls are not returned, we will make it our focus to repatriate them. But for now our focus must be to get them the attention they need now. While at UNICEF we copy these files, post and email copies to us and UNICEF in Geneva and to Connor at ICE as promised, and then return with all of this hard evidence to Bucharest. Presented properly we can close the Pied Piper's operation and get the support we require to hit future Pied Pipers as they rise. With our effort, the authorities and governments will come to realize that the threat of human trafficking is as serious as terrorism. That is what we came here for. It's what Radu gave his life for.'

Jakiv bowed his head for a moment before reaching over and spontaneously hugging his cousin, determined not to shed tears. Holding her by the shoulders he spoke in a measured tone. 'Tell me what you want me to do.'

ZURICH

Leaning against the round steel bars set into the concrete balustrade that bordered the high terrace, both men watched as the reflected city lights danced on the rippling Lake Zurich like

146

a cabaret of fireflies. With the onset of evening the familiar prestigious shoreline cast gabled shadows to complement the distant Alpine peaks.

'You know, Connor, one million people share this shoreline, yet it sometimes feels as deserted as when the Linth Glacier gouged it out twenty thousand years ago.'

'Hankering back to the last ice age eh?' said Brock.

Van Lederman pushed away from the wall and walked back to the seating area. 'Well, we have to admit there were fewer problems.'

'True, because of fewer people; and people do seem to have a habit of making more problems than nature. Still, it's how we grow, by solving them, isn't it?' Brock rested his arm on van Lederman's shoulder sensing how his boss was unusually morose. 'And Paul, the ice age you founded – it solves them effectively. What is it you wanted to share with me?'

Van Lederman smoothed his well-groomed silver moustache down with his finger and thumb, and looked hard at Brock with his steel-blue eyes. 'You are taking too many risks.'

'It's what special operations do,' replied Brock flatly. 'Now what did you want to share with me?'

'You're right. We – well, more I, I suppose – have a problem, in so far as I seem to be inextricably involved. And if we do not show clear evidence that I am not involved, the knock-on effect on ICE may be irreparable, certainly damaging.'

'This has to do with the briefing tomorrow?'

'It does. The fact is that as chairman of the advisory board of a company that appears more and more to be either the victim or culprit of a damning conspiracy, I will have to remove myself from any ICE investigation.'

'So, I take it that Buchanan will chair tomorrow,' prompted Brock.

'Sir Duncan is arriving tonight. I am having dinner with him later.'

'What do you want me to do?'

'I don't want you to give me any special treatment.'

'Paul, I said do, not *not* do.'

Van Lederman pushed his hand through his thick silver hair. 'OK, Connor. This is what I want you to do.'

*　　*　　*

147

It had not been difficult for Goryachev to locate the personal details of Connor Brock. The few details he had retrieved from the Tulcea hotel manager had been sufficient. He had simply sent the details to his current employer. An hour later he had all he required to fulfil his current mission, which he now set out upon without delay.

His persistent commitment to any undertaking to dispose of targets during Kosovo had won him the nickname of 'the Mortician' from former employer General Vlastimir Djordjevic. The general had subsequently fled to Russia to avoid the Hague tribunal for alleged war crimes, though no evidence of the assignments he had given to the Mortician would ever be traced.

As his flight approached Zurich airport, Goryachev reflected upon his recent failure. Mistakes had happened because he had stupidly relied on family, instead of more trusted professionals. Still, he thought, at least he had finally disposed of that imbecile cousin Doroshenko, which he should have done sooner. It would be as it used to be. If he, or rather his employer, wanted something done properly, then he would attend to it himself. No more delegation or slip-ups. It was what his employer wanted.

Twenty-Six

Seven people sat around the black oval table, the screens in front of them switched off. The atmosphere was serious with an air of nervous expectation. Van Lederman was elegantly attired in one of his dark blue suits and, as always, wearing a tie, deep gold in colour, with a crisp white shirt. To his left sat his operation chief, Carl Honstrom, Brock and Ferguson, similarly in suits. Sitting opposite was Professor William Steinwright of BioGenomics Research and Kurt Williams, the ICE director from the Washington office, who was momentarily absorbed in his Blackberry.

To van Lederman's right at the head of the table sat Sir Duncan Buchanan. Having chosen to wear a formal blue suit, in unusual preference to one of his signature herringbone sports jackets, his broad figure consequently looking somewhat slimmer, Buchanan quickly dispensed with introductions and familiar small talk and brought the meeting to order.

'OK gentlemen, I thank you for attending this ICE briefing at short notice. Our objective today is to see what immediate action is required to address, and hopefully resolve, a serious issue that has been brought to our attention. As is of course very often the case, such an apparently simple objective confronts a highly complex situation; and from the information we have uncovered to date, we have a number of interrelated illegalities.'

Buchanan momentarily paused, as if searching for the right words. 'Namely, and at the risk of oversimplifying the heinousness involved, we are dealing with drug-related human trafficking, black market organ transplants, baby abduction for adoption and foetus farming for embryonic cell supply.'

Everyone present continued to place their full attention on Buchanan's rugged face, with its broad nose and green eyes, topped with a rich mop of greying red hair. 'However, it is the

149

last element that has been brought to our attention by Professor Steinwright here. As everyone around the table is aware William Steinwright is the chairman of BioGenomics Research, based at Donaueschingen, and one of Europe's leading companies. You also know that Paul is the company's advisory board chairman, and has in fact called this meeting. So, William, if I may turn to you first, please, to share the information you have.'

Steinwright, whose personal mantra since he had reached the age of sixty-five had been 'Don't retire; re-inspire', appeared to have aged ten years, his legendary enthusiasm severely dampened. Quietly and succinctly he related what he had already shared with van Lederman following his meeting with Dr Su-Yeong and Sophia Lefrington. 'So,' he began to sum up, 'BGR has two immediate challenges. What to do with our drug Neurofribiline, and to discover who, within our organization, has introduced non-voluntary, contaminated embryonic cells.

'With regard to the first, I have decided to adopt a policy of doing nothing, which means to say that as we are in the period of awaiting licences from our launch countries, including the US, we will delay the whole process. Almost always the delays are from the bureaucratic administration side, never from the pharmaceutical side. However, my view is that we simply hold fire; if we allow ourselves the time to recheck Neurofribiline in its entirety, we may contain shareholder damage.'

Steinwright leaned forward. 'If, of course, we find that our product has been compromised because of the substances used – not by contamination but rather by embryonic maturity – then naturally the drug will be pulled immediately. Arguably – and I admit it in hindsight – perhaps more focus could have been on development than on marketing, but the fact is it has happened. As for person or persons guilty of causing the dilemma, I have turned to Paul and ICE for full assistance on the matter.'

'Thank you, William,' said Sir Duncan. 'We'll hold questions for now; please just make a note of any you have as they arise. Paul, can you bring us up to speed from your perspective?'

Van Lederman was seated in his usual confident, relaxed manner, his hands resting on the table without any sign of nervous fidgeting. 'Because of my position at BGR I immediately called this meeting as soon as William contacted me. However, because of other coinciding events, my concerns are somewhat different from William's, though they still impact on BGR.

'First, with direct regard to BGR – and William and I are agreed on this – it appears that the current crisis has been ignited from the inside. Full investigation has not been implemented before this meeting but the fact is that stem cells, cord blood, indeed all embryonic tissue that forms the very basis of BGR work have been supplied in an illegal and certainly an immoral and unethical form.

'From the elements of contamination the donor supply cannot be voluntary, as it provides evidence of a controlling drug that removes free will. We believe that this type of supply must have been requested, by person or persons as yet unknown who are closely involved in our research and development. We can surmise at least one reason: because working with such a quantity of almost impossible-to-acquire material allows the boundaries of research to be pushed way beyond what we are legally allowed to do. Now, though it might well surprise most of us sitting here, we can also assume that, were it not for the contamination, the supply would never have been questioned. Understandably you may ask why.

'Simply,' continued van Lederman, 'because, just as a person enjoying a steak gives no thought to the slaughterhouse that supplies it, a scientist working with an embryonic sample gives no thought to where his specimen comes from. He or she sees it differently. William has, of course, taken containment measures, by cancelling all future embryo supply with immediate effect. Alarmingly we have learned that there appears to be gross misconduct in the supply procedure, which indeed affects at least twenty suppliers. Until we have concluded a fuller investigation, we are unable to share more.

'Second, which also directly affects BGR, we now have good reason to believe that Hans Duisen and the de Brouwers were murdered; yet I have to inform you that the autopsies have concluded natural causes and death by misadventure respectively.'

Though van Lederman paused to take a sip of water before continuing, his audience of six made no attempt to interrupt, other than Buchanan, who prompted him with a nod of his head.

'As everyone present is aware, a scientist, Professor Ron Patrowsky, was indisputably murdered. And we know why: for collating evidence on behalf of Hans Duisen. Patrowsky was a neurosurgeon specializing in the influence stimulant drugs have on dementia. Herr Duisen we know was a major shareholder in a Balkan clinic founded by the de Brouwers. We do know that Herr Duisen was intent on liquidating his interest in both the clinic and, surprisingly at the time, BGR, and we can assume it was for valid reasons. We also know, now, from evidence that Patrowsky was able to collate before his death and which we were able to recover, that the Balkan clinic was involved in the illegal supply of living foetuses, including directly to BGR; and also the illegal trafficking of babies for adoption and the illegal supply of stolen organs via a structured black-market network.'

The Dutchman's steel-blue eyes looked at Brock. 'We also know from eyewitness accounts that such produce, from what we shall call this macabre farm, came directly from abducted orphans and trafficking of young persons.'

'Persons kept drugged, hence the contamination discovered at BGR,' added Buchanan categorically.

'Correct; and now we also know, from our own research, some more facts, some more bizarre than enlightening, but nonetheless cause for concern,' said van Lederman, who then motioned for Carl Honstrom to take over.

The Swede nodded before continuing seamlessly. 'With few leads to follow up, when we first learned of the deaths of de Brouwer and Herr Duisen we undertook as detailed a cross-check of assets as we could to see what transpired. The first clear joint ownership that came up was the Balkan clinic, and we sent Connor and Matt to follow up. More recently, however, we have uncovered a network of assets all owned by the de Brouwers, yet increasingly, and somewhat surprisingly, funded by the Duisen Foundation.'

'Why surprisingly?' asked Buchanan.

'Because it was believed that the de Brouwer empire was self-funded. However, it would appear from our investigation that though asset-rich, the family were highly geared. One of the principles of the de Brouwers, and no doubt a commendable one, is to hold on to their investments for the long term, often for generations; and indeed there have been several trust vehicles set up to accommodate this. The bizarre thing is that in the past three years their investment focus shifted from commercial to more altruistic, particularly research; and they have borrowed heavily to do so. For example, the Balkan clinic – which has, I hate to admit, impressively relocated overnight to as yet unknown where-abouts – is one of five fully funded clinics that the de Brouwers founded that we know of and—'

'Five! There are others?' interrupted Brock coldly.

'We must not assume that they are operating illegally, Connor,' said Honstrom. 'Much of the de Brouwer's philanthropy was setting up medical centres and hospices around the world to reduce human suffering.'

'That was the view of the director general of the Izmail clinic, Paul,' said Brock. 'We should investigate each of these clinics without delay to confirm they are bona fide.'

'We'll get to action in due course, Connor,' commented Buchanan firmly, swivelling his green eyes to Connor as he added, 'Please continue, Carl.'

The chief of field operations nodded at Brock, his grey-blue eyes and light complexion unfazed. 'Research projects on the scale that the de Brouwers invested in, whether driven by commerce or altruism are of course the proverbial bottomless pit when it comes to funding demands. Their initial investment of almost a fifth of BGR was immense, though its current capi-talization has more than delivered an adequate return.

'Yet again, however, the shares are held in long-term trust and therefore not liquid. But they can be used for security against borrowing further funds as required. Indeed we have learned that the Duisen Foundation effectively owns the de Brouwer interest in BGR. We are unable to know the details of the trans-action, but under the simple default terms of any loan, if it is not repaid, the de Brouwer family trusts will lose ownership.'

'That's impossible,' blurted Steinwright. 'It would mean . . .'

'That poor Stephan has inherited a drowning white elephant,' commented van Lederman.

'It would mean someone could launch a takeover which would be impossible to defend! Paul, currently our market price is at an all-time high. If the press got a whiff of any of this our shares would crash overnight. They would be worthless!'

'It would appear that someone is playing a game with you,'

offered Brock. 'A house of cards game – they can choose to either let it be or blow it down with the slightest of effort.'

'Possibly,' said Honstrom. 'Though it is baffling as to why the de Brouwers, who were hands-on operators, would put themselves in such a position. However, on a final point, we have uncovered something which once again, I'm afraid, directly links back to BGR.'

Steinwright audibly groaned. 'More? How can there be more of this?'

'I'm afraid it does add to the mystery of their deaths, though it also enlightens us on one point – which is where the contamination originally came from.'

'What, who?' enquired Steinwright in earnest.

'Last year the de Brouwers invested in Giramonte Pharma, the Milan-based drug maker.' Honstrom looked across the table at Kurt Williams. 'And Giramonte Pharma, we have just learned from our friends across the water, is the manufacturer of what Brock referred to in his Balkan clinic report as the Pied Piper drug.'

Twenty-Seven

'Do you want to take it from here, Kurt?' offered Honstrom looking across the table to his colleague.

Williams, the only one arguably dressed down, wearing slacks and a blazer, nodded apprehensively. 'OK, well, in the past year, as most of you are already aware, communication with various US services has improved. Let's say they owe us after the Subedei[1] affair. What was formerly a one-way street for us has become two-way, so now when we share intelligence we actually get something. Not always, but on this occasion we have. That is to say, something has been intimated, rather than expressly shared. It goes with the territory that what we get may be miscommunication, not that they may have done wrong research. It may be – well, they might get it wrong. Suffice to say we don't know for sure.'

Buchanan raised his eyebrows. 'What? Kurt, you sound like a politician. What actually are you trying to say? And this time make it clear.'

Williams flicked back the large lock of hair that tended to fall over his forehead, before glancing first at his Blackberry and then at Brock, who returned the look enquiringly. 'OK, well, when they learned from us about the drug we believed was being used to facilitate trafficking, which is a major concern for the US from an illegal immigrant perspective, they said they would get right back to us.

'Hey, and – surprise – they did, almost immediately. It seems that the development of a series of serums was one of many angles of interrogation at Guantanamo. Put it this way: it's where trial tests were performed. Initial success of the drug stimulated a project termed Infiltrate, which intended to release selected inmates and return them to Afghanistan with a view to their

---

[1] From the novel *GodSword* by Emerson Cole

being re-infiltrated into al-Qaeda. The expectation was that at worst they would cause peripheral damage, at best kill Bin Laden. Who knows, like many projects following 9/11, a ton of money was invested, but it never got past the testing phase. Apparently in some cases the drug began to mutate, cloning itself within the host. After several apparent suicides at Guantanamo attracted the wrong kind of media attention it was shelved.'

Williams leaned back nervously. 'So, you can imagine, they were none too happy when they discovered that their Infiltrate serum had not been destroyed as instructed, but actually sold to parties unknown.'

'Giramonte Pharma?' asked Buchanan.

'No – they, er – they were simply the manufacturer and for a number of reasons, not the least being that old Giramonte was a good friend of the services, as I understand. What I also understand to be the case is that his playboy nephew, Umberto, who recently became the head of Giramonte has, after incurring some sizeable losses, resorted to doing things he ought not to have been doing.'

'Selling the Pied Piper, or Infiltrate serum,' prompted Buchanan, his Scots temperament becoming slightly frustrated at the American ICE director's hesitancy. 'Do we know who to?'

Williams sucked his lips in and clenched his mouth, all his body language shouting signals of discomfort. 'We do, Sir Duncan. We do. I, er, in fact received notification by my Blackberry . . . just as the meeting started.'

'Excellent, then who's our culprit?' boomed Buchanan.

Williams reached for his Blackberry as if wanting to verify for himself. 'Remember this is not confirmed, however . . .'

'Names, Kurt,' said the Scotsman impatiently. Williams looked across the table at his colleague. 'I'm sorry Paul, but it appears that the . . . uhh, the initial order of one hundred thousand capsules was instigated by Messrs van Lederman and Steinwright of BioGenomics Research.'

BUCHAREST

Sonja had grabbed a couple of hours' sleep in the car and then in her own bed before rising early and spending several hours either on the phone or faxing and emailing to her network of colleagues at La Terre des Hommes, La Strada in Berlin, Ukraine, Bulgaria and Romania, as well as the respective offices of UNICEF. She learned from London that they had already taken action in closing down the destination that the girls arriving at Luton had been taken to, placing the girls in a detention centre, rather than co-ordinating efforts to truncate the operation. Two men had been arrested and released on bail; no doubt they were already on the way to Eastern Europe by now.

In Berlin, La Strada had made a formal request for the police to visit the address Enescu had provided, which had been ignored. Evidence was required; no warrant would be forthcoming on hearsay, particularly at such a prestigious address.

Her contact Lisselotte Hessinger was apologetic. 'I'm sorry, Sonja, our challenge is that since prostitution was legalized, the police do not give much attention to such requests. During the World Cup last year, forty thousand women were brought to fulfil demand. Even a three thousand square metre brothel was constructed opposite the stadium at a cost of six million euros, while the German Football Federation donated just two thousand euros to assist our anti-trafficking efforts. Though the police accept that many of the women are being trafficked, with four hundred thousand registered prostitutes in Germany now, it is not big on their agenda – even though a good portion are forcibly registered.'

A positive yet obtuse response was received from the Romanian authorities; Sonja sensed the hidden agenda. 'It is good to learn that you have acquired such evidence, Ms Brezvanje. You must get it to us immediately. It is vital that it does not fall into the wrong hands, particularly bearing in mind our recent membership of the EU. As soon as we have it we will look into the closure of the orphanages you refer to; though I have to advise you that we have limited powers, as they are no longer state funded. When can you get us it? Do you want us to collect? You have not sent it to others, I hope; that could put us in a delicate position and undermine our investigation, of course.'

Sonja replaced the receiver with a heavy heart and dialled the UNICEF offices in Geneva. 'Yes, Sonja, we have received the evidence,' replied Claudia Akermann in response to the first question. 'On preliminary cursory inspection, yes, you're right: it's dynamite.'

'I knew you would think so! We have everything we need for you to go for him.'

'Well, I know that you are already aware that our resources are more than stretched, but let me assure you we are going to do everything we can.'

'Thank you, Claudia, but can I press you for what and when?' asked Sonja, trying to keep her voice sounding level.

'Later this week we will immediately lodge a strong complaint to the Serbian authorities insisting that they take action in accordance with the Hague directive on trafficking. We will ensure publication to help our case; hopefully that will prompt them to action.'

'And the girls we delivered to your Belgrade office?'

'Our office there has already recommended prompt repatriation when they took them to the police station, though I understand they had to take three of the girls to hospital as they went into catatonic fits.'

Sonja felt a pang of guilt, though she knew she had done everything she could at the time. 'Oh no, it was only yesterday I was with them. Your Belgrade office promised that they would take the girls directly to hospital!'

Claudia momentarily paused before continuing, 'I am sure they did the utmost their powers allowed them, but they had to inform the police first. Look, there's no easy way to say this but I'm sorry, Sonja, one of the girls has since died. We are hoping to find out why and I will let you know as soon as we know.'

The pause this time was from Sonja, who could not bring herself to respond immediately. Jakiv had been right.

'Sonja, I promise you we will continue to monitor but I'm afraid that's all we can do. We are a charity, not a law enforcement agency. Our strength is to raise awareness for action.'

'And publish impressive reports,' said Sonja coldly, her voice thick with disappointment.

Claudia Akermann surveyed the huge pile of correspondence that cluttered her office in the Palace des Nations. She nibbled nervously at her lip; it was not the first time she had experienced similar calls. 'Sonja, what you have achieved is outstanding. The evidence will help to close down this operation. But you must understand that we are dealing with an industry worth over twelve billion dollars to the likes of this Pied Piper, or Kastrati, as we now know. We are like a gnat annoying an elephant. But we do what we can to alleviate suffering, though we cannot stop it.'

'Nor will we ever while the authorities support the perpetrators more than the anti-traffickers; and even the economies they work for are in part supported by the industry.'

Claudia Akermann nibbled her lip again. 'Listen, Sonja, we both know that you are right, but we do what we can. The way to really give them misery though is to hit them hard where it hurts. The evidence we have will close the operation down, in time, let me assure you of that. But if you were to obtain evidence of his banking and finance, that would be a different matter. All liquid assets could be frozen and material assets requisitioned under the Hague stipulation. It takes time but they are prevented from starting another operation.'

'I'll see what I can do next time,' said Sonja sarcastically, yet thinking how right she had been to follow Brock's advice in not releasing Kastrati's laptop containing all of his banking details, or his wallet. She would hit Kastrati hard all right. She would use his assets to support her operation. She would take them. 'OK, Claudia, but please keep me posted on your progress, particularly the girls. I want to get them home within three weeks. I made a promise, though that is impossible as one of them is no longer alive.'

'And I promise you, Sonja, that my office will do the very best we are able to. Take care.'

Sonja replaced the receiver with a sigh and glanced at her watch. Her team would be waiting for her. The drive back had taken far longer than anticipated and she had agreed with Jakiv that it would be better to get some rest before they all met up, shared the news about Radu and planned what they were going to do next. Jakiv had called Natalya and Georghe to inform them they would all meet the following morning.

Ten minutes later she had walked the short distance to the jaded French-bourgeois corner building which housed her office. As she approached the third floor she felt her cellphone vibrating with a message. She went to look at it while at the same time she recognized the sound of her office phone ringing; she was surprised how long it was taking for it to be answered. Ignoring

159

the message she pushed her phone into the back pocket of her jeans, quickly opened the door and came to an abrupt halt. Natalya was slumped in her chair behind the desk, her unscarred cheek covered in dark dried blood.

'You're late,' hissed a man she didn't recognize. 'Yes,' added Januz Kastrati. 'And neither of us likes to be kept waiting.'

'That's preposterous!' boomed Buchanan, the colour draining from his ruddy complexion.

'I did warn you that there was often misinformation fed to us,' agreed Williams. 'I could call to verify their source, though it is only two in the morning there.'

'I don't give a damn what time it is! Call them, Kurt, now!' Buchanan turned towards van Lederman. 'Paul, comments; and William?'

'Did I personally sign this order?' said van Lederman without emotion, and more in statement than question, as the US ICE director was busily dialling. 'If not, and as I am obsessive about reading any document I sign, I would surmise that our names are being used.'

Steinwright looked ill, having shrunk into a complete wraith of his former self upon the latest burden of news. 'All supplies of such a nature need to be countersigned by two directors, either non-executive, such as Paul, or myself. You have to believe me that I have absolutely no knowledge of such an order.'

Kurt Williams placed his Blackberry on the table. 'No reply,' he said. 'I'll keep trying.'

Buchanan placed his broad palms face down on the board-room table. 'It would appear that this is more serious than we envisaged, Paul. It may be that we, ICE, will be unable to proceed with this investigation, as it would seem—'

'That somebody has effectively removed ICE out of the picture with one simple stroke,' added Brock.

'It would seem, Connor, that we will have to hand the investigation over to others,' said Buchanan. 'However, I see no reason why we should allow ourselves to be compromised by circumstantial evidence. I propose we should ascertain more tangible information during, shall we say, the next forty-eight hours?'

'Seems a fair proposal, Sir Duncan,' said Brock, voicing the agreement of everyone present.

'Good. So, I believe that you, Connor, have your own avenue you are pursuing; William, you will ensure containment and with Carl's assistance seek to uncover your enemy within. Paul, I understand you are attending the de Brouwer memorial service planned for tomorrow?'

'Yes, at their estate near Brussels.'

'OK and I will personally go and visit this Umberto Giramonte.'

'You think that's wise?' asked Kurt.

'What's the difference? It might not make a jot of difference but I want to eyeball the man myself. And Kurt, I want confirmation and verification on the intelligence you have. Carl, you also have to uncover every bit of information on these other clinics and all assets of Duisen and de Brouwer.'

'Pete Kenachi's working on it as we speak, Sir Duncan.'

'Good, the more information we have, the stronger our position, because, gentlemen, if this load of shit hits the fan we're all going to be taken to the cleaners!'

Twenty-Eight

Leaving the boardroom on the second floor of the neo-chateau building, Brock and Ferguson took the wide stone staircase down a level and entered Kenachi's Kingdom, as it had been termed. The techie, who was third generation American-Japanese, was immersed in conversation with a woman whose long black curls hid her face from view, a face which Brock knew would be animated.

'Connor! This is excellent,' said Cassie enthusiastically, prompted to turn by Kenachi's nod upon their entrance.

'Good,' said Brock in short reply. 'Pete, you need to focus on the addresses of those clinics. Sorry, Cassie, we will have to delay your research for the moment.'

'No worries, Connor,' smiled Kenachi. 'I logged on to the network of Global Company Registrations – all one hundred and ninety-two of the world's listed countries, plus all the sixty-two erroneous ones, either unlisted, not recognized or just plain confused, including Taiwan, Greenland, Western Sahara, Vatican, Palestine, Bermuda and Puerto Rico, to name a few. Cookies directed at all the recently added references and names Carl gave me this morning are smoking them out, rounding them up and sending them all our way as we speak.' Kenachi looked at the holographic clock seemingly suspended from the ceiling above him, which revealed the world time zones. 'The final list will be with us in a couple of hours.'

'As long as that?' offered Ferguson sarcastically.

Brock remained serious. 'Cassie, I need you to go downstairs for a moment; grab a coffee. Matt, will you take her down? I'll join you in a few minutes.'

Matt nodded as the archaeologist stood up, allowing her natural enthusiasm to be temporarily deflated. 'Oh, OK; well, see you later, Pete.'

'Thanks, Cassie,' said Brock, turning back to Kenachi as the door closed. 'Listen, Pete, as soon as you have the details, I want you to learn everything you can about the five private clinics. Everything, Pete. What they are selling, buying, giving or taking. Whose, the whys and wherefores; right down to patients, specialities, even the nurses and part-time cleaners, and of course contact details including locations.'

'Will do,' said Kenachi without question. His immediate report was to Honstrom, but if Brock requested something he knew that his chief would always confirm the request.

'I understand you have deciphered a schedule from Patrowsky's memory stick.'

'Couldn't retrieve all files, and I suspect that is because they were corrupted before they were copied, or truncated during transferral. But what I did get, though not extensive, does provide information on organ transplant hospitals and clinics and details of monetary transactions between lawyers and agencies that dealt with the Izmail clinic.'

'And those references have already delivered details of the five clinics owned by the de Brouwers?'

'Yup, about which we'll hopefully know a whole lot more soon – though no promises. If it's been programmed I'll get it. All depends on what has been programmed.'

'Thanks, Pete, and all common links – you'll be able to collate?'

'Will do.'

'Good,' nodded Brock. 'Give me a call – oh and Pete, I need to be the one to see it first. OK? Can you print me off the report?' Kenachi leaned back in his chair, passed his hand through his collar-length jet-black hair and tilted his head to one side. Though his eyes were inquisitive, he replied matter-of-factly: 'No worries, Connor, though no promises, as I said. I can't guarantee that anything will come up at all.'

'Understood. Now, how did you get on with Cassie Kaligirou?'

'Interesting story, but her research is very disjointed. However, when I get round to programming all the info she has brought, we'll see what my little Izanami delivers,' said Kenachi, indicating the wide console in front of him.

Brock looked at the state-of-the-art networked computers which the technical prodigy had recently installed. 'Izanami? The Japanese goddess?' he said.

Kenachi looked surprised. 'You know Japanese mythology?'

'I lived there for two years, before the days of ICE,' offered Brock. 'As I recall, Izanami could give birth to anything, couldn't she?'

'That's right,' replied Kenachi, pleased that Brock was aware of the meaning behind the name he had given his new creation. 'She created the islands of Japan, the centre of technological brilliance of course, and thirty-five gods.'

'Including the god of fire, who became her burning nemesis.'

'Yes, but that's just part of the story,' he said, unfazed. 'Still, interesting you choose that term. Isn't it bizarre how you see or hear a word and then again within a short time?'

Brock inclined his head. 'Meaning . . .?'

'Your archaeologist lady,' replied Kenachi. 'The meaning of her name is the first factor my little Izanami defined.'

'Cassandra?' offered Brock. 'The one whose prophecy is ignored?'

'No, her middle name: Adrasteia; the Greeks and Romans identified her as Nemesis – she whom none can escape!' Kenachi laughed. 'So you'd better be careful, Connor.'

Brock grinned. 'Right, I'll watch my step. Anything else?'

'Well, I'd better not steal her thunder,' said Kenachi, wanting to continue the amusement. 'So I should let her tell you, though there's not much, yet. Apart from the fact that if her grandfather's research proves correct she could be the wealthiest woman alive. So you'd better keep on the right side of her!'

'Yeah, well, thanks for the advice, Pete. I'll see you later.'

Brock went quickly down the stairs which led directly into the building's central atrium. Elegant yet functional Corbusier seating of tubular chrome and white leather occupied part of the stone-floored meeting and recreation area. Ferguson and Cassie were sitting between the Seattle-style chrome coffee bar and the imposing yet tranquil sculpture that allowed water to flow, slowly and steadily down from a blue-white hanging stalactite on to a rising stalagmite of similar, almost translucent, hue.

'Matt has just been enlightening me as to the significance of this,' offered Cassie waving an arm towards the structure as Brock joined them.

Brock raised an eyebrow. 'Really?' he said.

'Yes, apparently . . . well, you already know about it, I'm sure,

164

Connor,' said Cassie. 'After all, it's in your building. But it is a metaphor depicting the symbiotic relationship required for transitional growth and proves that what befalls us helps us to grow, but can also destroy us if we rely solely on its nourishment.'

'That which nourishes our rise can lead to our fall,' added the Irishman sheepishly.

'You make a fine philosopher, Matt. And he's absolutely right. *Quod me nutrit me distuit* – "What nourishes me destroys me." An ancient Latin quote that first appeared on a portrait, believed to be Christopher Marlowe, and then adapted by Shakespeare in a sonnet: "Consumed by that which it was nourish'd by."'

'And the actress Angelina Jolie of course, talking of plays,' interrupted Ferguson. 'She's had it tattooed on her sexy navel – so I read somewhere, anyway.'

Brock shook his head at his friend. 'We're going to have to up your reading material, Matt,' he said pleasantly. 'ICE, Cassie, intends the metaphor to show how too much growth too quickly can lead to an addiction to power – as in "absolute power corrupts absolutely" – even with slow steady growth; if the need becomes dependent on one source, whatever it may be, the resultant dependency can destroy.'

Cassie nodded. 'So if the growth is too fast, the stalactite has not the strength nor substance to hold fast and crashes down, destroying everything in its path.'

'Just like the US energy giant Enron, which ultimately destroyed the livelihoods and pensions of everyone involved,' said Brock.

'But at the right growth there is joining. And the gulf is bridged,' offered Cassie.

'Yes, something along those lines. However, the most important factor is that Paul van Lederman knew the artist and liked the sculpture.'

'And there was I believing all these meaningful tales!' put in Ferguson.

'Belief is what makes things meaningful, Matt,' said Brock. 'Such tales inspire us, make us think. That's what any artist or writer desires: to open an emotion. Take myths of gods, goddesses or stories of treasure. We desire them to be true. And all myths, call them folklore, tradition or legend, are based on some originating element of truth. And in so wanting to

165

discover the truth we directly influence our perceptions. We perceive what we want to perceive. We even pass on our perceived truisms that we find meaningful to our offspring. For example, Cassie, why did your father want to call you Adrasteia?'

A fleeting shadow passed over the woman's face. 'Oh, Pete told you that. Great, isn't it, being named after a dark avenging goddess? The sort of thing you go around telling everyone you meet, isn't it? But remember, Nemesis is also the goddess of divine justice.'

'Your name is Nemesis,' asked an increasingly confused Ferguson. 'I thought we were talking about art?'

'I think Connor has been intimating that what is meaningful to the parent can be an unwanted legacy for their children to fulfil. He believes that I am obsessed with something my father and grandfather were obsessed with – which I admit they were, and they lost their lives chasing their obsession. Well let me tell you something, Mr Know-it-All!' added Cassie, indignantly. 'Yes, I do believe in their work, Lysippos and the treasure – they were killed for it – and I don't care whether you think it is myth or truth!'

'Good; and I believe in you too, which is why you are here,' said Brock firmly. 'I ask why your father called you Adrasteia and you fly off the handle.'

'Well, I have been the butt of my supposed peer group's jokes for a long time. You just hit a raw nerve.'

Matt leaned forward conspiratorially. 'He's always doing things like that. You try working with him. By the way, can anyone tell me who this Lysippos fella is?'

'A sculptor,' said Cassie curtly before continuing.

'Listen, I was called Cassandra, Troy's most beautiful daughter, after my grandmother. The mythical truth is that Cassandra was given the power of prophecy by Apollo so he could seduce her. She refused and ended up being raped by Locrian Ajax, given to Agamemnon, and murdered by his wife Clytemnestra and her lover Aegisthus because no one would believe what she foretold.

'OK, got that? Good; now, I was called Adrasteia because my father named me with the epithet 'Adrasteia' used of Rhea Cybele in her role as the Mother who punishes human injustice. Both my father and grandfather believed that the perfect image of her, created by Lysippos in bronze, was secretly removed before the first sacking of Constantinople. My mother told me that my father's letter proposed the name Adrasteia for his new baby daughter because he had found the statue and the family would be rich and famous in her name. That's the mythical truth if you like. The reality is that my mother lost a husband the week I was born and honoured his last wish before embarking on a solitary life dependent on cleaning work and handouts from the university, providing her daughter with a life of ridicule whenever her name becomes known. There, anything else?'

'Did Lysippos do stalactites as well then?' asked Matt.

Cassie looked at the serious face of Ferguson before bursting out laughing. 'What?'

'When you work with him all the time you realize he's always doing things like that,' said Brock.

'You could say that I see my role as releasing the tension this fellow seems to have a knack of building up,' commented Ferguson. 'He's always rubbing people up the wrong way. I tell him to get a life, but I don't think the poor lad knows what it is.'

'Which I am inclined to agree with,' said Brock. 'Tomorrow, Cassie, you should be able to work with Pete and see what his little Izanami delivers for you. In the meantime I suggest you enjoy Zurich and your hotel. Unfortunately I will be fully occupied for a few days, though I'll keep in touch. In the meantime I think you need some assistance with your research, so I'm going to ask a friend of mine to spend some time with you. I know you'll like him. Matt, we'll meet later on; there are a couple of things I have to do.'

Matt leaned forward conspiratorially again. 'Well, I'd be delighted to show the sights to Cassie – we could visit the Kunsthaus art museum if you like.'

'You like art?' asked Cassie.

'Well, it's all this talk of sculptors. By the way, is this Izanami fella one?'

Twenty-Nine

Sonja had ignored her first instinct to run, and instead coolly walked over to Natalya, ignoring Kastrati. A stunning blow caught her in the stomach and she doubled over in pain, gasping for breath. Petri Paloka went to hit her again but was stopped by the other.

'Careful, Petri, we need her to be able to talk. Then, and after I have finished with her, you can deal with her as you like.'

Sonja swung her eyes around the room, gasping again as she saw Georghe Enescu slumped behind the door. There was blood on the wall behind him and on the floor beside him. She looked directly up at her assailants coldly. Strangely she felt unafraid; angry contempt was her dominant emotion. She rose slowly, trying to ignore the pain billowing from her midriff and, unable to speak, continued towards Natalya.

Kastrati noticed the look with some surprise. He was accustomed to exerting control and the resultant look of fear and acquiescence that it stimulated. He watched as Sonja approached her assistant. Here at last was the woman who had had the insolent audacity to interfere with his business, yet, despite swearing to tear her apart as soon as he got his hands on her, he allowed her to do so. 'Ah yes, little Natalya, my little ferret who ran away from Turkey. She now has the perfect face for modelling, don't you agree? More even. Mind you, it's all down to you. I offered her the perfect face or just to tell me where you were; and she chose the face. It is what she wanted when we first met. But now you are here anyway.'

Sonja felt tears of anger, frustration and grief spring to her eyes as she felt for a pulse. 'You murdered them both,' she said as she closed Natalya's unseeing eyes.

'Both?' offered Kastrati innocently. 'Don't you mean all three?'

Sonja's heart missed a beat and she couldn't swallow or breathe. Poor Jakiv too, she thought. 'Three?' she asked.

'Well, it's your team; can't you count? First, the captain of your little boat; and you've just experienced how impetuous Petri here can be.'

'Radu,' Sonja said to herself.

'What do you expect after your team tried to destroy our livelihood?'

'Livelihood?' Sonja spoke slowly, the sheer contempt in her voice as cutting as a sharp scythe. 'Is that what you call making money out of slavery? Look at you; you have this high idea of yourselves as important businessmen. But you're nothing but slavers, the lowest scum of the earth. Do you think you scare me? I was raped and sold into slavery before I was a teenager. Scum like you aren't even men, let alone part of the human race. You profit from the suffering of others.'

Kastrati clapped his hands together slowly and sarcastically. 'Do you think words will stop me? Do you think that your annoying little jabs at my business network will stop me? Close us down? You stupid woman, wake up to the real world! Sex and corruption are what keeps the world turning. You can't hurt those who do the spinning.'

'You're right. If I destroy you, another will take your place. But eventually it will stop. We just have to confiscate what makes you spin. You think I don't know the real reason why you are here. You wouldn't bother coming here to just close us down. And I bet you are already planning alternative networks and routes. No, it's because I have all the trappings of your pseudo-business that make you pretend to be a man. Your bank codes, passwords, accounts, all of it – all your millions.'

Kastrati narrowed his black eyes menacingly. 'And you are going to give them back to me,' he said softly.

Sonja stood erect and stepped directly towards Kastrati, staring back at him. Then she threw her head back and laughed. 'Ha, after you have destroyed everything that would have made me give it you? You are a good businessman indeed! You think I value my life? Go on, kill me now! I have already given your computer and all the back-ups we took from your slime-hole into the hands of another for safe keeping. At this very moment I expect they are being opened, raided – or would

169

you understand it better if I said trafficked! How does that make you feel, all your wealth being abducted, eh? Miserable perhaps? Out of control? Lost?'

No woman had dared to talk to him before in that way, and losing control Kastrati viciously struck out at the face that stood up to him, smashing the back of his hand into Sonja's mouth.

The woman looked up at him in contempt. 'Go on, finish it! And then run and hide in your own scum!' shouted Sonja, blood and spittle flying from her mouth as she did.

Kastrati raised his foot to stamp hard on the disrespectful mouth that continued to insult him, stopping his action at the last moment. Standing behind him Petri Paloka was confused. 'Why don't you finish it Januz?'

The other whirled round to him grabbing Paloka by the lapels and lifting him off the ground, using him as a channel for his anger. '*Të qifsha marrtë!*' he cursed viciously as he pushed the other backwards. 'Because she's right! If I don't get the accounts back we're finished. Another will take over!'

Kastrati paced across to the other side of the room. His one ray of hope following the damage done at Belgrade was to receive a call from Remik Kostina, whose network had traced the anti-trafficking team to Bucharest. Further research had easily confirmed the identity of the founder of La Strada des Enfants as Sonja Brezvanje. At first Kastrati had cursed to himself when he thought how Kostina, who never took any of the risks, was telling him that Romania was Kastrati's responsibility and to pay them a visit to sort it. But when Brezvanje's picture and details came through on Kastrati's cellphone he recognized the woman who had trailed him to Izmail, and who he was certain was responsible for the Belgrade fiasco. He had purposely not divulged to Kostina what had happened for he knew that the Crocodile would seize the opportunity to put one of his own in Kastrati's place. And now, if he could not get access to his accounts it would become a reality. He was lost.

At that moment Jakiv Teslenko entered the small office and Kastrati's luck changed.

Brock thought of Paul van Lederman as he walked briskly along the wide Mythenquai which presided between Lake Zurich and the grandiose yet highly functional buildings, mostly occupied by banking and insurance giants. The main reason ICE had been able to initially establish its headquarters prestigiously close to the lake was due to the relationship between the giant reinsurance company, UnionRe, and its former CEO, van Lederman. UnionRe were the landlord for the ICE headquarters and the current CEO, Carina Reisner, a powerful and attractive woman whom Brock knew had more than a professional interest in him, sat on the board.

It had been twenty years since Brock had first been introduced to van Lederman by his father, Cameron Brock, so he had known him for much of his life. Or at least thought he did. He believed that van Lederman was implicitly trustworthy. Indeed, since the man had recruited him just four years ago he had always delivered – even saved Brock from a death penalty in Egypt. He knew a little of the Dutchman's background – that after graduating from The Hague University the somewhat rebellious individual had preferred to seek adventure rather than join the family business as expected, so, to the dismay of his father, left the Netherlands and joined the Foreign Legion.

It had been there van Lederman had met Cameron Brock. Both often admitted how their wilder sides had been channelled into disciplined characters able to follow through whatever they believed in. While Cameron Brock stayed with military life and was currently a NATO advisor, van Lederman had entered the corporate world, gained a PhD in business administration and joined UnionRe, eventually rising to CEO.

Brock also knew that when van Lederman's executive position had come to an end, having reached sixty years of age, he had become an advisor to the EU on security and investment. This was at a time when corporate governance scandals, pension fund calamities and volatile stock markets hit Europe and he saw his retirement plans disappear. And this, coupled with witnessing the increasing terrorism and economic terrorism that impacted upon his previous employer, UnionRe, stimulated him to found ICE, which he succeeded in doing in partnership with Sir Duncan Buchanan and their considerable networks. Other than the fact that he was a workaholic, had never married nor had children, though he looked upon Brock as both a protégé and son, van Lederman kept himself to himself. Brock, who

171

was inclined to do the same, respected this. And he was convinced of his friend, mentor and employer's innocence.

Brock arrived at the houseboat that had been rented by ICE solely for the purpose of his visits to Zurich. He preferred living either close to or on the water. Ever since the death of his wife he had cut all ties that reminded him of a homely situation and insisted upon a houseboat as part of his recruitment. Even though living on the water was actually forbidden in Zurich, van Lederman had delivered on his promise, as if recognizing the transient lifestyle demanded by Brock's free spirit, and somehow received a unique dispensation during the summer months, which suited Brock.

Upon opening the door, Brock became aware of a slight odour foreign to the usual aroma upon his arrival. Yet, bizarrely, the smell was faintly recognizable. He had not noticed it last night and he felt a familiar tingle as the hairs rose on the back of his neck.

Thirty

Though its external boarding had been recently renewed due to the more severe Alpine weather the houseboat structure, originating from Florida, was accustomed to, its eighty-two-foot length belied its luxurious apartment style accommodation. Standing in the rosewood panelled entrance Brock could easily survey the open-plan saloon to the front deck area. He listened for any noise out of the ordinary, certain that there either was, or had recently been, another person on board, while his mind fought to remember where he had last experienced the odour.

Quickly Brock paced across to the saloon doors to verify whether they had been forced open. No damage. He reached for the marlinspike that lay on the brass-cornered rosewood desk. Used for untying knots or splitting ropes, it had been a convenient paperweight-cum-letter-opener; now it could be a useful defence tool if required.

Although there was no immediate visual evidence, Brock remained certain that an intruder had recently entered each room as he went from cabin to cabin. In the master cabin he stood stock-still for a couple of minutes slowly studying every aspect of his room. Nothing seemed to have been touched. After a further five minutes of searching he returned to the saloon, opened the cooler, poured himself a glass of water and settled down on a worn buffalo-hide settee – the one item he had introduced to the boat.

Brock removed his cellphone from his pocket, placing it next to the marlinspike on the leather cushion beside him, lifted his feet on to the teak sea chest that functioned as a coffee table, and stretched out. He raised the glass to his lips, sipped at the cold water, picked up his phone and dialled a number.

'So, *mon ami*, what do you want?' a voice answered the call without preamble.

'Now come on, you know that's unfair. I don't always phone you for that reason,' Brock argumentatively mocked.

'The truth is often unfair, Connor. But as ever your timing is always right. You must think that I wait by the phone for your calls.'

'You mean you don't?' enquired Brock, hearing a loud chuckle from the other in response.

'Of course I do. But in case another might want to call me to ask about my health, what part of my brilliance can help you?'

'OK, my friend,' laughed Brock. 'You win. I need your brilliant mind.'

'Of course you do,' chuckled Ahmed Amuyani again in his customary manner.

Cameron Brock had rescued the outspoken academic from a death sentence in Tehran in 1979. For as long as Brock could remember they had hotly debated subjects as diverse as cabbages and kings. Brock considered the Iranian, a tenured, jovial professor of history at the Sorbonne, one of his closest and wisest advisors. 'Right, Professor, what do you know about Lysippos?'

'Lysippos,' said Amuyani. 'To whom do you refer – man or myth?'

'I assume they are one and the same.'

'In one sense they are, in another they are not. It depends on whether you have one or not. Do you have one?'

'I don't but I know a lady who says she knows where to find one.'

'So a lady is involved in it? Well, enough said; I take it you would like me to meet her? Tell me all about her; is she pretty?'

Brock sipped at his water. 'Like a Lysippos.'

'Oh, so you do know a little about the legendary sculptor?'

'Not really, and it would seem there is conflicting opinion on whether any of his bronze works are in existence.'

'Ah, and you are right. I remember a visiting professor at Tehran University in the early seventies giving a lecture on him. A real authority on the subject, he delivered a compelling argument how priceless Lysippos bronzes had been spirited away before the first sacking of Constantinople. Now, what was his name? I've never been good at remembering names.'

174

'No, Professor, you haven't – and I have told you before, it's Istanbul. Anyway, would it be Kaligirou by any chance?'

'Do you know I believe it was? You see, just talking to me, and my brilliance rubs off on you.'

'Of course it does,' mimicked Brock.

Amuyani chuckled. 'Which proves my point, again, that you should have been an academic. And by the way it was Constantinople for the period you are referring to so I am right again.'

'So it was Kaligirou?'

'Yes, I already said so. As I said, he delivered an impassioned lecture on how Emperor Constantine chose the city of Byzantium as the capital of the Holy Roman Empire, renaming it Constantinopolis. His research lay in what happened to the city's treasure almost a millennium later. In fact it was Kaligirou who stimulated my interest in Mediterranean and European history.'

'Did he say what happened to it?'

'Come on, Connor, the lecture was a third of a century ago!'

'I thought you were brilliant?' said Brock with mock sarcasm.

'Touché – or should I say touchy?' replied Amuyani before laughing himself into a fit of coughing. Brock waited. 'However, I do know that Constantine, and following patriarchs, continued the practice of building a huge treasure of Grecian art, including many Lysippos bronzes; always the first choice for emperors in the ancient world, of course.'

'Of course,' Brock repeated.

'Anyway, the general opinion among archaeologists and academics is that many of these were destroyed following the rape of the city during the infamous crusade of the early thirteenth century. Some may have been stolen, though due to the size it was more likely they were melted down for weapons. Any that were lucky to escape were almost certainly destroyed during the city's final sacking by the Ottomans in the mid-fifteenth century. Indeed, the last emperor of the city was also Constantine. Interesting circle, eh? Anyway, Kaligirou passionately believed otherwise.'

Brock took another quick sip of water and placed it on the sea chest. 'As did his son and granddaughter,' he commented.

'Well, I'm sure they would. He was a very passionate man,

175

very passionate about Grecian artefacts and always chasing sponsorship through his lectures. But I think I recall hearing that he died a few years afterwards – I was still in Persia at that time of course.'

'That's correct, Professor: lost, presumed dead, possibly under suspicious circumstances. His son too, apparently, but the person I want you to meet is his granddaughter – Cassandra Adrasteia Kaligirou, though she prefers Cassie.'

'I'd be delighted to, *mon ami*! Interesting name, *non*? Adrasteia was one of the subjects of Kaligirou's lecture. I actually remember that he made a comment which the audience took as a joke but which he was quite serious about. Now what was it? Ah yes, she who none can escape would herself not escape from him. He was convinced he knew where to look.'

'So, Ahmed, can I fly you down to Zurich? I know Cassie will love to spend time with you.' 'And me with both of you! As ever your timing is good. It is the summer! I am on holiday and my time is my own.'

'Great! My office will organize a flight and meet you. I have a couple of things to do out of town, but I will look forward to hearing what you have both come up with upon my return. Pete Kenachi is involved too.'

'So, your time is still not your own, Connor. I keep telling you, as a lecturer you would have more holidays.'

The phone suddenly felt heavy in Brock's hand. 'Thanks, Professor, but I do all right. Now I have to go. See you soon and thanks again.'

'My pleasure, *mon ami, au revoir!*'

Brock dropped the phone to his side, and lifted his glass, slowly drinking the cool liquid. He paused and sniffed at the glass. Once again he became aware of the familiar odour. He couldn't make up his mind if it was the water or perhaps it was a new detergent his cleaner was applying. He finished the glass and went to pick up his phone to make another call.

Instantly the memory of where he had first encountered the odour came to him. He picked up the glass again, which seemed heavier in his hand than earlier. Yes, it was the same smell he had noticed in the mortuary at the Balkan clinic. He stared at the glass, and through it saw the distorted reflection of someone appear in front of him. He went to jerk his legs from the sea chest and jump up, but his usual quick reactions were absent. Instead he simply stood up and slowly sat down again. It was as if his muscles had begun to go on strike. His mouth felt numb. His eyes tried to focus through heavy lids on the man he now recognized as the one who had tried to kill him in the delta wetlands: Doroshenko's cousin, the Mortician.

'What did you expect?' said Goryachev gleefully. 'You're far too dangerous to incapacitate easily, and I admit I'm getting too old to do so in a more traditional way, not that I would enjoy doing so. Anyway, we have already tried that and I need to – how shall I say? – interrogate you first. To know what you know.'

'I thought I smelled something rotten.' Brock spoke the words but felt like his mouth had been anaesthetized by a dentist preparing for an extraction.

'Sorry, didn't catch that – "yelled something forgotten", you say?' Goryachev chuckled. 'You didn't think I'd forget you, did you? Perhaps you are not so clever. I coated every glass and cup just in case you picked up one at random. A man's fridge tells a lot about him you know. Large bottles of water are for pouring from, not for drinking from. Clearly you are a man of – how do you say? – etiquette.'

'You son of a bitch!' Brock allowed himself to fall on to his side as the glass slipped from his fingers.

'What's that you say – "run of rich"? Yes, it is rich, isn't it? But don't you worry; we'll have plenty of time to talk sensibly together later. That particular drug only incapacitates the muscles, though you might well enjoy an initial rest as a bonus. Which, my friend, you will need, because after the preliminary stage you will be fully compos mentis, in a manner of speaking anyway, and there will be no opportunity for rest again, I promise you. Now if you'll excuse me for a moment, we need to get underway. See you later.'

Goryachev laughed to himself as he turned and left the saloon, allowing Brock to simply stare after him.

Forcing himself to stay conscious, Brock rationalized that, perhaps, as the drug had been imbibed rather than injected directly into the bloodstream, it might take longer than his intruder anticipated for his victim's immobilization. His mouth had reacted to it first. He knew he must do whatever he could to prevent the drug pervasively entering his bloodstream, however futile it might be. Slowly he forced his middle and fore-fingers down his throat as far as he could. His body reacted and began to spasmodically retch. His face lying against the leather was soon wet with water and bile. In slow motion he dragged the arm that was trapped under him to wipe his face. As he did so his fingers touched his mobile phone.

Brock's focus momentarily changed to seeking help. He concentrated on feeling for the first digit, which was speed-dialled not to his voicemail but linked to the ICE emergency line. He pressed the button and went to push the phone down between the middle sofa cushions. In doing so he felt the marlin-spike which had already nested itself there and he pushed that too out of sight. Brock began trying to flex the muscles of his arms and legs in turn. They responded but not enough to move quickly or stand. His muscles felt weak but his mind did not feel cloudy. He closed his eyes and concentrated on counting as he continued to flex his muscles.

Goryachev had already ascertained that the twin 4.3 litre Mercruiser V-6 Baravo II engines were, as expected, perfectly maintained. Within fifteen minutes he had cast off and was at the helm navigating the houseboat into deeper waters.

Thirty-One

T he sound of someone talking caused Brock to open his eyes. His intruder was back in the saloon and on the phone. Brock tried to move his fingers with success. He convinced himself that he could achieve greater movement when required. How much he wouldn't know until probably it was too late. But he would play for the only thing he could: time.

Goryachev looked away from the phone with a sigh. 'You must have been born under a lucky star. Evidently you know considerably more than I thought, and I haven't even started interrogating you yet.'

Goryachev eyed him suspiciously before quickly walking toward him and striking him hard across the face with the back of his hand. Brock's head snapped back as the force pushed him to slump further into the sofa. Despite pain ricocheting across his face, Brock purposely made no response and simply looked blank, as though comatose. Inwardly he was pleased. If he could feel the hurt of that, it could only mean that in spewing out the majority of the drug its effect had not been so immobilizing as anticipated. Goryachev was standing next to the coffee table, which was covered with an array of cutting devices Brock recognized as coming from his own galley and all of the belts from his wardrobe.

Replacing the phone to his ear, Goryachev continued his conversation. 'Brock's still in preliminary stage. Another ten minutes and he won't be able to stop talking. Having parts of you that necessitate amputation while being fully conscious, without pain, is a great military tool the Americans invented. Of course to saw off limbs as an interrogation tool is my own little adaptation.' The Mortician paused as he listened to the response.

'Don't tell me what I should do or not do!' he continued.

179

'You have already given me to understand he has to stay alive until we have it. But remember your irresponsibility is not my responsibility and I don't have to answer to you or do anything for you. I suggest you leave it to me now and let us see what happens. I will call you later.'

The Mortician placed the phone in his pocket and turned back to Brock. 'Listen, my friend; I came here to carve you up. You see, I have a reputation to consider. If you share what you know along the way that is a bonus. But for me it is not essential. However, you are lucky because it would seem that some do-gooder lady friend of yours has given you something for safe keeping; something belonging to a friend of a friend. Something that is promising to keep her alive for a little while longer. You too, in fact, and we can't have that, can we?'

The heavy-set man moved to within a hair's breadth of Brock's face. 'Because, Brock,' he said in a soft voice as cold as ice, 'I intend to kill you; let us be clear on this.' The man stood up, smoothing the shaved pate of his head with his ham-like hand. 'The good news, you will be pleased to learn, is that all you have to do is tell me what I want to hear and you will enjoy a relatively painless death. I am sure that your friend too will be offered the same deal. And if you don't think that is a good deal, trust me, you soon will.'

Brock tried to stop the confusion influencing the blank expression fixed on his face, all the time his mind whirring with the possibilities. Who has given me what? It must be Sonja Brezvanje. Hell, they must have her too! I must do something! But what can I do? I must play for more time. He closed his eyes. It seemed like a moment later when he reopened them. In fact ten minutes had passed.

Goryachev was leaning over him. 'So how are we feeling, Brock? Better? Ready to talk?'

Brock made a groan.

'Good, then let me explain what is going to happen. I am going to ask you a question and you, in return, are going to give me an answer; but only the right one, of course. The drug has dulled your physical nervous system, which makes you almost immune to physical pain but not to the mental or emotional anguish of what is happening to you. It's a bit like a heavy dose of LSD, which stimulated some people to painlessly drill holes in their head to release the demons within – only more so.

'Each time you try to refuse, give an incorrect answer, even tell me something I don't want to hear, well' – Goryachev used his left hand to gesture what he intended to do over his right hand – 'then I will cut off one of your limbs, slowly. You of course are physically unable to stop me doing so, though you will know it is happening to you. It is quite bizarre I am told, but incredibly effective. Let me show you how it works. Is your name Connor Brock?'

Brock groaned again.

'Now come on, I know that you can speak. It may be slurred, but the drug is designed to impair the major muscle groups, not the minor. In this way lifesaving bodily responses work. If not, I would never know when to cut off something, would I? What is so excellent is that I don't even require bonds to hold you down; in fact you would even be willing to assist were you so able. The drug also breaks down all resistance to willingly telling the truth. So, again: is your name Connor Brock?'

'Yes,' replied Brock.

'Good; see – it works. Now, do you know Sonja Brezvanje?'

'Yes.'

'OK, have you recently been to Belgrade?'

'Yes.'

'Good, now did you take a number of items from Januz Kastrati – who, a little bird tells us, is known to you as the Pied Piper. Is that correct?'

'Yes,' replied Brock again.

'Good; you see – it's easy, isn't it? Though I admit that none of these are the questions I was going to ask for myself or my employer. We can get to those in good time. Oh, and remember: please feel free to make as much noise as you can. No one will hear us, or at least pay any attention to us. Did you enter Kastrati's private apartments?'

'Yes,' said Brock.

'Now, Kastrati's personal computer; did you take it?'

'Yes.'

'And do you have it now?'

Brock's memory flashed the image of when he had given the

computer to Sonja. His brain wanted to say no and he fought to override it. 'Nes,' he said.

'OK . . . that's good. Now where can I find it?'

'Not here,' said Brock.

Goryachev looked pensive. 'OK, then do you know where I can find it?'

'No,' said Brock, not being able to help himself.

'Now that's a shame,' said Goryachev with an almost impatient glee. 'A wrong answer; then we will have to get to work to help you remember.'

With a superhuman effort Brock slid his left hand around the marlinspike as Goryachev sat down beside him on the sofa and turned his back to select the large serrated bread knife taken from the galley and one of Brock's belts.

'Tell me, are you right or left handed?'

'Right,' said Brock. The Mortician leaned over and attached the belt to Brock's upper arm and though he pulled it excruciatingly tight Brock did not flinch. The man stretched back to pick up a smaller knife and poked hard at the leather to make a hole for the buckle sprocket, spearing Brock's arm as he did so. Still Brock did not flinch as the tourniquet was put in place.

'There,' said the psychopathic Goryachev, who was clearly enjoying himself, 'that's so we don't have you bleeding to death too soon.' He then lifted up Brock's right hand, pulling it towards him so that the top of the wrist became exposed. He continued his explanatory dialogue for his victim's benefit. 'Although the hand is the smallest part of the body's limbs, this one is of course your most valuable. Which, I am sure you agree, makes it the best one on which to start. I used to start with the fingers but there is something far more psychologically exciting in going for the whole hand. There's no turning back, you see. The secret is in making it last a long time.' Deftly he tested the blade by cutting through the leather strap of Brock's watch, allowing it to fall to the floor.

'Good! Very important to keep a selection of sharp knives; it makes cutting flesh so much easier, doesn't it? Now don't worry, you won't feel any pain, so just enjoy the show. You see, I said you would lend a hand, didn't I?'

Goryachev laughed at his own joke as he began to saw very slowly through the exposed flesh. Brock could not be certain that his fervent command to his left arm had fully worked until he heard a gasp of pain emit from his torturer's set mouth. The sharp spike entered the soft flesh just below the side of the ribcage.

The wound caused the man to drop the knife, spring up and step back in surprise, falling backwards over the sea chest and crashing to the floor as he did so. Brock, with blood seeping from his right wrist, grabbed the discarded knife and stood up in an attempt to follow through his attack on his tormentor. His faltering legs caused him to lose balance and he fell awkwardly to the floor.

With the marlinspike still sticking out of him the larger man got back on his feet and stood over Brock seething with rage. He snatched at another available blade on the table, a curved filleting knife, and lifted his arm to strike hard at the victim who had dared to attack him. Brock, trapped helplessly between the chest and the sofa, pushed desperately with his legs to avoid the coming onslaught. The first swipe narrowly missed Brock's exposed stomach by millimetres.

Goryachev steadied himself before falling to his knees across Brock's legs to pin him down. His breathing rasping and without rhythm, he raised the blade more carefully this time, intent on mortally wounding his prey. Brock saw the poised knife and instinctively tried to brace himself for the inevitable.

Blood spurted over Brock's neck and face, covering his eyes, nose and mouth in its sticky metallic substance as Goryachev fell upon Brock. Though feeling no pain this time, Brock waited for death to overtake him. He felt his body lighten as if a great weight had been lifted off him.

'You have to stop rubbing people up the wrong way, Connor,' said Ferguson in short breaths, attempting to sound calm as he pushed aside the body of the dying Goryachev; whose neck still spewed a fountain of blood from the carotid artery which Ferguson's own blade had sliced.

Brock's eyes locked with his tormentor's as they both lay on the floor. The Mortician's hand moved inexorably to his side pocket and his lips stretched across his bloody teeth into a knowing smile.

A moment later an explosion tore the houseboat apart.

Thirty-Two

Georghe Enescu regained consciousness in a pool of his own blood. For a moment he thought he was at home in bed, then realized how hard the bed was and how excruciatingly stiff he felt. His head hurt and his face felt wet and sticky. Someone was talking to him. Why could they not just let him sleep? He wanted to strike out at them for disturbing him and then the realization of his worst nightmare began to flood back to him. He had been sitting chatting with Natalya, drinking coffee, when the door had opened.

'Come on, Georghe, you must stay awake now, help will be here in a moment,' said the woman as tears freely rolled down her face. Madame Saradiu occupied the office above. She had earlier heard raised voices, which was unusual, so on her way out to lunch had taken the opportunity to knock on the door to see if she could bring anything back for them.

Madame Saradiu had cried out when she'd recognized Natalya's limp body propped in her chair, the side of her face grotesquely mutilated. She had also recognized the fashionable neck scarf she had recently given to her as a present. It was tied too tightly around her neck. A moment later she had noticed Georghe. Though the pulse was faint he was still alive.

Sonja was too numbed to feel the jolts of every pothole that Paloka seemed intent on hitting. With their hands roughly bound behind them and their mouths gagged with tape, both she and Jakiv tried to lean their backs together with their legs pushed against the van sides in an attempt to endure the ride.

Sitting in the front of the Mercedes van, alongside Paloka, Kastrati considered how the unexpected bargaining card had put him back in the game. It had been easy for them to over-power the younger and less experienced man, though Jakiv had fought like a tiger. The sharp blow to his head was about to be followed by another heavy strike when the woman had screamed in protest. She had then been persuaded to give them what they wanted in return for not killing the boy.

Willingly she had shared the fact that the person who had taken the computer was Connor Brock, who still had it. Kastrati had called Kostina, who had promised to get back to him without delay. And his luck had been in. Ten minutes later he had learned that a friend of a friend of Kostina's had already put a contract on Brock's life.

'I can give you the contact details of the person conveniently able to get what you want from Brock,' said Kostina. 'But my friends are also curious to know what it is that is so important to a man in your position.'

'He scuttled my boat and I want revenge, that's all,' offered Kastrati.

'Then you have little to worry about because he has been a thorn in the side of my friends too. He is going to be disposed of. Now, have you resolved the Bucharest situation for me?'

'He can't be!' shouted Kastrati. 'Brock has something of mine. I have only just learned from these people in Bucharest. They are working together to destroy us.'

There was a pause before Kostina spoke. 'Tell me, Januz. Tell me everything or I will terminate this call now.'

Reluctantly Kastrati had shared how all the records of his network, operation and finance had been compromised. In turn Kostina told Kastrati how infinitely stupid and negligent he had been, before giving him Goryachev's cellphone number.

'You had better retrieve what you have lost,' said Kostina coldly before terminating the call.

Shrugging off the implied threat, Kastrati had immediately called the number.

'The contact has Brock,' he relayed to Paloka as he snapped his phone shut. 'He is going to call us back within the hour. We have time to visit the woman's apartment – just in case the bitch has the computer hidden there – then we will return to Belgrade.'

'And if she has?' enquired Paloka.

'Then we don't need them any more and we can travel lighter.'

'I hope it is there, Januz; I will enjoy making her suffer.'

Kastrati glanced at Paloka thoughtfully. 'Why not? It will prepare her for when I send her to our colleagues in Turkey. Then I will sell what is left of her.' Kastrati laughed. 'Very fitting,' he added.

With the underbelly of the houseboat ripped in two, the heavier stern began to sink fast. Alongside it, the ICE motor launch, usually available for ferrying executives across the lake to avoid traffic, was lifted out of the water knocking the two crewmen off their feet. Carl Honstrom, who had been about to enter the saloon behind Ferguson, after having followed him aboard as soon as they were close enough, was thrown into the water.

Ferguson grabbed Brock and dragged him towards the rising outer deck. 'Wait!' shouted Brock. 'They have Sonja. We need to question him.'

Ferguson glanced back at the glazed expression of the man whose life he had just shortened; Goryachev was still smiling. 'Not possible.'

Brock floundered like a newborn giraffe dropped from half its mother's height into the world and trying to get its balance, walk and run within a few minutes of birth for its own survival. 'Then get his phone,' he shouted. 'He was going to call them back. Their number will be on the phone. Matt! It's in his pocket.'

Ignoring Brock's plea, Ferguson continued to support and drag his partner across the saloon to the deck and surveyed the carnage that surrounded him. The fuel tanks that had been set to be part of the explosion had already destroyed the rear end. A splintered ragged deck was the only thing between them and a gaping watery void that hungrily sought to suck the fast-listing vessel from the surface like an oyster off its shell. 'Then let's hope he floats to the surface,' said the Irishman as he launched both of them into the water.

The cold water seemed to shock Brock's muscles into action so that Ferguson did not have to drag his limp body so much. Two minutes later a similarly sodden Honstrom was helping him aboard the ICE launch. The three of them and the launch's two-man crew watched as the last remnants of Brock's houseboat sank beneath the surface.

'Well, you've lost your dispensation, that's for sure,' said Ferguson. 'There's no way the burghers of Zurich will allow another houseboat on the lake.'

Brock ignored his colleague's attempt to lighten the moment. 'They've got Sonja, Matt,' he said, thinking how the only point of contact with her had just entered a watery grave.

Ferguson looked at the surface as air bubbles continued to rise. 'And we've got you, just in time, eh?'

Brock turned to his friend and colleague. 'Yeah, thanks, Matt. Good timing,' he answered looking at his gouged wrist. 'That reminds me. I need another watch.'

Hristo Amaut smiled at the little girl who had been brought into his new office overlooking the Dneister River in Odessa. 'They tell me your name is Anna,' he said. 'Tell me, Anna, how are you feeling today?'

The young girl fingered the new dress she was wearing nervously. After being taken from the smelly tank she had been vigorously washed and a nasty woman in a white coat had put something into her arm and removed something. The next day she was placed in her room on her own and given a doll and colouring pens to draw with.

'Where is Mother Govrovych?'

'Oh, she is well,' said Amaut. 'She wishes you well and says you are to be a good girl. You are a very special girl indeed and we want to make sure that your time with us is nice.'

'Why am I here?' asked Anna.

Amaut stood up from his desk and walked over to the girl, carefully taking her hand. 'Because you are a very special little person and we want to take great care of you. So, tell me, what can we do or get for you to make your life easier? Some more clothes, sweets, toys perhaps; anything at all?'

Anna lifted her wide blue eyes and looked directly into the director general's dark brown eyes before she answered. 'Could you please let my father know where I am?'

Thirty-Three

S ophia Lefrington watched the pleasant but unremarkable
Liège countryside from the comfort of the burgundy vintage
Rolls-Royce Silver Shadow II.

One of only a few, made to celebrate the company's seventy-
fifth anniversary in 1979, the longer wheelbase model, providing
extra length for passengers, was dubbed the Silver Wraith II.
Other than the initial greeting at Brussels airport, merely a nod
of acknowledgement, the car's quiet, unassuming chauffeur had
not spoken a word. Sonja was convinced he did not speak at
all, let alone a language she understood. His silence and grim
expression did not improve her mood. With the glass partition
the chauffeur insisted on having closed, Sophia had only her
own thoughts to occupy her. This was not the time to be called
away, though she was acutely aware of the fact that she could
hardly excuse herself from the de Brouwers memorial service.

Sophia settled back into the polished, almost worn, hide
seating, stretched her legs and thought about how Stephan's
insistent call last night had been ill-timed. Her research at
Donaueschingen with Dr Jon Su-Yeong was more important
and the Korean had wanted her to stay and help him.

'I think you are the only one I trust,' he had told her. His
research partner Kim Seokhung, similarly a biogenetics specialist
from Korea, had disappeared without even saying goodbye.

'Why would he do such a thing as that?' Su-Yeong had asked
of her before trying to urge her not to go at such a critical time.
But, as Steinwright had aptly pointed out to them both, they
needed a great number of embryonic cells and the fact was that
there were none available until the current crisis was over.

All supplies had been cancelled until further notice and all of the stocks had been secured and could not be used. Then Stephan had called, requesting, even demanding, before finally pleading with her to drop what she was doing and to come to the de Brouwer home in Belgium immediately. Both van Lederman and her father, travelling separately, would be joining them later, along with other close family friends.

The recently completed de Brouwer estate occupied a former abandoned hospital, a madhouse, as Stephan had previously referred to it. Built at the end of the nineteenth century, local folklore argued that it had been the site of Charlemagne's birth-place and would be cursed from the moment the first stone was laid. No one could explain why, as the revered founder of Europe held no grudge against the place. Yet, as if to add credence to local gossip, the hospital soon became notorious until it was closed a century later in the mid-1980s. It had then been left abandoned for twenty years, suffering the further ignominy of falling into vandalized neglect.

Two years earlier Simone de Brouwer had discovered the over-grown estate now known locally as Le Valdor Castle and persuaded her husband to make it their new home. Enormous expense transformed the building into high-tech comfort while restoring its classic gothic features of heavy coigned walls and steep-roofed towers over the tall entrances. Within six months of the de Brouwers taking occupation, however, the locals did not seem surprised to learn that their new neighbours had come to their demise through an unfortunate accident.

Whether it was the stories her fiancé Stephan had shared with her or the menacing security that witnessed her arrival, Sophia shuddered with foreboding as the Rolls swept silently through the wide electronic gates that had opened upon their approach. She immediately threw off the morose feeling upon noticing Stephan, who was on his way down the wide steps to greet her

.

Inside an expansive room the height of two floors – originally the amphitheatre where visiting doctors had learned how to perform lobotomies, among other experimental operations – sat two people in high wing-backed chairs. Though air-conditioned the room smelt old, musty. There were no windows and the elec-tronic heavy double-lined doors could not be accessed from outside the room, without the occupants releasing the override.

Only a select few invited guests and one trusted servant were allowed entry. One of the room's occupants, a woman with very pale, almost translucent, skin cast her dark eyes towards a bank of monitors. Dressed in an elegant black dress, the youthful-looking woman's figure, poise, and the almost sensual energy she exuded, belied her sixty years.

'They seem made for each other,' she said, her full red lips hardly moving.

'Well, we did plan it,' said the silver-haired gentleman opposite her.

The woman picked up a small remote control that lay on her lap and used it to zoom in on the young couple, turning her gaze back to her companion when they moved out of sight.

'Speaking of plans, what is happening?' she asked coldly. 'It would seem we have had nothing but problems to overcome over the past two weeks.'

'I agree, but we are still on schedule. We must hold our nerve.'

'Nerve! Do you think such mundane events affect my nerve? I just tire of interfering busybodies. First we have that sanctimonious manipulator Duisen to contend with; and then the infernal turncoat coward Patrowsky. As for that idiot Amaut, he gives more hassle than any of our other clinics put together. He complains about his self-proclaimed Pied Piper; then it's your snooping ICE and Brock. And the unscheduled move was not cheap, let me tell you.'

'Since when has money been a problem?' said her distinguished companion. 'As for Brock, well, I would imagine he is no longer a problem by now. And as for Amaut and Kastrati, well I understand that a perfect match has finally been discovered, which would not have happened without them.'

The woman sniffed haughtily not wanting to be mollified. 'I still want Kastrati taught a lesson – demanding a percentage; how dare he make demands!'

'From what I understand from our Berlin friends, he has already been taught a lesson; and I have no doubt that Kostina will teach him another in due course. In the meantime Kastrati must deliver another consignment – Kostina will give him the address. There are orders to fulfil.'

'Yes, we must continue supply. But the network must change.'

The man leaned towards the woman. 'There will always be a

supply. And it is wise to review the network periodically. The Kastratis of this world fulfil a role, and their ambitions go with the territory. It is almost inevitable they want more, which is why we have—'

'Goryachev,' completed the woman. 'I know, but my point is that our time seems to be always spent on fixing things that have gone wrong.'

The silver-haired man stood up, walked over to the side of the room and poured a clear liquid from a crystal decanter. His tailored blue suit accentuated his height and lean figure. 'I assure you, my dear, things have never been so well fixed. Within forty-eight hours Steinwright will be out, I will control BioGenomics Research and you – well, you will control all de Brouwer assets.'

'Until Stephan's thirtieth birthday – next year.'

'That is not a problem, and something we have planned for.'

'You have planned for.' The woman's eyes momentarily watered as they noticed the image of the embracing young couple captured once more by another unseen camera. 'They are indeed passionate for each other. I seem to remember that we were like that once.'

The man looked at the woman as he sat down opposite her again. 'Our passions are as strong as they always have been; we have simply redirected them in another mutual direction.'

The woman placed a blue-veined hand on the man's. It felt as cold as ice. The woman noticed the momentary shudder. 'Perhaps if my affliction had not been so consuming we might—'

'Then we would not have been driven to achieve what we have,' interrupted the man.

'But we seem no nearer a cure,' said the woman quietly.

'But your admirable alternative works as well as it always worked for you! Look at you. You could pass for Sophia's twin sister.'

The woman pulled her hand away, her face hardening into the expression he had become increasingly accustomed to seeing over the years: an almost regal beauty yet with cold merciless resolve. 'Under the circumstances that's an inappropriate phrase. Anyway, we must go,' she said, abruptly rising. 'They will be expecting us.'

The man rose and went to take the other's arm. 'You will talk to Sophia later?'

'You are sure she will co-operate?' replied the woman.

'She is a scientist with great promise. I believe that between us we can persuade her.'

'You do understand that she must be with us. There can be no half measures. This is not a game.'

'No it is not, and she has always been part of the plan. In which case, if necessary, you will have to insist.'

In a flustered state Stephan led his fiancée to the west wing of the mansion. 'This is our room – well, rooms, I suppose. It will be the first time I have stayed here too. Mother prepared them for me, but for the last six months I have been in America with you.'

'You seem preoccupied, Stephan. What is the matter?' asked Sophia upon entering the suite; ignoring the co-ordinated panelled and silk-papered decor and elegant, functional furniture she knew his mother would have insisted upon.

'I was about to ask you the same thing.'

Sophia pulled her fiancé over to the ottoman placed at the end of the king-size bed. 'What is it?' she asked.

Stephan allowed himself to be seated, keeping his head down. 'I have just discovered something about my mother that I didn't know.'

Sophia placed her hand softly under her fiancé's chin, lifted his head and looked deeply into his blue eyes. 'Tell me,' she said quietly.

'And it seems that the estate is more complicated than first imagined,' continued Stephan, 'according to Leon Werner, one of the executors of my parents' estate. You will meet him later. He explained my inheritance comes into effect when I am thirty, which I knew, but prior to that, under Belgian law, control goes to previously named trustees. Without going into detail, de Brouwers is now effectively controlled by my mother's twin sister; who is also my father's cousin.'

Sophia look confused, 'You never told me your mother had a sister, let alone a twin.'

'That's the point. I didn't know until yesterday.'

'What? I thought the de Brouwers' strength was based on family retention of all assets? How can you not know?'

'Tell me about it. I didn't believe it either until I met her. But

192

the woman is the spitting image of my mother, though she appears much younger. She reminds me of my mother when I was a child. Well, in looks, I mean, not character. She seems harder than my mother ever was, though we were never very close anyway. It's strange, come to think of it; I don't miss her as much as I thought I would. I miss Papa though. I miss him very much.'

'What's her name?'

'Solange Hampton de Brouwer. She's a widow – husband died of cancer, years ago according to Werner, though she doesn't like to talk about it. In fact she doesn't like to talk about her past at all.'

Thirty-Four

Kastrati was like a man possessed. Standing in the woman's apartment he had just ransacked, he tried calling again. Still no reply and he had already left six messages on the voice-mail of the contact interrogating Brock. 'Call me!' he shouted. 'You must call me!'

Paloka kept his distance. He had seen others killed just for looking at Kastrati when he was in a rage. Continuing to search through every room once more brought no sign of either the computer or any of the sought-after back-up discs or codes. Sonja Brezvanje might have lived simply, but whatever she owned had been torn apart or stamped on.

Kastrati burst through the door and bounded down the stairs, taking them three or four at a time. Reaching the Mercedes van parked in the street he ignored the looks of a passer-by as he tore open the door and grabbed the bound Sonja around the neck. Three times in quick succession he viciously smacked the woman's gagged face with his hand. 'Where is it, you stupid slut? Where is it?'

Jakiv desperately tried to turn his body, succeeding in kicking Sonja's attacker in the leg. Instantly Kastrati turned on him, pounding the young man senseless with heavy repeated blows to the head, continuing to shout obscenities and rain blows down on his face long after the body had stopped moving. He roughly tore at the tape on Sonja's mouth, tearing her lip in doing so. 'Tell me where it is!'

Sonja screamed back incoherently as two builders, working on the adjacent building and attracted by the noise coming from the rocking van, poked their heads in the back.

Kastrati noticed them and viciously kicked out, catching the man leaning closest to the open door directly in the face, breaking the man's nose and teeth. His partner watched as his friend fell to the ground, blood blossoming from the wound. For a bizarre moment both he and Kastrati looked at each other. His frustration temporarily satiated, Kastrati shrugged, pushed the man aside and began to step out of the van.

Overcoming the initial shock at what had befallen his workmate, it was the builder's turn to become enraged. As Kastrati stepped out, not expecting any reaction in the slightest to his own actions, the man kicked out hard with his hobnail boot at the bent knee of his friend's attacker. Kastrati felt a sharp pain as his leg was knocked from under him and he toppled to the ground.

The bricklayer had hands the size of the bricks that he carried up and down scaffolding on his hod, and was known for his quick temper and bar-room altercations. He kicked again and again at the fallen Kastrati, before resorting to using his huge fists. Howling with rage, Kastrati tried to get up but this time was kicked from behind by the man whose nose he had broken.

Despite Kastrati's skill as a street fighter he was unused to being on the wrong side of unfair odds. Lying on his back using his hands to protect himself, Kastrati kicked out at his new aggressor, catching him directly in his genitals, then began to raise himself up. The man's workmate took the opportunity to launch a solid blow to the side of Kastrati's head, sending him crashing again to the ground. The workman raised his boot to stamp down on Kastrati's exposed face and stopped halfway, a look of consternation coming over his own face. A moment later he coughed blood from his mouth as his lung, punctured by Paloka's sharp blade sticking in his back, collapsed.

Kastrati scrambled to his feet, punching the wounded man in the throat as he fell to the ground. Within seconds the Mercedes, tyres screeching like a banshee, was speeding the Pied Piper and his pet rat away from the scene.

Sonja, her face numb with pain, listened to the screaming obscenities emanating from the front. With Jakiv unable to support her back, she was thrown to her side when the van hit a jarring pothole full on. With any final vestiges of hope fading she lay there hurting all over; it felt as if the nerves in her muscles were uncontrollably twitching. She became aware that it was her cellphone vibrating with an incoming call. Forcing her tied hands into her back pocket she pulled the phone out, felt for the familiar key, pressed it and quickly turned over so that her head was over the phone.

'Listen to me, you son of a bitch,' said Brock.

'Connor, it's me,' Sonja whispered.

Brock waited while Pete Kenachi proceeded to triangulate the open call with Sonja's cellphone. What seemed an eternity later, yet in less than a hundred seconds, three satellites had picked up the signal and an icon flashing like a tiny beacon on the wide plasma-screen wall map began marking the route of the Mercedes as it left the city of Bucharest heading west-south-west on Autoroute 6 towards Craiova in the direction of Belgrade on the Danube.

Thinking of every conceivable alternative, Brock had considered that Sonja's kidnappers would have her phone and called it. Sonja had quickly whispered what had happened and where she currently was. She had told him that Kastrati's laptop and files were still in Georghe Enescu's minibus, the one in which they had originally followed the Pied Piper.

'Then we give him what he wants but on our terms,' Brock had instructed.

'Thanks, Petri,' Kastrati said following a lengthy pause while the adrenaline that had fuelled their mutual outbursts had dissipated.

'You have done the same for me many times,' Paloka replied as he sped down Autoroute 6.

'I won't forget it. Might even get you another boat,' laughed the other, breaking the tension. 'Now, let's try these bastards again,' he added, dialling on his cellphone.

After listening to the voicemail, Kastrati terminated the call and gazed out of the window without speaking. Then, as if having made a decision, he made another call.

'I take it you have it or you would not be calling,' said Kostina, answering on the third ring.

Kastrati smiled broadly. 'That's right,' he lied. 'I have retrieved everything from the woman. She had it all along.'

'Good. Have you told the contact? I don't want him wasting his time.'

'I did call him. No answer, but I left several messages for him.'

'Then he must be busy. Januz, we should meet and very soon. We need to discuss rebuilding your network.'

'And what has that got to do with you?' asked Kastrati insolently.

Kostina paused. 'You're right. So long as you continue delivering, what do I care?'

Kastrati smiled to himself. 'Good; anything else?'

Another pause. 'Yes, Januz. Regarding the order for next week, I will transfer payment to your account today.'

'Wait, Remik, I will be changing the accounts – just in case they have been compromised.'

'Fine, let me know. I will give you the address now. Remember it.'

Kastrati wrote down the address as it was relayed to him. 'Odessa, eh? It will cost more.'

'No it won't; it's still Ukraine – and, Januz, any delay on my order and – well, let's just say it will not reflect well on you,' said Kostina, who then terminated the call.

Kastrati ignored Paloka's enquiring look and pointed at the sign for the town of Ghimpati. 'Turn off here, Petri, I need food.'

Ten minutes later after pulling into an industrial area, Paloka went over to a food kiosk. Kastrati opened the back of the van and surveyed his captives. He pulled out Jakiv, looked at his swollen face and felt for life signs. 'He'll live, for the moment. Now tell me, where is it?'

'Brock has it,' she said.

'That's my problem, you see; I know Brock has it but I don't know where to get hold of Brock.' Kastrati placed his hands around Jakiv's neck. 'Now we will stop the games. How can I contact Brock?'

'He told me that if I needed to contact him I was just to call his office and they will immediately patch me through.' Sonja looked at Kastrati's cynical expression. 'He told me!' she shouted.

'Number?'

'I don't have it with me – I can't remember it. Internet! You can get it from the Internet!'

Kastrati shut the doors in time to grab the sandwich Paloka passed him. 'We need the Internet, now,' he said.

* * *

197

Ferguson took the call. 'Brock?' asked Kastrati without preamble.

'It's his business partner, Ferguson. Brock's not here; how can I help you?'

'I am Januz Kastrati. Brock has something of mine.'

'Ah, the Pied Piper fella. Yes I know all about you. You must be referring to your computer he's keeping safe for you.'

'Good! Now here's the deal. You give me the computer and all the files and I let your friends live.'

'Oh, I can't do that. You see, we don't negotiate with terrorists,' offered Ferguson matter-of-factly.

'What? I am not a terrorist, you fool. But I am serious. I am holding a woman, Sonja Brezvanje. A good friend of Brock. She told me to contact him.'

'Brock's not here. In fact, I don't know where he is. Do you know where he is?'

'No! Listen. Do you have my computer?'

'Yes, indeed, I'm here looking right at it.'

'Where is here?'

'Zurich, in Switzerland; can you not tell by the number you called?'

Though relieved to learn that the computer was within his reach, Kastrati could not believe the conversation he was engaged upon.

'Find Brock and tell him to call me on the number I am about to give you. Tell him we have to meet.'

Ferguson took down the number. 'Where shall I tell him you want to meet him? Do you have an address?'

Kastrati rolled his eyes. 'Tell him to meet me at my Belgrade office. He knows where that is. But tell him to call me!'

'Will do, and what if I can't find him?'

'Then you will have to take his place.'

'Assuming I am persuaded, where would you be inviting me to?'

'Belgrade. I will give you the address of my office.'

'If you're referring to the eighth floor of that tower block where you keep all those girls like caged animals and that crass apartment where I lifted your computer – oh yes, I think I know that place.'

Kastrati squeezed his phone tightly. 'Listen, you stupid fuck! Are you playing with me?' he shouted.

'No, you listen to me you dog-shite,' said Ferguson with a voice like granite. 'If you harm a hair on that woman's head, I'll tear your head off and play football with it.'

Kastrati laughed. 'Ha! At last, we understand each other. OK, Mr Ferguson, meet me at my office with the computer tomorrow morning . . .'

'We'll meet at the airport, the Swiss-Air check-in desk. I will call you at dawn tomorrow with an exact time when I know my flight schedule and, when I do call, I want to talk to Sonja or no deal. Capice?'

Kastrati knew he had to agree. They had his computer. All he had was a worthless woman. 'I agree,' he said imperiously.

'Good, now piss off!' Ferguson terminated the cell without waiting for a response.

'Your psychology is interesting,' said Brock as the vehicle they were travelling in entered the private airfield.

'It's called reverse; it apparently opens up the aggressor in tactical negotiations.'

'He considers what we have is more valuable than what he has,' admitted Brock grimly. 'Let's hope Sonja is able to switch her phone back on in a few hours and send us another signal.'

Ten minutes later Brock and Ferguson were in a Sikorsky S-92 helicopter speeding at 295 kilometres an hour towards Romania.

'We can assume the target is travelling at an average of a hundred kilometres an hour to Belgrade, giving them about a four hour drive,' said Brock to the pilot as he briefed him through the headsets. 'At our cruise speed we should rendezvous with them in about three and half hours between fifty and seventy-five kilometres west of Belgrade.'

'With this low payload we have enough fuel to get there and back to Vienna before refuelling,' confirmed the pilot. 'But twenty-five clicks is a pretty large window of opportunity.'

'Well we will have a clearer signal to guide us in approximately three hours' time,' said Brock.

'Well, no worries then. Give us that and we can set you two right down on top of it.'

'Good. Our operations man will patch the signal through to us as soon as he has it.' Brock mentally crossed his fingers in the hope that the signal would indeed come through. He surveyed the expanse of water that shimmered below them as they passed directly over Zurich. There, lost in the depths of the vast lake, was his former temporary home, now a permanent watery grave to his would-be killer who perhaps had been a key to many unanswered questions.

Brock took from his pocket the folded envelope Kenachi had given to him earlier. Inside was an all too brief schedule of the information he had requested. Other than names and addresses of lawyers, agents and hospitals which might prove to be leads, the list was a disappointment. He had hoped it would provide more tangible evidence of what he was looking for. There were three addresses for clinics in Europe, one in the Guangzhou province of China, one in Mexico City and one in the African Democratic Republic of Congo. Brock recognized the Ukrainian address at Izmail. The other European ones were in Belgium, Geneva and another in Ukraine at Odessa; two of them, Belgium and Odessa, were listed as abandoned hospitals awaiting planning permission for development.

There were then a series of addresses taken from Patrowsky's disk, in London, Berlin, Boston, Dubai and Vienna. Brock clenched his teeth in frustration. That was one hell of a lot of leads to follow up within a short period of time. And none of them promised to provide the answers that van Lederman needed.

Paloka pulled into a service station at Craiova to refuel. 'It's damn hot. Want something to drink?' he asked.

Kastrati nodded. 'And get some more food,' he said as he got out of the car and went round to open the rear doors. He surveyed his female prisoner leaning against the windowless side as he would an animal that had disobeyed him. She had managed to manoeuvre Jakiv's lividly bruised face and head on to her lap. 'Your friends are bringing my computer back,' Kastrati told her triumphantly. 'You see how worthless your efforts are?'

Sonja did not reply.

'Tomorrow morning you will talk to him and then we will see what will happen to you. I will get what I want and they — well, they will get one of the Pied Piper's drugged-up zombies. One who will be all meek and mild before either becoming aggressive or simply, well, dropping dead. It depends on the dosage and I am no expert.' Kastrati removed a small metal container from his pocket, the size of a pencil case, and waved it in front of her face. 'But I believe we have enough for you and your toy boy here.'

Sonja looked into the black eyes of her captor. She hated him with every fibre of her being, knowing that he had killed or almost killed everyone she loved. But she must stay alive, if only to destroy this monster. She swallowed and motioned with her head to the unconscious Jakiv. 'Will you give us water, please?'

Kastrati smiled maliciously at her before climbing into the van and seizing Sonja by the hair. 'You know, your friends warned me about harming a hair on your head. The thing is,' he said tugging her head towards him with a rough jerk, 'they have no idea who they are dealing with! When I've finished with you there won't even be a hair worth giving them!'

The returning Paloka looked in and Kastrati motioned to be given a bottle of water. He unscrewed the top and took a long swig before retightening the lid and pushing it into his jacket pocket. 'Aaah, that's better. Lovely and cool! It's so hot this summer, isn't it? Water, you want water?' he added, pushing her roughly to one side and exiting the van. 'Well, to borrow an expression from your friends, piss off! In fact, drink your own piss,' he added, laughing at his own joke before slamming the door shut.

Two hours later Sonja felt the vehicle slowing again. Jakiv had regained some form of consciousness and she whispered for him to remain silent and still. Carefully she dialled the number she had painstakingly stored following her brief conversation with Brock. After pressing 'send' she lifted the carpeted flap of the spare wheel housing and slipped the phone inside. Now she could only hope that her battery had enough charge. As she withdrew her hand the doors were suddenly pulled open.

Thirty-Five

Fifty members of close family and friends gathered in groups in the vast dining hall of Le Valdor Castle following the funeral service of Simon de Brouwer and his wife Simone at the private chapel, adjacent to the castle.

Solange de Brouwer, her arm linked with the arm of Sophia Lefrington, stood with Paul van Lederman and Leon Werner. To her right were Conrad Lefrington and her nephew Stephan de Brouwer. 'Thank you, Paul, for delivering such a moving eulogy. I know I speak for the whole family when I say how much we appreciated your tribute. It was very fitting.'

'Thank you, my dear. It was both an honour and a privilege,' replied van Lederman before turning to the younger de Brouwer. 'Your epitaph for the family was beautiful. As I have said before, you serve the memory of your father and mother admirably.'

'Thank you again, Paul.'

Solange smiled, her full ruby lips slightly parting revealing film-star teeth. 'Now, Paul, Leon, I am going to ask if you will kindly excuse us. I have been longing to spend some quality time with my nephew, his delightful Sophia and her distinguished father – my new family. Please continue to enjoy, I believe there are many you know here.'

Van Lederman watched as the woman led her new family out of the room, shaking his head in amazement at how similar to Simone she was, yet even more beautiful. He then frowned as he watched her place her arm through Conrad Lefrington's.

'She's a remarkable lady, isn't she?' offered Leon Werner.

Van Lederman looked at the tall Swiss banker, gauging his age to be similar to his own. Despite Switzerland being a village, they had not previously met; though, as many of the old-school Swiss private bankers mixed only with themselves, this was not a surprise. 'Yes, quite remarkable. Indeed, I did not know she existed until today. You're based in Geneva, Herr Werner?'

The man, of medium build, though looking painfully thin in an untailored suit that was at least a size too big, shook his head. 'Lausanne, actually. Yes, I have acted for the de Brouwers for many years; though it would seem that, like me, Solange Hampton de Brouwer has preferred the quieter corridors to the halls of fame.'

'You are the executor to the de Brouwer estate?' enquired van Lederman.

'I have indeed had the honour of being retained for that purpose; but I am afraid I must ask you to excuse me too, Dr van Lederman. Much to do, you can imagine.'

'I understand, Herr Werner. Here's my card; your client Simon de Brouwer was a dear colleague, let me know if there is anything I can assist you with.'

Werner glanced at the card before inserting it into his top pocket and returned a thin smile. 'Thank you; goodbye.'

Enclosed in the former amphitheatre, soundproofed and away from interruption, Solange spoke in a level, controlled voice. 'Let me come straight to the point,' she began. 'We have not the time to waste over social niceties. De Brouwer is one of the great families of Europe and it is in trouble. Against the counsel of leading advisors, my deceased cousin, Simon, made a series of unwise decisions that have brought us to where we are.'

Solange noticed a protest rising in Stephan. 'And now is not the time for recriminations either. Simon's motives were correct and we are going to honour his intent. However, strong and quick action must be taken.' She looked hard at Stephan and Sophia in turn before continuing.

'First, de Brouwer have an enormous investment in BioGenomics Research, a company which is about to crash.'

Sophia's mouth and eyes opened wide. 'How can you know that?'

'Because I am a de Brouwer! I could see what was happening, even tried to explain it to my cousin, but he would not listen.'

'But Professor Steinwright will resolve the issue, I am sure he will. It must not be allowed to crash,' said Sophia.

203

'Steinwright is part of the problem, Sophia. Our only option is to take control. The way we do that is to allow it to crash.'

'But the de Brouwers will be wiped out!' shouted Stephan.

'Conrad, explain,' said Solange.

'Listen Stephan: shares can operate under a law of reverse physics. What is forced down can be bounced back up. Currently de Brouwers shares are controlled by the Duisen Foundation, and unless loans that have been drawn down are settled they will have control of all of de Brouwers assets. But Duisen is also heavily extended through its investments in BioGenomics. If it crashes and de Brouwer defaults on loan repayments, the Duisen Foundation becomes worthless.'

'Well if everything becomes worthless, how can that help us?' said Stephan.

'Because of reverse physics. Within less than forty-eight hours news will hit the market that will slash one hundred billion paper value off BioGenomics as minority institutions and shareholders will take their money and run. At the same moment de Brouwers will default on its loans to Duisen. With no one at the helm of Duisen, other than a group of lawyers and advisors protecting fees, we will snatch the opportunity to purchase all their BRG shares, as well as the stock that will inevitably be dumped on the market. As the bounce-back inevitably happens, fuelled by positive news timely released, we will have control of BGR, de Brouwers and Duisen.'

'I understand what you are implying; but how?' Stephan asked in frustration. 'Our shares will be worthless too. If we haven't got funds to buy all these shares flooding the market, then de Brouwers will be the next Enron!'

'Not a comparison, Stephan,' said Lefrington. 'True, they did not have the funds to buy when the shares crashed, and their own pension fund was already in hock. We do have funds. We have Lefrington Industries and the new de Brouwer estate combined. It has already been ratified that Lefrington will take over the Duisen holding in BGR – an option that they cannot get out of. It's just that after the day after tomorrow the price will be about ten per cent of what I would have had to pay.'

'But our de Brouwer assets will still be frozen?' said Stephan.

'Your father's, already in probate, will be; but not your mother's. Under Belgian law, she has to be missing for several years before anyone can freeze her assets. During that period, their control, under the terms of her living will, has passed to Solange's guardianship.'

'But theirs was a joint investment in BRG, wasn't it?'

'That's the beauty of it. Your mother did listen to her twin sister. That is why the loans were taken out with Duisen. It was the only way your father could maintain his investment. Your mother's assets, which are numerous, are unencumbered. You see: perfect security.'

'My father passionately believed in improving the lot of mankind,' said Stephan quietly. 'I thought my mother did too.'

'She did, and above all she believed in longevity!' retorted Solange animatedly. 'She was a de Brouwer too, remember, first and foremost. She wanted longevity for the de Brouwer estate; she did not want to see it lost through unproven genomics. The fact is that her action wisely protected the assets which will allow us to fund a new empire. An empire that your father, Stephan, would have been proud of.'

'What positive news will be released?' Sophia asked. 'If bad news causes it to crash, what news can be released to cause such a bounce, as you put it?'

'Simple. First the announcement that BGR is rife with fraud, illegal and immoral manufacture of drugs, including contamination, coupled with fraudulent and misleading press releases, will force an imminent crash. Within a few days, the statement that the de Brouwer family, with its faultless reputation, has taken full control, dismissed the board and brought in new management will be released. Furthermore an announcement will independently be released to the press that ICE has been instrumental in a fraudulent cover-up. From a rising-market perspective BGR will be exonerated from blame. Finally we rename BioGenomics Research 'De Brouwers Lefrington Research'. The market will respond by revaluing the capitalization to a hundred billion dollars.'

Solange's dark eyes sparkled. 'Meaning that the de Brouwers future inheritance is saved – an inheritance led by your marriage. The future is yours, De Brouwers Lefrington!'

Sophia looked accusingly at her adopted father. 'Papa, we are not even married, yet already you seem to be orchestrating my future.'

205

'Not at all, Sophia, even if it might seem that way. This is a simple matter of choice. Either we take this opportunity or your future husband is a pauper.' Lefrington held his hand up. 'Again, it is simply a matter of choice and I am choosing to take up the opportunity.'

Sophia looked at her fiancé. 'Stephan, this seems too complex, to me, to be a simple opportunity. You must have known something about all this.'

'I promise you, Sophia, this is the first I have heard of it. Look, darling, we're only in Europe because of your project!'

'Listen to me, Stephan,' said Lefrington. 'You know about hedge funds. You have even discussed the opportunities with me. You must agree that the complex opportunities such funds offer are not far removed from the opportunity our families have here. Both promise huge success or huge failure. We are timely placed to succeed if we hold our nerve.'

Solange leaned forward towards the younger woman. 'Sophia, you are a scientist,' she offered. 'Stephan tells me that your research project involves developing a cloning procedure that would allow vaccines to be duplicated at a cost that would allow poorer nations to develop.'

'That's true. That is why I joined BGR.'

'And partly why I invested in it,' added Lefrington.

Solange laid her hand on the younger woman's arm. 'Sophia you must see that Steinwright has been managing on behalf of the shareholders and not science? Cutting corners – anything to get quick results.'

'I can't believe that!' said Sophia, her voice rising in disbelief.

'Did you know that one of the leading research scientists has left?'

Sophia's brow furrowed. 'What do you know about that?'

'Because Dr Kim Seokhung, the brilliant biogenetics scientist, has already joined us at a clinic my sister set up.'

'My mother never told me about such a clinic,' said Stephan.

'Simone never told you about many things though, did she?' replied Solange, a cold edge entering her voice. 'However, the fact is she was interested in longevity and she set up the clinic to investigate the genetic elements that are conducive to achieving it.'

'But why would Dr Seokhung leave BGR. There is no other facility with such state-of-the-art resources in the world?'

'True, but if the resources required are not available he would have to go, wouldn't he? Isn't it true that Steinwright has just stopped all supplies of embryonic cells? How can a biogenetics scientist conduct research without a constant supply of the material? He or she can't. How can you achieve success with your own project without those resources? You can't.

'Yet the simple alternative we are offering you, my dear, means that you can. Think of it: unlimited resources and funds to develop what you want. Where else would you have the opportunity? Not America, at the moment, which is why you came to Europe. Even the European leader in stem-cell research has failed to secure the funding promised by its government.'

'It's true that's what my father wanted,' said Stephan.

'Exactly, Stephan!' said Solange. 'And think how proud he would have been to know that you will be fulfilling his dream. Listen, Sophia, I am travelling there tomorrow; why don't you come with me? Then, when the dust has settled at Donaueschingen, you can go back there if you choose to. Meanwhile, I would counsel against returning immediately. You cannot afford to sully your reputation at such a young age when the press run riot.'

'Whereabouts is this clinic?' asked Sophia,

'On the Black Sea, Odessa; we will leave in the morning.'

Thirty–Six

Paloka leered menacingly at the woman as she quickly retreated into the van. The ferryman's wiry arm shot quickly towards her, his fingers catching her blue blouse, bloodstained from both her own mouth and Jakiv's wounds. Tugging it hard towards him, Paloka ripped the material at the buttons and Sonja was pulled to her side. With his other hand he reached for the woman's flesh he had exposed, stroking it softly before pinching it hard. As Sonja twisted back on herself out of his grasp, Paloka laughed without attempting to grab her again. 'Don't you worry,' he said. 'I'm not going to force you. I will wait until you beg me to touch you, like an ugly whore.'

'I'll be dead before I let you touch me!' shouted Sonja defiantly.

Paloka smiled, revealing a row of even but tobacco-stained teeth 'Makes no difference to me, sweetie, so long as you're still warm! Just like your little assistant,' he teased maliciously.

Paloka slammed the door shut and went to the vehicle's passenger side now they had changed drivers.

Sonja waited for the vehicle to begin moving again before kicking hard at the doors with both feet in frustration.

The front-seat occupants of the black Mercedes heard the noise and enjoyed a joke Paloka made over it. They did not notice the helicopter that passed over them at an altitude of 1800 metres. Kastrati, now driving, turned off the E70 fifty kilometres west of Orsova, to follow the more direct, though slower, country road that skirted the Danube.

Following Brock's instruction, the Sikorsky S-92 flew in a wide circle and located a suitable quiet landing area ten kilometres ahead of their oncoming target. The pilot had already sought permission to fly across Romanian and Serbian air space, agreeing to land at Belgrade airport.

'We're fortunate this area is not busy,' he said. 'Still, we can only drop you guys without landing and you call us when you need picking up. I'll take the opportunity to refuel, then we can take you home to Zurich.'

'I prefer you to stick around,' countered Brock. 'We don't intend to be long – can't be, in fact. Then I want you to take us all to Vienna.'

The pilot looked at his co-pilot and back to Brock. 'We can't push it! But I'll make up some reason, see what I can do. You have twenty minutes max.'

Landing in a recently cut field, Brock and Ferguson quickly made their way to the road. 'It's tight, Connor, rendezvous in about eight minutes,' said Ferguson.

Both scanned the area looking for anything that would stop the vehicle. 'Over there,' said Brock, pointing to one of the three vehicles parked just off the road. 'We need to hot-wire one.'

Two minutes later Brock and Ferguson were driving slowly along the road. 'Have you ever thought of simply taking the more traditional package tours?' asked Ferguson, innocently sitting in the passenger seat of the antiquated Fiat truck he had just stolen.

'We'll send the owner a cheque.'

'He'd probably prefer a new truck; we wouldn't want to be taking the man's livelihood away.' Ferguson turned his body round to look through the back window, keeping his eyes on the road behind. 'OK, Connor, I see it: third behind us. Keep it steady; we want a blue Citroën and white van to overtake us first.'

Brock studied the rear-view mirror. 'I see them,' he confirmed, keeping his speed below thirty kilometres an hour. 'And we're coming to a straight section.'

The old woman driving the Citroën, her eyes not leaving the road for a moment, had the look of someone not used to overtaking. Following quickly as if in hot pursuit, the white van tore past, just making the manoeuvre as a vehicle approached from the oncoming corner.

Brock increased his speed as the Mercedes approached. By the time the next overtaking opportunity arrived, a minute later, both vehicles were taking advantage of the road and travelling at seventy kilometres an hour.

'You know that the insurance companies are getting wise to this forced rear-ending of luxury vehicles by crap trucks,' said Ferguson. 'We may not be able to make a valid claim.'

'Just be ready to brace yourself for whiplash, Matt,' replied Brock. A few seconds later Kastrati increased speed and began tailgating in preparation to overtake.

Brock anticipated it. He sped up too and the Mercedes was forced to draw in closely behind him due to an oncoming vehicle. Brock gripped the steering wheel and forced his head against the rest. 'Now!' he shouted.

When the battered truck in front of them unexpectedly came to a sudden stop, Kastrati instinctively slammed on his own brakes. The Mercedes with its ABS reacted immediately, yet with a travelling speed of over twenty metres a second, smashing into the solid truck only a metre ahead was inevitable.

Paloka, his feet up on the dashboard, in the process of cleaning his nails with his knife, was flung forward when Kastrati braked, hitting his head against his knee before the airbag first inflated upon impact then exploded as Paloka's knife punctured it.

Although also not strapped in, Kastrati was at least able to brace himself against the impact by holding firm to the wide steering wheel. Instantaneously his own airbag inflated, obscuring his vision, but within seconds he was feeling for the door handle to get out of the vehicle.

He looked at the damage the impact had caused before throwing his arms up in the air and storming towards the truck, screaming obscenities. With his head jutting forward from his shoulders in aggressive accusation, hands balled into fists, he reached the offending driver's door. Whether the driver was injured in the crash or not his stupidity was going to be punished.

Seeing the face at the window, he came to a halt, uncertain recognition registering in his face. 'You!' he said.

Brock took advantage of Kastrati's momentary pause of confused realisation. 'Me!' he returned, throwing the full force of his opening door into the man's body.

Brock was on Kastrati before the other had time to recover; his fist, thrown with full weight from the shoulder to the rising target, smashed into Kastrati's face, breaking his nose. Kastrati, as if impervious to pain, flayed his fists at whatever body parts they could reach. Brock aimed a kick down on Kastrati's knee, following up with a stunning blow to the man's sternum. As Kastrati fell again, Brock kicked him twice, catching him first in the groin and then the stomach. Despite being doubled up in pain, Kastrati rolled away down the bank seeking escape. Brock dived after the fleeing man and they both fell down the bank. Teeth bit into Brock's forearm as it closed around Kastrati's head.

Brock raised his other fist, driving it into the side of Kastrati's face. As the other was forced to let go, Brock head-butted, delivering a jarring blow to Kastrati's already mashed nose. Kastrati roared in pain and anger as he once again lost his balance. Clambering on the soft ground he tried to get up before sliding on to his side, where he clawed at tufts of grass, turning his face towards his attacker. Brock, on higher ground, aimed a kick, catching the exposed jaw full on. An audible crack came from Kastrati's jaw as he fell back further into the muddy bank.

Brock dragged the groaning man by the scruff of his neck back to the road. Paloka was sitting in the passenger seat, a large lump on his forehead, his hand still holding the handle of the knife that had pierced his heart, killing him instantly. 'Well, mine was easy,' announced Ferguson.

'Good, tie this piece of slime up, Matt,' Brock said as he went to pull open the rear doors. Both Sonja and Jakiv were leaning against the back of the van. 'Hi, Sonja; you OK?' he asked.

Sonja nodded as she shuffled nearer the doors and Brock leaned in to pull her out. 'Yes, but I'm worried about Jakiv,' she said.

Brock untied her hands and went to climb into the van to untie Jakiv. Sonja's freed arms circled his waist.

'Thanks, Connor,' she said, hugging him fiercely.

Brock held her tight in return 'We need to move, Sonja.'

'Where's Kastrati?' she asked, pulling herself out of the embrace.

'Enjoying a dose of his favourite medicine,' he replied.

'He will,' said Sonja quietly as she climbed back into the van to check on Jakiv.

Brock went around to the front. Vehicles continued to pass by slowly as they looked more out of curiosity than to see if help was required. 'We have got to go. Is this vehicle movable, Matt?' he asked.

'Radiator busted but still movable. No problem with the truck though.'

'I'll take the Merc; Jakiv's in a bad way. You go ahead in the truck.'

They lifted the bound Kastrati in a co-ordinated fireman's lift and threw him into the back of the Mercedes. 'Sorry, Sonja, he will have to ride with you for a short time.'

Sonja said nothing.

As Ferguson pulled away in the truck, part of the Mercedes fender fell off. Brock picked it up and threw it into the truck and kicked the larger portions of debris to the roadside before walking past the crumpled hood and into the driver's side.

Brock looked grimly at the corpse sitting next to him shrouded in the airbag's white blood-spattered material. 'Mercedes spend millions on safety and people like you just ignore it.'

In the back Kastrati's eyes glared back with shared hatred at Sonja while she removed the metal case from his pocket. Though dented, the contents remained intact. She opened it. His expression turned to abject terror as he helplessly watched her prepare the phial he had intended to give her.

Coolly, she stabbed the needle into his arm, pushing the syringe to the hilt. Sonja grabbed his head by the hair, pulling his bloodied face roughly towards her. With her lips inches from his she whispered in a voice as cold as ice: 'Now let's see who the zombie is. Goodbye, Mister Pied Piper.'

Sir Duncan Buchanan's presence and height were intimidating to Umberto Giramonte as the Scotsman was shown into his office. 'Coffee?' asked the Italian following their introduction.

Buchanan sat down. 'No, thank you,' he replied before pausing to allow the assistant who had accompanied into the room to exit.

'Well, Sir Duncan, what brings you to Milan?'

Buchanan looked long and hard into the eyes of Giramonte before coming directly to the point. 'I would greatly appreciate your co-operation on a special order made directly to Giramonte Pharma, signed by Messrs van Lederman and Steinwright. When, and how, was it initiated, how much for and how was the payment transferred?'

'You are indeed forthright, Sir Duncan. Why do you ask?'

'Simple – Paul van Lederman is a close friend and colleague and I believe he is being set up – admittedly innocently perhaps, as concerns yourself and Giramonte Pharma, but set up nonetheless.'

'So you require the same proof I have already been persuaded to give the people who will have furnished you with the accusation.'

'I have not received nor seen any damning evidence. Anything else is just circumstantial.'

The head of Giramonte Pharma turned towards the laptop on his desk. 'OK, I will give you what I gave them.' After a few moments he turned the computer around towards his guest. 'That is the bank statement that corresponds to the period of payment. You see the receipt of three million euros? That represents the hundred thousand units at an agreed price of thirty euros. Payment was requested in advance for this order, because, as you perhaps already know too, we were not . . .'

'Authorized to produce the drug,' added Buchanan.

'Partly; but this was an unknown client, and bearing in mind preparation, we were not going to manufacture any quantity before payment was effected, naturally.'

Buchanan studied the onscreen statement. 'There's only a number for a reference,' he said flatly.

Giramonte nodded, pulled back his computer, pressed 'print', spent a few moments more on the keyboard, pressed 'print' again and swung the computer back towards his uninvited guest. Onscreen was a purchase order with the same reference. The signatures at the bottom were van Lederman's and Steinwright's. Giramonte reached over to his personal printer behind him and handed both hard copies over. 'It's all I have. The order was initiated over the phone.'

'You sell an unauthorized drug on the basis of an anonymous conversation?' shot back Buchanan.

'Not at all; on the basis of receiving three million euros. But you did not come here to discuss my ethics and I have been reprimanded, indeed threatened, about them already. You are here about the ethics of your colleague. I of course asked the caller's name and he told me it was William Steinwright of BioGenomics Research. I merely emailed him that order insisting upon authorization and payment in advance. You see the email address corresponds, of course.'

The muscles in Buchanan's jaw flexed as he clenched and unclenched his teeth. 'This is no proof other than of a set-up,' he said more to himself than Giramonte.

'I have given you what I have. The onus is not on me to prove otherwise,' offered Giramonte, standing up, indicating that the meeting was over.

Thirty-Seven

Sonja went through Kastrati's pockets for other drugs or weapons. She removed all contents including his phone, another wallet, a passport and Albanian driving licence, and the piece of paper he had recently written on. Then, within a few seconds of retrieving her cellphone from its hiding place, it rang.

'Sonja? It's Georghe, are you—'

'Georghe! Thank God! I thought you were dead!'

'I thought you were dead. I've been trying for ages, left a dozen messages. Are you OK?'

'Yes, and I'm with Jakiv. Where are you?'

'Hospital – Madame Saradiu found me. They killed Natalya. She's dead. Sonja, it's my fault!'

'It's not, Georghe. It was Kastrati, the Pied Piper!'

'I know, I recognized him, but they told me their Berlin friends sent them. That's where I lost my phone! Little Natalya is dead because of my stupidity. You told me not to go and I wouldn't listen.'

'Stop it, Georghe, that's enough! Listen to me. We have Kastrati. You must now rest. I will come to the hospital. I promise.'

'Wait, Sonja, I—'

The mobile battery expired.

Brock drove into the field gate that Ferguson had opened as the Sikorsky approached. He pulled open the rear doors, immediately sensing something further had happened. He looked questioningly at Sonja. 'Is Jakiv OK?'

Jakiv nodded. 'My mother always said I have the head of a mule,' the young man added, trying a weak smile. 'Though I am as hungry as an ox.'

'As soon as we get airborne we'll sort something out.'

Sonja reached for Brock's arm. 'Connor, we need to get back to Bucharest.'

'We need to get out of here and we're going to Vienna,' said Brock firmly. 'As for this slime-ball, we need to get him into custody and get rid of his pet rat.'

Sonja stepped out of the van keeping hold of Brock's arm. 'Please listen to me, Connor. I need to return to Bucharest and we are already in Romania, not Austria. Georghe is alive but Natalya is dead and I promise she will not have lost her life for nothing, or Radu! Kastrati's files are in Bucharest and I need to get them now. As for Kastrati, he will no longer be giving any further trouble.'

Brock looked at Kastrati lying on the floor. He pulled his head around and forced open his eyes. He could only see the whites. 'What have you done to him, Sonja?'

'I injected him with the Pied Piper drug he was going to give me.'

'How much?'

'All of it.'

Brock looked at the woman before turning to watch Matt as he heaved the body of Paloka into the aircraft. Turning back, Brock pulled out Kastrati, bent down and lifted him on to his shoulder. 'Can you help Jakiv, Sonja? We need to get airborne.'

'Promise me we will first go to Bucharest.'

Brock looked at the woman. Even in her bloodied, dishevelled state she managed to appear vibrant and stunning. Her eyes blazed with an ice-blue fire of determination and conviction. He realized how attracted he was to her.

'Bucharest,' he said.

Two minutes later the aircraft had lifted and was circling back on itself as Brock briefed the pilot.

'We're already cleared for Romanian air space; though all this changing of my flight plans – you owe me a big one, Connor,' said the pilot. 'We can refuel at Bucharest. You still want to go to Vienna?'

'Yes, we have to go to Vienna.'

The pilot turned and raised his eyebrows. 'Well, I'll take a bet that you change your mind. And if you do, perhaps you would be kind enough to inform me before we take off next time,' he added in mock sarcasm.

During the forty-five-minute flight, Brock and Matt took time to debrief both Sonja and Jakiv. Finally Sonja repeated the conversation she had had with Georghe Enescu. Brock registered the mention of Berlin.

'Do you think Kastrati is a subordinate to someone in Berlin?' asked Sonja.

Brock shrugged. 'It's worth following up. Matt, you go to Vienna and follow up the lead from Pete Kenachi's list, then Geneva. You know what we're looking for. Do whatever it takes. I'll get out here – do what I can before flying to Berlin to follow up our lead there.'

'And who watches your back, or mine for that matter, while we're racing around Europe?' 'I'll text you the Berlin address I'll get from Georghe. We can co-ordinate to meet there before we go to Odessa.'

'Odessa?' enquired Sonja, removing something from her pocket and passing it to Brock. 'This was in Kastrati's pocket.'

Brock looked at the address, recognizing it as the same address as the other Ukrainian clinic on the list Pete Kenachi had given him – the abandoned hospital. He looked over to the prostrate Kastrati. 'Pity he can no longer talk,' he said, casting a reproving look towards Sonja before going through to the cockpit and putting on the available headset.

'Slight change, but you don't win the bet,' he said to the pilot. 'You're returning with Matt to Vienna.'

'And the body we couldn't help but notice you brought onboard? We prefer not to land at the airport carrying it. Too many questions, you understand.'

Brock glanced back to look at the former ferryman and then Kastrati, before surveying the woods that covered the lower slopes of the Carpathian Alps to the west. 'Find a quiet place,' he said, 'where we can dispose of our excess baggage.'

Five minutes later and despite the vortex of turbulent air, generated by the spinning blades hovering over treetops, which seemed intent on sucking her out, Sonja leaned out of her seat. She watched as the two traffickers responsible for dealing out so much suffering disappeared into the thick undergrowth.

As Brock pushed the door shut Sonja experienced no sense of guilt. Though she knew Kastrati was still alive, albeit, she assumed, in the irrecoverable zombie-like state he had promised

217

her, the man's actions had succeeded in removing from her any remaining vestiges of conciliatory kindness she might have previously had towards human traffickers. He had shown neither mercy to Radu or Natalya nor pity to countless other unfortunates, whose short lives he had truncated for his own greed. Revenge felt good to her. No more would she accept compromise. This is how she would now like to treat all traffickers, seeing everyone in the image of the brutal trafficker who had first raped her; and she would use Kastrati's fortune to aid her cause.

Solange de Brouwer surveyed her naked body in the full length mirror in front of her. Though her figure appeared firmer and suppler than that of a woman half her age, she shivered with self-disgust. She put on her robe and moved towards the refrigerated cabinet that was integral to the rich rosewood furniture. Removing a bottle of thick dark red liquid, she filled one of the crystal glasses placed on the adjacent shelf and began to slowly sip until the glass was empty. With each sip her self-disgust diminished, replaced with an arousal of indefinable pleasure that started in her groin and began to sweep through her navel, breasts and limbs. She breathed a sigh of relief as the self-imposed addiction began to be satiated.

Feeling the smooth soft sheets around her she recalled how the first doctor that her mother had secretly consulted had thoroughly investigated her naked, marked body. His diagnosis was that her self-mutilation to suck her own blood was induced by low self-esteem. His treatment was to mix with more friends. Her mother had immediately allowed friends to sleep over, something she had never allowed before. At one of these she had discovered, accidentally, the excitement of sucking blood from a friend's finger who had inadvertently given herself a deep paper cut. From that moment she had covertly sought out blood whenever she could.

Later, during her mid-twenties, a specialist had diagnosed it could be Renfield syndrome, so termed by Harvard professor Dr Richard Noll, who had named it after Dracula's insect-eating assistant Renfield. She had laughed at the comparison but was drawn by the condition attributed to it – where if a child experiences sexual arousal involving blood before puberty, it can lead

218

to an addiction towards blood as both a stimulant for sexual arousal and a source of self-confidence.

When she confirmed to the specialist that she derived pleasure from sucking her own blood, the doctor termed it autovampirism, as delineated by Noll. The specialist prescribed that she try to remember what might have happened to her as a child and then seek psychotherapy to overcome it.

At the same time she was diagnosed as suffering from a rare blood disorder that could become cancerous, though her excellent health astounded the doctor. Convinced that her addiction was a natural response by her body to alleviate her affliction, and maintain her youth, she continued to keep secret the craving she had developed for human blood.

Marriage, soon after, had brought great wealth and she had been able to maximize her indulgence, one which unintentionally led to her and her husband opening a clinic. From her visits there, unbeknown to her spouse, she indulged further, took a lover and with him began to develop a business far more profitable and certainly more exciting than any of the de Brouwers' other interests. And one that she ardently believed was justified by the demand.

Lying down on the bed, she smiled at the pleasurable feeling coursing through her veins. The fulfilment of her own desire was enough to justify her actions; yet as for profit, wealthy customers paid fortunes to ensure healthy donors matched urgently demanded organs and body parts. She simply fulfilled the demand. And in doing so was able to locate not only a supply of fresh young blood and high-protein human sweetbreads to enjoy, but also to locate a liver and marrow that matched her rare blood group.

At last! For she had inherited one of the rarest blood groups; so rare that she had memorized the specifically coded O Rh negative: D- C-E-c+e+, M+S-, Le(a-), K-, Fy(a+b-), Jk(a+b-) CMV-, indicating the lack of common antigens and uncommon antigens it contained. Only one person in a million was born with such a type.

Now, after years of searching, she would receive her new organ and marrow from a healthy young donor. At the same time her fortune would be assured, giving the power she also craved and allowing her to indulge in the ongoing research required for her greater longevity. She would be a queen of the future.

A knock at the door broke her reverie. She waited for the trio of taps before swiftly moving to the door to unlock it.

'Ah, my very own Konrad Lefrescu,' she purred, playfully pulling him towards the bed, her former ill-humour gone. 'I was just thinking of the time we first met.'

Lefrington noticed the empty glass, and the sickly metallic hint of blood in the air. 'You have not called me that in a long time,' he said somewhat reproachfully, quickly closing the door behind him.

The woman pouted. 'Well, perhaps I should do so more often. It sounds so much more romantic than the American Lefrington.'

'Still, I'd rather you didn't,' said Lefrington sternly. 'We have Stephan involved now. Our secrets must remain just that.'

The woman looked at him, her pout turning into a cruel sneer. 'And Sophia, of course. Poor girl, I wonder how she would feel to know that her marriage to Stephan is turning your own son into your son-in-law. How delightfully incestuous your plan is.'

Lefrington did not return the smile. 'What great empire has not been built that way? At least Sophia is not blood-related to her future husband. Our son is not interbred, as he might well have been.'

'Are you implying that de Brouwer inbreeding is the cause of my affliction?' shot back the woman in rising defence.

Lefrington looked at the volatile woman he had known for thirty years, since she was a new bride recently married to her cousin, the powerful Simon de Brouwer. She was almost as beautiful as when they had met during her extended honeymoon on the Black Sea. With the money he had unexpectedly come into and the fortune she had married into they had built an adoption and organs-for-sale business targeting the very wealthy.

'I'm implying we must be careful, Simone,' he said gently but firmly. 'There is too much at stake. As for Stephan and Sophia – they love each other – a marriage of interests, yes of course – but we cannot dictate how their hearts feel.'

Simone de Brouwer smiled. 'We will – be careful I mean; but don't expect it to stop me enjoying our true names when we are alone.'

PART FOUR

Separating Wheat from Chaff

Thirty-Eight

Fully aware that functioning on auxiliary was an unwise option, Ferguson slept during the flight. Arriving at Vienna International airport he cleared customs, took a taxi to the Hotel City-Central on Taborstrasse, purchased a new shirt from the adjoining store, checked into the hotel, requested toiletries, freshened up and then, much to the surprise of the receptionist, checked out again.

Thirty minutes later he entered an elegant baroque building, briskly climbed the staircase with its ornate balustrade and reached a short corridor. A wide panelled door to his right opened and a slightly rotund gentleman with overly oiled hair and a nondescript suit stepped out. The man was about to close the door when a voice called out to him. He spoke a few words, received a reply and then closed the door. Hearing the name of the man he intended to see, Ferguson spontaneously knelt down to tie his shoelace.

Max Adler walked slowly, his head down as if the weight of the world was on his shoulders. He approached the entrance of an underground car park and made his way to the first lower level, which was reserved for local business. He pressed the digit on his key fob, opened the door and got in.

'Max Adler?' enquired Ferguson, as he opened the passenger door and sat down in one fluid movement.

The lawyer's eyes opened in shock.

'Max Adler?' repeated Ferguson

Adler's initial expression of disbelief, thinking he was the victim of a mugging, slowly changed. 'Who are you? How do you know me?' he demanded, all the time feeling rising panic.

'My name is Ferguson of ICE, Investigating Corporate Espionage. We have reason to believe that you have innocently been involved in a baby-trafficking racket.'

The lawyer's brain focused on the word 'innocently' and he visibly relaxed. However, hearing 'been involved' still held dire implications. The confidence of hearing the first helped him to address the second, by reverting to his legal training. 'Whoever you are, I advise you to get out of my car immediately. Any discussion must be dealt with through my office – and the courts if necessary,' added Adler for good measure.

'OK,' said Ferguson. 'They said you would have that reaction. I only wanted to help you before the reporters surrounded your building tomorrow.'

'What?'

'And you and I both know that when they get hold of something, it's much worse than when lawyers get involved.' Ferguson made to get out.

'Wait!' shouted Adler. 'What do you mean reporters? I demand you tell me now!'

The Irishman relaxed back into his seat. 'You forget, Herr Adler, I came here to ask, not tell. This is how it works. You give me information I want and you don't see me in court and, much more importantly, you don't see your picture spread over the front page. With the evidence we have, the media will have a party at your expense. I can see the headlines now: "Adler feeds on baby-trafficking", or something similar – reporters are so good at catching people's interest to sell their newspapers or get you to tune into the news, don't you agree?'

Ferguson watched as the colour drained from the lawyer's face before continuing. 'Hey, I don't want to see you again so it doesn't have to be like that. Now would you not agree that is a simple and agreeable negotiated settlement, as you soliciting people call it?'

Adler viewed it as a caught-out lawyer would view it. 'What information?' he enquired, wiping his sweating hands across his knees.

'This is how it is: your name has come up as being a customer. Which, I repeat, we are viewing as innocent for the purposes of our investigation – in relation to baby-trafficking.'

The lawyer in Adler tried again to wriggle out of it like a worm turning on the hook that held it, though he did not have to feign the shock he was feeling. 'This is outrageous! How dare you make such accusations! I am an adoption co-ordinator and could never be associated with trafficking.'

'Well we already know who these people are and that they have been duping many others. Let me repeat, we are not interested in you. We are in the process of building more evidence against them. All we want from you is confirmation of names or contact details.'

'Well, I'm not certain how I can help. I can assure you that my suppliers are all bona fide. Do you have a specific supplier in mind?'

Ferguson sighed. 'Max, I thought we had just settled this point. OK, to be more specific, does Amaut's Ukrainian clinic at Izmail help at all?'

Adler closed his eyes in resignation. Recently he had found it harder to believe that what he did brought happiness. Following the Williamsons' agonizing scene in his office when they had returned their catatonic baby, which had died a few hours later – he had returned the balance that had been earlier transferred and he'd have to tell other clients that their planned delivery dates would have to be cancelled – he now questioned his work. The money had motivated him, yet his debts were enormous and he had to make the promised transfer tomorrow. Perhaps it was good that it was over.

Bizarrely he became aware that his hands had stopped sweating. Lifting his hands he turned them and studied the palms. He smiled. If his condition was panic-related, as the doctor had diagnosed, then why were his hands dry?

Ferguson looked at him quizzically. 'I already said your future is currently in my hands,' he said. 'Now I am going to have to press you, Max. It's a time thing.'

Still smiling, Adler removed a pen and small notebook from his inside pocket. Removing his cellphone from his trouser pocket he began to scroll down his list of contacts. He wrote down numbers and names. He handed the list to Ferguson followed by his phone and wallet. 'Here, you had better take these too. If you had been a real mugger you would have taken them anyway. The people on that list might even believe it.'

Ferguson nodded as he took the items. 'You know I can't promise that you won't become accountable to the authorities for your involvement,' he said.

Adler shrugged. 'The authorities are no threat – I am a lawyer; but Austria is a village, and the mud sticks for all to see when you slip over.' The man rubbed his palms together – they were still dry. It was as though the fear of being found out had been far worse than actually being found out, which he found a relief. It was true he had always found the stress of having to make a decision greater than the decision itself. He looked at Ferguson, having made his decision.

Over the next thirty minutes Adler explained everything, concluding with how he had been approached by someone based in Berlin. 'He said it was because my practice specialized in family, custody and adoption that he had come to see me with a proposition. He told me his network could provide unwanted babies from Eastern Europe to prospective parents.

'My initial response was that it did not interest me, particularly as although some of my work related to adoption, most of it involved divorce and such clients were not interested in more children. However, he said he could provide parents from America who were desperate to adopt. He wanted to instruct me to act as the adoption co-ordinator. Again it did not interest me that much until he told me how much money was involved.'

'And that did interest you,' offered Ferguson.

'Payment from adopting parents was to be in two tranches,' Adler continued. 'The first was to reflect my commission in full, and never refundable under any circumstance, having been agreed as a finder's fee and for professional services. Naturally that interested me. Why would it not? I don't have to find the child or the parent and yet get paid well for it and in advance. The paperwork was a formality less tedious than divorce, when you know the system.'

'And the second payment?'

'The balance, representing two-thirds of the agreed amount, I transferred to an account in Switzerland.'

'What about delivery of the babies from Eastern Europe? How is the transfer made?' asked Ferguson.

'I believe, as you said, that there were other co-ordinators, but, for myself, I imagine that Vienna was chosen as it is a natural hub with an international airport. Most of my clients would fly in with details of their future baby already on their passport.

'They would receive their baby at one of the hotels close to the airport, take a short boat trip down the Danube to Slovakia and then fly from Bratislava to join a connecting flight to the US from another hub, usually Amsterdam. However, with more select ones, where the client had paid handsomely to provide semen to impregnate the donor, I preferred that it was handed over directly at my office, due to the sums involved.'

'Did you not concern yourself about getting caught?'

'Not at all. Why should I? All the paperwork was in order. We are a recognized adoption agency and keep appropriate facilities. The baby arrives with a nurse at around the same time as the adopting parents, who receive it, pay and depart. All in all it is a very rewarding event.'

Ferguson looked at his watch. He would need to return to the airport for the flight to Geneva he had earlier booked. 'The man who first approached you – apart from his being from Berlin, what can you tell me about him?'

'That he is Bulgarian for a start.'

'I thought you said he was from Berlin?'

'I said based in Berlin. He took a call while he was here and I recognized the language. I mentioned it after the conversation and he freely volunteered that he had moved to Berlin from Sofia in Bulgaria in the early nineties. He saw great opportunities.'

Ferguson looked at the list of numbers. 'Which one is he?'

'Kostina – Remik Kostina.'

'And he is the one you transfer the money to?'

'No, he is the one who approached me. I have hardly spoken to him since. He allowed me direct contact with the clinic – Amaut, as you mentioned. As for the transfers, I believe it to be another. He has an accent which is hard to define. Though he always speaks to me in German, I don't believe it is his mother tongue.'

'And his name?'

'I don't have a name for him, just a number.' Adler pointed at one on the list. 'There – that one.' Adler paused and looked again at his hands, feeling them. They were still dry. 'But I have recently had occasion to call him.'

'Why was that?'

'In the past year I have been approached independently by

individuals and couples seeking adoption. To have our own introduction in such a way naturally leads to a greater profit. I secured
several confirmation deposits, which actually reflected fifty per
cent of the full payment. Then unexpectedly I was informed
that the babies could not be supplied.'

'Why was that? Do you know?'

Adler was silent for a few moments. 'Amaut told me that they
had been terminated,' he said quietly.

'So why call the money man, not Kostina?'

'Because money usually talks, and I've always had the feeling
that Kostina was the front man for the other. Anyway, he was
the only one who answered.'

'What did he say?'

'He told me that I had to be patient and pay him what I
already owed him.'

'OK, Max, I have to go. I already have your details. I'll call
you if I need anything else.' Ferguson exited the car, leaving the
lawyer staring at the palms of his hands.

Ferguson felt good as he left the car park. What he had
thought would be a fruitless trip to Vienna had turned out to
be fruitful and relatively easy. He heard his cellphone demand
attention and retrieved it. The display read 'Honstrom'. 'Carl,'
he said light-heartedly.

'Is Connor there?'

'Now, if you're after speaking to Connor, then did you not
know that it's a hell of a lot easier to call his number?' said
Ferguson wryly attempting to be humorous.

'It's Paul,' said Honstrom.

'Look Carl, I'm not Connor, and you're not Paul. Now if
you're looking to confuse me, then be careful; as an Irishman
I could take offence.'

'Damn it, Matt! Will you shut up and listen!' Ferguson stopped
in mid-stride; he had never heard Honstrom's voice so unchar-
acteristically frantic. 'What?'

'It's Paul van Lederman – he's disappeared.'

Thirty-Nine

At the hospital Jakiv had refused to be admitted, insisting on just being patched up. Sonja persuaded him otherwise.

'I'd rather you stayed with Georghe,' she reasoned. 'We all need to debrief, but he needs one of us to be with him.'

'I think he would prefer that to be you,' Jakiv argued obstinately.

Sonja was in no mood to be conciliatory. 'Jakiv, I need to see about Natalya. With you looking like that, what are they going to think? Georghe needs someone now – he witnessed her murder. Now for once just do as I bloody say and stop arguing against everything I decide.'

When Brock accompanied Sonja to visit Georghe Enescu he asked him to relate his recent Berlin experience and the address of the property. Later, when they arrived at Jakiv's apartment, they located the minibus parked where he had described. Sonja had wanted to stay at Jakiv's apartment. On Brock's insistence, however, they drove the short distance to check into the Intercontinental Hotel at Nicolae Balcescu Boulevard; but upon entering the room it was clear she was still reluctant.

'How am I supposed to do what I have to do here?'

'Well, above all it's safer. And from a practical perspective this is an executive suite. You have Internet, fax, bar, room service. It's a mini-office, which is why I took it for you. There's a boutique for clothes. And it's clean, which young Jakiv's was not, I am sure you agree. What more could you want?'

'A battery charger – my phone is completely dead,' she retorted. 'Anyway, staying in executive suites and buying from classy boutiques is expensive. And why do I need to be safer now?'

Brock placed the box containing Kastrati's personal laptop and files on the table, peeled off his light leather jacket and threw it on to the chair. 'Sonja, they trashed your office and your apartment so it's conceivable that they will check out your team's apartments in due course, isn't it?' he said countering her argument.

'Except that "they" are no longer around,' she retorted.

'Bearing in mind that "they" were directed right to you by another "they", to follow Georghe's reasoning, which I actually agree with, this is an unwise assumption.'

Sonja crossed her arms. 'Unwise?'

'Yes, and let me say that under normal circumstances I would question the wisdom of leaving such valuable material on the roadside after the hassle of obtaining it. However—'

'Unwise as in "stupid woman" – is that it?' shouted Sonja, the stress finally getting to her.

'However,' continued Brock ignoring the outburst, 'the mistake certainly saved your life, and kept you alive until—'

'You saved it – is that what you mean?' interrupted the woman, her face flushed. 'You must be wondering why you are bothering with such a stupid woman.'

Brock sighed heavily, walked over to the window, turned and leaned against it, his arms crossed. Inclining his head to one side he surveyed her as if in contemplation. 'Well, now I suppose it is beginning to cross my mind. So, let me think. Is it the bruised foundation and bloody lipstick or the abrasive communication style you insist on applying that I find so appealing? Or is it perhaps the torn bohemian clothes; or maybe even the sweaty odour cologne you insist on wearing that motivates me to help you?'

Brock shook his head, his mouth beaming a wide cheeky smile. 'No, it must be your sense of timing, that's what it must be.'

Tears streaming down her cheeks, Sonja ran towards the man who was so infuriatingly handsome, despite his own bedraggled appearance, and fell into his opening arms, pressing tightly against him. He returned the embrace as the woman sobbed her heart out, letting the pent-up grief and horror of the past hours pour out of her.

'I should call the police – they will be looking for me, thinking I am involved,' she said between sobs.

'Why? They already have Georghe's statement of how they were attacked by traffickers who killed Natalya. They're looking for the description he gave to them of Kastrati and his henchman.'

'Then I should be attending to Natalya. No one else will – we were her only family.'

'Right now there is nothing further you can do and she would prefer you stayed safe so that you can continue to do what she joined you for in the first place. Listen, let it go, Sonja. Attend to what is important in life – your life. There are other Natalyas who are depending on your work. They don't have anyone else either.'

'You are right, about everything,' Sonja said finally releasing her grip and looking up into the deep-azure eyes above her. 'I'm sorry. I must wash, get some fresh clothes. Then—'

'Well, I must wash, get fresh clothes and fly to Berlin,' interrupted Brock.

Sonja looked pensive. 'You have to leave so quickly?'

In answer Brock reached for his black jacket. He felt for the new phone that Kenachi had given him earlier and swore under his breath as he could not find it. It must have fallen from his pocket during his fight with Kastrati. 'Just great,' he said. 'Two phones in one day.' He reached for the remote control, turned on the television, pressed the 'information' button and located the flight departures page. 'It appears that the next flight to Berlin is first thing in the morning, Lufthansa,' he added as he picked up the desk phone and looked back at her.

Sonja brushed back her hair, wiped her face and smiled nervously as she walked towards the bathroom. 'Then perhaps my timing is not so bad after all,' she said coyly, closing the door behind her.

Brock booked a flight with Lufthansa, kicked off his shoes and lay down on the bed, stretching out his tired limbs. Intending to call Ferguson in a few minutes, he fell into a deep sleep almost as soon as he closed his eyes.

Brock caught the 06.05 Lufthansa flight from Bucharest, changed at Frankfurt, arriving at Berlin at 08.55. Acquiring another phone with prepaid card he called Ferguson, who relayed the message about van Lederman before briefing him about his Vienna trip.

As they were already both at their intended destinations, Brock decided they should complete their respective tasks; then whoever finished first should go directly to Brussels, keeping the other informed. Brock then called Honstrom, who had no further news about van Lederman, other than that the disappearance had been narrowed down to when the Dutchman was travelling by car from Liège en route to the airport.

Brock arrived at the office of Friedrich Neumann, holding a new slimline black leather attaché case. The receptionist sat behind a plate-glass screen like a bank teller and spoke with the use of a microphone. She did not return Brock's acknowledging smile.

'Herr Neumann does not see anybody without an appointment,' said the woman with relish. 'Do you have one?' Her voice sounded artificially metallic.

'Of course,' said Brock confidently, causing the receptionist to look first surprised, then perplexed, as she had no recollection of an appointment made for this time. 'Do you think I would get up at dawn and fly all the way from Switzerland to Berlin if I did not have an appointment?'

The receptionist tapped her computer. 'Are you sure? What is your name?'

Brock looked at the clock that hung on the panelled wall of what he was convinced was a former bank. It read 10.29. In the corner above it he noticed a camera directly aimed at where he stood.

'Brock, ten thirty, my office in Zurich made it a couple of days ago.'

'I'm sorry, Herr Brock. We have no record of it on our computer.'

'In my experience computers are never the problem,' said Brock with clear annoyance, 'it is their human programmers who are, and so clearly my appointment was neglected, and not entered at the time when it should have been. Now, excuse me, but I have not flown into Berlin this morning to be told, as a client, that I am mistaken. Is Herr Neumann in?'

The receptionist's aloofness had diminished, replaced with concern. 'I will have to check; please take a seat, Herr Brock, and excuse me for a moment.'

Brock paced up and down, occasionally glancing at the clock, knowing that he was being monitored by the camera. Three minutes later he was shown into a large square office filled with highly polished ebony furniture and deep-buttoned black leather seating. He was offered refreshment, which he declined, explaining he had enjoyed a good breakfast while waiting for this rendezvous.

Two minutes later a short, stocky man with a balding head and thin lips made an entrance. He was immaculately dressed in a single-breasted Brioni suit, grey with a thin blue pinstripe, blue buttons and a blue double-breasted, lapelled waistcoat. Brock noticed that the diamond-studded Rolex on his wrist had to be worth at least a hundred thousand euros.

'I sincerely apologize if there has been any misunderstanding, Herr Brock,' said the man, his brow furrowed with concern. 'I am Friedrich Neumann at your service, *mein Herr*.'

'It's good to meet you, Herr Neumann; you have been highly recommended,' offered Brock in return.

The lawyer's thin lips parted in a wide smile, revealing cosmetically perfect teeth. 'I am pleased to confirm that all of my clients have become so via word of mouth. Now, I know that your time is valuable to you; how is it I can advise you?'

'I am here on behalf of my father, who, having enjoyed a rather too full life of indulgence, with the finer fluids of life, is urgently seeking a liver.'

Neumann nodded. 'That should not present too much of a challenge, other than locating the right donor, of course. May I enquire as to his blood type?'

'AB,' said Brock.

Neumann pushed his lower lip out and turned his mouth down in thought. 'Of the four types, that is the most recent. O, the oldest, is compatible with all the four types of O, A, B, and AB. But only AB is compatible with AB. It may take a little time.'

'Well, time is something that we do not have much of.'

'And naturally you have investigated more traditional channels?'

'He is on several waiting lists, but – well, the family has decided to take more command of the situation,' said Brock, allowing his eyes to rest on his attaché case, placed by his side.

Neumann noticed. 'Quite right; such decisions should be

definitive and not dependent on myriad unknowns. However, the timing and type have to be reflected in the price, you understand?'

'Of course, that is not a concern. Though one of my father's concerns is where he would have the operation. Can it be at a hospital of his choosing or do you recommend?'

The lawyer nodded. 'It can be very much his choice. However, we prefer with a delicate operation such as this that the time period between extraction and insertion is as short as possible. For that reason we prefer that the operation is conducted at a clinic we recommend. Of course, should you choose your own we would ensure delivery in good time. In any event we are, of course, not liable for any rejection during the operation or indeed after it. Our role is to ensure healthy compatible organs at the right time.'

'Understood,' said Brock. 'I believe that the preference would be to take your recommendation. Where are they located?'

'Well I understand you are from Switzerland, so I can recommend one in Geneva. How does that sound?'

'Sounds good, though we do have a country home on the Black Sea which we thought would be excellent for convalescence following the operation.'

Neumann held up a finger. 'I have an idea; just bear with me a moment while I verify something,' he said as he began to peer at his laptop. 'Your father's in luck, Herr Brock. A new clinic has recently opened on the Black Sea, in fact. I requested verification of when it would be available for transplant operations only yesterday and the confirmation is now in. It is available from next week.'

'Now, that does sound good. Where exactly?'

'In the Ukraine – Odessa, in fact, right on the Black Sea. I have not yet had the opportunity to visit it myself but understand it to have state-of-the-art facilities as well as occupying a very private and quiet setting.'

'Excellent! Now I suppose I should enquire as to practicalities,' said Brock, his eyes straying to the case again. 'I understand that something was required on agreement. Is that correct?'

Neumann nodded pleasantly. 'Correct – a finder's fee, half of which is refundable should we not locate the required organ in the agreed time – which has never happened to date, I hasten to add.'

'And, very importantly, what time period can my father expect?'

'As soon as we have agreement, I would imagine. We may require some good fortune to locate one to suit your timing, but even with AB we should be able to locate a compatible organ and transplant within a week.'

Brock's mouth opened in genuine surprise. 'That's excellent service, bearing in mind the AB type.'

'Now, you see why my business is via word of mouth; every one of my clients remains a satisfied ambassador. However, once again such speed of delivery is of course reflected in the price,' said Neumann with clear pride.

'I do, indeed, and of course it would be. Which, may I enquire, is in the order of how much?'

The lawyer looked directly into Brock's eyes in anticipation of his reaction. 'Professional services are a hundred thousand euros on agreement and a further hundred thousand upon delivery.'

Brock's face was a mask, giving a slight nod of the head in acknowledgement.

'Good, now perhaps we should attend to the immediate practicalities,' offered Neumann, his own eyes shifting to the attaché case this time.

Brock stretched out his hand to reach for the handle, pulling it on to his lap. 'Naturally my father would be fascinated to know about the donor; would that be at all—'

'I have to stop you there, Herr Brock,' interrupted Neumann, holding up his hand. 'It is our policy to never discuss any details of the donors. Suffice to say, however, that donors are located using our excellent network, which follows all the right avenues.'

'I would imagine they are, but my father is a very old-fashioned Catholic. So, you can understand there has been some difficulty in persuading him that organs from the – well, black market – which I know is perhaps indelicate to mention – are bona fide. But I'm sure you have come across similar circumstances. What's your advice for reassuring him?'

Neumann bristled at the term his visitor had used, before sighing as though bored at having to explain something again to a child. 'I believe that the issue is choosing either life or death, Herr Brock, not moral or immoral. I am not going to alarm you with the statistics of patients who do not have a choice other than to die because there is either no liver available or they cannot afford it in time or money. Do I think that, given the option, they would choose life? Well, most certainly they would.'

'Herr Neumann, I am in agreement; it is just that my father is worried that the organ he receives will have been harvested from another without consent.'

'Then you must reassure him that, as the person donating the liver will already be at death's door, via an accident, for example, this is a way that they can provide for their loved ones; for often there is no insurance to provide for them.'

'So, I can tell him that consent is always received?' asked Brock.

'Of course, and that family's dependants are always generously provided for; again reflected in the price, of course.'

Brock nodded in understanding as he went to push open the two gold-coloured latches of the case.

Forty

T he sleek twin-engined jet soared elegantly away from Liège airport at 1200 metres a minute. Levelling out at its optimum altitude of 11000 metres, the Cessna Citation X achieved its maximum cruise speed of 934 kilometres an hour, a smidgeon below Mach 1. Heading south-east it was due to reach its Black Sea destination in 150 minutes. Of the eight seats in a double club arrangement, four were occupied: two at the front by Sophia Lefrington and Solange Hampton de Brouwer, and two at the rear by the older woman's personal entourage. One of them Sophia recognized as the chauffeur, whom she smiled at as he passed her carrying the glass of water his employer had requested, though no acknowledgement was returned. She turned to the woman opposite.

'Solange, I never met her, but Paul van Lederman told me that Stephan's mother and you were identical twins. Were you close?'

'We were certainly very alike, though I was perhaps a little more independent than she.' Solange laughed. 'It's bizarre though; I feel that somehow she has become even more part of me. But tell me, Sophia, how about you? I understand from your father that he adopted you as a little girl. Do you remember your parents or siblings at all?'

'Yes, I was not that young, and I do remember my family. I remember playing with my two brothers, and I was close to my sister, but not so much to my mother. As for my father, he disappeared when I was a baby.'

'Then it is good that you have such a wonderful man as your father today; indeed, fortunate that he chose you to adopt.'

Sophia's pale-blue eyes momentarily burned like blue ice, something which did not go unnoticed by the older woman, who was intent on watching for every reaction. 'I believe I was sold before I was adopted; it is something I remember very well. But yes, I guess I am fortunate.'

'And fortunate too that you have been able to follow the work that interests you; such research demands wealth, time and sponsorship. What led you into the field of biogenetics?'

'Well it was a number of factors, I suppose,' began Sophia. 'In tracking my roots, my adoptive father had somehow learned that my two brothers had died during an outbreak of pertussis, or whooping cough, a preventable disease that incredibly still kills over two hundred and fifty thousand children a year.

'My mother, being poor and illiterate, according to my father, was so convinced that it was a disease of poverty, she sold me so I could have a more fortunate life, as you say. The mortality rate for children in Ukraine is four times higher than Belgium, for example.'

Solange raised her eyebrows 'From my own interests in Eastern Europe, I am aware that child mortality is higher, though I was not aware it was four times.'

'Very few are aware, which is why at Stanford my interest grew in researching prevention through gene modification to gain immunization from disease even before birth. We can do it; we just need to raise awareness of the benefits.'

'Well, I for one am certainly aware of the benefits,' commented the older woman.

'With respect, Solange, you are very rich and literate. Of course cures already exist but too often they are only available for the very rich. By identifying susceptible genes and adapting those through a cloning procedure, vaccines can be duplicated at negligible cost and, hopefully, lead to natural immunization in future generations.'

'Then longevity must be of interest to you too, is it?'

'Yes, as a by-product of an improved quality of life, resulting from natural immunization, but not as an end in itself,' replied Sophia.

Solange leaned forward. 'Surely you agree that having longevity, while retaining health, vitality and youth is a desire of every human; certainly every woman?'

Sophia looked at Solange sitting opposite, noticing how bright her eyes were and how her skin seemed as smooth as her own, though she knew her to be over twice her own age. 'It would seem that you have already achieved it, Solange. Look at you; you're living proof that attitude and purposeful industriousness are the best ingredients for longevity!' Sophia threw out a playful laugh. 'Unless you have discovered some secret potion of course.'

'I have,' replied the other, her expression serious.

'Then you must share the secret,' said Sophia light-heartedly. 'Woman to woman.'

'That's exactly what I was hoping you'd say. You see, my dear Sophia, I have, in a way, but I need you to help me to develop it further. To support the work that Dr Kim Seokhung is currently working on. It follows your own interest, though takes it much, much further.'

'In which way?' asked Sophia quietly, as yet uncertain if the older woman was serious or not.

'By re-engineering proteins,' said Solange. 'Already, as you are aware, they are being utilized to treat cancer and blindness, indeed many afflictions. And already we can repair damaged hearts by injecting the patient's stem cells from their own marrow. And we know that stem cells regenerate, and that stem cells from hybrid embryos, ninety-nine point nine per cent human and nought point one per cent animal, have huge potential in their regenerative ability.

'And of course we know that the right embryonic stem cells at the right time will provide the re-engineering that will stimulate longevity. With good farming we can harvest the embryos that will be genetically superior, allowing for both natural immunization from cancer and healthy long life. Think of it, Sophia! We can harness the wide potential of stem cells to grow new organs as our own begin to malfunction – livers, hearts, kidneys – even regenerate our skin to youthfulness.'

'Admittedly,' said Sophia, impressed by the woman's passion, 'but as it costs at least twenty thousand dollars for just one injection of a million stem cells, that would require altering natural selection to achieve a form of Aryanism, which would benefit only the very wealthy. Be careful, Solange,' added the younger woman, in a light-hearted vein once more. 'The next thing is they'll be accusing you of designing a superior race only the very rich can afford.'

Solange looked as if she had been stung. 'And what is so wrong about wanting that, for one's self and family?' she retorted.

'Isn't that what today's natural selection is about? We no longer live in the jungle evading predators. Make no mistake, it is wealth that keeps the world spinning, yet most people are more interested in putting the brakes on. Do-gooders with no idea of what wealth can achieve insisting how it should be distributed! We live in a world that depends on the strong to generate wealth, not the weak, who would lead us into ruin. The survival of wealth is what counts!'

Sophia felt uncomfortable but could not refrain from saying what was on her mind. 'With the healthy and fit cells of poor babies used to regenerate the weaker and wasting cells of the rich adults, I suppose?'

'Is that not the way it has always been?' argued Solange, her voice rising. 'The wealthy seek to enhance the duration and quality of their lives and in so doing the rest of mankind inevitably benefits. I believe you are in danger of being one of the wealthy hypocrites you misguidedly have distain for. You attend the world's best university while living in luxury and enjoy state-of-the-art technology at your fingertips for your research.'

Sophia felt her stomach churn. 'You're right, I do! But I am sure of my motives. I want to provide for the poor; you seem to want to take the only thing they have.'

'Oh, don't be so sanctimonious, Sophia. In time you and Stephan will control one of the world's leading family empires. With great wealth comes great responsibility – a responsibility to protect it for future generations, not to give it away. By all means support chosen charities to soothe your altruism, but your duty will be to do what is right for our own dynasty. That is why you were chosen.'

'What do you mean, chosen?'

Solange looked momentarily flustered. 'I didn't mean chosen, I meant groomed. It is what you have been groomed for.'

'Well, what do you mean, groomed?' demanded Sophia, her own voice rising, alerting the entourage seated behind her.

'By your father of course; naturally he wants the best for you. But never mind that; please listen to me Sophia. Let me explain something to you of the utmost importance. I may appear the picture of health but I am dying. That is the reason I am going to Odessa. Recently my internal organs have started to break down. My kidneys are showing signs of malfunction and my liver is wasting away; but a matching donor has at last, miraculously, been found. I also require a bone marrow transplant, which the donor can also supply.'

'But the donating marrow must be alive. How can the same donor give you their liver?' Sophia looked appalled. 'You intend to take their liver at the same time! Without a liver they will die!'

'Calm yourself, Sophia! Listen to me; the young girl has been in an accident, and is already on life support, that is how we located the match. She is going to die anyway.'

Sophia took a deep breath, finding it hard. 'Why are you telling me this? I am not a surgeon. This is not my area of expertise, yet you talk as if I am to be involved.'

'I do, because you are already very much involved.'

The younger woman's brow furrowed in confusion. 'Involved? How?'

'I need you to assist Dr Kim Seokhung to develop the stem cells that will regenerate my other organs and generate replacement organs, which I can store for future requirements.'

Sophia felt as if her head was spinning, making her sick; she tried to shake it. 'Such requirements will involve creating stem cells through embryonic cloning of the compatible donor's eggs.'

'The young girl has just entered puberty. As such we have access to the full quota of eggs we females are born with – millions, every one compatible. We can fertilize as required, extract the stem cells from them as the embryo grows, and then freeze them, thus ensuring a continuous supply.'

Sophia looked horrified. 'You are serious, aren't you? I am a scientist. But what you propose is ethically wrong.'

'Now there you go all sanctimonious on me again. You're a scientist; the end always justifies the means of research, to use your jargon. As for my personal motives, it is because I have a very rare blood group—'

'So do I,' interrupted Sophia, 'but that is no reason to—'

'Yes, my dear, I know you do,' Solange cut in again. 'Indeed it happens to be the same as mine. Our blood can only be found once in every million people, which makes us very special, doesn't it? But, in my case, I have also developed a rare blood affliction, a symptomatic association that rejects any incompatible organ. An affliction that is likely to happen to you too, in time, my dear. Does that change things for you, knowing that what you develop today will ensure you live tomorrow?'

Sophia found it increasingly hard to swallow; her mouth felt numb. 'That is what you meant by me being chosen,' she said meekly, her words slurring.

'Under the circumstances, that's very perceptive of you, my dear. You have been part of a long-term plan, but don't worry, no harm will come to you; it's just that, as well as your future help, I will need some of your blood for my operation, just in case more is required for transfusion.'

Sophia felt her glass slip to the floor, the muscles in her hand no longer responding to her command.

'Forgive me, Sophia, but I can't have you disappearing on me for the next few days, can I? Soon you will be better, you will marry Stephan, and we can develop our future requirements together as a family.'

Sophia struggled to focus, not hearing the words she struggled to speak, 'You're insane. Stephan——'

'Thinks you're very special too,' added the woman as Sophia passed into unconsciousness. 'And as Stephan is my only son, he's very special too.'

Forty-One

'On second thoughts perhaps you should verify the amount,' offered Brock, rising to his feet. He carried the case over to Neumann's desk, holding it with both hands, placing it directly in front of the lawyer. 'It's all in high-denomination notes.'

Neumann nodded and flicked the latches, his expression turning to one of consternation upon not seeing what he expected to see; the only contents were a roll of duct tape and a memory stick. Brock had already removed from his pocket the replica German army service pistol he had purchased earlier from the historic memorabilia store opposite the central station. He placed the cold steel of the 1938 Luger against Neumann's neck.

'What do you want? I have no money here!' shouted the lawyer.

'I want you to be quiet,' said Brock menacingly, pushing the barrel into the lawyer's throat. 'Or you will need a black-market vital organ replacement yourself. Now, I only want information from you, that's all. In a few minutes I will be gone, leaving you unharmed. If you don't give me the information then I will harm you. It's a policy I was recently introduced to. I want you to plug in the memory stick and copy over your database of addresses relating to supply.'

Neumann looked confused, so Brock repeated his instruction. 'I want to know where the organs and spare body parts which allow you to fulfil your black-market orders so promptly come from.'

Neumann shook his head. 'If I do that I sign my own death warrant,' he whispered hoarsely, his Adam's apple finding it hard to swallow.

'Well, you know what they say about people who play with fire. Now, Hristo Amaut's address in Izmail, for example, I already have. I have seen the empty corpses of children, drugged children who gave no consent to have their organs untimely ripped, or their body parts torn limb from limb, according to a delivery schedule.' Brock saw the lawyer's eyes widen further in shocked surprise. 'Good, I see you understand me at last. Then go ahead and do it.'

Within five minutes, Brock had the stick in his pocket and had securely bound Neumann's arms and legs to his chair, disconnected the laptop and placed it snugly into the attaché case with Neumann's mobile phone. 'Yes, I'm sorry about that, I need to take this too, though I am sure you have back-up, so it is not really too much of an inconvenience for you, is it?'

Brock then wound the duct tape around Neumann's head three times, gagging his mouth. 'Now, just one more thing,' said Brock, his eyes like flint as he drew himself close to the lawyer. 'After I have gone and you have been released you will want to hurt me, to get back at me, make phone calls et cetera. Well, this is what I advise you to do and I want you to be clear on this. Understand?'

Neumann nodded.

'Any such action and this computer will automatically be sent to the right authorities. Any such action and you sign your own death warrant at the hands of your own suppliers – because I will confirm to them that you have gone against them. The only action I want you to take is to carry on with your work specializing in locating organs for transplant. But from this moment you do it legally. If, at any time, I hear you have gone back to your old ways, then I will personally remove your black heart and sell it to the lowest bidder – without your consent!'

Sonja felt no emotion as she effected the first transfer from Kastrati's account. At first she had sat in silence at the amount of money that the account contained, dumbstruck at the unexpected eight-figure number.

A secondary feeling of guilt was fleeting as she rationalized that what she was about to do was not stealing; it was requisitioning funds that would be used to repatriate and compensate. The third emotion she felt, as the few clicks of her mouse made the transfer, was genuine excitement. For some reason she had expected to see the money transferring in a download dialogue box as if in some movie. All that happened was a confirmatory message acknowledging the transfer instruction.

On Brock's advice she had already advised her bank that a wealthy benefactor wishing to support her cause against the trafficking of young people would be making a significant transfer. Naturally she expected the bank's discretion if she was going to keep the account there. Unwanted publicity was against the wishes of the benefactor. They had confirmed that they fully understood and promised to confirm when the donation arrived.

Her feeling of elation at joining the ranks of the super-rich and becoming one of her bank's best customers turned to despair as she opened Kastrati's email account. Over the next hour she learned the full extent of the Pied Piper's network of prostitution, Internet pornography and trafficking. Though she once again baulked at the fact that the reservoir of money she now had access to was being fed by the network, she would take Brock's advice not to have a knee-jerk reaction. The more she understood, the more effectively she could irreparably damage the network.

Calming herself, she continued to read recent emails that confirmed imminent delivery of young orphans to Izmail. Some had been as young as nine years old. Tears sprang to her eyes as she came across the identity photos that had been taken of children trafficked to the lightless basements of Istanbul or the massage parlours of Birmingham in the United Kingdom – prisons of iniquitous misery Natalya had escaped from, and in which she believed her own sister had died.

Angrily she clicked 'receive' and immediately several new messages began to download. The first from a Leka Varoshi, desperate for Kastrati to contact her, stated how much she missed him, apologizing in advance that she would keep calling his cellphone.

Another was from Remik Kostina congratulating him on retrieving his property and confirming that he would make payment as soon as new details had been received; a third was from Hristo Amaut, explaining that the forthcoming order was to be delivered to an address at Odessa, which he had detailed below. It also informed Kastrati that having spoken to his employer he was now able to discuss terms. They would do so when he arrived. The message asked to confirm delivery and dates.

Yet another from the US demanded to know why the Internet video link available to their members had been stopped. If it was not reinstated they threatened to agree new terms with another supplier. File after file of damning evidence highlighted the untouchable arrogance with which Kastrati had built his empire. It listed the orphanages he had taken over, even the names of the bureaucratic palms he had heavily greased to take them over. Reading it she knew that he had always intended to kill her as soon as he had retrieved his computer, assuming she would have already accessed the files.

Sonja closed the computer down, feeling emotionally and psychologically exhausted. She opened the minibar, removed a bottle of vodka, opened it and drank it down, not bothering to pour it into a glass or add ice. A minute later she had made her decision. She would go to Odessa and rescue the orphans.

Picking up her phone she went to call Brock, then thought better of it. He would only attempt to dissuade her. Breathing deeply she scrolled through the contact list, locating the Kiev number she had not called in over five years. Her heart pounded in her chest as she pressed the dialling button and listened to the tone as it connected. It answered after a few rings.

'Sergei? It's Sonja – Sonja Brezvanje.'

A pause. 'Sonja! Is that really you?'

'Sergei, I need your help with something.'

'Sonja! Straight to business, eh? and there I was thinking you were calling to see how I was.'

'How are you, Sergei?'

'Good. I run a legitimate business now. Times have changed, commerce is the future and at my age, well, one's perspective changes! But how about you? – are you still in the protection business yourself? I mean the anti-trafficking business.'

The ex-army sergeant, ex-policeman, and subsequent ruler of Kiev's protection rackets had been seriously attracted to Sonja, offering to go legitimate if she would be his wife.

'Sergei, listen to me. I am able to pay and I don't care how much.'

'Then your kind of protection pays much more than mine used to.'

'That's because your henchmen were overzealous. I told you before, if you keep breaking the legs of people you are trying to protect, how can they pay you for protection when they can't work?'

'True, very true, my lovely Sonja. But somehow I get the feeling that you require some leg-breaking done. Am I right?'

'I'm calling because I have to pay a visit to Odessa in the Ukraine and will require both protection and aggressive force.'

After a slight pause Sonja heard that the tone in Sergei's voice had at last become serious. 'I promised you before, Sonja, that I would always protect you as a loving man protects the beautiful wife he loves. Just because you chose not to marry an old bear like me does not mean that I will not honour my word. Now forget money, tell me when you are coming and I will personally meet you in Odessa.'

'But not on your own,' said Sonja. 'You will bring some of your hench—'

'Associates, Sonja,' cut in Sergei. 'They are my associates. I told you I am in legitimate business now. The term you insist on using is no longer appropriate.'

'Associates then; you will bring some?'

'Of course! Protection could hardly be termed protection without an abundance of muscle and artillery.'

Brock had checked into the Berlin Hilton at Mohrenstrasse, spent an hour studying the information on the memory stick before emailing the contents to Zurich and securing the laptop in a hotel safe-deposit box. He then took a taxi to Bachenhofstrasse.

'Is it number six you are visiting?' asked the driver as the black Mercedes turned into Bachenhofstrasse. Brock looked at the driver's reflection in the rear-view mirror, noticing he was smiling. 'Why do you ask?'

'In case you want me to wait for you,' grinned the driver. 'Unless you will be taking your time, of course.'

Brock understood. 'I'm actually visiting number twelve.'

The driver looked disappointed.

'But that's a good idea,' added Brock. 'I would like you to wait for me. Tell me, what is number six – an embassy?'

'It is more than just that, my friend,' replied the driver grinning again. 'Word on the street is that it is Berlin's most exclusive

247

club, if you know what I mean. Only the very wealthy come here. Before 1989 it was a government building. Indeed, I remember it; I was born not far from here. Most of the larger residences in this street were taken over by the Russians. In the last fifteen years almost all have been restored to their former Prussian splendour, number six being by far the best; but then with the fees I have heard spoken of we must expect that, no?'

'Is it invitation-only?' enquired Brock.

The driver reached number twelve, stopped the car, turned round and nodded his head in understanding. 'I could find out for you, let you know when I pick you up later, if you want me to.'

'You can do that?'

'Gives me an excuse, doesn't it?'

'OK, excellent,' said Brock, handing over a fifty-euro note, representing double the amount of the fare on the meter. 'I won't be long, about fifteen minutes. See if you can get me an appointment; I'll make it worth your while, and you can wait for me.'

The taxi turned around as Brock walked to the rear of number twelve and back down towards his real destination. Arriving at number six he discovered that the rear was as impenetrable as the front he had noticed earlier. The veritable fortress would certainly keep people out, or in. Georghe Enescu had been lucky.

Fifteen minutes later the wrought-iron gates of number six opened immediately the taxi had spoken into the intercom; two minutes later Brock was shown into the club's deep-red-velvet-festooned parlour.

Forty–Two

Ahmed Amuyani surveyed the papers strewn over the wide table as he re-entered the room carrying Andreus Kaligirou's journal. Since his arrival from Paris he and Cassie Kaligirou had been collating the information extracted from the journal and the information that Kenachi's computer, Izanami, had delivered.

Cassie looked up. 'You look pleased with yourself.'

Amuyani smiled broadly. 'Let's just say that I am a genius; though a little help from Izanami has been useful, I do admit.' The Iranian professor placed the journal on the large round table and picked up one of the small bottles of water. 'Cassie, I think it is time for us to review and reflect concisely on the information we have before us,' he said removing his round spectacles and walking around the room looking at the jotted notes that had been placed on the walls.

'First, the lost treasure of Constantinople that so absorbed both your father, Adonis, and grandfather, Andreus. What do we know? Well, from the old Venetian Doge's campaign journal of the Fourth Crusade, we learn that his nephew, Count Marcus Dandolo, and the usurping Emperor, Alexius III, both disappeared on the same night; Enrico's scribe records that the count and his men were killed by the Emperor's bodyguard as they tried to prevent Alexius fleeing the city.'

'Though Villehardouin's memoirs record that there was no love lost between the old Doge Enrico and his nephew,' said Cassie. 'This means we can assume that his nephew's disappearance was a useful excuse, since with Dandolo out of the way there would be no dispute over inheritance, all of which went to Enrico's side of the family.'

249

'Perhaps,' said Amuyani, nibbling at the end of his glasses arm, 'one could argue that Enrico did away with his nephew, but we are both of the opinion that it is more likely that he simply took advantage of his nephew's disappearance. Therefore we must look to the motives! Studying the motives is a proven method when trying to determine history,' he said pointing his still unopened bottle of water at Cassie.

'So we know Alexius was motivated by wealth and power to usurp the throne from his brother Isaac. Which he did, and then blinded Isaac before imprisoning him. The action of pulling one's enemy's eyes out was, may I say, a brutal but effective medieval practice. After all, they only killed emperors as a last resort; they were far more valuable as a ransom. Indeed, the blind Isaac was restored to power with his son until both were killed by Boniface and his crusading cronies. However, I digress; it's a habit I'm afraid, my dear. Now, where were we? Oh yes – we also have it on good authority from Villehardouin, and I quote: "The usurper, Alexius, took off his treasure and abandoned the city." So we can assume that he was not inclined to give up his newly acquired wealth, and no doubt intended to use it or organize resistance against the new regime.'

'But he was motivated to abandon the city, pronto,' added Cassie.

'Indeed he was! But we know that he was never able to regain power and lived in poverty. And we also know from Enrico's campaign journal and Villehardouin's memoirs that Count Dandolo and his small band were renowned as an elite group of professional soldiers whose skill and prowess had already been proven at the ports Zara and Dyrachion.'

'Which leads to the assumption that Dandolo was not killed, disappearing instead with the Emperor's treasure, which he would be loath to give to his uncle,' said Cassie.

Amuyani unscrewed the top of his water, took a long sip and nodded. 'Experience of his uncle's acquisitive tendency would indeed motivate him to do such a thing. So, if we follow your grandfather's line of reasoning, young Dandolo would have chosen to keep the treasure and disappear. Probably using the same boats required by the Emperor to ferry such booty.' The professor paused as he drank once more from his bottle.

'Right, now, what do we know about the treasure? Well, we

250

know from the record, *The Alexiad*, written by the Byzantine princess, Anna Commena, daughter of Alexius I, that it was an incomparable hoard of treasure collected by her father, including a series of Lysippos bronzes. Yet we also know that in the eyewitness account of Nicetas Choniates, *On the Statues*, destroyed by the Latins, there is no reference to the Lysippos bronzes . . .'

'Nor in Gunther von Pairis's eyewitness testimony, *Historia Constantinopolitana*, which lists all the relics and statues of saints that were stolen . . .'

'Allowing us to arrive at your grandfather's postulation: that the works of Lysippos were among copious amounts of precious gold and silver artefacts, jewellery and money taken by Dandolo. And we can surmise his motive would be to found his own dynasty, perhaps one big enough to challenge his uncle, given the opportunity. History is crowded with dynasties being lost and regained. Just look at Constantinople.'

Cassie stood up from the table with a sheaf of papers. 'Right, and we know from these primary sources that, following the sacking of Constantinople in 1204, the Tsar of Bulgaria, Kaloyan, unexpectedly inflicted a crushing ambush at the Battle of Adrianople on the crusader army led by Emperor Baldwin I, Count Louis I of Blois and the Venetian Doge Enrico Dandolo.'

'And sharing the motives for the previous ambush,' prompted Amuyani.

'Absolutely! The chroniclers refer to a professional group of mercenary knights, led by a nameless count, who were instrumental in Kaloyan's victory. Baldwin was captured, Blois was killed and Doge Enrico was forced to retreat with the remnants of his defeated army.'

'Mercenary knights motivated not so much by money, but something they really needed: a province.'

'And in recompense the mercenary knights requested and were given by Kaloyan a territory north of the Danube and part of the Dobrogea Plateau to the south.'

'Known in more recent times as Izmail, of course!' added the professor thoroughly enjoying himself. 'Not that it would have been called that in the thirteenth century, you understand. The initial "I" in the name would have been added during Turkish domination, due to the same feature of their

251

language that transformed Stanbul to Istanbul. However, forgive me; there I go digressing again, though often these digressions prove to be useful, you know. Now, naturally the knights' recompense included the great fortress recently completed by Genovese merchants. So, my dear Cassie, in view of the supporting evidence, I am of the very strong opinion that Andreus Kaligirou's thinking was right that the family dynasty we know of as Dobrudza of Dobrugea Province, was founded by Count Marcus Dandolo.'

'Which for me confirms that the Lysippos was at the Izmail fortress as my father's picture reveals,' said Cassie enthusiastically.

'Good,' said Amuyani, enjoying being in the company of the enthusiastic young woman. 'Now, there was another ambush . . .'

'An ambush involving Dandolo, or Dobrudza, and his mercenaries with Kaloyan, which this time succeeded in killing the old Boniface in 1207.'

'Yes, it does seem that the hot-headed count built his fortune and exacted his revenge, not through strategic diplomacy, but with tactical ambushes. Now, there are no further references to the Dobrudza family to be found for over one hundred and fifty years. Then, finally, after one hundred and fifty years of building the Dobrudza coffers, they are recorded as being one of the many dynasties crushed by the Ottoman invasion of the fourteenth century, an onslaught that drowned the Bulgarian Empire in a flood of their own blood.' Amuyani paused to drink from his bottle of water.

'So, Cassie, we can assume that was the end of the Dobrudza dynasty, as indeed it was for all the feudal families in the Balkans. Of course, if they had only stopped their despotic feuding and fought together against their common enemy, they would have checked the Muslim invasion so determined to establish a world-embracing Islamic empire, and driven them back to Asia. However, when you—'

'Yes, professor,' interrupted Cassie, learning quickly that it was necessary to keep the convivial man on track. 'So we can strongly assume, therefore, that the descendants would have hidden it, as my grandfather believed.'

'Well, that's what usually happens, Cassie – whatever was left of it. Now, where was I? Oh yes – the references your grandfather tracked down in the Ottoman chroniclers of the fourteenth century. They outline how in 1372 the fortresses from the Balkan foothills to the Danube began to fall one by one, pillaged for their treasure, excepting Izmail, which was "found wanting", according to the eyewitness chronicler.'

'Surely that is confirmation that the treasure had already been removed to safety.'

'Or is it simply telling us that there was none? So, let's review the motives. Why did the chronicler mention Izmail specifically, and that it was found wanting, meaning empty in today's terminology? I am of your grandfather's opinion that there were other motives involved than the spread of Islam. Countless fortresses were destroyed except Izmail, which to me means they either gave up without a fight or it was empty because they had already departed. In which case there was no need to destroy it, was there? Either way we must assume, Cassie, that there is little point looking at Izmail.'

'But what about the co-ordinates on the back of the photo my father sent to my mother?'

'The ones which relate to the fortress at Izmail, which was found wanting – I mean empty?'

'Yes, the treasure could have been hidden. My grandfather's notes spoke about the location being in the lee of the fortress—'

'Well, let's come back to that later, shall we?' cut in Amuyani. 'First let's continue to follow the motives. Let us consider another factor Izanami graciously delivered,' said the professor, picking up several sheets of printed paper. 'First we know the bronze statue, similar to one in the photograph sent by your father, is universally acclaimed by art experts to be an original Lysippos. It was sold to an Italian private collector in 1976—'

'The year I was born!' put in Cassie.

Amuyani tried to appear patient at being interrupted. 'A factor that has not gone unnoticed, my dear. Now, it was for an undisclosed sum, though believed to be many millions. Called, as you already know, the Boxer of Thermon, it was bequeathed to the city of Rome upon the collector's demise in 1998. Indeed, according to Izanami, no one knew the collector had had it in his possession since 1976, until his estate was realized.'

'And it is the same one that my father is holding in the photograph he sent to my mother,' said Cassie.

253

'Which leads us to assume that your father and grandfather discovered the whereabouts of the hidden Dobrudza or Dandolo treasure and—'

'Were killed for it! Which brings us back to what I have been trying to tell everyone, though no one seems to—'

'Yes they do, which is where we are now. But to finish what I was saying, we can assume that they were motivated to keep the secret for some reason.'

Cassie looked confused. 'What do you mean?'

'Well, I instructed Izanami to collate all the artefacts of Grecian or Byzantine heritage sold between 1976 and 1977. The only Lysippos it came up with was the Boxer plus four other artefacts comprising gold jewellery inset with rubies. The same collector purchased these.'

'From the same source, I bet.'

'Almost certainly; look at the motives. If more had been available it would have been available to him, or another private collector. The fact was that whoever took the items your father and grandfather found did not know the exact location of the mother lode, assuming that to be the Emperor's treasure, otherwise he would have been motivated to sell those to his eager collector. That means that the treasure either only amounted to those few items or your grandfather was motivated to keep the location of the lode secret.'

'Because he knew his life was in danger!'

'Perhaps, but that is something we will never know. However, we can assume that the money paid by the collector made somebody very rich, so perhaps they were no longer concerned.' Amuyani paused to sip from his water bottle.

'Now, young lady,' he continued conspiratorially, tapping Andreus' journal, which lay on the table, 'let us consider the marginal jottings your grandfather made – particularly the one that you believe specifically indicates location.'

Cassie reached for the journal, opening it at the page marked by a yellow Post-it sticker. She read it aloud: '"Lysippos sleeps in a fordable part of the river, where the barren ruler is shaded in the lee of a fortress. When the time is right, take ten paces south and twenty-three west; then look for the exact spot eleven long by thirty-five wide and then look to recognize my sign."'

'Now what do you consider that to mean, my dear Cassie?'

'That at some measurable position in the lee of Izmail fortress is the entrance to the treasure,' said Cassie. 'And I told you I went to Izmail to find the location where the photo was taken because I believe that is the starting point.'

'And I told you that it could not be Izmail fortress because it was found wanting.'

'So how do you interpret it then?' Cassie said, impatience resonating in her voice.

'Well, as I briefly told you this morning, I was fortunate to meet your grandfather in Tehran in the early seventies. He was a very interesting man, very interesting—'

'I really envy you!' Cassie felt compelled to interrupt. 'Everyone I have ever spoken to who knew him said the same.'

'Indeed,' nodded Amuyani in understanding. 'I remember how unusual his lecture style was, almost delivered in a Homeric fashion. In his lecture he would often juxtapose ancient and modern terminology.

'Anyway, in reading his marginal note I got to thinking it may be telling us something very simple but in an old-fashioned way. For example, "Lysippos sleeps", means that he is hidden deep underground, as a warrior who sleeps in Hades. A fordable part of the river I was uncertain of so I requested Izanami to help me. While waiting I considered the words "barren ruler". Now, the ancient term for a Byzantine ruler is *saccea* – indeed the term first appears in Anna Comnena's *Alexiad*, which you remember also first records the great treasure of the first Alexius, later stolen by the third.

'Now, not far from Izmail there is a town called Isaccea and, of course, you will recall my earlier rambling that Turkish influence placed an "i" in front of names. At the same time I checked up on what the word *saccea* meant in Romanian, and discovered it means "barren". So, feeling pleased with myself I returned to Izanami, who had calculated the most fordable route of the Danube. And what came up but Isaccea, located on the right bank of the Danube, in Dobrujea, Romania, about thirty-five kilometres from Izmail? Apparently it has been inhabited for thousands of years because it is one of the few places in the lower Danube that can be forded.'

'But what about being in the lee of a fortress?' Cassie asked.

'Well, let me tell you. Because of its vital strategic position it was fortified by the Romans, becoming the most important military post in the region, Noviodunum.'

'But the numbers on the back of the photo – what about those?'

'They are indeed our confirmation, if we were not wise enough to translate the riddle.'

Cassie looked perplexed. 'What?'

'Well, Izanami verified the position of Izmail Fortress.' Amuyani picked up a paper and passed it over to Cassie.

Cassie looked at the numbers printed on it: Longitude – 45° 21' 00" N, Latitude – 28° 50' 00" E. 'That was why there were no seconds,' she said. 'There weren't any required.'

'And if, as your grandfather says, "when the time is right take ten paces south and twenty-three west; then look for the exact spot eleven long by thirty-five wide" – well, Izanami subtracted what she took to be actually minutes and seconds of longitude and latitude, not measured paces, and came up with 45° 16' 1" N and 28° 27' 3" respectively, which was of course—'

'Isaccea,' finished Cassie. 'I have been looking in totally the wrong place. How frustrating it is that riddles seem so simple after they have been solved.'

'I would imagine that neither your father nor your grand-father wanted to serve up on a platter something that had taken them their lives to solve. Though I am at a loss to know how he came to discover it in the first place.'

'Well he spent his life at it. But what about the last section – "recognize my sign"? Have you any idea what that means?'

'None at all, so I suggest we go and find out.'

'Great idea; when?'

'Well, I'm on vacation and Connor instructed me to do what-ever it takes to assist you; so, well, it strikes me that to do that we must go to Romania.'

Cassie stood up quickly, knocking her chair over. She ignored it. 'To Isaccea, now?'

Ahmed Amuyani theatrically pointed his right arm, holding the bottle, to the ceiling. '"To follow the signs", to quote Andreus; and there's no time like the present.'

Forty-Three

'It's been our pleasure, Herr Smithson.'

Brock returned Mira Luga's broad smile. 'It's been good of you to give me a tour at such short notice,' he said as they returned to the parlour. 'It is only by chance that I learned of your establishment and I know it will make my regular visits to Berlin less tedious.'

'We promise to make them memorable, and I know that our girls will look forward to seeing more of you. Now, might I suggest that we attend to your membership details? Places are limited so I recommend that you secure yours with payment. We don't want any disappointments, do we?'

Brock nodded. 'Not at all; let's do it.'

The madam glanced at the ornate French clock behind Brock that stood on the marble mantelpiece, her long black-and-red satin dress rustling as she swept forward towards him. Pushing her arm through his she guided her prospective member down a corridor. 'We have members arriving soon,' she said quietly, leaning towards him in a conspiratorial fashion, 'and as our policy is to guarantee maximum discretion, we'll go to my private office. I will arrange some refreshment.'

Sitting in a wide leather chair in front of a highly polished nineteenth-century Prussian desk, Brock filled out the short membership form, writing fictitious personal and banking details. The door opened and a moment later a beautiful blonde girl, no more than eighteen, dressed in a petite French maid's uniform, entered carrying a silver tray with decanters and bottles. Placing the tray on a flamboyant antique table she coyly curtseyed and left.

For the benefit of his host Brock smiled appreciatively at the girl's gesture. A faint bruising on the girl's mouth was evident. 'If you let me have the bank details, Madame Luga,' he said, keeping his eyes on the departing girl, 'I will make the transfer later today. You understand that as my visit was unexpected for both of us I would prefer . . .'

'Of course I understand, Herr Smithson; that will be acceptable. Now, you have seen a selection of our facilities and we offer a service equal to if not better than any of the finest hotels. The membership fee of twelve thousand euros allows you access to everything including a select choice of lady for company every month. The monthly subscription can be at various levels starting at five thousand a month, which includes dinner, drinks and of course allows you to partake of our adoring companions, and rises according to the degree of your requirements. Indeed, talking of drinks, please always help yourself to whatever you want at any time – which is another of our club's policies.'

Brock stood up and walked to the drinks tray, choosing a bottle of water with its seal unbroken. He poured a glass and surveyed the room, noticing the photos on the wall. 'You have certainly got it right here, Madame Luga. Whatever and whenever for the taking – what more could I want? I'm not surprised that you have to limit membership.'

'We believe exclusivity is worth paying for,' said Luga as she noticed the light of her desk telephone blinking. 'Please excuse me for a moment,' she added, picking up the handset from its cradle.

Brock nodded and politely absorbed himself in looking at the various pictures around the room. He heard the woman greet someone on the phone in German, and listen for a short time before replying, making enquiries of her own, before finally acknowledging instructions detailed.

'That's a good one of you,' commented Brock, as Luga thoughtfully replaced the receiver.

'Excuse me?' asked Luga looking towards her guest studying a small photograph on a table in the corner of the room.

'All four of you seem to be sharing a huge joke,' added Brock.

Madame Luga left her seat and rustled over to the picture. 'Hmm? Oh yes, but that's quite a few years ago now, I have to admit. The picture was taken just as the gentleman on my right did indeed make a joke. He is founder of our establishment, Herr Kostina, whom I know will look forward to meeting you as soon as your membership is confirmed.'

'Is it not possible to meet him now?' said Brock, recognizing the name from his list as well as overhearing his name spoken in the recent telephone conversation.

'Unfortunately Herr Kostina is away on business.'

Brock had already heard the woman mention Odessa during her telephone call.

'And the tall, distinguished gentleman, and the other woman on his arm. Are they founders too?' enquired Brock.

'Well, discretion prevents me from revealing their names, until you are a confirmed member, you understand, Herr Brock. However, he is certainly one of our founding members; indeed, it was his idea to introduce our highest level of service. Should you choose to subscribe to the highest level, I can assure you that the network you would associate with would be of a very influential nature; though you do need to be invited to join by existing members at that level.'

'As one would expect, of course,' said Brock turning quickly towards the madam and inadvertently spilling his drink on to the woman's chest, causing her to utter an exclamation of surprise.

'How clumsy of me, Madame Luga; I'm so sorry,' said Brock, as the woman walked across the room for a serviette from the tray and began to dab at her wet dress.

'No harm done,' replied Luga 'It's only water. And it was my mistake for leaning so close to you.'

A few minutes later Brock was inside the taxi. 'I thought you would be longer,' grinned the driver as they turned out of Bachenhofstrasse. 'Did you get everything you wanted?'

Brock studied the photograph he had quickly removed from its frame while Luga was preoccupied with drying her dress. 'I certainly did,' replied Brock with a grim satisfaction, recognizing the tall man in the picture.

Ferguson's visit to Geneva was unproductive. The taxi driver knew the exclusive retreat located outside Montreux overlooking the shores of Lake Geneva. The pleasant receptionist happily confirmed that the clinic specialized in organ transplants. The dialogue continued in an amiable manner until Ferguson suggested that there was evidence that the clinic's supply of organs for transplant might be coming from the black market without their knowledge.

His request to meet with the director general of the clinic was politely refused and she refrained from further discussion. Calmly she handed Ferguson prepared contact details of their lawyers, suggested he make enquiries through the appropriate channels, and firmly requested he leave the building immediately, calling security to ensure he did so. By midday he was on board an Airbus leaving Geneva bound for Brussels.

Dagmar Stahl, of Börse Online was the first to receive the tip, anonymously. The usual dilemma was whether to run with it before verification. She checked the current share-price position, which had reached an all-time high since the company's incorporation four years earlier. She called the company, whereupon a spokesperson, other than confirming that there was to be a shareholder announcement later in the week, declined further comment.

The tip received confirmed the doubts she had already raised to her colleagues. She decided to advise her clients accordingly. If they could get out now, they would preserve their original investment, maybe even make a profit. Though hesitant due to the anticipated fall-out, her quick action was endorsed by her colleagues when CNN transmitted a report by the reporter Kate Drew three hours later.

Steinwright watched the screen in his office as the share price he had worked so hard at maximizing crashed. By the close of business, twenty-six billion dollars had been wiped off the capitalized value of BioGenomics Research.

Forty-Four

Sophia Lefrington's recurring nightmare was more vivid than she had ever experienced before. It seemed that the deepest recesses of her memory were being accessed. A voice she had not heard since she was a little girl was talking to her. Desperately she fought to open her eyes. The image of the man she had witnessed cruelly raping her sister came into her mind. He was looking at her now, turning towards her, appraising her, stroking her face. She couldn't move, she screamed, but made no sound. The face, that pockmarked face, was now as vivid as it had been since her first nightmare, fifteen years ago.

'You are right, Simone, the scraggly little weed has indeed grown into a beautiful wallflower. Whoever would have imagined?' Kostina said, keeping his eyes directed at the comatose Sophia as he felt the smoothness of her skin.

The woman pushed herself gently against him, nudging him with her arm. 'Wealth, Remik, makes the difference. Think of the alternative. If you had had your way and she had ended up on the street, her soft beauty would be tainted with the hardness of poverty.'

'Then she was extremely lucky that her blood matched yours, wasn't she?'

Simone placed her hand on the Crocodile's arm. 'It is I who was extremely lucky that you discovered the match. It has taken fifteen years for us to locate another match. Fifteen years!'

'It is Konrad you must thank,' said Kostina, patting the hand of his long-term employer. 'Had it not been for his insistence on testing the blood of every girl we ever received, then this one would have ended up on the streets like her sister.' The Crocodile's scarred hand affectionately patted the woman's again.

'Mind you, I must admit that even I was surprised when he also insisted on adopting the girl when it was discovered her blood matched yours. He must love you very much, Simone.'

'Yes, dear Konrad, perhaps he still does, in his own way; but as I repeat, Remik, it is wealth that makes the difference.'

Kostina turned towards Simone de Brouwer, a thoughtful expression on his face. 'It does make you wonder how our dear Konrad would feel if another match had not been found at such a critical time? He would have to give her up for good.'

'You have known him almost as long as I have, Remik. Why should he feel anything? Sophia was always part of a plan. But we have a match, so she simply forms a different part of the plan.'

'Did you know that it was I that renamed her Sophia?'

Simone raised her eyebrows. 'No, he never shared that with me, I assumed it was her birth name, not that it really mattered.'

Kostina grinned. 'I agreed with Konrad that if he were going to adopt her and give her his name, then I should have an involvement too. After all, we were partners in everything, at that time. I am Bulgarian, born in Sofia, and I named her after my country's capital. So, our little wallflower carries both our chosen names: Sophia Lefrington.'

LIÈGE, BELGIUM

Conrad Lefrington looked through the two-way mirror at the fully dressed man stretched comfortably over the top of the satin-quilted bed as though in a deep sleep. 'Enjoy your rest, Paul; you are going to need it when you wake up in a couple of days' time.'

'Was it really necessary to drug him?' Stephan asked, standing by his side.

'I didn't want to, son, but we could not really take the chance that he might cause a difficulty at such a critical moment.' Lefrington placed his hand on the younger man's shoulder. 'You don't mind me calling you son, do you? You're almost as good as; and if I'd had a son I would have wanted him to be just like you.'

Stephan turned to look at his future father-in-law, a man he respected but found hard to get a handle on. 'You adopted Sophia; did you ever consider adopting a son as well? With due respect, sir, money would not be a barrier.'

262

Lefrington smiled, delighted that he had so easily deflected the younger's man's focus of attention away from van Lederman. Stephan had a lot to learn, but he was doing so fast; already he was an unwitting accomplice to the Dutchman's abduction. 'Well, let's just say the opportunity never arose, though with you as Sophia's choice, I consider myself a very lucky father.'

Stephan turned back to the glass, about to say something when Lefrington's cellphone interrupted them. He spoke into the phone curtly: 'Hold' – before looking directly at the man he knew to be his son. 'Excuse me, Stephan; I need to take this call. If you go to the room that was planned to be Simon de Brouwers' study, I will meet you there. It is yours now, you know.'

Lefrington watched Stephan leave the room, before returning his eyes to the phone in his hand. He had recognized the ring-tone as that of the more private of the two phones he carried, the number of which was exclusive to only the most vital members of his network – a network started in 1989, which successfully supplied Eastern European girls, babies and organs to meet specific orders. In the last five years he had added China, India, Africa and Latin America, making a global network that generated millions a month – a vital cash flow allowing him to increase his investments, as well as absorb his losses, as a venture capitalist.

Lefrington released the 'hold' button. 'Yes, Mira?'

A minute later, his jaw clenched from the news, he switched off the phone and turned back to look at the motionless van Lederman, his own face now sharing the shallow pallor of the drugged director of ICE.

On her way to Bucharest bus terminal, Sonja went via the hospital. Jakiv Teslenko was sitting on the chair next to Georghe Enescu's bed at the end of the ward. Both men were clearly very depressed and had been commiserating with each other.

'Have you been to the office?' Georghe enquired.

'Not yet, and I can tell you that we will not be returning there permanently, Georghe.'

The news did not improve the atmosphere of tense depression. 'I see,' sighed Georghe. 'Then Natalya—'

'We won't have to, because I have great news!' exclaimed

Sonja, causing Georghe to look more alert. 'Unexpectedly La Strada des Enfants has become the beneficiary of an extremely generous legacy. At last we will be able to achieve what we have always wanted. As soon as you are better, we will be doing things differently and on a much grander scale.'

'More promises?' Jakiv said, his face swollen and livid with bruises.

Sonja placed her hand on the young man's shoulder. 'That's right Jakiv, more promises. Some of which I am going to put you in charge of fulfilling – like repatriation of those girls in Belgrade, for a start. I want you to attend to that as soon as you can. First there is something I must do, which means I will be away for a couple of days and—'

'Where?' interrupted Jakiv more with concern than suspicion.

'And I want you to attend to things in my absence,' continued Sonja, ignoring the interruption.

'How? On fresh air, with no office, no vehicles and no phones?' retorted Jakiv, sarcastically, his depression making him angry with himself at being so helpless in protecting Sonja and Natalya, whom he had grown so fond of. Taking it out on Sonja was how he had chosen to handle it.

'So, here is a schedule of what I want you to do,' said Sonja brightly as she handed over the list she had prepared. 'I want you to agree terms for all of this; we can settle up upon my return.'

Both men stared at the long list, which included making preparations for Natalya's funeral, securing large new offices, vehicles, state-of-the-art computers and databases. The first item on the list was to purchase the orphanage at Brasov, Natalya's former home. Georghe was the first to speak. 'But this is going to cost a fortune, Sonja. How are we going to afford all this? It must be a very generous legacy.'

'Trust me Georghe, it is.'

Knowing about the Pied Piper's computer and why the man had been so desperate to retrieve it, Jakiv looked slowly up towards Sonja's face. While Georghe continued to study the list, Jakiv gave Sonja's eyes a studied look, his eyes asking the question that was on his mind. Georghe did not notice the mutual nod of acknowledged understanding that passed between the others.

The cloud of depression seemed to disperse from Jakiv as he got to his feet and lightly tugged the list from Georghe's fingers. 'How we afford it is not our problem, Georghe. She's the boss, and if she says get it done, then let's get to it!'

Georghe joined in with Jakiv's enthusiasm. 'Five minutes ago we thought La Strada des Enfants would be out of business. Where do you have to go, Sonja?'

'I have found out where our orphans have been taken: Odessa. I am going to bring them back.' Her colleagues' expressions of shocked concern were very plain to see.

'Don't worry; I'm not so stupid as to go on my own. I have arranged professional help, lots of it.'

Jakiv stepped towards Sonja, opening his arms to embrace her, pulling her close so that he could whisper in her ear. 'I see Brock's philosophy is rubbing off. Now we can keep the promises we make, Sonja. Give him my best.'

'It's not Brock,' returned Sonja. 'He has done enough to help our cause and I can't expect him to do any more.'

Jakiv pulled back in surprise. 'Then who?' he asked.

'You remember Sergei?'

'Kiev?' Jakiv whistled. 'I would rather face the Pied Piper again than him.'

Georghe Enescu looked bewildered. 'What do you mean – Sergei? Who's he? And what about Kiev?'

Jakiv did not take his eyes off Sonja. 'You don't want to know, Georghe. Be careful, Sonja, promise?'

'I do promise; and I promise much more for the sake of Radu and Natalya,' said Sonja before reaching to clasp each of the men's extended hands, to form an embracing trio. 'I promise that La Strada des Enfants will no longer settle for being a voice battling bureaucracy. We will do whatever it takes! Our actions will make the difference.'

Within the hour, Sonja Brezvanje boarded the bus heading towards Izmail. From there she planned to take the train that circled the Black Sea bound for Odessa. Though she could now afford to fly, as the only scheduled flight took hours via Vienna, she considered it to be too costly in time. She had made her decision; she would delay the action no more.

When she arrived in Izmail she made another decision.

Ferguson's phone rang as soon as he was able to switch it on upon landing at Brussels. His voicemail informed him that Brock was flying directly to Odessa. In the message Brock had detailed his instructions. Ferguson called Honstrom to say he was on his way to Le Valdor Castle at Liège, and would report in within two hours. An hour later his taxi swept through the opening gates of the de Brouwer estate.

Periodically keeping an eye on the tumbling share price of BGR, the focus of Lefrington's attention was primarily on the monitor relaying the audio-visual details of the ICE investigator talking with Stephan de Brouwer.

'There's nothing further I can add, Matt. Paul had arranged his own car, we'd already said our goodbyes, and – well, we assumed he had gone directly to the airport.' Stephan reached for the glass of water on the table beside him.

'We?' enquired Ferguson.

Stephan paused to think. 'Myself and my fiancée's father, Conrad Lefrington.'

'Did you actually see him drive off?'

Stephan looked momentarily blank. 'Well, not exactly; I just assumed the car had arrived. This is a big property, as you see.'

'Is Mr Lefrington still here?'

'No; he had to leave soon after. I am here on my own now.'

'Interesting that they did not leave together,' said the Irishman.

It did not matter that Ferguson had been trained to recognize the signs that the man was lying, because Stephan de Brouwer was so uncomfortable about having to do so. Short of physical coercion, there was only one other option available to him: to look around.

'You're right, this is a big place. You could certainly get lost on your own, Stephan. It looks really impressive. Do you mind if I have a look around?'

Stephan de Brouwer was hesitant. 'OK, I'll show you myself.'

'Well, I have a few calls to make; do you mind if I just wander around on my own? I promise not to get lost.'

Stephan looked surprised. 'Do you usually ask to wander around people's homes?'

Ferguson leaned forward, his green eyes levelled at de Brouwer. 'No, Stephan, just when my boss inexplicably disappears. Surely you can't have an objection. You said you "assumed" he had gone to the airport; and in my book, "assume" spells "ass", "u" and "me". So I really would like to put my mind at rest.'

Stephan paused, uncertain – then looked at his guest and nodded. 'Yes, of course.' He stood up as Ferguson's phone rang. 'Excuse me, Matt; I'll let you take your call.'

Lefrington adjusted the monitoring levels of the ultra-sensitive microphone, enabling him to catch the whole conversation of the incoming call.

'Matt? It's Cassie Kaligirou here.'

'Hi, Cassie, what is it?'

'I can't get hold of Connor so I thought I would give you a call instead.'

'Yes,' said Ferguson, 'people seem to have a habit of doing that. So what did you want to tell Connor then?'

'No, I want to tell you too, Matt. It's just that Professor Amuyani and I are going to Romania. We've tracked Lysippos to Isaccea.'

'When are you going?'

'The professor insists there is no time like the present.'

'Now? Well, be careful, Cassie; you know what happened last time.'

'We will, and don't worry; we're not going anywhere near military bases. I read the signs all wrong. Anyway, I'll text you where we're staying.'

'OK, give the professor my best; oh, and that Lysippos fellow – when you see him, that is!' said Ferguson laughing.

Despite another major fall in the BGR share-price monitor, Lefrington stared transfixed at the monitor displaying Ferguson.

Forty-Five

S tretched out in the back of the bus Sonja had requested him to bring, Sergei Redofski slept for most of the 400 kilometre drive from Kiev to the north-west of Odessa, leaving the driving to the five men who accompanied him. He intuitively awoke when they were close to their destination.

Making his way to the front of the bus he had to stoop as the ceiling was too low for his two-metre solid frame. Sergei motioned for the driver to slow down as the former nineteenth-century summer home of a courtier of Imperial Russia, later used as a hospital until it was abandoned, came into view. Situated on the north-eastern terraces, close to the Dneister River, the neoclassical Italianate structure was enclosed by a recently built high wall that matched the residence's limestone construction.

'Pull off here,' Sergei said to the driver as they approached a convenient parking area. He pointed at one of his men to open one of the large food containers Sonja had also requested he acquire. 'We will wait here, and enjoy breakfast. I don't know about you but I could eat a horse!' he boomed.

The bright July morning sun was prevented from filling the enormous room by the heavy black drapes that covered the wide windows. Hristo Amaut, Ivan Karnovitch, Tereza Ditschec, Kim Seokhung and Remik Kostina were among the team of twelve people surrounding Simone de Brouwer's bed. An anaesthetist was preparing to administer the preoperative as Simone was issuing final instructions.

'With Gregor absent, I have requested Remik to take charge of my personal protection while I am here. He will have final say on everything – is that clearly understood, Hristo?'

268

'Fully understood, madam,' replied Amaut, trying not to show how uncomfortable he was as his authority was publicly usurped in front of his staff. He had got used to tolerating Goryachev, but this Bulgarian was another matter. 'Do you know when Gregor will be returning?' he enquired.

Simone looked at Kostina, who answered on her behalf. 'We have reason to believe he may have been permanently detained. When Madam returns home I will be leaving one of the team to head up security.'

'Will we return to Izmail in due course?' asked Tereza Ditschec hesitantly.

Simone settled a cold look on the gynaecologist before turning to the Korean doctor. 'You are fully prepared, Dr Seokhung? You will remove all the eggs while the blood, marrow and other organs are being removed?'

The Korean nodded in earnest. 'I can assure Madam that everything on my part will be effected perfectly.'

Simone turned her attention to another. 'And the candidate, Dr Karnovitch – you have confirmed that all organs are healthy, and you do not envisage encountering any problems?'

'All is in excellent order, madam, and with the simultaneous extraction and insertion I can assure you that there are no risks involved.'

When she was alone, and like anyone about to undergo an operation affecting one of their vital organs, Simone reflected on her life.

She fervently believed in the work that, following her addiction and later affliction, had absorbed her life. Longevity was a cause in itself. It was the next step in the evolution of the human species and anything, including disposing of her husband Simon, was justified by it.

Why he had been so morally misguided still shocked her. His way would have led to her death; it was simply a matter of survival of the fittest. Given it over again she would still have done the same. Faking her own death had brought her to the exciting edge that would propel her to the pinnacle of what she had sought – what she deserved to achieve.

Smiling contentedly she closed her eyes, allowing the preoperative anaesthetic to do its work.

* * *

'What made you change your mind about contacting me?' asked Brock as he drove the blue BMW X3 he had hired toward the north-west of Odessa.

'Because I remembered that the first time I saw you was entering and exiting the Izmail clinic. Later I recall how your visit there prompted you to relate how that trafficking was the tip of the iceberg. After you had risked your life to help me, I thought it wrong to hinder your investigation with my plans.'

Brock looked across at Sonja Brezvanje and grinned broadly. 'I thought it was just because you were missing me so much.'

The woman smiled back, her pale-blue eyes almost twinkling. 'I can't think why. You did not give me much reason to; as I recall, you fell asleep.'

'Well, I'm really glad you got in touch, because Matt and I were on our way here; but the fact that you had arranged support made me alter my plans.'

Sonja placed her hand on Brock's leg and squeezed playfully. 'And I thought it was just because you were missing me so much!'

Ten minutes later they became serious as they passed the high limestone walls of their destination. Two minutes later they saw a luxury travel coach parked at the side of the road, with a group of tough-looking men standing aimlessly around it, as if it had broken down.

After Sonja had been lifted off her feet and twirled around in a bearlike embrace, Brock's hand appeared small as it was shaken by Sergei's oversized paw. At one metre eighty-eight it was rare that he had to look up to someone's eyes. On this occasion he liked what he saw. Through the hard exterior of the battle-scarred face he recognized a man who lived by a certain set of principles, even if his practices might be questionable.

'I said any old bus would do!' said Sonja as she entered the air-conditioned coach with its airline-comfort seating and tables.

'Sonja, you only deserve the best!' exclaimed the grizzly Sergei. 'Is that not why you called me? Anyway, I told you I was legitimate. Well, this is one of the legitimate interests I am involved in – tourism!'

Over the thirty minutes, with every member of the coach crammed into the central facing seats around the tables, they discussed their forthcoming strategy.

'OK, Connor, I understand,' concluded Sergei, his gaze level. 'But I have to warn we only rescue young people. All other non-combatants will be considered collateral damage. I have lost too many men from alleged non-hostile collaborators. Only the children are innocent here.'

Brock nodded. 'I understand, but I will at least try and negotiate with Amaut if he is here. He is a key to my own investigation.'

Sergei pulled at his barbarous beard. 'As you wish.'

'And Sonja – she stays here.'

Sergei looked at the woman he knew from Kiev. 'As she wishes.'

Ditschec pointed the needle upwards before applying a little bit of pressure on the syringe. The liquid was forced out, expelling the air from the tube. She took hold of the little girl's right arm, located the vein and injected the preoperative anaesthetic. 'There, now that is all the pain you are going to feel, I promise you; and that little pinprick was nothing for a brave girl like you, was it?' Ditschec removed the needle from the girl's arm and discarded it with the syringe attached.

Anna was not convinced. She disliked being taken from the little room they had given her and the new doll she had made her friend. Her pretty dress had been taken away too and she had been told to put on a white apron that kept opening at the front. 'But that is the fourth needle!' she argued, suddenly beginning to feel tired. Why does everyone have to keep sticking pins into me?'

If Ditschec had once felt compassion, she could not remember. So far as she was concerned this was just another street urchin, though they had all been told to take particular care of this one. She could not reason why; for it was the end result for all the girls that she dealt with. 'Because you are very special; good, I see you are ready to go to sleep.'

Even though the room was white, Anna saw all the colours of the rainbow as her heavy eyelids began to close. She tried to speak, wanting to ask if the lady could see them too.

Ditschec motioned to the waiting orderlies, who expertly transferred the unconscious girl to a gurney before wheeling it swiftly down the corridor to the operating theatre.

* * *

The delivery van, opportunistically requisitioned by Sergei's team, pulled up to the heavy steel electronic gates and pressed the intercom, only to be refused entry. No deliveries whatsoever were allowed access today. The driver argued that he had got up before dawn to make this food delivery, after fresh fish had been demanded. After ranting for several minutes he opened the doors of his van and began angrily dumping the open polystyrene boxes he had supposedly been sent to deliver, directly beside the two stone gateposts. He shook his fist at the camera on top of the gatepost. Then, seemingly in a further fit of rage, he searched the area for a large stone before throwing it at the camera, successfully knocking it to one side. He got back in his vehicle, reversed into the road before driving back the way he had come. In its new position the camera was unable to monitor the persons who had exited the van.

Having been alerted by one of his security team as to what had transpired, Kostina immediately sent one of his men to investigate.

Standing in the observation enclosure on the first floor, Hristo Amaut was able to survey clearly the ground-floor operating theatre. A mass of green cloths and tubes almost covered from view the three patients on the operating tables. A separate anaesthetist sat at the head of each of the three females, patients who shared a blood type so rare that it made each of them one in a million. In the centre lay the eldest of the three patients. To her left lay the young woman she had brought with her. Amaut had neither been informed nor enquired as to why the young woman had not been chosen over the young girl to be the main donor.

He looked at the smallest of the three, lying to the right of his employer. The girl was currently surrounded by the largest team. As he watched the two almost simultaneous incisions, first into his employer's flesh and then into the girl's, Amaut closed his eyes tightly, regretting he had got to know and, indeed, like Anna – the optimistic little orphan who waited each day for her father, convinced he would soon collect her.

'Smells like fish,' reported the man sent to the gate. 'Yeah, it's fresh fish and a whole lot of it by the looks. The ice it's packed in is melting fast!'

Kostina made a decision. 'Bring it in – no point in letting our own food rot in this heat. I'll send Toruk to help you, and then we will open up. Don't forget to reposition the camera.'

The gates began to slide back as Toruk drove up in a black Volkswagen van to join his colleague. After turning around, he reversed the vehicle into the now fully open entrance to facilitate the loading. Swiftly they began lifting the boxes from the two posts. Concentrating on ensuring that no fish slipped out of the slushy polystyrene boxes, neither Toruk nor his colleague heard the dull coughs of the silenced Steyr semi-automatic pistols switched to single shot. Each of the bull-nosed lead bullets entered its target without exit, as intended.

Brock, arriving with the rest of the team, under the cover of the VW that blocked the entrance, nodded briefly at the two killers' cold efficiency. Quickly he stripped the jacket off one of the dead bodies and slipped it on as the corpses were both loaded into the van with the fish and the rest of Sergei's team. Brock climbed up on the gate and repositioned the camera before getting into the van. Already inside the zone his special operations training had taught him to enter, he mentally ticked the success; the whole team were inside the perimeter with two hostiles down. The gates closed behind them.

Though he was not medically trained, Amaut had learned enough to know how to recognize a diseased liver. He knew that, as the body's biggest organ, it can be as much as 80 per cent destroyed and still function. At such a point it was beyond recuperation and transplantation was the only viable alternative, the only other outcome being death within weeks, possibly days. The colour of the older woman's liver was not a healthy deep purple-red; it was a ravaged grey sallow red.

Karnovitch had miscalculated the extent of disease. The woman began to haemorrhage quicker than anticipated. Additional blood was required. He nodded to his colleague to commence blood transfusion from the patient to his left: Sophia Lefrington.

Forty-Six

B rock drove slowly, following the gravel road round to the rear of the premises in the assumption that both men and fish would be expected at the kitchens. He parked the van close to what appeared to be the rear entrance, adjacent to a black metal fire escape. Brock was about to get out when the rear doors of the jeep burst open.

Sergei, remarkably agile despite his bulk, charged towards the kitchens with a loud battle cry, his earlier bonhomie having undergone a bizarre metamorphosis to crazed beast.

The face of a man appearing at the open double doors was a mixture of confusion and shocked surprise as he instantaneously took in the spectre of a grizzly bear-like human bearing down on him with a Heckler and Koch automatic pistol in each of his giant paws. A split second later the surprised man was falling to the floor, his body riddled with eight bullets from head to groin. Pushing him aside, Sergei crashed into the large open kitchen area, his fingers tight on both triggers.

As bullets flayed through the air in a lethal maelstrom, two of the occupants dived to the floor, immediately returning fire. Like a lion intent on tearing the throat out of its prey, Sergei threw himself at them, focusing the last remnants of his pistol's magazines at them, killing them instantly.

Of the five other occupants in the room, two were already on the floor — one dead, one wounded. One had fled and the remaining two were now returning fire haphazardly, bullets successfully hitting the invader. A second later they were distracted by three more hardened killers charging at them with weapons blazing.

Kostina, about to join Amaut in the observation room, had halted in mid-stride upon hearing the first outburst of rapid gunfire.

Instantly he had turned on his heel and thundered down the wide staircase that led from the first floor to the central front entrance hall, spiriting an automatic Glock pistol from a shoulder holster as he did so. He bellowed instructions at the five men standing there, each carrying a machine pistol. Two raced off to guard the operating theatre as Kostina swept towards the lower stairwell leading down to the kitchens like a killer bullshark, his personal armed ramora parasites sticking close to his side.

Tereza Ditschec waited, ready to commence her own work as soon as her surgeon colleague gave her the go-ahead. Dr Seokhung stood in observation of Ditschec's extraction of the girl's Fallopian tubes, womb and uterus. Karnovitch, having finally stemmed the haemorrhaging of his primary patient and prepared her body for organ insertion, moved towards his secondary patient to begin removal of the donor liver.

The crescendo of firing caused everyone in the theatre to instantly freeze, nervously looking from one to the other in mutual consternation. In unspoken unison they looked up towards the first-floor observation window in anticipation of receiving some informative signal from Hristo Amaut. The director general stared back at them, his face a picture of confused alarm. He stood momentarily transfixed, before turning and rushing out of the observation room.

Brock, followed closely by two of Sergei's team, sped up the fire escape to the first floor. The half-glazed door was locked from the inside. Stretching up his arms he grabbed at the protective balustrade that continued above him to the next level. Swinging his body he kicked at the door with the full force of his legs. The door flew open with a crash, though barely audible with the continuing cacophony of gunfire below.

Brock raced along the corridor, noticing a man hastily exiting a room at the end of a wide staircase. Both men instantly recognized each other.

As Brock gave chase and his team followed he was unaware that another person had tagged on to his team; Sonja Brezvanje was determined to locate the stolen orphans before they were hurt in crossfire.

*   *   *

275

Karnovitch's eyes, vividly wide above his surgical mask, searched his colleagues' questioningly. 'What is going on, Tereza? What should we do?' he exclaimed, his hands still poised above the exposed liver to be transplanted.

'It is not our problem. Let that fool Amaut handle it. This is our problem. Damn it, Ivan! We are in the middle of a life-threatening operation on our employer. If she dies, that's us finished. Don't you realize that Kostina will kill us? We have no choice but to continue with the operation!'

Karnovitch looked at Seokhung, who nodded, confirming the same answer his eyes gave. Karnovitch nodded, carefully placing one hand to the side of the organ, while holding his other palm upwards to receive the surgical clips required to stem the arterial flow after he had commenced cutting for extraction.

Amaut ran down the steps, knowing Brock was hard on his heels. In frightened desperation he ran towards the operating theatre, rationalizing that there was safety in numbers. He was brought to a halt by two armed men in front of the double doors. Holding his arms high, the director general shouted a warning, unaware that the instructions Kostina had given them moments before had been explicit.

Amaut felt his legs give way and he crumpled to his knees, sliding to a stop. Dumbly he gazed at the spots of blood that appeared on his white shirt around his navel. The man who had shot him momentarily stood bolt upright before being sent crashing through the double doors behind him, a gaping wound in his chest.

Brock swerved at full pelt to avoid the raking onslaught of bullets that the remaining guard directed in a sweeping movement towards the shooter who had killed his colleague. Brock heard the grunt of one of his team behind him before diving headlong at the surviving guard, his outstretched arm shooting. Brock's bullets tore the man's throat out a split second before he rammed into the crumpling guard. Crashing through the operating theatre, he rolled over and was back on his feet in a split second. There was a time-stopping pause before most of the surgical team screamed and fled to the side of the room. Karnovitch stood transfixed, a scalpel poised in his right hand.

'Stop!' shouted Ditschec. 'We are operating! You must stop!'
Another time-stopping pause.

Brock's voice was granite as he spoke. 'Quiet! And don't move! Not a muscle. Not yet! I know all about the kind of operations you specialize in!' Without taking his eyes off the three surgeons, who had remained in their positions, he instructed his remaining team member to cover him as he assessed the situation.

Kostina met with unexpected ferocity when he reached the kitchen area. He saw the head of the man on his right take a bullet, snapping it back, as his own weapon simultaneously downed the shooter. A second later they were back on the stairwell in forced retreat.

He leaned against the wall, confused. Simone had insisted that he come to Odessa after she had been unable to make contact with Goryachev; but he had not expected to be involved in a mini-war. Simone and Konrad had not told him everything; why the hell should ICE be involved with him and why did this Brock, whom Amaut, as well as Simone and Konrad, had warned him of, have some sort of vendetta against their operation? What difference could it make to him?

Hearing gunfire above him, Kostina instructed his remaining men to not let anyone pass, while he went to the aid of his employer. He had to protect Simone; he knew that too much was at stake for them to lose her. Crossing into the long corridor from the entrance hall, he saw a woman quickly going from door to door, looking for something. Silently he paced towards her. As if sensing his presence, she turned back and their eyes met, prompting them both to look at each other in shocked recognition.

Brock looked at the face of the patient closest to the three surgeons. It was the face of a young girl, no more than ten years old. He looked hard at Karnovitch. 'Have you removed anything?'

Karnovitch shook his head, slowly.

'Is she ill? Dying?'

The surgeon shook his head again.

Brock reached up and removed the scalpel from Karnovitch's hand, before moving to the head of the centre table. He looked at the face of the woman. Though her skin was firm, under the operating light she looked in her early sixties.

'Have you removed anything?'

Karnovitch nodded.

'What, you son of a bitch?'

'The liver,' said the surgeon, tilting his head to the ravaged organ still lying in the silver bowl at the adjoining table. Brock quickly glanced at it. 'You were about to replace it with this child's liver?'

Karnovitch nodded.

Brock moved to the third table. 'And this one; another organ?'

Karnovitch shook his head. 'Transfusion,' he said, adding, 'for her,' when he saw Brock's enquiring look. 'All three carry a rare blood type,' he said, pointing at Simone. 'She needed it for the transplant.'

Brock looked down and stared at the face of the young woman for a full five seconds, completely disoriented at what he saw.

A short burst of gunfire felled the man covering Brock.

'And we are going to let them continue with the transplant!' Kostina shouted from the doorway, his arm held tightly around the neck of Sonja Brezvanje. 'Drop your gun and move back!'

Kostina walked into the room dragging Sonja in an armlock alongside.

Another burst of gunfire resounded through the house. Brock held the other's gaze, the man Mira Luga had pointed out to him as the founder of her club. 'No, Remik. No deal.'

Kostina looked momentarily surprised. 'How do you know me?'

'The Grim Reaper always knows the names of those he comes for.'

'Are you Brock? Listen to me, Brock, or whoever you are, we have enough dead between us today. Why do you want to die? Drop the gun now or I will kill this girl in front of you now, and then you! As for what is going on in here, this team is trying to save a life. What difference does it make to you?'

Brock looked at Sonja; their eyes locked. He had never seen her look so defiant. 'It makes a difference,' he said, slowly lowering his gun and pointing it directly at the head of the middle patient in front of him. 'What about you?'

The look of satisfaction on Kostina's face visibly altered to abject panic at Brock's unexpected action. 'Wait!' he shouted. 'What point is there in killing that woman?'

'Because it makes a difference to a little girl's life,' Brock said looking at Sonja.

'Then we have an impasse,' replied Kostina. 'One which I am sure can be overcome with the payment of a large—'

Kostina's head jerked. Amaut, his torso a blanket of blood, was still kneeling in the doorway, the weapon he had just fired resting between his knees. Sonja, freed from the Crocodile's grip, actually turned on him, blocking Brock's line of fire. In an almost demonic fury she tried to kick out hard at her aggressor's genitals before being pushed roughly away.

The Crocodile lurched to the outside of the room, firing at Brock. A bullet caught Tereza Ditschec directly in the face as she desperately tried to get out of the line of fire; the back of her head exploded in a crimson cloud as the sharp-nosed metal projectile exited. Brock stopped himself from following as he heard Sonja shriek over the screams of the nurses. Turning swiftly around he saw her standing at the head of the end patient.

Brock shouted for silence before raising his gun at Karnovitch, while pointing at the patient to the surgeon's right with his free hand. 'Fix up this little girl now, and you live, understand? If she dies, so do you.'

Karnovitch nodded, motioning to Seokhung to take over from the nurses that were still cowering in the corner of the room.

Brock shouted at them while pointing at the end patient where Sonja stood. 'And you! Attend to that patient now! Then attend to that man,' he added, pointing at Amaut. 'Now get to it! Move!' The anaesthetists and nurses scurried to take up their stations.

Brock went over to put his arm around Sonja's shoulder as she continued to stare down at the deathly pale face of the young woman before her. The anaesthetist who had hurried over shook his head as though any action he did would be too late. Removing the oxygen mask fully revealed the stunning resemblance that was plain to see.

Silent tears coursed down Sonja's cheeks while she gently stroked the woman's hair, her own hand visibly shaking. She looked up into Brock's eyes. 'It's my sister, Connor; it's my little sister.'

Forty-Seven

Amuyani removed his battered panama hat and used it to fan his face. 'This is hotter than I remember even Tehran used to be; trouble is, I have got used to air-conditioned lecture halls – must be years since I have been on a field trip.'

'It's more interesting, and fun too!' Cassie replied as they made their way through Isaccea towards the two-thousand-year-old Roman ruins of Noviodunum at the top of the small town. 'Everything is so much different in reality. Take this town. Hard to believe this was once a major Roman strategic outpost.'

'And now it just has a population of a few thousand, but the heavy floods of the last ten years mean it's no longer a fording place.'

'That's what worries me, Professor, after the dykes were destroyed by the floods last year many of the areas that my grandfather mentioned might now be inundated.'

With a mock severity Amuyani looked at the young woman with whom he had spent the last twenty-four hours. 'Now then, Cassie, that does not sound like you. We're here, are we not? We are crossing each bridge as we get to it, are we not? Forget the floods; once we have the signs we will be home and dry, as the saying goes.'

Cassie punched the old man playfully on the arm. She had already begun to treat him like the grandfather she had never had. 'You're right, Professor, come on – race you to the top!'

Brock looked at one of the men lying among the carnage of the kitchen floor, the man's white cooking apron red with blood. 'Collateral damage?'

In answer Sergei roughly kicked the man over on to his stomach; the apron separated, revealing a weapon.

'Yours is an unusual strategy, Sergei' said Brock without emotion.

'So I have been told before, but it works for me.'

'You OK? I heard you were hit.'

'I am crazy, but not stupid, Connor.' He pulled open his jacket. 'Specially designed body armour, Russian-made of course, light and protective – well, let me put it this way: I don't notice the extra weight.'

'You risked your life and those of your men for something you confessed to me earlier held no concern for you.'

'Connor, I risked my life for Sonja. Whatever I do, my men follow; they are loyal.'

Brock held out his hand. 'Glad we're on the same side, Sergei.'

The big man smiled as he shook it. 'Like you, Connor, I do what I have to do.'

Sonja did not leave the side of her sister, anxiously watching the colour slowly restored to the pallid skin as the transfusion was reversed.

As for the older woman, other than removing her from the incremental anaesthetic, none of the surgical team paid her any attention. For a brief moment she regained the lucidity of consciousness. Being the closest person to her, Sonja noticed the flickering eyes open, the mouth trying to form words, and moved closer.

Simone de Brouwer's eyes flickered recognition. 'Sophia, is it finished?'

Sonja turn to glance at the anaesthetist as he finally removed the tubes from her sister's arm, before lowering her lips near to the woman's ear. 'Yes,' she said. 'It is finished.'

'You're lucky to be alive,' said Brock as he entered the room and walked up to the bed.

Amaut raised his bushy eyebrows. 'Choice, Mr Brock. If I had not killed Kostina, I would have bled to death.'

'Let us hope that he does too.'

'He still lives?'

'He got away,' replied Brock flatly.

Amaut squeezed his eyes tightly shut. 'Why? How?'

282

'We were busy, but I have not come here to talk about Kostina.'

'I don't imagine you have,' offered the director general resignedly.

Brock removed a photograph from his pocket. 'I want to talk about the man Kostina is with. You recognize him?'

Amaut nodded.

'Conrad Lefrington,' said Brock, more in statement than question.

Amaut nodded.

Brock pulled up a chair. 'I'm listening,' he said. 'Start at the beginning. Tell me everything.'

'Is she dead?'

Brock nodded. 'The woman wanting a new liver – yes, she is dead,' he said.

'She was my employer,' began Amaut.

DONAUESCHINGEN

With two days' growth of silver stubble, and eyes appearing almost bruised blue-black from lack of sleep, Professor William Steinwright looked more like an ageing junkie than an esteemed academic.

Earlier in the day he had received the announcement that the trustees acting for the Duisen Foundation had been forced to liquidate their shareholding. Now that the capitalized value of BioGenomics Research had dropped by as much as 90 per cent, the market anticipated that survival relied solely on a white knight coming to the rescue. The media, however, having got wind that there could be a criminal investigation forthcoming, thought this to be highly unlikely.

For two days Steinwright, with the support of Carl Honstrom and his team, and Dr Jon Su-Yeong, had undertaken a thorough investigation. They had discovered that since their inception over half of their embryonic supplies had come from a series of companies ultimately owned by De Brouwer Research. This had risen to almost 100 per cent in the last six months, which Su-Yeong believed coincided with the time period during which contamination had been introduced.

'The six-month period ties in with the order date for drugs from Giramonte Pharma,' agreed Honstrom.

'Which is also the time when my errant colleague, Kim Seokhung joined us,' offered Su-Yeong. 'If you remember, he insisted on being involved in overseeing our embryonic supplies, as he considered them currently insufficient for his work.'

'Does anyone know where the hell he is?' Steinwright asked.

'I think we must assume that he forged the signatures,' said Honstrom. 'He had access to your offices and the boardroom; there are enough minutes of meetings recorded, so it's hardly a difficult task. As to what his motives were or how he facilitated payment, that is confusing.'

'To bloody well destroy the company, that's why, Carl, damn it!'

'But he's a scientist, William, not a corporate raider,' Honstrom replied. 'What could possibly be his motive, and anyway, you're forgetting the money involved in the purchase of the drug. There has to be someone else behind it.'

Steinwright slammed his fist on to his desk. 'Which is what Paul believed, and now he's vanished along with Seokhung!'

Honstrom raised his hand as his cellphone emitted a shrill tone from his shirt pocket. 'Connor! Where the hell are you?' he shouted before he fell silent and focused on listening.

Five minutes later the call ended and he turned to the others' expectant faces, slowly returning his phone to his pocket.

Steinwright could not contain himself. 'What the hell is it, Carl?'

'It would appear that our very own Simone de Brouwer has been our Nemesis. She apparently faked her own death.'

'Simone, alive?'

'Well, she's dead now,' shrugged Honstrom. 'But it was her clinics that supplied us with all our contaminated supplies, which according to Sophia Lefrington was intended to bring BGR down, incriminating ICE at the same time.'

'But why? What on earth would be the point?'

'A very simple idea, in essence, apparently – one that would allow Simone, with a partner acting as a white knight, to take full control of BGR. Then subsequently make an announcement that would rally the shares following the acquisition.'

Steinwright's face was florid. 'Who? The white knight – who is it?'

'According to Sophia it is her father.'

284

'Conrad Lefrington!'

Honstrom nodded. 'It seems that Paul, having investigated Lefrington's background, had intuitive doubts about the man. He asked Connor to seek tangible evidence that would confirm his suspicions.'

'Well, it seems that Connor has it now!' boomed Steinwright. 'We can be exonerated.'

'Unfortunately he doesn't, William. From what Connor has told me, the evidence will be at best treated as circumstantial. It would seem that nothing directly links Lefrington to any wrongdoing, particularly with BGR. Indeed, there is more evidence against you and Paul.'

Steinwright's face had returned to a sickly pallor. 'But what about his daughter!'

'His word against hers – not that the courts are really interested in family disputes; and how long will that take anyway?'

'Too long,' said Steinwright morosely. 'It would be too late for us. Lefrington will take over, and I will be under arrest. As for ICE, Carl – well, without Paul, the media will most certainly implicate us.'

LIÈGE, BELGIUM

Stephan's hands visibly shook as he placed his phone down on his dead father's desk. He then repeatedly shook his head slowly in disbelief at what his fiancée had just told him.

To learn that his new aunt, Solange, was actually his mother, Simone, and not a twin, was one thing. To learn that she had arranged to fake her death and murder his father, and then had been prepared to take the blood of the woman he loved, was too much. The emotions of shock, anger and grief culminated in an ascending scream of desolate rage and brought two members of staff running, who were immediately thrown out of the study.

Ferguson, finishing his third tour of the house, had his ear to the phone in the frail hope that in calling van Lederman's own cellphone he would hear it ringing. Reaching Stephan's office he found it in total disarray, the man himself sitting on the floor, his head in his hands.

Ten minutes later, Stephan led Ferguson to a concealed lift

shaft and the lower-level rooms it accessed. Paul van Lederman still lay motionless.

While Ferguson checked his employer's vital signs, Stephan's mind continued to churn with questions. Sophia's father must have known; but far more importantly, if what she had told him was correct, how could he allow the daughter whom he claimed to love so much to risk her life?

Stephan banged his fist on the door of the adjoining room, then, in receiving no answer, proceeded to try to break it down. After two attempts he went back into the room where Ferguson and van Lederman were and lifted up one of the heavy chairs. As Ferguson turned to see what was happening, Stephan threw the chair against the large wall mirror, smashing it to pieces.

Without comment, Ferguson got up from the bed and helped Stephan knock out the remaining glass. Both men stepped through the opened partition. Apart from the image of a news reporter on a television screen confirming that the share price of BGR had bottomed out, the room was empty.

Forty-Eight

Perched on a stone step among the ruins of the fortress of Noviodunum, Amuyani placed his Blackberry into his pocket and turned back to the page that had been taped into Andreus Kaligirou's journal. It was a sketch made during the archaeologist's visit to the Louvre over thirty years earlier, detailing a marble statue of a winged female holding a wheel. Below were the words: 'Nemesis dedicated by Ptollanubis 2nd Century; found in Egypt'. To the side of the sketch a poem had been put down: 'Hymn to Nemesis' by Mesomedes, with the first and last lines heavily underlined. Scribbled in the margin was the word 'Guardians'.

He called out to the young woman busy looking for signs that matched something in her grandfather's journal, motioning for her to join him as she raised her head. 'Cassie, there are two lines of this poem underlined: the first and the last. The first line takes the underline to the wheel the statue is holding; and the last line takes the underline to the word "Guardians"; I think I have an idea.'

Cassie dusted her hands off. 'What?'

'Well, your grandfather's journal is in two parts, relating to either before fourth century BC, the time of Lysippos, or from the Fourth Crusade.'

'I know, but that's because those are the two events that he was investigating,' said Cassie.

Amuyani pushed his panama hat to the back of his head. 'Then there must be a good reason that he inserted these pages.'

'And your idea?'

'Well, I know this statue. I live in Paris and have seen it in the Greek, Etruscan and Roman rooms on the ground floor of the Louvre. I also know that Mesomedes was the Roman Emperor Hadrian's poet. Both are from the second century AD.'

Cassie shrugged. 'But they also both relate to Nemesis, or Adrasteia, who he seemed to be obsessed with. That could be the reason.'

'But he wasn't, Cassie; he was obsessed with finding long-lost Greek art stolen in the thirteenth century, including the famed Lysippos. Remember, it was your father who wanted you named after the Lysippos statue he claimed would make them rich. So why are we directed to Hadrian?'

Cassie crossed her arms, 'OK, tell me.'

'Well, Cassie, where we are standing is on the grounds of a Roman hilltop fort.'

'I can see that. To look for any sign my grandfather may have left. So, are you saying that the fort that used to be here was built during Hadrian's rule?'

'Well I was about to, quite so. Hadrian was one of the good emperors, who sought to maintain peace through fortifying his empire with walls and forts, including the Danube frontier. And indeed such fortifications became his legacy; but what is not so common knowledge about him is that he died childless—'

'A barren ruler!' interrupted Cassie. 'So this is the right starting point!'

Amuyani held up the journal. 'Now then, this last line of the poem that Andreus underlined: "down into Tartarus", along with the word he jotted down, "Guardians". Let us consider that for a moment. You will recall that I tried to apply Homeric thinking to your grandfather's words, "Lysippos sleeps", meaning that he is hidden underground, as a warrior who sleeps in Hades.'

Cassie nodded.

'Well, in Homer's *Iliad*, Zeus asserts that Tartarus is as far beneath Hades as heaven is high above earth. Of course, Tartarus was supposed to be much bigger than Hades, which was for the dead. Tartarus held prisoners, guarded by three giants, each with one hundred arms.'

Cassie shook her head, 'I'm sorry, Professor, you're losing me. What does all that signify?'

Amuyani looked surprised. 'Well, isn't it obvious? We are looking for a cavern under a cave.'

Cassie put her arms on the old man's shoulders. 'My dear Professor, we still have to find a cave.'

Amuyani stood up. 'Haven't you been listening? Don't you

remember your own mythology? Look!' he said pointing. 'The cave we are looking for must be right over there! The journal has already told us to follow the signs!'

The young Greek archaeologist looked into the distance at the Macin mountain range, the oldest in Romania. She had been so intent on detail she had not seen the beauty of the big picture. The Northern Dobrugea Plateau stretched from the great Danube River, rising to a peak of almost 500 metres, the whole province interlaced with lagoons, fed from underground channels of the Casimcea and Taita Rivers, which meandered through the country. The lowering afternoon sun in the west bathed the vista in a myriad colours, its fauna and flora containing Mediterranean species indigenous to the region, which was much milder than the rest of Romania. Viewed from the river the range had looked like mountains, yet from the fort ruins they now appeared more like small hills. Amuyani was pointing at three almost uniform hillocks about 400 metres in the distance. Each hillock was covered by an outcrop of protruding rocks, some at least three metres or more in length. 'The Hecantonchires,' she said to herself out loud.

'Exactly!' shouted Amuyani. 'The guardians of Tartarus – "where the barren ruler is shaded in the lee of a fortress", to quote Andreus.'

'We still have to locate the entrance.'

'Then, Cassie, we will continue to follow the signs,' he said confidently.

'You're a genius, Professor. How can you remember so much?'

Amuyani shot her a sheepish glance as he removed his Blackberry from his pocket. 'Well, I admit to having a little help from Izanami,' he said, 'though I had to prompt her of course.'

'You're still a genius!' shouted Cassie, jumping up and down and clasping both his hands in hers. A moment later she was skipping him around in a circle, blissfully unaware that their joyful antics were being watched.

Three executive jets were in the air. The de Brouwers Citation X that had earlier returned to Liège airport was once more en route to Odessa with Ferguson and Stephan de Brouwer on board. Carl Honstrom was on board the ICE Learjet 60, returning to Zurich with van Lederman under the supervision of three medical specialists. A Gulfstream IV, designed to take off from short runways yet capable of intercontinental flight, carried Conrad Lefrington to Berlin for an arranged press conference.

Even before the BGR share price had bottomed out, Lefrington had already secretly executed the option held with the Duisen Foundation and, with Simone's proxy, which Leon Werner had ratified, he would have control of the de Brouwer shares too, declaring to the market that a white knight had been found.

The fact that he had not heard from Simone, Remik or even Sophia did not unduly concern him. After the initial shock of hearing from Berlin about an unexpected visitor called Brock who had taken a photograph, he had settled down to the fact that everyone knew what was expected of them. There was no way his two long-term partners would allow Brock to get the better of them and even if they did, he had taken great care to cover his own tracks.

Lefrington sipped at the glass of Cristal champagne his steward unobtrusively placed in front of him. Yes, he was untouchable, and by the end of the day after tomorrow, he would no longer need his former partners, he would be on his way back to the US, one of the richest and most powerful men in the world.

ODESSA

Sonja spoke with each of the thirty-five girls they had located in locked wards on the second floor of the clinic. Aged between ten and thirteen, almost all of them were from Romanian orphanages. Each had been kept slightly sedated since her arrival.

'There are fewer than I imagined,' said Sonja as they boarded them on to the coach. 'We counted almost two hundred at Belgrade. Where are all the older children, and the pregnant ones?'

Brock had already learned their fate from Amaut. 'Thirty-five is a success, Sonja. And you've destroyed the network.'

'Kostina got away,' she replied coldly.

'You've still destroyed the network. If he lives then . . .'

'Then I will destroy him too,' she interrupted. 'Thanks to you, I now have the means.' Brock looked at the woman questioningly.

290

'That's good, Sonja, but use them wisely, not just for vengeance and retribution.'

'That man was the monster Georghe witnessed strangle an innocent girl in cold blood. And he is indirectly responsible for Natalya's death. He is responsible for all this!'

Brock stayed silent.

'Connor, I knew him! He raped me when I was thirteen! He was the one who took my sister away,' cried Sonja. 'He was the one who threatened to kill her if I did not work for him. And then told me she had died on the streets herself anyway. Almost fifteen years and he is still wreaking misery and killing. Fifteen years! How many have died? Why should I not wreak vengeance and retribution? If it was your sister or daughter, you would. I know you would! You have already proved to me you live by your own rules.'

'Yes, I do what I feel I must do. What I feel to be right. And you must do what you feel you must too, Sonja, but it seems to me your life has gone full circle. You have a family again, your sister and already thirty-five dependents. You have been given the means to build, not destroy; to do what is right; to make a difference.'

Sonja held Brock's gaze before moving quickly towards him, burying her face into his chest as she wound her arms tightly around him. Slowly he raised his arms to gently stroke her hair. A minute later she pulled away. 'My sister enjoyed meeting you; we owe you a lot.'

'It is good you have found each other. The pain and shock of what she has been through and discovering things about her father—'

'You mean the man Kostina gave her to. She was not just sold; she told me she was chosen for her blood. She overheard Kostina and Simone de Brouwer talking about her, thought she was dreaming. She believes the man adopted her to keep her close to Stephan's mother. They must have been lovers or partners.'

Brock removed the photo from his pocket and passed it to Sonja. 'Perhaps she's right; Kostina and Lefrington perhaps were partners too, that picture must be ten years old. One of the women works in Berlin for Kostina, the other is—'

'Simone de Brouwer.'

Brock spoke quietly. 'Tough on your sister . . .'

'You know what? I believe she is even tougher than me, Connor,' added Sonja, passing the photo back.

Brock grinned seeking to lighten the tension of the conversation and pending farewell. 'Someone tougher than you! That is just not possible! You scare me – even Sergei, though he won't admit it. You are the most tenacious, tough, resolute and infuriatingly beautiful woman I have ever met!'

Sonja walked towards the coach, turned and smiled ruefully as she boarded the first step. 'My sister and I have great plans you know, Connor. We must share them with you. Why not travel with me and Sergei to Bucharest?'

Brock moved swiftly towards her and kissed her on both cheeks. Sonja put her hands up to his face and returned the kiss on his lips. 'Please?'

Brock shook his head, 'There are things I still must do, Sonja.'

As the coach departed, Brock looked at the photo again. It seemed clearer in the daylight. There was something about Lefrington he hadn't noticed before. He had recognized the man from the image Paul van Lederman had passed him in Zurich, when he had shared his intuitive concerns about the man. But now there was something else, something familiar.

Ferguson returned from transporting Stephan de Brouwer and his fiancée from the clinic to Odessa airport, gently landing for a second time on the grounds of the former imperial summer home. The Irishman sat in the Bell Jet Ranger he had hired at the airport, keeping the single turbine turning while he waited. A few minutes later Brock exited the building and ran toward the helicopter keeping his head low.

'Much to clear up?' enquired Ferguson through his headset as he guided the Bell to rise at a steep angle towards the Dniester River.

Brock repositioned his own headset comfortably as he looked down at the vehicles making their approach, their wailing sirens carrying through the air. 'There will be,' he replied.

'Good of someone to make an anonymous tip-off to the authorities.'

'Contract killings are rife here,' offered Brock. 'Now, what the hell are that Kaligirou woman and Ahmed Amuyani doing?

Why did you let them go off on their own? If anyone is going to wind up in trouble with the authorities, those two are.'

Ferguson sniffed the air around Brock. 'Can you smell fish?'

Brock sniffed at his jacket, thinking that how he smelt was the least of his problems. 'Well, it's been a long day,' he replied curtly.

'Well, Connor, we have a whole sixty minutes before we arrive at Isaccea. Tell me about it,' offered Ferguson, seizing the opportunity to initiate a mutually beneficial debriefing.

Brock surveyed the graduated terraces of the Ukrainian port 2,000 metres below, watching how they seemed to abruptly truncate as they met the vast expanse of the Black Sea. As Ferguson veered toward the coastline following a route that would take them over the Danube delta and over Izmail, he thought of when he had first met Sonja Brezvanje.

'We made a difference,' he began.

Forty-Nine

Cassie found it first – a small gap on the second hillock about a third of the way up. An outcrop of rock that possibly centuries ago had been forced to defer to the greater strength of gravity, due to the hollowness within its foundation. Though the entrance was not clearly evident, inside the small cave was clear evidence of human visitation with an array of signs that modern man was intent on leaving, including beer bottles, cans and cigarette butts and packets.

Removing their powerful field torches from their backpacks they searched the cave before sitting down with their backs against the cave wall looking at each other.

'There must be another, Professor. This cannot possibly be it. Look at the mess in here!'

'Then we are not looking closely enough, because why otherwise would Andreus direct us here?'

'OK, let's do it again!' Cassie got up to search millimetre by millimetre while Amuyani opened the journal. 'Applying your grandfather's classical thinking we can't expect to just stumble upon it, though; as I have said before, it is beyond me how he located it himself. But the last line of the poem led us to the first cave; so perhaps the first line will lead us to the cavern. Otherwise why would he mark the poem so?'

Cassie turned back, shining the torch directly into Amuyani's face. 'The poem starts with "winged balancer of life" and the line goes into the wheel – I know it by heart,' said Cassie. 'We must look for a wheel somewhere or something that . . .'

'Acts as a fulcrum in a natural balance which only moves in a certain way. Why don't we . . .' Amuyani paused as his phone began to ring.

'Connor, *mon ami*!' he said as soon as he heard Brock's voice. 'How wonderful to hear from you; your timing is once again, perfect. How do you do that?'

'Don't try and placate me, Professor. Where the hell are you?'

'Not hell but Hades actually; high above Tartarus.'

'What? Listen, Ahmed; Matt and I have just landed at Isaccea.'

Amuyani looked at his watch. 'My goodness, it's time for tea, I had forgotten how hungry I was. We'll meet you at our hotel, the Romania, in about thirty minutes. We will fill you in with all our news.'

After a couple of glasses of malt whisky, followed by a steak dinner and wine, which the four of them enjoyed together, Brock felt more relaxed. 'Well, I admit, Professor, your perceptive thinking seems to be working.'

'Simply following the signs, my dear Connor; as I have always said, follow the signs.'

'I thought you always said follow the motives,' said Brock playfully.

'Same meat, different gravy, though it still aids the digestion process, eh? A process of elimination, you could say, eh? Every sign indicates a motive, and every motive leaves a sign.'

'Talking of which, Cassie, do you have the photo you showed me before, the one of your grandfather and father holding the Lysippos?'

'Yes, Connor, just a minute,' she said reaching into the small bag fastened around her waist, taking out the photo.

Brock looked at the photo, removing the one he carried a few moments later. He passed them both to Ferguson. 'What do you think, Matt?' he asked.

'Could be the guy's father; certainly looks like him.'

'Except that Cassie's photo is about twenty years older.'

Matt studied the faces closely. 'Well, if I had to make a bet, I would not make it a large one; but I would bet.'

'What?' demanded Cassie, looking perplexed. 'Let me see what you are looking at.'

Ferguson passed both photographs over.

Cassie studied them, her look of consternation slowly giving way to shock. 'That man in your picture looks like the man standing next to my father.'

295

Amuyani took the photos and studied them. 'The hair might be grey but the crown of the head still causes unevenness to the left. The corner of the left eye also bears an idiosyncrasy. I would make the bet.'

'How did you get this, Connor? Who is this man?'

'A very wealthy and influential man, apparently.'

The colour drained from Cassie's face. 'What do you mean, very wealthy – how?'

'According to Paul van Lederman, his name is Conrad Lefrington, a first-generation Swiss-American, having moved to the US fifteen years ago with his nine-year-old adopted daughter after a successful career in a variety of import and export businesses. The interesting question, which Paul's research raised, was that prior to 1976 no record of his name appears. It was not until I looked at his image in a different light that I felt I had seen him elsewhere; then I remembered your photo, Cassie.'

'But he must know something about the Lysippos! If my father and grandfather disappeared, then how did the Boxer of Thermon get sold to that collector?'

Brock leaned his elbows on the table. 'Well, based on what I have recently learned and keeping to the motives and signs, as our good professor keeps advocating, I would say the man could know something about your father's and grandfather's disappearance.'

'You mean he killed them!' shouted Cassie, causing other diners to look up from their tables.

Brock paused to allow their neighbours to return to their own conversations. 'Before we jump to conclusions, why don't we focus on following the signs? What do you think?'

'Excellent idea, *mon ami*!'

'Sounds good to me,' added Ferguson.

Brock looked across at Cassie, who continued to study the photographs, biting her lip hard as tears silently trickled down her face. 'Matt, can you sort out what the professor thinks we need,' he said quietly. 'We'll leave at dawn.'

Brock leaned over to the woman as the others diplomatically left the table. None of them noticed the table of four diners across the room that continued to surreptitiously observe them.

* * *

Kostina reached Berlin just after midnight. The wound he had sustained had broken his arm and the people he knew in Odessa had welcomed the opportunity to assist him, knowing that the Crocodile would be in their debt. Mira Luga had rushed out to him as soon as he arrived and led him to the private rooms on the first floor.

Lefrington put down his phone. He then returned to finalizing the statement to be delivered at the close of business the next day. The girl he had recently chosen to be his latest Berlin mistress was massaging his shoulders. As Kostina entered, the former virgin discreetly retreated from the room.

'Simone is dead,' Kostina said matter-of-factly.

Lefrington visibly paled. 'The operation was not a success?'

'Operation! It was a bloody war zone down there. I was lucky to get out alive. None of my men were as fortunate!'

'Brock?'

'And a bloody army; killed everyone.'

'Sophia?'

'I didn't stick around to find out after I was shot in the back. But her sister was there with Brock.'

'What do you mean, sister?'

'The older sister; the one who got away fifteen years ago. I only recognized her because she looked so like Sophia; I thought it was her.'

'Sophia must be OK then,' said Lefrington.

Kostina leaned forward in his chair and looked hard at the man opposite him. 'Simone is dead, Konrad; it's finished.'

Lefrington stood up. 'What do you take me for, Remik? Do you think that I did not make contingencies for such events? Simone was becoming more of a liability every day she lived.' Lefrington picked up his notes and made to leave the room. 'I've only just started!' he added.

'What about Brock? He will come after you.'

'Why – what has Brock got on me?' replied Lefrington innocently. 'Anyway, somehow I don't think he will be able to.'

The arc halogens and generator that Ferguson had hired with the jeep made the cave appear larger, flooding every crevice with light. Ferguson had quickly scraped back the debris and loose earth on the area he had been detailed to, revealing an area of rocks. 'Just my luck to get the toughest part of the whole bloody mountain to dig.'

Brock looked up from his own section. 'And there's you always telling me you have the luck of the Irish.'

Ferguson changed his shovel for a pick to pry the rocks out. After removing several he found part of a bloodstained glove. 'Connor, look at this. These stones have been placed here by human hands. Looks like someone hurt themselves in the process.'

Brock began to help Ferguson remove the rocks until the edge of the hole was waist-high while Amuyani and Cassie shone the lights on to the base. Ferguson and Brock worked in unison to lift a heavy stone out revealing a wooden plank. Ten minutes later a series of planks was revealed. Ferguson stamped on one hard, his face turning to an expression of shock as the whole plank gave way and his leg went into empty space. Brock jammed his feet against the sides and carefully pulled Ferguson back up. They both stood at the sides looking at each other.

Ferguson whistled soundlessly. 'And there I was thinking it was always you putting your foot in things, Connor.'

Brock picked up a stone and dropped it through the hole. It fell for a second before hitting something. 'It's deep enough to break a leg, Matt.'

Twenty minutes later, secured with a rope, Brock had cleared away the planks and was lowered by the others. He reached firm ground and swung his torch from side to side. It was a small cave, similar in size to the other. Against the wall was a pile of rags.

Brock carefully pulled the rags to one side, revealing two heavily decomposed corpses, their huddled bones protruding through rotted flesh.

Finding a place above the entrance of the cave, Cassie leaned back against a protruding piece of rock and carefully held the grimy pages of writing Brock had discovered delicately wrapped in a tobacco pouch. They matched the pages of her grand-father's journal. They had been written by Adonis Kaligirou, her father.

Father is dead. There is nothing left and I write this with the last of the light. It is my fault. We had realized our dream and my stupid impatience smashed it. Father wisely wanted to return later with our own team. He was wise to once more disguise the vault on our visit. Wise to send his journal home. Wise to send the picture home. Home, a place I will never see again. How stupid to have trusted Lefrescu. I was so blind. But he is blind too. We sit on a king's ransom and he left us here to rot, believing there was nothing but the case of gold and jewels he took. Yet I would trade every piece of this Byzantine treasure, and every Lysippos, to hold my darling Demetria and my baby. I swear on Adrasteia below me, that blessed dealer of justice, that my vengeful curse will follow Konrad Lefrescu throughout eternity for killing my father and me.

Adonis Kaligirou, 1976

Fifty

Cassie got up slowly, determined to visit the lower cave, though Brock had advised against it. As she neared the entrance she heard Ferguson shout a warning cry followed by a series of gunshots in rapid succession. She retraced her steps to hide behind the rock. At the bottom of the hillock she could see their jeep. Another jeep drew alongside and a man, his ear to a phone, got out. A moment later she saw three men vacate the cave, talking. She could not hear what they were saying. One re-entered the cave while another sat down by the entrance. The third walked quickly down to the vehicles to join the other, whereupon both jeeps were driven away. Cassie pressed against the rock, breathing heavily, desperately thinking what she could do.

Brock sat on the floor of the lower cave to look at Ferguson's leg. 'Well, at least it's not broken, Matt.'

'So you were wrong then!' snarled Ferguson, clearly in discomfort.

'Well, I was referring to a normal leg, not one of your legs; they're as hard as old English oak!'

'Don't you mean Irish oak?'

Amuyani sat down beside them. 'Do you think Cassie's all right?'

Brock looked at the hole. 'I don't know, Professor, I don't know. But there's little point in just waiting around. We will keep working on locating this vault Adonis wrote about. It may offer an alternative exit or at least give us something to help us climb out.'

'Anything else?' said Ferguson.

'Yes,' said Brock. 'I think we should sing, as loud as we can.'

*   *   *

Her heart beating furiously Cassie made her way silently down the slope, inch by inch on her stomach, until she could see the man sitting outside the entrance, holding a gun. She saw him remove a packet of cigarettes, shake one up and put it in his mouth. Replacing the packet in his shirt pocket he removed a disposable lighter. Experiencing difficulty in lighting it he placed his gun on the ground next to him, freeing his hand to cup the light against the wind. Cassie took the opportunity to throw a stone further down the hill. The man immediately picked up the gun and peered over. As he did so Cassie stepped quickly towards him clutching a rock in her hand.

The man heard the noise and quickly turned, the stone catching him full in the face. He cried out as he fell, grabbing Cassie as he did so. Falling on top of him they began to slide down the slope, Cassie fiercely clutching her rock. She felt her hair pulled back and ignoring the pain swung the rock into the side of his head as hard as she could. He shrieked in agony and the gun fell from his grasp. Though he desperately sought to recover it, the momentum of a woman fighting for her life coupled with the increasing slope caused him to slide faster on his back. Using both hands to protect himself from the frenzied attack, he was unable to protect his head, which smashed into the first protruding rock it encountered.

Adrenaline pumping through her veins, Cassie pushed herself up and searched for the gun, snatching it up as soon as she spied it a few moments later. Surprised at its weight, she began to make her way up the slope, being careful not to drop it.

The man inside the cave was getting angrier. 'Quiet! What have you got to be so happy about! You can't even sing! Shut up!' he shouted repeatedly.

'Because we are down here with the treasure and you are up there without it,' shouted back Brock, before he continued to sing, his voice amplified by the acoustic characteristics of the cave. The raucous noise reverberating throughout the enclosed cave caused the man to put his hands over his ears.

With the memory of her father's words fresh in her mind Cassie refused to compromise, having firmly decided that a third generation of Kaligirous would not suffer the same fate. What she had started moments earlier she would finish. Her father had been right to name her Adrasteia, for the adrenaline-fuelled blood that now flowed through her veins made her burn with the injustice inflicted upon her family. She would do whatever was required of her. She heard the singing as soon as she entered the cave, inwardly knowing that, even though it had a remote possibility for success, Brock was causing a distraction. His confidence in her ability filled her with courage.

When the man turned as if sensing her, she immediately fired and kept shooting until her gun was empty, unaware that she too had been hit in return fire.

Fifty-One

The information earlier detailed over the phone by Brock from Odessa was more powerful than van Lederman had ever anticipated. The ICE Learjet 60 flew the 670 kilometre trip from Zurich in under an hour and a half, van Lederman insisting to Honstrom and Steinwright that he was fully in command of his faculties.

He had also insisted that Leon Werner accompany them, informing him that the de Brouwer proxy was invalid as Simone's dead body had been found, and a death certificate was forthcoming. Werner had initially refused until van Lederman reminded him that under Belgian law all immediate assets passed to the son and heir of the parents' estate, unless proved otherwise, and Werner's duty could only be to the son of his clients, namely Stephan de Brouwer. Finally he had persuaded Stephan de Brouwer and Sophia Lefrington to meet him at Berlin airport. Both had readily agreed. They arrived with five minutes to spare.

Conrad Lefrington, waiting to make his entrance, was unaware of their presence at the Crown Plaza until the door of the private room he occupied opened and his adopted daughter entered, leading the others behind her.

Twenty minutes later an impatient audience unexpectedly received Professor William Steinwright.

Steinwright walked confidently to the podium, with almost a spring in his step. 'Ladies and gentleman of the press, thank you for coming. I am William Steinwright, chairman and chief executive officer of BioGenomics Research, and I have a statement to make. Following that I will be happy to receive questions from the floor.'

Steinwright paused, not for gravitas, but to calm his furiously beating heart with a deep breath. He would stick to the truth.

'Following an excellent growth record over the past four years our shares recently reached an all-time peak, due to our announcement of our drug Neurofribiline. Then, as you are aware, following a series of rumours, and indeed serious accusations, our shares crashed, losing as much as ninety per cent of their value within a forty-eight-hour period. I would like to first address the rumours and accusations, some of which are indeed true.'

Steinwright paused again, aware of the utter silence other than his own voice. 'First, the unfortunate deaths of BGR's three major shareholders. Our investigation has discovered that these were not accidents as originally perceived, but murder.'

This time several gasps were audible around the room.

'Though continuing police investigations do not permit me to provide further details, suffice to say that those authorities will be releasing their own statement in due course.

'Secondly, the accusation that our embryonic products were contaminated, indicating that they had been supplied under coercion. This has also been found to be the case. Here again the offenders have been identified and are in custody. Again it would be irresponsible of me to pre-empt any forthcoming statement.

'Thirdly, our drug, Neurofribiline. Though I personally believe that this will become the most beneficial drug available to man since penicillin was developed, it is true that we will be withdrawing the drug for further tests. Its recuperative powers for Alzheimer sufferers and other degenerative diseases, including Parkinson's, I believe will be proven when it is released in due course.

'Finally, it has been rumoured that we are under criminal investigation for malpractice. This is false. The truth is that we have been instrumental in bringing in the authorities, including ICE, because it became apparent that our company was being manipulated by unknown parties for nefarious gain. ICE has indeed learned that the same instigators, instrumental in our demise, were linked to the murders of our shareholders, the contamination and the possible corruption of our products.

'Notwithstanding this, the fact remains that our shares are now worthless and for our company to survive and restore the confidence of our shareholders and regain the value of our shares in due course, we will need a great deal of support. For this reason we have found a white knight who I believe will instil confidence into our remaining shareholders, encouraging them to hold their shares and once again consider them to be an excellent long-term investment.

'It now falls upon me to introduce to you this benefactor, but before I do so I would like to add that following this meeting I will be tendering my resignation, as I believe that it also falls upon me to take full responsibility for what has transpired. To ensure that the interests of the white knight, existing shareholders and the company are served, we have already identified one of Europe's most respected personalities to replace me and we will be announcing this in due course. In the meantime allow me to introduce you to Stephan de Brouwer.'

With a tourniquet tied tightly around her left leg, Cassie made a lasso with one end of the rope before slipping it over the nearest protruding rock at the entrance. With the help of the rope, Brock swiftly climbed out and helped the injured Ferguson and Amuyani up before retrieving the other man Cassie had attacked outside. Both of the men were dead.

Five minutes after donning the jacket of the man who guarded the entrance, Brock saw one of the jeeps return with both men. He waved at them to come up and join him before leisurely entering the cave. Both of the new arrivals were incapacitated within seconds of entering.

'I am going to ask you once only,' said Brock. 'Who sent you?'

The elder of the two men spat at him. Without hesitation Brock shot both of them in the right foot.

'Who sent you?' repeated Brock, his voice like granite.

'Our employer!' screamed the younger of the two, desperately trying to remove his left foot away from Brock's pointed gun.

'Of course he did. What is his name?'

'Konrad Lefrescu.'

'You mean Conrad Lefrington?'

305

'We only know him as Lefrescu.'

'Where is he?'

'His family is from Izmail, but he owns property here.'

Brock looked at the others. 'What were your instructions?'

'He told us to watch you and if you entered this cave then . . .' The man fell silent.

'Then what – you were to dispose of us?'

The man slowly nodded and lowered his head.

'You are going to take us to this property.'

BERLIN

Lefrington stood slowly up and made to leave, turning towards the man opposite him. 'Well, Paul, good show. Destroyed the company in one fell swoop, eh?'

'The shares will rally; it merely means that it will not be under your sole ownership, or influence. No longer a legitimate vehicle for your illegal fuel, eh?'

'You have no evidence against me, Paul. You may have won this time, but there will be other opportunities. There always are.'

Van Lederman's steel-blue eyes bored into Lefrington, with a mixture of contempt and disgust. 'You seem to forget that you drugged me.'

'Me? You are hallucinating, Paul. Why would I do such a thing, in Stephan's house of all places?'

'Yes, a fine man, Stephan. His father would be proud of him.'

Lefrington smiled. 'Now that, Paul, is something we can both agree on.'

'Children are what life is all about, but like you, Conrad, I am childless. Though I think I would prefer that than have a daughter who hates me,' Lederman goaded.

'Do you think that concerns me? Sophia's a grown woman. Her life is her own. Now, if you will excuse me, Paul, this delightful drink we have had together is over. I have a plane to catch.'

Van Lederman stood up after Lefrington had left and carefully picked up the glass the other had been drinking from, placing it into a plastic bag he removed from his pocket. 'No, Conrad, it's not over yet.'

*   *   *

306

The unusual silence was more disturbing for Kostina than any unexpected noise. He glanced at his watch and called out for someone. 'Mira, where the hell are you?' His arm in a sling, he got out of bed and walked on to the large landing and began to descend the wide staircase. There was not a sound. He glanced at his watch again. It was only early evening – where the hell was everyone? He saw a figure standing alone in the entrance hall. Though the light was dim, he recognized the person. 'You! What the hell are you doing here?'

The light accentuated the woman's distinct beauty, high cheek-bones and finely chiselled nose above her uniform mouth; the pale-blue eyes were as cold as ice. 'I've come to end a night-mare,' she said calmly.

Kostina shrugged. 'What for? You seem to have done all right for yourself. I made you what you are.'

'True, which is why I am here.'

Kostina moved menacingly towards her. 'What do you want with me, you mad bitch?' he spat.

Rather than flinch the woman also took a step forward. 'I already told you: to end a nightmare.'

Kostina pulled back his good arm to strike at the face in front of him, but was unable to do so, as it was suddenly caught in a vice-like grip. A moment later there was a dull snap as the arm broke.

The Crocodile screamed as both of his broken arms were pulled tightly behind him and upwards. 'I did not kill you, or your sister! Why do you want to kill me?' he yelled.

'I don't want to kill you,' said the woman, shaking her head. 'No, you and I have come full circle. I want to sell you! My friend Sergei here has arranged for you to spend the rest of your life in Chita Oblast.'

Kostina's eyes widened at the name of the infamous place in eastern Siberia. 'You are sending me to prison. Ha! That will not keep me!'

'Not prison – the Gulag slave camp there which Sergei assures me does exist, despite firm denials. But first I need to avenge what you did to my sister and hundreds of other young girls.'

Kostina desperately tried to move as the bear-like man holding his arms and two associates forced him to the floor, spreading his legs wide apart. 'No, you can't. Your father is—'

307

'Ah, but I can,' interrupted Sophia Lefrington coldly, a blade appearing in her hand. 'As you just said, you made me.' The Crocodile screamed. The woman got up to leave. 'And now I have unmade us both.'

Epilogue

Amuyani had been delighted to be invited to visit Cassie Kaligirou's authorized archaeological dig. When he arrived he was shown directly into the cave and down the ladder. The young Greek woman limped swiftly up to him. 'Professor! You were right about the fulcrum!'

'You found Tartarus?'

Cassie nodded, grabbing his hand.

Amuyani looked perplexed at the pneumatic drills and the chunks of stone and debris lying around. 'From the look of this, my dear, the fulcrum did not work very well.'

Cassie nodded again. 'Grandfather and father destroyed the balancing mechanism from inside Tartarus so that it would not reopen when they closed it. We didn't realize that until after we were forced to use other means and then found his notes in the last journal.'

'Can't say I blame him,' said Amuyani thoughtfully. 'He must have done it in case Lefrescu decided to ever come back. I would not want my life's search—'

'Come and see, Professor. I want to show you something!' Cassie eagerly pulled him towards a ragged hole, revealing steps hewn out of the granite.

Amuyani followed Cassie, descending slowly into a dark cavern that contained a lagoon. Cassie took her guest's arm and walked down to the water's edge. 'Grandfather believed that this whole area was formed three hundred million years ago during the Palaeozoic era. For aeons the water has risen, frozen and cooled. From Roman times to the medieval age this cavern would have been almost dry.'

'And the river strategically fordable,' added Amuyani.

'Grandfather wrote that Dandolo stored Alexius' treasure here through an empty underground channel, taking from it as required with his Dobrudza dynasty adding to it over a couple of centuries.'

'Which is why the Izmail fortress was discovered to be empty when the Ottomans arrived; the famed wealth was never kept there.' Amuyani scratched his head. 'But that does not explain the entrance we were led to.'

'Grandfather believed that during the great floods of the mid-fifteenth century, the water level reached the heights it is today – remember, Professor, only last year the dramatic floods destroyed twenty-nine bridges – forcing Dandolo's descendants to make another access. Well, they simply went straight up, constructing a counterbalance stone to conceal their hidden hoard yet provide easy access.'

'One still wonders how Andreus found this entrance.'

'Serendipity.'

'Meaning we unconsciously gravitate to whatever is most dominant in our mind, stumbling almost accidentally upon that which we seek.'

'Exactly right, Professor, and grandfather was so certain of what he was looking for that when he saw something that looked right he took it as a sign to investigate.'

'The Hecantonchires,' said Amuyani.

Cassie nodded. 'Like any good Greek academic, he was a scholar of Greek mythology. So he searched the area and stumbled upon his Tartarus by accident.'

'Those clues he left were his – as he said, "follow my signs".' Amuyani shook his head in incredulity.

'After their discovery they lifted out a number of items to the next level. A statue, and a case of gold and jewels intended to fund the whole project later. While my father went into the town for help, grandfather shut the concealed vault.'

Amuyani nodded, understanding.

Cassie looked down. 'Father went into the town for help. They met with Lefrescu, who helped them carry what they had found back to their base at Izmail.'

'Taking a photograph of the Lysippos in front of the Dandolo, or Dobruzda, family home to send home,' concluded Amuyani.

Cassie turned the professor around, motioned him to stay still and returned to the ladder they had just descended. She flicked a switch, bathing the whole cavern in bright light.

For a moment Amuyani stood there blinking as his eyes became accustomed. His mouth dropped open and a moment later he removed his hat and threw it to the ground in disbelief.

Stacked in an orderly fashion were dozens of wood and bronze cases. The lids had all been opened, revealing mounds of silver and gold coins, rich ruby and emerald jewellery and artefacts. Behind them on a slightly higher level stood a number of perfect statues, appearing lifelike as athletes, warriors and Olympian gods; each one a Lysippos.

In the centre stood a magnificent work of art, a perfect female form with raised wings billowing from her back. Wielding a sword in her right hand, a pair of scales in the other, her expression, though beautiful, was deadly serious, as one determined to act against the wicked with inflexible vengeance: Nemesis, the divine goddess of justice.

SANTA CRUZ, US

Sitting on his terrace watching the full midnight moon over the Pacific Ocean, Lefrington was surprised to hear his private cellphone ringing in the other room; it had not done so for a long time. Without voicemail it continued to demand attention. He chose to ignore it.

'I just wanted to confirm that this was the right number,' said Brock stepping on to the terrace. 'Max Adler, among others of your network that we have been busy dismantling, gave it to us.'

'You must be Brock,' said Lefrington pleasantly, appearing only slightly unsettled at the sudden appearance of his unexpected guest. 'Allow me to offer you a drink.'

Brock sat down in the adjacent seat. 'No thanks, I'm still on duty, as they say.'

Lefrington looked at his watch. 'Even at this time?'

'I prefer to stay with European time,' replied Brock.

'Well, I am indeed flattered that you have flown halfway around the world to talk to me personally; certainly it must be above and beyond the call of duty. What is it you are so desperate to tell me?'

'I always believe that the best encounters are face to face; though I know you don't hold to that view, Lefrescu.'

Lefrington blanched at the name, but again quickly recovered. 'Conrad, please, and it's Connor, isn't it? We both seem to know each other well enough, and indeed you are a resourceful and remarkable man. How is everything back in dear old Europe?'

'Sophia and Stephan got married. You were not missed.'

'Good; I think that the sign of a father's success is when the child becomes their own person, even though she was adopted; and she was one in a million.'

'They have adopted a little girl too, about the same age as when you adopted Sophia; miraculously she is one in a million too. Lovely little girl called Anna de Brouwer. The name Lefrington has been dropped.'

'Ah well, but history does have a habit of repeating itself, doesn't it? Now, enough of the pleasantries, Connor, get to the point; I'm tired.'

Brock removed a piece of paper from the inside pocket of his jacket and passed it across. 'Well, I would have come earlier but there was so much to sift through we had to wait till the right time. I wanted to give you the headlines that will be appearing in all the papers tomorrow – both sides of the Atlantic.'

Lefrington opened the folded sheet and read it. His face drained of colour.

'Paul recovered your DNA from the drink you had with him. It matched the DNA that forensics extracted from the bloody glove you tore when you were burying the Kaligirou men alive at Isaccea. You are being indicted for murder; I believe the police are on the way here now.'

Brock stood up. 'Oh, and by the way, you have a very interesting property at Isaccea. DNA there and in a certain club in Berlin link you to numerous other, shall we call them 'unseemly', activities. The papers we found in your cellar were very enlightening. If you are going to play with fire you really should burn such papers. My friends at the IRS and the FBI feel that they will be obliged to make an example of you, if you ever get off death row, that is.'

'Anything else?'

Brock nodded. 'Yes, a couple of things, which Sophia asked me to share with you. First, that she persuaded Stephan to take a DNA test. Guess what? – it didn't match yours. Simon de Brouwer was his father. Simone lied to you; seems that your

312

lover used you as much as you used her. Which apparently your erstwhile partner, Remik Kostina, did too. He was another one who liked to play with fire, but for some reason chose not to burn incriminating evidence about you. It makes really interesting viewing.'

Lefrington felt a sudden tightening in his chest. 'What was the other thing?'

'From Sophia? Oh, just that she too was very glad you were not her real father.'

Lefrington remained silent.

'Well, I have to go. Been invited to a grand opening tomorrow of Sophia and her sister's new foundation; did you ever meet Sonja Brezvanje? She is truly an amazing woman.'

Lefrington did not notice Brock leave the terrace, or hear the car that departed the house. He stood up, letting the sheet of paper slip between his fingers. He walked down to the beach, kicked off his shoes and entered the water, not stopping until he was forced to swim. He continued to swim far from the shore until he was so exhausted he could not take another stroke. Slowly he sank beneath the surface.

BUCHAREST

The announcement that the Natalya and Radu Foundation, funded by Sophia de Brouwer and Sonja Brezvanje, had taken ownership of five orphanages across Romania and was opening many more received both support and praise from charities and government departments. La Strada des Enfants, its funds greatly boosted by a legacy bequeathed to Sophia from her adopted father's estate, opened offices throughout the Balkans with a mission to fight the trafficking of children.

During the celebrations Brock excused himself and returned to the suite booked for him at the Intercontinental Hotel. Throwing his clothes on to the bed, he stepped into the shower and closed his eyes, enjoying the luxurious power-shower that sprayed his body with stinging hot water like sharp needles. After a minute of being pulverized he switched the massage unit to 'normal'. A moment later the door slid slowly open.

'Good, I see you are wide awake this time,' said a naked Sonja,

313

stepping into the shower and winding her arms around his body in a firm embrace.

In the confined space Brock was pushed into the corner of the unit. 'I don't think it's big enough,' he said.

Sonja raised her face from his chest to his face, kissing him deeply as soon as their lips met. 'Trust me,' she said breathlessly, pulling Brock even tighter towards her, 'it's just perfect.'